DROWNED GRAVES AND RUINS
LITTER THE SEA OF FALLEN STARS.

Gray bodies knifed through the water around him.
In the next heartbeat, the distorted images of six sharks
appeared before him. One of them streaked for him and
he was unable to get away in time. The hard muscled body
slammed against him. His breath left his lungs and he felt
hot scratches that scored his chest from the impact.
When he glanced down, he saw that the wounds were deep
enough to draw blood. He knew the scent of the fresh blood
in the water would send the sharks into a feeding frenzy.
He shook his sticks into his hands and knew that
he was about to be torn apart.

"Don't try to be too much trouble, manling." The Blue Lady
stared into his eyes. "I find myself curious about you, but
that won't save you from my irritation."

AND THERE'S ROOM FOR
A FEW MORE . . . .

THE WILDS

The Wilds books explore the uncivilized reaches of
Faerun in four self-contained stories. From the jungles of
Chult to the bottom of the Sea of Fallen Stars,
a world of danger and adventure is waiting.

The Fanged Crown
Jenna Helland

The Restless Shore
James P. Davis

The Edge of Chaos
Jak Koke

Wrath of the Blue Lady
Mel Odom

FORGOTTEN REALMS

WRATH OF THE BLUE LADY

Mel Odom

THE WILDS

N · E · W · I · L · D · S

Wizards
OF THE COAST

The Wilds
Wrath of the Blue Lady

©2009 Wizards of the Coast LLC

Published by Wizards of the Coast LLC

Forgotten Realms, Wizards of the Coast, and their respective logos are trademarks of Wizards of the Coast LLC in the U.S.A. and other countries.

Printed in the U.S.A.

Cover art by Erik M. Gist
Map by Robert Lazzaretti

First Printing: December 2009

9 8 7 6 5 4 3 2 1

ISBN: 978-0-7869-5192-5
620-25022740-001-EN

U.S., CANADA,
ASIA, PACIFIC, & LATIN AMERICA
Wizards of the Coast LLC
P.O. Box 707
Renton, WA 98057-0707
+1-800-324-6496

EUROPEAN HEADQUARTERS
Hasbro UK Ltd
Caswell Way
Newport, Gwent NP9 0YH
GREAT BRITAIN
Save this address for your records.

Visit our web site at www.wizards.com

For my son, Chandler, who lives to go adventuring in dark dungeons and fight evil monsters! You take the tall ugly one on the right and I'll get the stinky one on the left!

And to Erin Evans, who threw me a lifeline when I thought I was drowning!

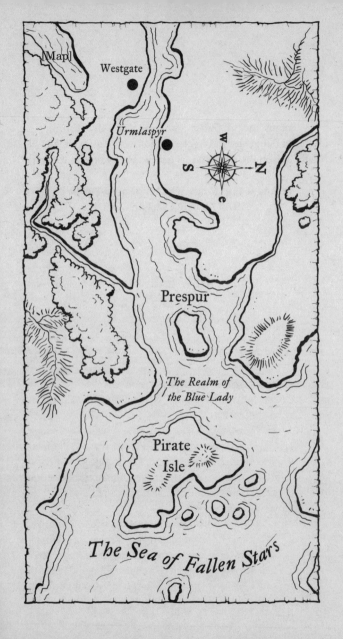

CHAPTER ONE

North of Cedarspoke, Turmish
Sea of Fallen Stars
Year of the Fallen Friends (1399 DR)

The woman's voice haunted Bayel Droust's dreams as it had for weeks. Images of nightmarish creatures scurrying across the ocean floor moved to the sound of her words. Dangerous, merciless monstrosities twice as big as the ship he sailed on. The dead the sea had taken walked through a graveyard of sunken ships and prowled watches they'd walked above the surface on her orders. Other things, small and furtive, darted through trees and brush the likes of which Droust had never before seen.

The woman's voice resonated in his mind. He still didn't know what tongue she spoke, and Droust was conversational in five Inner Sea dialects, three human, one Dwarvish, and one Elvish. He could make his way through a dozen more, but not hers.

Over the last few tendays, she had learned his language at an unbelievable speed

But her own inability to learn more than one at a time frustrated her. During those times, while kneeling before her and praying that she didn't take his life, he had grown afraid of her anger. When the dream ended and he woke once more each day, he felt as though a death sentence had lifted.

That night, though, the woman's words were sharper and more intense, like an awl digging into his brain. Something bad was about to happen.

Droust moaned as he listened to the woman. He was almost awake. He knelt there in that strange, undersea forest, the skeletons of dead sailors scattered on the ocean floor in front of him, and felt himself slipping away from her.

Wake, he told himself. Just wake up. She isn't real. But Droust was all too afraid that she was.

When she noticed him slipping from her, she turned to him, her face frozen in fury. *You can't escape me, Bayel Droust.*

Droust held his hands out in supplication even as he prayed for wakefulness. "Why do you desire me, lady? I am nothing. A poor sage who's been assigned a tiresome task."

You have skills I need, human. Knowledge that I require. Be glad that I let you live and don't merely pluck it from your corpse.

Rough hands closed upon Droust and wrenched him from his restless slumber full-awake into the dark cabin. At first he thought one of the woman's guards had seized him. He fought against his captors but it was no use. Strong, calloused hands managed him as if he were a child. His knees cracked painfully as they forced him to the floor of the ship's cabin.

"Bind his hands behind him." The voice was rough, but it was human. Droust considered that a blessing under the circumstances, but he was still confused. Had pirates taken the ship?

"He's not a mage. He's just a scribe."

"He's called up all this ill luck that's followed us. Do you want to take the chance that he doesn't have a spell or two up his sleeve?"

Droust whipped his head around in disbelief. He was being taken captive by the ship's crew, the same sailors that had sworn to protect him.

Someone yanked Droust's arms behind his back. Coarse rope bit into his wrists. He howled in pain but they ignored him.

"Why are you doing this?" Droust struggled against them but it was no use.

"Gag him."

An odorous rag slammed against Droust's lips hard enough to burst them. He tasted the salt of his blood but the pain felt distant and removed.

The woman's cries echoed within Droust's skull. He didn't recognize the words, but he knew the tone. They were commands, but he didn't know if they were to him or to something else. The pain in his head almost blinded him. He blinked at the massive figure that stepped through the crewmen.

"Belay that." Captain Porgad's rough voice rang above the rough crew manning the ship. He was a huge man with a fierce beard. He wore leather armor and protective fish-shaped charms around his neck. "He's no mage. Cursed is what he is. Don't gag him. We'll want to hear what he has to say."

Droust struggled and tried to break free. A handful of years past fifty, he still possessed his strength. But it was panic, not bravery, that drove him. He hadn't spent all his years as a scribe chained to a desk working on manuscripts and letters for the council to end up like this. He wasn't supposed to be at sea. He'd had no choice about his assignment, though.

Despite his best efforts, his captors held him. Someone struck him in the back of the head and told him to stop struggling. For a brief moment, the woman's voice went away, but it resumed only a few heartbeats later. Cutting agony followed her incomprehensible words. But she sounded stronger, closer.

Do not let them kill you, Bayel Droust, she said. Do not dare let them kill you before I get there.

Someone lit a lantern. Soft golden light filled the small cabin and gleamed against the lacquered wooden walls. Captain Porgad ran a tight ship. That was why the Grand Council at Impiltur had hired the captain and his vessel when they'd assigned Droust to his present mission.

What would those lords and ladies think of this ship and her captain now? Fear coiled more deeply within Droust when he realized that the Grand Council would doubtless never learn of his harsh treatment. These days, the Sea of Fallen Stars was an unstable and dangerous place. All of Faerun was.

Droust found his voice, though he didn't recognize it when he spoke. "Why are you doing this?"

Captain Porgad grabbed the lantern and held it close to Droust's face. "What is it the Grand Council has you doing out here, scholar?"

The bright light forced Droust to slit his eyes. The captain and his crew stood as dim shadows in the lantern's glare. They swayed gently as *Grayling* rolled on treacherous waves.

"I'm researching the waters." Droust hated the desperation he heard in his voice, but he couldn't hide it. "Since the Spellplague, the Sea of Fallen Stars hasn't been properly charted. The Grand Council told you; they want to know what dangers lurk in the waters." He said the council's name as a cleric might call on a deity. Surely they would know they couldn't hope to go against the council's wishes.

"Lies." Captain Porgad backhanded Droust to the floor.

"No." Sickness swirled in Droust's stomach as the pain in his face warred with the pain in his head. From the moment he'd stepped aboard *Grayling* he'd known he was among rough, superstitious men. They feared the stories of the lady, and the foul storm they'd blamed on him had blown them directly into her waters.

"We've seen the signs and portents, scribe. Did you think we'd stay blind to the danger we're in?"

"What?" Droust's heart nearly exploded in his chest. "Who?"

"The monsters and beasties the sea sends up." One of the sailors waved a sharp knife under Droust's chin. "The bad weather that follows us wherever we go of late." The speaker spat to ward off bad luck, but Droust knew that was a futile gesture. The lady was coming, and she was coming for him.

Droust had seen the monsters, sketched them in his journal, and written about them and the storms. He had checked the books he'd copied while readying himself for the voyage. Similar storms and creatures had been mentioned in those pages. Similar, but not identical.

Those pages had spoken of the horrendous monsters that Droust had seen in his dreams, with their illustrations of tentacled things and huge fish with more teeth than sharks. Through it all, though, the lady had remained beauteous. None of them had drawn her as Droust had seen her, though, which led him to believe that none of the authors of those books had actually dreamed of her. So why had he? What had he done that was so bad?

Reading by lantern light after the dreams of the lady had first started, Droust had become frightened. But he hadn't been so frightened that he told the ship's captain and crew of his fears. At best they would have turned around and abandoned the mission. At worst, they would have killed him and abandoned the mission.

You are lucky, manling. I will suffer you to live. As long as you have knowledge that I need. She sounded closer than ever. His head felt near to splitting.

Droust closed his eyes at that cruel promise. It would be

better if he were to throw himself onto the knife the man held at his throat. At least then he would die and be done with whatever evil the lady had in store for him.

"It's the Spellplague." Droust knew he should tell them she was coming, but he couldn't. They would kill him outright. "It isn't me."

"The Spellplague was fourteen years ago." Captain Porgad slapped him again. "I saw it happen with my own eyes." He shoved his broad, ugly face into Droust's. "But in all that time I've been out here, before and after the Spellplague, I've never had such ill luck."

There it was then: luck. The one thing that all sailors insisted must be on their side. They made donations to all the gods and goddesses that kept watch over sailors and the sea while in port. On the ship, they offered food and prayer to Umberlee, the Bitch Queen who didn't care for the lives of humans but sometimes spared them all the same. She commanded the wind and the waves, and she could remove them from the storms and give them safe passage. If she could be wooed. If they were lucky.

Droust had come between Captain Porgad and his crew and their luck.

"I've sailed *Grayling* for seventeen years without such ill fortune." The captain's bloodshot eyes narrowed. "Most of this crew has been with me nearly as long."

"*You* are the only new thing on this vessel." Porgad grabbed Droust's shirt and shoved him backward.

"That and the ill luck he brought." Someone slapped Droust's head.

In the dark, with his arms held behind his back, Droust trembled. "What are you going to do to me?"

"We gotta get rid of the bad luck." Captain Porgad pulled back into the darkness, somehow more frightening when Droust couldn't see him. "Gotta keelhaul you. We'll ask Umberlee to spare your soul and wash you of whatever curse has rooted within you."

Keelhauled. The thought of being dragged under the ship from stern to prow caused a sour bubble to burst in the back of Droust's throat. He'd never seen anyone subjected to that, but he'd read about it. And he was sure he'd drown before he was brought back up. Most victims—and that's what they were because no one suffered that harsh challenge willingly—drowned.

The storm he heard raging outside would make keelhauling him even more difficult. He wasn't going to be given a cleansing. He was going to be executed.

"Bring him." Captain Porgad stepped away. "Let's get accounts settled before this blasted storm wreaks havoc with *Grayling*." He turned and headed for the door.

If you let them kill you, manling, I will bring you back from death itself and torture you in ways you've never dreamed of.

Droust braced himself and fought against the crewmen trying to drag him from the cabin. The ship heeled sharply to port. Droust lost his footing and slammed against the bulkhead. The sailors tumbled against it as well. In the confusion of tangled arms and legs, Droust threw elbows and knees into his captors. They tried to fight back and maintain their holds on him, but the dark and the heaving ship confused them.

Despite the bad luck the sailors accused him of, luck was with Droust now. He swept aside arms that grabbed at him, ducked under others, and walked on anyone in his path. When he reached the cabin door, he opened it and hurled himself through.

Heavy rain drummed into him hard enough to sting his skin. He blinked against the storm's fury as he tried to get his bearings. The strong downpour dimmed the lanterns that marked *Grayling's* prow.

Lightning blazed across the sky and made the billowing canvas strung through the rigging stand out the color of yellowed corpse bone. The sails strained at their moorings and timbers creaked as they held tight. Water cascaded across the deck and splashed across Droust's bare ankles. In just that short time, rain drenched his light sleeping robe, turning the material heavy and cold.

"Get him!" Lightning blazed and lit Captain Porgad standing in the open cabin doorway.

Frenzied by the command, Droust ran forward.

Grayling lurched again, caught up in the power of the storm that buffeted her. Incongruously, a line of poetry from a book Droust had read while studying in Candlekeep wound through his frightened thoughts: *And lo, as the ship struggled in the sea's embrace, she gave in and allowed the vessel to win her over with hard driving need.* Tonight the sea would not be seduced and was as savage and as furious as a spurned paramour.

Another lurch steered Droust toward the mainmast. He tried to shift direction, but his bare feet slid across the slippery deck. His face collided with the rough wood. Pain filled his cheekbone and nose as splinters gouged his flesh. He staggered and went down to one knee as another lightning bolt seared his gaze.

The woman screamed at him so loudly her voice rang inside his head and made his teeth ache. Dazed and dizzy, he forced himself up. Before he regained his footing, two sailors crashed into him and drove him against the mainmast. The impact almost robbed him of his senses.

Thunder rolled over the deck and vibrated within Droust's body.

BAYEL DROUST!

The woman's voice cut through the scholar's frightened thoughts even as the sailors spun him around and looped rope around his wrists. They tied his hands together this time. His fingers went numb almost at once.

"Bring him!" Captain Porgad stood in the ship's stern. Lightning flared along his bared cutlass. "Bring him now before this storm takes us down!" He started up the sterncastle steps.

The crewmen dragged Droust. He fought them, kicking and elbowing, but his efforts failed and he got battered for his trouble.

The storm continued to rage. One of the sails ripped free of the yards and tumbled to the deck. *Grayling* foundered and lost control.

Captain Porgad lunged over the stern railing. "Tie that down! Save that sail!"

Black clouds swirled down from the sky and formed an inky cloud over the ship. The lanterns at *Grayling's* prow vanished, lost in the darkness or doused by the cresting waves. Crewmen shouted at each other, but the sudden rolling thunder swallowed the words.

Live, manling. Live that I may have you.

Unashamed and fearful of his life, Droust pleaded for his life. "Captain Porgad! Please! I've done you no wrong! None of this is any doing of mine! You're making a mistake! Don't kill me!"

Rain sluiced down the captain's craggy face. "I pray that you're right, scholar, for I've come to taking a liking to you." He turned his gaze toward the swirling blackness that surrounded him and obscured view of half his ship. "But your life is in Umberlee's hands now." He looked back at Droust. "This is the only way I've ever seen to break bad luck."

Crewmen held Droust's legs while another tied a length of rope around his ankles.

Droust wanted to ask if anyone had ever survived keel-hauling, but he was afraid of the answer. He tried asking for Umberlee's mercy, if she wasn't the Blue Lady herself, but the woman shouted inside his skull again. The pain of her voice drove him to his knees.

"Be strong." Captain Porgad clapped Droust on the shoulder. "One way or the other, this will soon be over."

White-capped waves slammed into *Grayling*. The ship shuddered like an animal in its death throes. The howling of the storm and the hammering of the ocean near deafened Droust.

One of the crewmen threw lengths of rope over the side as he raced forward. Three others followed him. All of them dived to the ship's deck as lightning touched the mizzenmast. Flames twisted up around the wet wood and stabbed into the angry sky like a torch. Even the downpour couldn't quench the fire.

Grayling twisted and heaved like boar fighting wolves. The crewmen holding Droust banged into each other, but they managed to keep hold.

"Throw him over." Captain Porgad held fiercely to the creaking railing.

The crewmen swept a thrashing Droust up from the deck and lifted him high enough to put him over the railing headfirst. He screamed until his throat tore. Black water surged at *Grayling's* stern. The obsidian clouds twisted and turned as they rushed forward and overtook the ship.

"No!" Droust kicked and fought to no avail. There were too many of them to resist. They were going to put him over. "Please!"

The woman screamed again, only this time the crewmen heard it as well. Her howl of unrestrained fury pierced even the storm's thunderous boom's like an unholy crescendo. Instinctively, they ducked. Droust's head thudded against the railing. For a moment he thought he imagined what happened next.

A feminine face appeared in the swirling black clouds. She was beautiful, but her gaze held a shark's merciless fierceness. Feral wildness clung to her and lent her regal bearing. She was tall and thin, long limbed. Her pointed ears stood revealed beneath her flowing mane.

She shouted, but her words were carried off by the wind. She pointed at Droust.

"She wants the scholar." One of the crewmen holding

Droust drove a fist into his side and knocked the air from his lungs.

"Then give him to her!" The second man shoved Droust toward the railing.

The crewmen redoubled their efforts to heave Droust over the side. The woman closed the distance, her eyes focused on Droust Then a spear and a long, lissome arm appeared out of the black clouds.

With unerring accuracy, the thrown spear plunged through the heart of the crewman to Droust's left and through the chest of the man behind him. Their hot blood splashed the scholar and brought momentary and grotesque warmth against the storm's chill bite.

The men, one dead and the other grievously wounded, sagged. Droust's legs and body dropped but he saw the woman stride out of the clouds.

"She's walking on water!" One of the nearby crewmen scuttled away, in awe of what he witnessed.

"Umberlee sent her! We've angered the Bitch Queen!"

Lightning blazed and reflected on the woman's seashell armor and small clam shell shield. A long sword hung at her side, but she left it there. She stretched forth her hand and closed it. When she did, the spear vanished from the bodies of the crewmen and reappeared in her grip.

"Bayel Droust." Her voice sounded loud during a lull in the thunder.

The headache throbbing between Droust's temples increased its unrelenting ferocity. It felt like his mind was slowly shattering.

"Let him go." The woman's words carried a curious inflection, as if she weren't used to the common tongue. Her black cloak twisted behind her.

Then Droust saw her inhumanly silver eyes for the first time.

Eladrin, the scholar thought.

"Arm yourselves." Captain Porgad lifted his blade and

stood his ground. Around him, his men took up cutlasses, battle axes, and belaying pins. Droust knew they would have run if they'd only had a place to go.

The woman vanished in a blaze of lightning. For a moment Droust thought she'd disappeared or fallen into the sea. In the next, she reappeared on the deck.

Highly trained and experienced in battle, Captain Porgad and his crew wheeled on the woman. She thrust the spear forward and pierced the captain's throat. Blood cascaded down the front of his blouse as he stared dumbly at the weapon that had killed him.

The death of the captain paralyzed the crewmen like spider venom for a moment, but—pushed by self-preservation and past combat experience—they rallied and attacked. With a gesture and a quickly spoken word, a blast of wind lifted the woman's attackers from their feet and knocked them backward. Three of them sailed over the stern railing and dropped into the sea. She gestured and once more the spear reappeared in her hand. Calmly, she turned to the three men standing near Droust.

"This will be your only chance to flee," she said.

The crewmen sprinted amidships. One of them heaved himself over the sterncastle railing and crashed to the deck.

The woman focused her attention on Droust. He pushed his feet against the deck and tried to inch away.

"Bayel Droust," she said.

The scholar didn't know if he heard her musical voice with his ears or inside his head. He gazed at her.

"I don't know you." He didn't hear his own whisper.

"But I know you." She stood effortlessly in the midst of the storm's onslaught.

Renewed fear locked cold fingers around Droust's heart. Her announcement sounded like a threat.

She approached and gazed down at him. Her skin shone blue in the glare of lightning. The water elves, the *alu'Tel'Quessir*, that lived in the Sea of Fallen Stars were sometimes blue like that. But this was no sea elf.

"Lady, I thank you for my life." Droust didn't know what he was supposed to do. Instinct told him he wanted as far from her as he could get.

Grayling strained against the storm. Her timbers continued to creak and a few of the yards snapped off to jerk at the ends of the rigging. Hoarse voices sounded from amidships. The sailors would regroup and try to attack. Onboard the ship, they had nowhere to go.

"You will pay for it." A cruel smile curved the woman's lips. She slid her shield up her arm and transferred her spear to her left hand. Then she grabbed the front of Droust's robe and lifted him with no apparent effort.

Before Droust could attempt to stand on his own, the woman kicked the stern railing. Wood split and fell away. She strode forward and dropped at once, still holding onto Droust as if he weighed nothing.

A scream ripped from the scholar's throat as the sea sped up at him. He expected the cold water to engulf him. Instead, he stopped only inches above the heaving surface. The woman righted him and turned back to gaze at the ship.

Grayling drew away and remained barely visible against the swarm of black clouds. The lanterns serving as her running lights faded one by one, but the fire atop the mizzen remained bright.

The woman gestured with her spear. The storm's fury lashed the ship. Lightning struck *Grayling* repeatedly and lit fires along her. Winds ripped away her yards in a tangle of rope, then snapped off her masts. A black wave rose up and heeled her hard to starboard.

When the wave passed, *Grayling* was gone. The storm abated, breaking up with astonishing quickness. Stars peered from the black sky.

"What have you done?" Droust demanded in a hoarse voice.

The woman released Droust and he started to plunge

through the water. When she caught him again, this time by wrapping her long fingers around his head to buoy him, he was submerged to his waist.

"Bayel Droust." She eyed him calmly. "You will pay for the life I give you. If you don't, I will take it back." Then she squeezed her hand.

Pain filled Droust's head. He would have sworn he heard his skull fracturing. Incredibly, he felt her fingers sinking through his flesh, through his bone, then she touched his mind.

Until that point, Bayel Droust had foolishly thought he'd known what pain was. The Blue Lady taught him the true meaning of it.

Bayel Droust woke, thinking he was rousing from another nightmare. As he gazed around, he saw that he was inside a ship, but it was one that was unfamiliar to him. Light issued from outside the vessel, but everything held an unaccustomed blue tint.

"No." He pushed himself up from the strange bed and walked to the porthole to look outside. Just before he reached it, a school of small fish swam inside the room. As one, they turned and darted away from him. "Not *here!*"

The undersea world spread all around him. Strange trees and plants, things that should not have grown at these depths, stood all around. Before he could move, a vine reached for him and tiny teeth latched onto the palm of his hand. Droust yanked his hand away and burning pain invaded his flesh.

He put his mouth to the small wound and tried to suck out the poison. As he spat, he watched the spittle pass slowly before him then spread out. Mesmerized, he waved his hand through the spittle. The blob broke into parts and spread out like a spider before disappearing, absorbed into the sea.

"This can't be." He whispered so lowly he scarcely heard himself. He took a deep breath to reassure himself. He wasn't drowning. He was underwater and he wasn't drowning.

Trembling, walking on legs that he felt certain would betray him and collapse beneath him, he walked toward the cabin door. When he pulled on it, the door moved slowly and he felt a lot more resistance to his effort than he should have. He could move freely under the water, but the door couldn't. Whatever the spell was that allowed him to breathe and walk normally, it didn't have the same effect on the ship.

Outside, Droust peered up at the blue, blue water. At some distance, he wasn't certain how far, the blue turned to black. There was no hint of the sun. He had no idea to what depth he had sunk. High above, sharks and other things circled through the water. Ivory bone, limbs as well as skulls, lay half-buried in the sand and vegetation that had a stranglehold on the sea bottom.

"Droust." The familiar feminine voice drew the scribe's attention at once.

When he glanced up, he saw the Blue Lady standing on the sterncastle of the wrecked ship. A tentacled monstrosity Droust couldn't identify lay coiled and restless on the deck behind her. Its great eye kept watch on him and never blinked.

"Yes." Droust wanted only to flee, but he knew he wouldn't get far.

"I have given you your life that you may serve me."

Droust swallowed hard. "I understand, lady."

She gestured and the water around Droust seized him and lifted him to the sterncastle. Droust didn't try to fight. He was still bruised and battered from his harsh treatment at the hands of *Grayling's* crew. He came to a rest in front of her. The monster lying behind her flicked out a tentacle with blinding speed and stopped within inches of his flesh.

Droust stared at the suckers that lined the underside of the tentacles. "What is it you would have me do?"

"I have walked your dreams. I know you for what you are. You are a scholar. I have learned much from you, but I would know more."

"Anything, lady." Droust was so scared he thought he was going to throw up.

"This is my realm." The Blue Lady waved at the strange land spread out around them and the shipwrecks scattered about it. "What little I have left of it. This world is new to me. You will be my guide as I secure my empire. More than that, you shall help me find a way to leave this place once I'm ready."

"Lady?" Droust peered at her in confusion.

The Blue Lady frowned and anger radiated from her. "Those who cast me forth from the Feywild bound me to this piece of land they sent with me. Only a powerful spell can set me free."

"I'm no mage, lady. I'm but a scribe."

"I know that. But you read books." The Blue Lady waved to the sunken ships. "Aboard these ships, there are books. You will locate and read those books. Some of those books will have spells."

"Spells like that won't be revealed in just any books. "

"I know that. I have brought down mages as well as ordinary sailors and merchant ships. Somewhere in those books, you will find the knowledge that I need."

"Lady, there was one such book that I had in my hands, but I don't know if it had the magic you seek."

"What?"

Immediately, the beast flicked out a tentacle and wrapped it around Droust. The cold flesh lay hard and heavy against him.

The Blue Lady shoved her cruel, beautiful face into Droust's. "You had such a book? Where is it?"

"I don't know, lady. I swear. Perhaps it's still aboard *Grayling*. It's a history, perhaps more, by a Shou monk named Liou Chang. He wrote histories about his people and the monastery. He also knew the secret of opening magical gates that allowed people to travel from one place to another. I was studying his books. They're very precious. Few of them remain in existence. The monastery was attacked and razed to the ground at one point by General Han, a man who swore vengeance against the monastery and the Standing Tree Order. Han knew the secret of opening the gates to transport his troops."

"The monk wrote of this?"

"Yes, lady." Droust was squeezed so hard that he almost couldn't get his answer out. "I believe that Liou wrote down Han's secrets. The monk was the last man to talk to Han before he was executed."

"You had this book and you let it slip away?"

"Lady—" Droust thought quickly. He didn't want to point out that her decision to sink the ship, and the crew's intention of keelhauling him, had removed him from those books. "Perhaps those books are still aboard *Grayling*."

The Blue Lady waved her hand and the monster unwrapped its tentacle from Droust. The scribe fell to the deck and gasped for his breath as fish swam impossibly around him.

"Find your ship, manling. And find those books."

"But you have to know that the sea may have harmed the books." Droust peered up at her. "If they are ruined, I can't read them."

"I allowed no harm to come to any books."

Only a short time later, they stood on *Grayling's* deck. the ship lay broken in pieces in a canyon. All hope of finding the books by Liou Chang that Droust had brought with him instantly disappeared. A thorough search of the cabin only frustrated the Blue Lady and alarmed Droust.

"They were lost, lady." Droust stood before the Blue Lady and prayed for a quick death.

"Then you will find them." The Blue Lady's face held threatening anger like an unleashed storm.

Unable to stop himself, Droust gazed at the wide open sea in dismay. "Lady, those books could be anywhere."

"You will find them. There is not another reason I would suffer you to live. Do you understand?"

"Yes, lady."

"Then get busy." Without another word, the Blue Lady launched herself into the sea and swam away.

Feeling an inch from death, Droust watched her go, then he looked at the immense forest and tried not to think that the task she'd set before him was impossible. Then he started his search for books, beginning with the immediate area around him. The books couldn't have fallen far,

Unless they were caught in a current or still afloat with the wreckage above. Or any of a dozen other reasons Droust could think of.

Captain Porgad's body had landed on the deck of this ship at the foot of the mizzen. Small scavengers were already at work on his body, feasting on his eyes and crawling through the gash at his throat. Droust couldn't help feeling that could be him at any moment.

CHAPTER TWO

I told you they were Nine Golden Swords warriors."
Kwan Shang-Li gazed at the group of rough looking
men standing in the gloom gathering in the alley
behind Ottard's Alehouse. The night truly hadn't
gotten off to a good start and it looked like things
were going to get worse.

"Feh," his father grunted. "Those thugs could
be anyone's."

The Nine Golden Swords was a criminal
organization that operated out of Westgate. They
robbed, raided, and sold protection to businesses.
According to his father, they were far too coarse
to have any interest in Shang-Li and his father's
plans, and were nothing to worry about.

However, there was no mistaking the identity
of the warriors. To anyone that would know, the

tattoos on the arms and necks branded them as Nine Golden Swords warriors. Shang-Li discreetly pointed these out.

"Evidently they like the alley as a staging point for burglary as much as we do." Shang-Li glanced up the tall, crooked tower not far from the alley.

"If this book wasn't as important as it is, I'd say leave them to it. Let them deal with the wizard. He will kill them all."

"Do you think Kouldar's defenses are that good?" A slight trickle of fear ran through Shang-Li, but he felt excitement as well. His father had always considered that mixed feeling as a failing. Shang-Li lived for the rush of adventure. That was one of the first things that had led him out of the Standing Tree Monastery and out into the world.

"He's supposed to be one of the best wizards on the isle." His father shrugged. "I do not believe the Nine Golden Swords would have anyone skilled enough to defeat his defenses."

"You know I've got to break into that tower tonight."

His father clapped him on the arm. "Perhaps you will be lucky."

"Thanks."

"We'll find out later." His father nodded toward the Nine Golden Swords warriors. "In the meantime, it would be better if they didn't get brave enough to attempt to break into Kouldar's tower tonight. Maybe if we reasoned with them."

Shang-Li stared at his father. "We're going to *reason* with the Nine Golden Swords? For all we know, they're after the books too."

Kwan Yung was a slightly built man with gray hair and a forked beard. He stood only as tall as Shang-Li's shoulder. Kwan Yung was full-blood Shou but he had married an elven ranger in spite of his family's traditions, and had only one son: Shang-Li.

At twenty-four, Shang-Li was barely considered an adult by his father. His father had contributed his dark, buttery complexion and the black hair Shang-Li wore close-cropped. His pointed ears and turquoise eyes came from his mother, and from somewhere between the two he had ended up with a lean, compact build. He wore leather sandals and a black server's uniform that fit him loosely. The small leather pack over his shoulder showed years of hard use and had accompanied him through his travels for the last twelve years.

His father grunted in disappointment. "Perhaps reasoning with them *is* too much to ask."

"Knowing the Nine Golden Swords are here is going to alter our plan."

His father shot him a look. "Our plans altered the moment you broke the last jar of hot sweet-and-sour sauce and angered the most dangerous pirate on these isles."

"It was an accident." Shang-Li hated the way the lie sounded so false in his ears.

"An accident that got you fired and earned you a death threat from Captain Trolag. As I recall, that wasn't part of the plan."

It wasn't, and Shang-Li was embarrassed he'd jeopardized the plan. Not only that, now that his father knew about the incident, Shang-Li knew his father would never let him live it down. Once they returned home, Shang-Li trusted everyone at the monastery would hear the tale. Years of woe stretched out before him.

And then there was Captain Trolag's death threat. Captain Trolag had brandished his displeasure and menace around like weapons. Few on the Pirate Isle would stand against him, and Captain Trolag stayed away from those men. Instead, he enjoyed stringing up men too helpless to defend themselves. The corpses of three that had angered the captain that morning danced from gibbets at the harbor entrance. Shang-Li had seen the dead men from the kitchen window where he worked at the Blinding Onion.

Had worked. Shang-Li's dismissal from the tavern had come suddenly and without any chance of misinterpretation. He'd been surprised at how much getting fired from the tavern had stung. The job had merely been a cover, but he had worked hard to do his job well for as long as he had need of it.

Except for the mishandling of the spice tureen. That was truly unfortu—

"I'm not convinced that the sweet-and-sour sauce was mishandled by accident," his father said, interrupting Shang-Li's thoughts.

"Maybe we could deal with our friends here now, and talk later?"

"If you must."

Shang-Li walked out of the shadows and approached the Nine Golden Swords warriors standing in the alley. He kept his hands open, showing no weapons. His server's uniform from the Blinding Onion offered no clue as to who he was.

"What do you want?" A large man stepped forward and put his hand on the hilt of his sword.

Shang-Li stood his ground and expanded his senses, reaching for Moonwhisper, the horned owl that he'd taken as his animal companion. After three years, the effort of connecting with the predatory bird was as natural as breathing.

Moonwhisper sat in the shadows of a window high on one of the nearby buildings. He had already started to fidget restlessly when the men closed on Shang-Li. The owl watched the seamen closely, and through the bond that they shared, Shang-Li got a better look at the scene.

Through the owl's eyes, everything was rendered in black and white. But Moonwhisper's vision was sharp. Shang-Li felt the owl shift his weight and unfurl his wings as he leaped from the window. He took to the air soundlessly, earning the name Shang-Li had given him when he'd been little more than a struggling hatchling.

"Can you spare a few copper pieces?" Shang-Li waved at his father. "My father is sick and I need to get him to a healer."

Kwan Yung coughed theatrically and walked over as well.

"Go away." The big man waved a threatening hand. Like all the others, he was Shou, golden-skinned and black-haired, covered in tattoos. "I'll kill your diseased old father before he comes close enough to get me sick."

His father stopped. "Have things changed so much in the world, Shang-Li, that an old man in the streets can't rely on the kindness of strangers?"

Shang-Li seized the big man's outstretched hand, pinched the nerves deep in his palm, then round kicked him in the face. "The kindness of strangers is something you find in a book. Did you really expect to find it here in the Pirate Isles?"

Another warrior lunged with a spear, intending to skewer Kwan Yung. The old man side-stepped the spear thrust, then swayed effortlessly forward and chopped the man in the throat with the edge of his hand. The warrior dropped to his knees, abandoning his weapon and holding his bruised throat as he tried to force his breath in and out. "The kindness of strangers must be a lot like good service in taverns," his father said. "It can't be found anymore."

Shang-Li didn't reply. His father had always been good at ferreting out his lies.

His father persisted. "Did you spill the tureen on purpose?" His father caught a man's sword lunge, redirected it, and then slammed his elbow into the man's temple. The Nine Golden Swords warrior dropped like a rock.

You just can't leave it alone, can you? Shang-Li thought. His father always expected perfection from him. "It was the last night at the Blinding Onion. The captain had become insufferable since he got into port a tenday ago. I hated waiting on him."

Shang-Li held his arms down at his side, twisted his wrists, and shook his hands to free the fighting sticks holstered there. Short and iron-capped, the wooden fighting sticks barely reached from Shang-Li's wrist to his elbow.

With one whispered command, however, they nearly doubled in length in the blink of an eye.

His opponent thrust his sword forward, intending to pierce Shang-Li's throat. The young Shou batted the sword to the left with the fighting stick in his right hand, then followed the motion and turned to his left. He completed the turn and slammed the stick in his left hand into the man's temple.

The big man's eyes rolled up into his head and he sank to his knees. Shang-Li snap-kicked the unconscious man in the face and knocked him back into his fellows as they scrambled for their swords and knives.

"That's no excuse." Kwan Yung scooped a loose cobblestone from the alley floor with his foot and hurled it into the face of another attacker. The rock hit solidly and the man screamed in pain as he fell backward.

"I wasn't trying to excuse myself." With a quick spin, Shang-Li confronted the three men closing in on him from the rear. He swung the sticks quickly, blocking his opponents' blades with harsh *thwacks* that filled the narrow street. A quick step to the right took him to the man on the outside of that group. The pirate swung his long sword at Shang-Li's midsection but stepped in front of his fellows to do so.

Shang-Li caught the sword between the sticks and turned the weapon aside. Metal slid along the reinforced wood but stopped just short of the Shou's hands. He shifted the trapped blade quickly and put the tip against the ground. A sudden stomp snapped the blade like kindling, and Shang-Li jumped high into the air and swung a roundhouse kick into the man's jaw. His head spun to the side at the impact and bone broke. He slumped into an unconscious heap.

"Your impudence has jeopardized our mission here." His father picked up a fallen spear, expertly spun it to block the blades of two attackers, then knocked one of them out with the haft. He ran at the second, used the spear to leap above the man's sword strike, and kicked him in the head. His father landed gracefully and spun the spear again.

"The mission isn't jeopardized." Shang-Li heard the survivors of their attack closing ranks, then charging at him. Driving his feet hard, Shang-Li ran up the wall of the nearest building. Just as gravity claimed him and stopped his upward path, Shang-Li pushed himself backward and flipped high in the air. He landed on one of the men, one foot on his opponent's shoulder and one foot on the man's head. Burdened by the unexpected weight, the pirate sank to the ground.

Moonwhisper sped out of the darkness and raked his heavy claws across the forehead of one of the men. The heavy sweep of the owl's wings cracked in the air. The razor-sharp claws parted flesh easily. Blood ran down into the wounded man's face and he retreated while clawing desperately at his head to find out how bad the damage was.

His father snorted disdainfully and swept the retreating man's feet from beneath him, then rapped him on the skull.

Shang-Li cringed a little. There was nothing as irritating as that snort.

"You had to cause a scene, Shang-Li. You couldn't leave well enough alone. You had to let that man know that he couldn't control everything."

"I think he believed it was an accident." One of the Nine Golden Swords warriors halted a dozen paces away and unlimbered a crossbow. Shang-Li reached inside his belt and took out two throwing stars. He flipped them into the air smoothly. The disks whirred across the intervening distance and buried themselves in the man's elbows. The armor he wore might have stopped them. The warrior howled in pain and the crossbow dropped from his hands. He turned and fled. Shang-Li allowed him to escape.

"Then why did Trolag offer an immediate bounty on your head even after you were fired? Why did you flee the Blinding Onion like a monkey with his tail on fire? And how could you possibly think we'd last any longer on our quest with you a wanted man?"

Shang-Li sighed. "The Pirate Isles are filled with wanted men."

"They don't want each other." Kwan Yung elbowed one man in the face that had made it to his feet, then kicked another in the head.

The crashing serving trays and plates during the escape from the Blinding Onion *had* been impressive. The act of discretion hadn't been one of Shang-Li's better escapes. But any escape he could walk away from . . .

"I am not happy." His father walked across the alley, which was now filled with unconscious Nine Golden Swords warriors.

Shang-Li shook his head in disbelief. "You're never happy."

"I trained you to always be subtle." His father held his hand in front of him and moved it with delicate precision. "You are supposed to be like water. You flow. You do not cause disruption. You do not ruffle feathers."

Shang-Li counted to ten in Shou, and then again in Elvish.

His father threw up his hands in frustration. "I blame your mother for this. She was impulsive. She could never pass by an opportunity for confrontation. You are like your mother."

And you could never pass by an opportunity for *discussion*, Shang-Li thought, could you, Father? Arguments had filled their house while he'd been growing up. A casual onlooker might not have believed his parents had cared for each other as deeply as they had. But they had loved one another more than anyone else Shang-Li had ever seen.

"Could we not bring Mother into this? We still have a book to liberate from a wizard's tower."

"If that task remains possible."

"It does." At least, as possible as getting that prize initially was. "We know where the book is, and we planned to get it tonight anyway. Now we have time to get some rest before we break into the wizard's home."

His father snorted again. "You talk as if that will be easy."

"*You* planned that part of the mission. *You* told me I had nothing to worry about." Shang-Li paused but his father never broke stride. "I *don't* have anything to worry about, do I?" He didn't relish breaking into wizards' homes. Thieves got killed—or worse—quickly while doing that.

"You cannot even serve a simple tureen of sauce without spilling it. How can you expect to break into a wizard's home even if I plan everything?"

"I could have served the sauce without spilling it. A child could have—"

"Hah!" His father wheeled to face him and threw a finger up into his face. "See? I told you that you angered Captain Trolag because you wished to."

Shang-Li bit back a sharp retort.

"This is why I wished to come along on this task. You lack discipline and this task is important." His father gazed up at him and the wavering light of the nearby street torch played across his face. Embers from the flaming bundles swirled from the iron cage but extinguished before they struck the ground.

The uneven glow highlighted Kwan Yung's wrinkled features and gray hair.

When did he start getting so old? Shang-Li wondered. He remembered his father as the man that had taught him to fight at the monastery, had taught him his love of books and history. His mother had given Shang-Li his wanderlust and shown him the mysteries of the woodlands. Pirates had killed her when Shang-Li had been fourteen. That was when Kwan Yung had lost part of himself.

"I could have done this, Father." Shang-Li spoke softly, hoping to prevent a further tirade. "But I am glad you're here." Mostly. "We haven't spent much time together of late. This could be good." Gods, he thought, please let it be good.

That caught his father off-guard. Kwan Yung regarded him suspiciously.

"I'm not going to forget that you spilled the sauce on purpose."

"That will make two of you." Shang-Li smiled. "I made sure the sauce was very hot."

Kwan Yung's hand flared out quickly and tweaked Shang-Li's nose hard enough that he barely kept from crying out or cursing. Either would have been a mistake.

"Pay attention." His father's voice lashed like a whip. "You need to focus. I would rather not report back to the monastery in shame after you ruin this opportunity to recover what was lost so long ago. Especially since the Nine Golden Swords might know about this prize as well. We cannot miss this chance."

Shang-Li rubbed his stinging nose and concentrated on breaking into the wizard's home. If he was fortunate enough to do that, there was a chance he might live to see morning.

Bayel Droust cowered in the chair of the small area where he worked. For all the years he'd spent under the sea as the Blue Lady's prisoner, he'd never become so jaded that he lost his fear of her. As the Blue Lady strode into the hull of the ship, Droust's guts threatened to turn to water, even though he'd asked her to come. He steeled himself and waited.

Outside the porthole by his desk, the verdant growth ran rampant, claiming the whole of the sea bottom that lay within the Blue Lady's power. Twitching vines that moved over their own accord wreathed twisted trees and warped bushes where horrible monsters dwelt.

Droust had given names to some of them only so he could tell them apart. Perhaps the whiptails, eye-piercers, and slashsails had started their lives as something else, either in this world or the one that the Blue Lady had been forced from, but they no longer remained recognizable as anything Droust knew. Some of them had been changed by the Spellplague, but others had been changed by the Blue Lady's protective spell over the area, and maybe others had simply lain under the sea so far that no one had ever before seen them.

Liou Chang's two books lay before Droust on the desk. He never went anywhere without them. They were his greatest burden, and they were the only things that kept him alive. That and the Blue Lady's power. He'd already lived beyond the normal life of a human, and still the years didn't touch him. If he weren't a captive, those added years would have been wondrous things.

The books were in the same pristine shape all these years later as they had been when Droust had first found them. Back then, Droust had thought only of ferreting out the information and selling it to wizards. But the book's code remained beyond his talent and skill, despite years of work. Fortunately, it was also beyond the Blue Lady's skill.

"Well? What is it?" The Blue Lady stood in the doorway. A group of kuo-toa stood behind her with their weapons bared.

"There has been a . . . problem with the recovery of the book in the Pirate Isles. The men in our employ have run into an obstacle."

"I don't want to hear about obstacles."

Droust shrank in his seat. "Nor do I, lady. Still, it might be our good luck this time."

"How so?"

"The obstacle they encountered is a Shou monk from the Standing Tree Monastery."

"How do they know that?"

"They know this one from previous encounters."

The Blue Lady thought about that, and Droust feared the dark thoughts that constantly paraded through her head. She directed her cold gaze at him. "You're certain this monk is after the same book we are?"

"Lady, the Standing Tree Monastery has been searching for Liou's books for hundreds of years. It was my good fortune when I happened on the two in my possession—"

"*My* possession. Do not forget your place, manling."

Droust bowed his head and raised his hands in supplication. "Of course not, lady. I spoke in error. I'm tired." Despite the longevity of the scribe's life, he still wearied as though made of normal flesh and blood. He'd almost forgotten what the sun looked like. Caelynna used others as go-betweens for the agents that served her on land.

"Your good fortune began when I needed someone who could teach me more of this world." The Blue Lady's eyes blazed. "That you had those two books was merely a blessing. And a curse. I should kill you for your inability to translate them."

Droust quavered. "Lady, I can still be of help to you. If I can learn the code that Liou used for these books, I can translate the books. I only need someone to show me. And I will be loyal to you." He had no choice. He wanted to live, and that shamed him most of all. Surely all of the Inner Sea would suffer the Blue Lady's wrath and more if she was successful in bringing her war to this world.

"Where are the warriors now?"

"Still in the Pirate Isles, lady."

"Contact them. Tell them to let this monk take his chances with the wizard and his books."

"Lady, I know—knew—the man that wrote that book. He was a ship's officer. He would have recorded where *Grayling* went down. You decided"—Only after Droust had pointed it out to her—"that exact knowledge of where the ship went down was dangerous. It's better if everyone believes a storm took *Grayling*."

"I know that." The Blue Lady drew herself up in haughty indignation. "But this book has served to draw this monk to us. We should not overlook the chance this provides."

"If this man is as good as the Nine Golden Swords believe at avoiding traps, he could get the book."

"Fine. Have them take it from him then. And while they're at it, I expect them to capture this monk as well. Both tasks are equal. Perhaps if he is so skilled at stealing things, he might be skilled as stealing sense from locked words."

"Yes, lady." Droust turned back to the spelled crystal he used to contact the Nine Golden Swords the Blue Lady had employed.

"Keep me informed, manling." The Blue Lady glanced up. "There is a ship sailing through my waters that I intend to bring down." She showed him a cold, cruel smile. "Pray that it doesn't harbor a scribe more cunning than you."

Droust cursed himself for being a coward, but he prayed that she wouldn't find someone to replace him. And he hoped that the monk died a swift death at Kouldar's hands. That would be far more merciful than falling into the Blue Lady's thrall.

CHAPTER THREE

Are you awake?"

From half-closed lids, Shang-Li watched as his father reached for his nose. Shang-Li blocked the move and took a half-step back. He glanced at his father as they stood in the alley where the encounter had taken place only a handful of hours ago. "Don't do that. I'm awake."

"You shouldn't have slept back in our room. You should have stayed awake and prepared. Now you're all befuddled. You move like you're older than I."

Shang-Li gestured to the small bag and the katana over his shoulder. "I was already prepared. And I needed sleep. Not all of us got to wash vegetables at the Blinding Onion. Some of us had to lift heavy trays of food and wash dishes."

His father waved the complaint away. "You complain far too much. Work is good for you. You could have studied. I brought books to read."

"I've read the books you brought"

"They're good books. I've read them before too. They're worth re-reading."

Before he could stop himself, Shang-Li sighed.

"Don't be insolent." His father slapped the back of Shang-Li's head. Shang-Li moved farther away.

His father stared up at the wizard's tower jutting up over the next building. The structure bent and twisted, and it gave the impression of a coiled snake. People in the city called it the Serpent's Tower. If he hadn't known, Shang-Li would have guessed that that the tower had been designed and built by dwarves deep into their cups.

Magic lurks in the mortar of Serpent's Tower, Brianthom the Traveler had written in his history of the Pirate Isle— one of the books Kwan Yung had insisted Shang-Li read again. *No one knows what secrets the edifice contains. If any thief has ever chosen to brave the tower's magical defenses, none has ever escaped with the tale. The Wizard Kouldar entertains only a few guests, and those seldom. None of them have ever seen the entire interior of the Serpent's Tower.*

As he looked up at the tower corkscrewing toward the dark night sky, Shang-Li admitted to himself that he was more nervous than he'd expected. He'd broken into the lairs of wizards on other occasions. He'd gotten away with his life. Usually someone that crossed a wizard and got caught didn't get the chance to learn from his mistakes.

"Stop fidgeting." His father stood placidly, as if they were planning to go for a walk instead of invading a wizard's stronghold.

Shang-Li adjusted the pack over his shoulder and didn't look at his father. "Mentally preparing myself."

"Do you think you will be finished sometime before the dawn?"

Shang-Li frowned at his father. He wished he knew what to say. Usually when he took risks like this, his father wasn't around. He'd thought of leaving a letter telling his father his innermost thoughts, not to blame himself for whatever happened, and that he cared for him.

The thought of telling Kwan Yung that in person was just too awkward.

"I told the others that you could do this," his father said.

For a moment, a flicker of pride sparked inside Shang-Li. "So do not embarrass me."

Shang-Li thought about telling his father that if anything went wrong he'd be too dead to worry about embarrassing anyone. But he didn't. He nodded and smiled. "I won't."

Then he shot across the alley, caught the edge of the low roof, and flipped himself up onto it with a lithe move. On top of the building, he lay prone and reached for Moonwhisper's senses.

The owl sat on the rooftop of a tall lighthouse that commanded a view of the town. Through the owl's eyes, Shang-Li saw himself lying on the building's rooftop, the river to the left of the Serpent's Tower, and the crooked edifice that earned the building its name.

At Shang-Li's urging, Moonwhisper fell forward and caught the wind from the sea with his wings. He glided toward the tower.

The tower's exterior was rough, irregular stone mortared into place. Shang-Li felt confident he could climb it if he had to. But that was a long way to go without being discovered by someone. He planned to cut down on that distance by a considerable amount. Wicked-looking gargoyles manned the roof and a widow's walk a third of the way down the tower.

From the widow's walk, an observer could watch the

sea in the distance. Someone with good eyes, Shang-Li felt certain, could identify a specific ship in the harbor.

Or a wizard could keep watch over his tower. The thought hung like sour grapes in Shang-Li's mind.

Moonwhisper glided by the structure, then came back around it in a tight, gentle circle to see all sides of the tower.

Satisfied with the reconnoitering, Shang-Li drew his senses back from the owl and became aware of his own body again. The cool wind from the sea rushed over him and carried the almost lyrical noise of the lines banging against the masts. Here and there, occasional voices sounded, but most of them belonged to drunken sailors stumbling through the streets.

The quiet time, only a few hours before dawn, softened the city. If Shang-Li hadn't known the place was a pirate stronghold, it would have looked like any other city.

Shang-Li glanced over the side of the building. His father was gone. Hopefully he would secure their escape vessel before it was needed. The dark ribbon of the river that cut through the heart of the city's more prosperous side ran beside the Serpent's Tower.

Only a few lanterns remained lit along the shores cluttered with small boats and transport barges. Most of those lights were stationary, the lights of guard ships sent out by pirates and, possibly, in the pay of the Nine Golden Swords.

He waited only a few moments more, until a black cloud scudded across the sky and masked the quarter-moon. A pall of darkness fell over the city.

Shang-Li stood, uncoiled a line and a padded grappling hook from his pack, and whirled the device beside him a few times. Then he cast, whipping his body with practiced ease.

The padded grappling hook sailed across forty feet and landed on the widow's walk with a barely audible thunk.

Shang-Li regretted that his father wasn't there to witness his success. But then he would only have found something unsatisfactory about it.

The cloud continued across the quarter-moon and no one was around to notice the line that suddenly spanned the distance. Knowing time was short, Shang-Li tied the line to the rooftop. The rope was made of spidersilk, weightless as a feather and strong as dwarf-forged steel.

When he'd finished, the line was taut. Slipping off his soft-soled shoes, he ran barefoot across the thin spidersilk. The line twisted and swayed a little as he passed, but he had no problems making the adjustments to keep his balance. The alley floor was forty feet below. Rats and other things rooted through the garbage and never noticed him pass.

A grin touched his lips and dimmed some of the unease that filled him. If the wild things didn't sense a predator among them, he was almost invisible.

But not against magic.

During his travels and adventures, that was one lesson he had learned the hard way. He paused at the other end of the line. The grappling hook hadn't appeared to set anything off, but a protective spell might be laid to sense flesh and blood.

Moonlight slipped toward him and slid along the spidersilk line.

Once you're focused on your goal, once you're committed, inaction is your enemy. His father's words came to mind. Shang-Li had drilled hard under the tutelage he'd received. He sipped a quick breath, then used the spidersilk's slight elasticity to aid his leap toward the widow's walk when it pulled back to its original length. He flipped forward, twisted, and landed almost silently on the jutting stone parapet.

For a moment he held still. His ears strained as he listened for sounds from within the tower. His body quivered like a tuning fork, waiting to feel any vibrations headed toward him. Nothing.

Then, an instant before the moonlight touched him, Shang-Li strode forward, shook his sleeves to free the sticks, and shoved one into the open window in front of him.

Shang-Li slipped a necklace from beneath his shirt and held it out before him. A sliver of dark blue crystal hung at the end of the silver chain.

"Mielikki," he whispered, "watch over me, because I'm going in dark places tonight."

The crystal spun quickly. The faceted sides glimmered blue from an internal light, but didn't flare up in warning. Some magical residue was to be expected given the surroundings.

Steeped in the shadows inside the room, Shang-Li breathed deeply and made himself remain calm. The scents of the room told him of the books, inks, parchments, wooden shelving, and furniture before his sensitive half-elf eyes adapted to the dimness.

A sweeping glance of the round room revealed the bookcases that reached at least fifteen feet from floor to ceiling. Books, all manner of books in many kinds of bindings, filled the shelves.

"Forest Mother," Shang-Li whispered before he could stop himself as he surveyed the books. Then he waited to see if his inadvertent expression of surprise would set off a spell triggered by voice.

When nothing happened, he let out a pent-up breath and gave silent thanks to Mielikki. Once again, the Forest Mother was looking out for him.

Memory of his father's voice jangled Shang-Li's thoughts. *She only looks out for those that look out for themselves. Have a care here, you great-footed oaf. Don't get foolish.*

Despite the fear that had tightened his belly, Shang-Li gave into the awe and curiosity that filled him. Outside of Candlekeep and the Standing Tree Monastery, the wizard's collection of books was the largest he'd ever seen.

He took a deep breath and broke the fascination that had fallen over him. For a moment he worried that the effect was part of an enchantment that had been laid upon the books.

However, he quickly dismissed that idea. As his father had told him, Ravel Kouldar wouldn't trifle with any magical spell that wouldn't kill someone outright. The knowledge hadn't been reassuring, but it hadn't been meant that way either.

Across the room, a large mahogany desk gleamed from the outside incandescence. The top had been cut from a single piece of wood that showed the rings under a heavy varnish. An inkwell, a clutch of quills, and candelabra sat on the desk. An array of globes sat in front of the desk. Besides the doors to the balcony, another set of doors lay to his right. Those led to the stairwell and the lower floor.

Shang-Li knew better than to try the doors. Those would definitely be protected. Every door in the tower would be sealed. He'd been surprised the windows hadn't been. His attention shifted to the three globes in front of the desk. Shang-Li focused. Don't get distracted, he told himself. Your father is out there now counting down the time you're inside.

But Shang-Li couldn't forego his curiosity. It wasn't every day that he invaded a wizard's sanctum.

Carefully, Shang-Li stepped forward and examined the globes. He recognized the first one as the world of Toril as it had been before the Spellplague brought lost Abeir back from where the twin world had been hidden.

While growing up, Shang-Li had read many books concerning the twin worlds and the wars the gods had fought to control them. Mystra's death a hundred years ago had broken the barrier between the worlds. A new continent had appeared in the Trackless Sea, and disasters had swept across Toril as the planet had become whole and less at the same time.

The second globe was of Toril as it was now. There were several unfinished areas he could have helped Ravel Kouldar fill in, but he doubted the wizard would be interested in his assistance.

Shang-Li longed to be out there exploring the newly arrived lands. As a historian for the monastery, he lived for the stories he found. And these days the stories were more like riddles, waiting to be solved.

The uncovered tales, pottery, weapons, and artifacts that belonged to cultures that hadn't been part of Toril for thousands of years made writing history even more difficult. Historians, those like his father that served as librarians and keepers of knowledge, fought over how things were to be labeled. Explorers, like Shang-Li, reveled in a world that still held secrets.

The third globe was even less defined. It held only patches of lands that had once been part of Toril and were no longer on that plane. Ravel Kouldar was evidently attempting to fill in some of the spaces with educated guesses based on what parts of Toril had slipped back across the barrier weakened by the Spellplague.

Shang-Li thought seriously of shoving all three globes into the magical bag he'd brought with him. The bag was nearly bottomless, capable of holding a great many things without increasing in size or weight. His father had given it to him the first time he'd left the Standing Tree Monastery. He'd also told him to fill it with worthwhile things.

Things go wrong when you try to do too much. His father's cautionary words curbed Shang-Li's zeal. *Stay with the plan.*

Reluctantly, Shang-Li turned from the globes.

With the magical crystal still held before him, Shang-Li walked to the wall on his left. He sidestepped a hanging skeleton, making sure to stay out of reach just in case, and stopped in front of the bookshelves. A ladder built into the shelving was attached from the floor to the topmost shelf to his right.

The time had come to find out how good the information his father and the monastery had gotten was. He knelt and gazed at the shelves.

In the time of Shang-Li's grandfather, a historian had happened on information that the Standing Tree Monastery had lost in a battle nearly three hundred years ago. An invading army under General Kirat Han had laid siege to the monastery and sought the riches they knew the monks had hidden within.

But he'd taken more than mere treasure.

The Shou kept journals written by monks that had served the monasteries. Wisdom and history resided in those pages, and all of it was irreplaceable. General Han had taken six of the books of Liou Chang, also known as Liou the Perceptive. The books had contained all of the monk's family history of the five other monks that had preceded him.

Most important of all, though, Liou had written about spells, which General Han had used to open gates around the Inner Sea. With that power at his command, the warlord had been almost unstoppable. The knowledge of those spells remained a threat as long as the book containing the information was at large.

General Han had executed Liou the Perceptive, then ordered the monastery burned to the ground and salt poured into the gardens. Ultimately, the survivors had rebuilt the monastery and exacted vengeance on General Han. The warlord soon fathered a traitorous son that gave information to the Standing Tree monks that allowed them to kill him.

Unfortunately, Liou's books had been hidden, scattered throughout General Han's doomed empire. The search for Liou's books had become legendary. Shang-Li had remained on the lookout for them for all his life. But he had never seen even one of those the monastery had recovered.

Four of Liou the Perceptive's books had been found and returned over the years. General Han had traded them to sages and clerics that desired the herbal magics contained in the pages. Those had been relatively harmless, but the monks hadn't known that until they'd gotten possession of them and deciphered them. Liou had always written his original manuscripts in code, and he'd created a new code for each manuscript. Liou had been laborious in his efforts, and each code had taken years to decipher.

Two of the books had at last been traced to an ill-fated historian, a man called Bayel Droust. Ravel Kouldar didn't have either of the two missing books, but he did have a journal of a ship's officer that had gone down on the *Grayling*. After hundreds of years of searching, the monks of Standing Tree Monastery finally had a clue as to where the ship had gone down, and what had happened to it.

Ravel Kouldar had recently hired a scribe to help him organize some of his books. Once the job was finished, Kouldar had planned to kill the scribe. The young man had kept his wits about him and barely made away with his life a step ahead of an assassin. In time, because he was one of those the Standing Tree Monastery had taught and who had learned of Liou's missing books, he'd reported his experience and the existence of the book mentioning *Grayling* to the monks only a short time ago. The monastery had worked quickly to take advantage of this bit of good fortune. Kwan Yung was given a ship and told to find Shang-Li, then travel to the Pirate Isles to verify the scribe's report of the sailor's journal.

Silently, Shang-Li stepped to the center of the room and faced the window squarely. He held up his right arm at his side, took note of where his shadow lay across the angle of the rectangle of moonlight streaming through the open window, and turned to face the bookshelves.

The tomes were expertly bound and expensive, and would have been worth quite a lot in certain circles, but none of them captured Shang-Li's interest.

He reached under the shelf and felt along the back for the hidden trigger the scribe had told the monks of. At first Shang-Li thought the scribe had made a mistake. The man had been nervous, scared. Working for a wizard like Ravel Kouldar, he'd have been a fool not to be.

Even investigating carefully, Shang-Li found no hidden release as was promised. His anxiety mounted and he listened for noises within the tower but heard only the beating of his own heart.

Then, after a second search, then a third, Shang-Li's callused fingertips discovered the barely discernable depression. It was there, only a small change in the wood.

He smiled and depressed the section of the shelving. The hidden door swung open and Shang-Li's fighting sticks slid smoothly into his hands.

Shang-Li forced himself to breathe out. Forest Mother, he prayed, protect the fools that believe in you.

Tense, Shang-Li hunkered down and peered through the opening. It lay along the floor, barely large enough for him to slide through. He saw only the thick, impenetrable darkness on the other side.

With a fighting stick in his right hand, he propelled himself through the opening and gracefully rolled to his feet in the darkness on the other side. He bumped against something and flailed for it. Almost immediately, the sound of ceramic shattering filled the room and chunks of an object ricocheted from his feet and legs.

Shang-Li flattened himself against the wall he'd come through. After a while, when he heard no one in the outer room, he breathed a sigh of relief and chose to believe no one had heard the awful noise. He lifted the necklace and the crystal and spoke another word.

This time the blue crystal glowed like pale moonlight.

The illumination slowly pulsed outward and filled the room.

Shards of an elaborately painted vase lay scattered on the floor. Valuable, Shang-Li noted, scanning the swirling decorations. A piece from a druid clan in Dragon Reach that had attained some prominence. Kouldar wouldn't be happy about that. Lifting the glowing necklace, Shang-Li swept his gaze around the room. Like the outer room, this one had floor-to-ceiling shelves lining the walls. Instead of books, though, other objects filled the shelves as well.

Multi-colored lights reflected from gemstones and precious metals and the locks of small chests. Weapons—swords and knives, and bows with quivers of arrows—lay among them.

Goddess of the green, Shang-Li thought as he held the glowing crystal before him. The scribe's story hadn't prepared him for the treasure trove that lay around him.

After spending a moment orienting himself, he searched through the book collections. Histories, studies of plants and animals, journals written by wizards, treatises of learned men who sought to understand spellcraft, and books about other lands filled the shelves. His quick mind grasped that in short order, though the topics appeared disparate. Kouldar was obviously a collector of some magnitude.

Grayling's lost log by her third mate was located with a clutch of books regarding other ships lost in the Sea of Fallen Stars. If Shang-Li hadn't been knowledgeable of those lost ships, he might not have made the connection.

Although the book showed wear and tear, it had obviously been well made. Shang-Li had expected a common sailor's log filled with rough, woody sheets, but the pages were pristine and white even after all these years—not a feat many could do and something that was paid dearly for. A few of the pages held stains from drink and food. Others had burn marks that scored the pages and had eaten holes in places. The pasteboards that held the pages together were thin wooden leaves bound in sturdy cloth. The author's name was mostly worn away.

Shang-Li had no doubt that this was the book he'd come for. The scribe had described it very well. Reluctantly, Shang-Li temporarily avoided the siren call of the tale preserved in the pages.

A warning itch tickled his scalp and he knew he was no longer alone.

"What interest do you have in that book, monk?" The voice was dry and deep, one used to command.

Startled by the proximity of the voice, Shang-Li shoved the book into the bag at his hip and stepped away from the speaker as he turned. By the time the book was gone from his hand, the fighting stick had dropped into place. He kept the weapon hidden.

The man chuckled derisively. "Don't worry. If I'd wanted you dead, you would have died never knowing you were in danger."

The light inside the room slowly gained strength as a floating sphere dawned a few feet away. Shang-Li glanced away from the light to save his peripheral vision. More of the room stood revealed. A man's shape, not ten feet distant from Shang-Li, appeared in the darkness.

The man was at least six feet tall. His dark maroon brocaded robes hugged his bony frame. Dark hair framed a withered face scarred by the pox. His nose was prominent between his close-set sunken eyes. He carried a staff with a purple stone at the tip.

"You're good, thief, but you didn't find all my alarms.".

Shang-Li forced himself to remain calm. He felt like he'd locked gazes with a viper. Kouldar's stare was cold and impersonal. He imagined the room in his mind, estimating the strides it would take to span the distances, the moves he'd have to make, and the cover he could seek. His chances of completing that were so small he didn't even count them.

Boldly, Kouldar strode toward him. The purple stone at the top of his staff glittered as it caught the light hovering in the air.

Shang-Li said nothing. He took a firmer grip on the book and rolled the pendant chain between his fingers to take up slack.

Kouldar took another step forward and smiled knowingly. "The scribe that was here. He was one of you meddling monks, wasn't he?"

Instead of answering, Shang-Li drew in his breath and charged his lungs. *Breathing is always a part of readiness.* The monks at the Standing Tree Monastery had taught him that as far back as he could remember. *No matter what you do, no matter the challenges you face, breathing should always be your first concern.*

Kouldar trailed fingers along the spines of the books nearest him. "I thought the scribe showed too much interest in some of the books I had him copy. I baited him, but he was very well trained. For a spy."

"He wasn't a spy." Shang-Li shifted slightly, falling into rhythm with the wizard's movements, prepared to leap in an instant. "He was merely a scribe."

"But he felt he owed you an allegiance." Kouldar trailed a covetous hand along a panther-headed statue of a winged woman. "I have studied that book you have in your hand."

Unconsciously, Shang-Li tightened his grip on the book. No matter what, he wasn't going to leave the journal behind.

"I suspected there was more to that journal than I perceived." Kouldar shrugged. "I was hoping to coerce the scribe to tell me all he knew. Without having to kill him or tip my hand that I had knowledge about that book." He scowled. "Evidently the man's sense of self-preservation was far stronger than his nerve. If I had known that he belonged to the Standing Tree Monastery as you do, I would have acted differently."

"I haven't ever heard of that monastery."

"Liar." The wizard raised a hand and spoke a single word.

Heat seared Shang-Li's forearms. He struggled to keep them at his sides. A moment later, the tattoos on his forearms glowed bright green and showed through his shirt sleeves. Both forearms held images of mighty oak trees with widespread branches and gnarled roots. Carp swam in a pool beneath the one on the left and a dragon lay curled around the one on the right. The symbols of the Standing Tree Monastery.

"You're one of those cursed monks. Always so secretive and stingy with your knowledge." Kouldar paused. "What is in that book that you find so important?"

Shang-Li didn't bother to lie. The wizard wouldn't have believed him. Cautiously, Shang-Li slid the fingers of the hand that held the necklace inside the folds of his blouse. The sharp points of the throwing stars held there grazed his fingertips.

"Your insolence doesn't matter. Neither does your naive resolve." Kouldar smiled again and the expression held only cruelty. "You will talk before I'm through with you. Every secret you know, every hidden thing you *think* you know, will be mine for the taking."

With effort, Shang-Li took a deep breath and throttled the fear threatening to break loose inside him. The naked threat of the wizard's power hung in the air. He deposited the necklace into the loose folds of his blouse, and slid a half dozen throwing stars into his callused hand. The blouse masked his movements but he couldn't help feeling the wizard knew about each move he made.

"Now." Kouldar pointed with his staff. "Give me that book."

Instead, Shang-Li snapped his wrist and flipped the throwing stars at the wizard. Before they struck their target, Shang-Li dived for the opening at the base of the wall.

CHAPTER FOUR

Shang-Li rolled to his feet and hurtled forward, racing for the window.

Halfway to his escape, thunder cracked behind him. The wall of books exploded outward. A few of them slammed into Shang-Li. Others littered the floor ahead of him and made footing treacherous. He slipped, caught himself on his hand and fist closed around the sticks, and pushed himself back up.

From the corner of his eye, Shang-Li saw Ravel Kouldar stride through the large, ragged opening that had been torn through the wall with his glowing staff in his hand.

A word ripped through the confusion rumbling through the wizard's den. The power of the spell blew cold air over Shang-Li and filled him with vibrating fear. He controlled the fear and kept it distant because he knew it didn't come from inside him. The emotion was a thing created by Kouldar's spell.

Something jostled on the room's ceiling, then dropped to the floor. The dark shadow obscured the window and Shang-Li instinctively turned to one side and bumped against a bristly surface that scratched his exposed skin. His foot slipped on the books and he fell, immediately scrambling to get once more upright.

A monstrous spider lurched toward him, its front legs raised as if reaching for Shang-Li. Taller than a man with several black, beady eyes peering out through the bristle of its hair, the spider twitched its fangs, ichor dripping from them as it sprang forward.

Shang-Li threw himself to one side and narrowly avoided the spider's legs. They thrust against the floor with power enough to cause small tremors. Enough to crush him.

In the moonlight, the spider's flesh stood revealed, shiny and pale; it was a golem. A masterwork to be certain— whoever the craftsman had been the spider looked lifelike, complete with striations in its coloring and the bristle of hair. But it was made of heavy clay.

The golem-spider reared again and spun with super-human speed toward Shang-Li. The forward legs streaked for him once more.

Gambling on his opponent's strength, Shang-Li leaped, put a hand on top of one of the legs, and vaulted upward. He flipped and his back thudded against the golem-spider's back. Before the creature could reach him or shift, he shoved himself to his feet and leaped through the window. Unfortunately, the golem-spider chose that moment to stand taller and the added movement threw Shang-Li farther than he'd anticipated.

He sailed across the widow's walk and headed for the long drop to the alley below. Frantically, he managed to catch the railing with one hand. His stopped his fall but felt his shoulder briefly separate and snap back in place. Pain flooded his senses and he nearly blacked out.

When he blinked his eyes, he realized he dangled from the balcony railing and faced the wizard's room. He cast his senses for Moonwhisper and found the owl perched on a nearby building. The bird fell forward and his wings unfurled to seize the night.

Shang-Li felt a moment of relief at the promise of help, but his hopes quickly fled. The golem-spider would destroy the owl if it landed a blow. Desperately, feeling the muscles in his arm quivering under the strain of holding his body despite his training, Shang-Li turned his attention to his survival.

The widow's walk quivered as the ponderous weight of the golem-spider trod upon it. The creature's legs curled over the railing and felt for prey.

Shang-Li reached into his bag and took out the padded grappling hook. He didn't trust his ability to make the cast back to the building he'd come from. Instead, he shook out the line and aimed for the gargoyle almost ten feet away.

The cast flew true and Shang-Li hauled the line to take up slack.

One of the spider's legs brushed against the back of Shang-Li's hand as he drew the rope tight. Immediately, the widow's walk shivered as the golem-spider eagerly changed positions. It leaned over the railing to peer down at him.

The golem-spider's fangs flashed as they worked in anticipation. It leaned over the railing and lunged for him.

Shang-Li released the railing and took up slack on the rope. For a moment, he dropped, then he reached the end of the line and swung like a pendulum under the gargoyle. The stone statue shifted a little with a low grinding sound.

He smashed against the rough surface of the tower wall. Warm blood spilled down his cheek and the burning pain proved too sharp to completely ignore.

The gargoyle shifted again, and this time rock fragments

pelted Shang-Li as he swung under it. He searched for another safe haven and spotted a second gargoyle farther down, sticking out over the meandering river.

Back at the widow's walk, the golem-spider rose on four legs and propelled itself toward him.

Shang-Li knew there was no chance the gargoyle would withstand the golem-spider's additional weight. As lithely as the thing moved, the wizard's guardian was still massive. When Shang-Li swung back under the gargoyle, he arched his body high and threw himself forward.

The golem-spider landed on top of the gargoyle and the structure tore free of the tower. Shang-Li landed atop the next gargoyle and struggled for his balance.

Skittering noises behind him drew his attention. The hairs on the back of his neck rose as he glanced down.

The golem-spider crept along the surface of the tower as easily as a true arachnid would, moving swiftly toward Shang-Li.

The distance to the alley floor was somewhere near thirty feet. A fair chance he'd turn an ankle in the fall. With the spider hot on his heels, that wasn't a plan for a hopeful future.

Desperate, Shang-Li ran his fingers along the stone. He found enough crevices to grab a tenacious hold. His hands sent bright, blazing messages of agony to his brain as his fingertips took his weight. As quickly as he could, he clambered down the side of the tower.

The golem-spider closed on Shang-Li rapidly. He gazed up into the golem-spider's multitude of eyes and reached into his blouse for more throwing stars. A deft flip of his wrist sent the sharp blades spinning into the creature's face. All of them bounced from the golem-spider's hide without doing any damage. It relentlessly continued to gain on him.

"Shang-Li."

He recognized his father's voice at once and snapped his head around. His father stood in the middle of a small transport boat along the river's edge. He held a pole in his hands.

"Shang-Li. Here" His father waved him toward the boat.

Shang-Li reached inside his blouse and took out the journal. "Meet me at the ship."

A grimace of displeasure tightened his father's face, but worry showed there as well.

Quickly, Shang-Li looked up at the widow's walk. There was no sign of the wizard, but light neared the edge. He held the journal up briefly so his father could see it, then he tossed it down and across the thirty feet of intervening distance. The cords around the journal kept it closed as it sailed. His father plucked the journal from the air.

Light dawned over the edge of the widow's walk. The wizard peered down as the golem-spider closed on Shang-Li.

"Go!" Shang-Li implored. "I'll meet you at the ship!" He ducked beneath the golem-spider's leg and felt vibrations course through the tower. Mortar trembled from the cracks.

Kwan Yung shoved the journal into his robes and grasped the pole in both hands. He pushed hard against the river bottom and swung his craft into the slow current.

"Hurry," his father admonished.

Even if he'd thought of one, Shang-Li had no time to utter a response. Moonwhisper brought him a moment's respite when he flew in front of the golem-spider's face. The creature struck at the owl but missed by several feet. The owl spun gracefully in the air despite the large wingspan and came back for another pass.

"Ignore the bird!" Kouldar leaned over the window's walk. "Kill the thief."

Across the alley, Shang-Li noticed a small balcony. From his precarious position, he couldn't tell exactly how far the distance was. But he was all out of choices. He pulled his knees to his chest, planted his feet against the wall, and pushed off with all his strength.

He was awkward and ungainly as he sailed across the alley, but his aim was true. He flew toward the balcony—

His fingers grazed the balcony's railing. It slipped through his grasp, but he managed to catch the bottom of the balcony and hang on. He dangled for a moment, not believing his good fortune.

Then, along the wall, the golem-spider crouched to pounce. In frozen disbelief, Shang-Li watched the long legs flex, and it leaped for the balcony as well.

Shang-Li swung forward and let go of the balcony. He crashed through a window and rolled across a hardwood floor just as the shriek of cracking timbers filled his ears. As he pushed himself up from the glass-strewn floor, the golem-spider and the balcony tore loose from the building and tumbled down.

Before Shang-Li could celebrate his good luck, a grotesque leg curled over the window's edge. The golem-spider hauled itself up to the window.

"Goddess," Shang-Li whispered miserably, "my father is with me on this quest. Haven't you tested me enough for one night?"

Motion behind the golem-spider attracted Shang-Li's attention and saved his life. He threw himself backward in the hallway as the wizard unleashed another fiery bolt from the widow's walk. Heat roiled over Shang-Li as he rolled backward in a desperate attempt to increase the distance between himself and his attacker. Flames licked the hallway and swarmed outward.

A nearby door opened and an older man stood there with naked steel in his fist. "What's going on? By the gods, you're making enough racket out here to wake Kelemvor's guests."

Shang-Li silently agreed. Kelemvor, the Lord of the Dead, would doubtless arrange passage for several people in the building if they didn't get out before the fire spread.

"Wizard." Halting to face the man with the sword, Shang-Li pointed back toward the window.

The golem-spider pulled through the window and scuttled through the flames, pausing as if to get its bearings.

The man with the sword eyed Shang-Li with open hostility and disbelief. "You riled *Kouldar*?"

"Wake everyone," Shang-Li entreated. "The building is on fire." The golem-spider focused on Shang-Li again, then sprang.

The man with the sword dodged back into his room and slammed the door. Shang-Li fled down the hallway only a heartbeat ahead of the spider. Other doors opened but closed even more quickly.

Through the window at the other end of the hall, the peaked roof of another building, this one no more than a couple stories tall, stood out against the darkness. Without pausing, Shang-Li crossed his hands in front of his face and dived through the window. Mielikki willing, the distance wouldn't be too great between the buildings.

Glass crashed all around him, spinning away and glinting in the moonlight. He landed on the other roof off-balance and tucked himself into a roll automatically. The night kaleidoscoped around him in a whirling mixture of night and stars.

On his feet again, he looked back and saw the golem-spider break through the window as well. Chunks of rock plummeted into the alley. Flames illuminated the hallway behind the creature as smoke spiraled up from the burning building.

The rooftop shook as the golem-spider dropped onto it. By then, Shang-Li was in full flight, lunging forward and powering his steps. Startled shouts rang out around him, and he could only imagine the tales that would be told tomorrow of a giant spider chasing a man across the rooftops of the pirate city.

Despite his best efforts, Kwan Yung was no longer able to see his son's frantic flight across the rooftops. The old man's stomach tightened anxiously, but he made himself breathe through it until his strokes with the pole against the river bottom were once more smooth.

Only his attempts to spot Shang-Li allowed him to spot the waiting ambush. Three Nine Golden Swords warriors ran swiftly to a low bridge that crossed the river. They held weapons naked in their fists and stared at him.

They were watching, he thought. We did not succeed in routing them. Kwan Yung put more force into his poling efforts but the small boat remained sluggish. The Nine Golden Swords warriors gathered before him, standing on the outside of the bridge now as they prepared to leap down at him.

Kwan Yung was glad Shang-Li was not there to witness his embarrassment. He'd fallen prey to their trap far too easily. You should have stayed in the monastery, Yung, he thought. That is what you're better suited for these days.

But he hadn't been able to let Shang-Li step alone into all the danger that now faced him. As a father, Kwan Yung hadn't been able to keep his son safe all the time, but this assignment was one of those times he'd had to try.

One of the Nine Golden Swords perched on the edge of the bridge and stretched forth his arm. "Give us the book, old man. Hand it over and you won't get hurt."

Kwan Yung snorted and took his pole from the water as the boat glided under the bridge. One of the men lifted a crossbow and fired. Moonlight glinted from the steel tip. Twisting, Kwan Yung let the deadly missile pass, then reached down for the curved boat anchor. With one quick flip, he threw the boat anchor and succeeded in wrapping it around the crossbowman's leg. Then Kwan Yung poled again to gain speed.

The boat glided under the bridge and the anchor line drew taut. As the boat shot out on the other side of the bridge, the anchor hauled the crossbowman off and spilled him into the river. One of the remaining warriors leaped down toward the boat.

Turning, Kwan Yung planted the pole in the center of the boat and caught the man in the chest; then he levered him to one side. The last warrior thudded into the boat and drew two heavy knives, quickly weaving a razored dance before him.

On his toes now, moving smoothly, Kwan Yung batted the knives away as they sought his flesh. The warrior was fast, but movement on the boat required fluid reflexes and uncanny balance. Kwan Yung kicked down on the port side, taking advantage of the drag created by the man captured by the anchor rope. The boat rolled over to the side and came out of the water, throwing the Nine Golden Swords warrior off-balance. Before the man recovered, Kwan Yung swept the pole around and hit him in the head.

As the man flew from the boat, Kwan Yung swung the pole again and knocked one of the knives into the air. Then he stepped toward the boat's stern to right it before it started taking on water. He plucked the tumbling knife from the air, then dragged the keen blade across the anchor rope and cut loose the tangled warrior.

Returning the pole to the water, Kwan Yung drove himself farther downriver. There was no sight of Shang-Li, but even across the distance, Kwan Yung heard the yells of frightened men.

The chase was not yet finished.

Minutes later and nearly out of breath, Shang-Li reached the harbor. Even though he'd doubled back through alleys, Shang-Li hadn't managed to lose his pursuer. The golem-spider remained tireless. Not only that, but the pirate watch had gone on alert and now patrolled the sleeping city as well.

Shang-Li charged through the knots of frustrated and tired pirates. He leaped over and zigzagged through those in his way, but a handful of guards rushed at him. As soon as the guards spotted the golem-spider lumbering in his wake, they fled too. Screams and yells trailed in his wake, not quite fast enough to get ahead of him and warn the people ahead.

Air tore raggedly through Shang-Li's throat despite his conditioning. All the climbing and running took its toll. His legs and back ached with the effort he expended.

And he was almost out of room to maneuver. The dock ended less than forty feet ahead. Despite the screams and shouts from the harbor, the men aboard the second ship ahead kept hauling on the block-and-tackle to hoist a net filled with cargo.

Shang-Li leaped for the net as the golem-spider thundered across the crooked wooden dock after him. Pirates dived from the docks as the giant creature knocked crates, barrels, bundles, and urns in all directions during its mad scramble to catch its prey.

The cargo net continued its upward journey, pulled by the cargo handlers. Shang-Li caught his left hand in the strands and made a fist. The rough fiber cut into his flesh but he didn't release his desperate hold. The load rocked slowly but strongly and carried Shang-Li along with it. Flailing, he latched on with his other hand.

One of the men below him noticed him and let loose a squalling curse. "What do ye think ye're doin'? Get offa there!" He glanced over his shoulder. "Kellam, get a pole and give that bonehead a knock between his lights."

Shang-Li scuttled around the net and felt the swaying load drop another few inches. His stomach flipped and he had to quell the impulse to dive into the water. For all he knew, the wizard's guardian could swim like a fish.

"By Gruumsh's diseased nostril!" Another pirate swore and pointed back the way Shang-Li had come. "Look over there!"

As one, the pirates' heads swung back along the dock. Closing quickly, the golem-spider leaped over a pile of crates and landed amidst a group of pirates drunkenly unaware of the danger among them. Mercilessly, the creature flung the howling men like ragdolls. They fetched up against ships in bone-jarring thumps or splashed into the harbor water. Those fortunate enough to escape the arcane creature's grasp fled like scalded hounds.

With a lurching creak, the cargo net plummeted almost a foot, leaving it scarcely more than fifteen feet above the deck. Shang-Li was certain the wizard's sentinel could leap that high without a problem.

"Hold that line, ye melon-headed lummoxes!" The pirate foreman stomped among his men. "Hold it or I swear I'll gut ye meself an' save the cap'n the trouble! We ain't gonna lose the cap'n's cargo!"

Incredibly, the men held the load in spite of their fear and the swinging mass. The rope that secured the net sang in protest of the ill-treatment.

The golem-spider poised beneath the swinging net and readied itself to pounce. Its four front legs stretched upward. Then its back legs flexed.

Move! Shang-Li told himself. He reached down and slid free the knife strapped to his right leg. It was an elven blade his mother had given him when he'd been just a boy.

The double-edged blade gleamed, straight and true. Elvish language that asked for blessings and guidance from Corellon Larethian scrolled along the spine in copper. Ridges scored the amber grips to provide a surer grip.

The net jerked sideways suddenly. Without looking down, Shang-Li knew the golem-spider had made the leap. In two desperate arm pulls, he reached the top of the cargo net, but one of the creature's legs curled around his foot. The limb tightened with steely strength and pulled. He thought his leg was going to tear from its socket.

Aboard the pirate ship, the lead pirate fought a losing battle. His shipmates had decided they were much too close to the golem-spider. The line jerked as another man abandoned the effort.

Blocking out the pain of his bruised foot, Shang-Li whipped the knife across the golem-spider's leg. The mystical power in the blade cracked the clay limb and managed to roughly shear it away. He yanked his foot up while the creature recoiled and rebalanced itself. The stump thumped noisily against a crate.

Turning quickly, Shang-Li grabbed the rope holding the net with his free hand, then sliced the rope beneath his fingers with the blade. The hemp strands parted in a snapping rush.

Relieved of the cargo's weight, the pirates straining at the other end of the rope fell backward and pulled the line through the block-and-tackle.

Shang-Li swung his body up and threw his knife arm over the top of the boom. He caught hold of it in the crook of his elbow. The bottom pulley pinched his fingers but he yanked them free before they were tugged inside. The rope shot through the assembly fast enough to send up a smoke trail.

Shang-Li held onto the boom arm and struggled to catch his breath.

Beneath the debris and wreckage held together by the cargo net, the golem-spider's legs twitched feebly. Most of the cargo had landed on the creature. In the next moment, the golem-spider's legs turned paler, then cracked and turned to dust. A wave of intense cold brushed by Shang-Li as whatever magic had been contained within the thing was released.

Danger!

Moonwhisper's warning brushed across Shang-Li's mind. The owl's thoughts weren't close to anything human, but Shang-Li understood them. When he looked over his shoulder, he spotted Kouldar striding along the docks. A small group of armed thugs surrounded him.

The thugs lifted crossbows and took aim.

Shang-Li sheathed his knife, gripped the boom with both hands, and quickly hauled himself into a squatting position atop it. The first quarrels cut the wind around him as he propelled himself toward the harbor water, but one of the later ones slid along his neck and under his jaw. Pain followed immediately and he hoped the quarrels weren't poisoned. A fireball impacted the boom and heat washed over his back.

In the next instant, the cool dark sea took him into its embrace and he dived deeply. The bright flash of the fireball briefly illuminated the depths. He swam with powerful strokes almost within arm's reach of the bottom.

Find safety, he told Moonwhisper. *Stay away from the ship. They might follow you. I will send for you when it is safe. Be safe until we meet again.*

The owl reluctantly headed back to shore.

As the remnants of the fireball flash faded, Shang-Li fixed his bearings in mind and swam toward *Swallow*. When he surfaced for air, he did it next to a ship. Safe in the shadows, he regained his breath and plunged under again.

Lungs near bursting , Shang-Li surfaced at *Swallow's* stern and gripped the anchor rope. He shook water from his eyes and a voice called down to him.

"Shang-Li?"

His father stood in the stern. Beside him, three archers held nocked arrows aimed at Shang-Li.

"Don't loose." Shang-Li held his hands above his head and spoke only loud enough to be heard aboard ship. "It's me." The salt of the harbor burned the wound on his neck and jaw.

With a wave, his father dismissed the archers. Then he frowned down in displeasure. "I would have thought you could have made a much quieter departure."

"No," Shang-Li said, "I couldn't. Else I wouldn't have gotten away at all." He took hold of the anchor rope in both hands and climbed up while bracing his feet against the ship's side.

One of the sailors extended a hand and caught Shang-Li's when he was close enough. Taking advantage of the sailor's strength, Shang-Li allowed himself to be hoisted aboard. His sodden clothing dripped water onto the deck.

His father stepped away and sniffed disdainfully. "The pirates obviously don't care where their filth runs. I'm surprised the sea elves haven't put up a protest."

"The *alu Tel'Quessir* don't enter these waters by choice, nor to they get invited to voice their complaints." Shang-Li accepted a towel from one of the sailors and began drying off. His father was right, though. He did smell foul.

The ship he'd dived from blazed merrily. Evidently the wizard's fireball had spread too quickly for the pirates to put it out. More like, though, they'd abandoned their posts out of fear for their lives.

"Where is Kouldar?" Shang-Li mopped at his face, hoping to rid himself of the stench.

His father stood with a spyglass to his eye. "The wizard was there? Did he get a look at you?"

"Not a good one. Not enough to know me personally."

"But enough to guess who sent you. Enough to guess we were involved."

"He already knew that we would be there. The journal was a trap. He knew someone from the monastery would come for it. He'll be looking for Shou ships." Cold soaked into Shang-Li as the wind picked up and rattled the rigging. Fatigue ached his bones but his mind remained as sharp as his elven blade.

"That shouldn't be a problem." His father's calm was

surprising. "There are plenty of Shou pirates in these waters as well."

The spyglass joints *snicked* in quick succession as his father collapsed the instrument and put it inside one of his voluminous sleeves. Now that he was aboard *Swallow*, he wore a more traditional robe, though without Standing Tree Monastery markings.

"You left a trail through the water." His father's words were thick with accusation.

Shang-Li returned his father's steady gaze. "I left no trail."

His father stepped forward and touched Shang-Li's neck with a finger. "So you say." He held up the finger. It was stained crimson.

Shang-Li cursed silently. There were things that could track a man's blood through water with the unerring accuracy of a shark.

His father wiped his finger on the towel. "Let us hope that it is not *enough* of a trail for the Nine Golden Swords warriors to pick up."

Dead men rained from the black water into the blue. Droust watched as he had so many times before, and the grisly nature of their deaths was not lost on him. Most of the men had drowned when the Blue Lady had taken their ship down. A merciful few of them died by Caelynna's hand when they stood against her. Even if they tried to escape, she killed them. They had no choice but to fight or die like sheep.

Droust didn't know if that lethal side of the Blue Lady's nature came from anger she felt at being marooned to a land unknown to her and abandoned at the bottom of the Sea of Fallen Stars, or if she had always been that vindictive. He suspected the latter.

She floated in the still blue sea and watched the dead men fall around her. One started to fall across her and she caught the body by one leg and threw the corpse away without a second thought.

The shambling monstrosities that lived in the brush darted out from their hiding places and took what the sharks didn't catch. Carnivorous vines slid slowly across the sea floor, but they still managed to reach their prey. Everything that lived within the underwater forest lived to eat other things. Droust often wondered if the forest had been like that before it had been pushed through whatever gate had brought the land to the Inner Sea.

"What do you want, manling?" The Blue Lady spoke without turning around to acknowledge him.

"I have bad news, lady."

She turned to face him then, and Droust though his heart would burst with dread. "What?"

"The monk escaped with the journal."

"Escaped Kouldar?"

"Him. And the Nine Golden Swords." Droust spread his hands. "Lady, if there was any way I could have known—"

"Silence!"

Droust closed his mouth and sat waiting. He had failed her all these years, and now his inability to capture the journal possibly endangered her. He didn't regret the last, but he feared her wrath. The Blue Lady was not one to live with failures or disappointments.

"There is nothing in that journal that can hurt us." She locked eyes with Droust.

"The location of where *Grayling* went down will be in that book. Farsiak would have taken note of that. And there will be mention of you."

"True, but you fools had no idea of who I was or what I desired." The Blue Lady tapped her chin in thought as she watched the stricken ship's debris fall into the canyon in front of her. "For all they knew, I was Umberlee herself risen from the depths to assert my ferocity for some inevitable transgression. Have you ever seen this book, manling?"

Droust thought but it was so hard to get to those memories so many years removed. "I don't think so, lady."

"That doesn't mean you didn't." The Blue Lady crooked her finger. "Approach me."

On shaking legs and feeling very fearful, Droust got to his feet and went forward. He hoped he didn't throw up or foul himself as he had in the past. She always punished him for those instances. When she shoved a hand toward his face, he flinched.

"Stand still."

This time Droust did as she bade, but it was a near thing because he didn't know if his heart or his knees would give out first. Then her hand, like a thing of ice, closed over his face. He closed his eyes, and screamed silently in pain as it felt as though she reached into his brain.

Images flipped through his mind. Then he saw Farsiak, very quick memories of the man on deck and down in the galley. The multitude of remembrances stopped when Droust saw the man sitting in the sterncastle working on a journal.

"Is this the book, manling?"

"Lady, I don't know." Droust's voice was an almost unrecognizable croak and a rasping pain through his throat. "This is a book I saw Farsiak with."

The pain inside Droust's head increased and he felt certain his skull would explode at any moment from the pressure of the Blue Lady's grip. He prayed for unconsciousness or death. Either was preferable to his current agony.

"The book still exists." Enthusiasm echoed in the Blue Lady's declaration. "I can feel it. But there is something more. Something that connects you to it."

"I don't know what that would be, lady."

"Did you ever touch it?"

"No. I swear to you."

The Blue Lady was silent for a time and Droust could

feel her raking talons through his thoughts. "You're telling the truth, manling. I would know if you were lying."

Droust doubted he had the strength to lie.

"But there is something of you within that book."

Droust gasped as he tried to collect his thoughts and answer her unasked question. Anything to make the savage pain desist. "Perhaps it is only the fact that Farsiak mentioned my name in the book. That can sometimes tie a person to another thing." Names had always held power.

Finally, the Blue Lady withdrew her hand and most of the pain ended.

Reeling on his feet, Droust slumped bonelessly to the ground.

The Blue Lady grinned. "There is more than just your name within that book, manling. There is yet another trap I can set. One that won't be so easily escaped as Kouldar's."

Droust doubted that the wizard's defenses and guardians had been easy to escape. Shang-Li the monk had to either be very good or very lucky. Droust didn't know which to wish for.

The sea continued to rain the dead, some of them in pieces that fell close to the scribe.

"When you regain your strength, go and search the ship." The Blue Lady swam upward. "You were in luck. The ship carried no scribes more talented than you. However, I do want to know what else it carried. When you have performed an inventory, find me."

"Yes, lady."

"And let your hired men know that I'm not happy with their progress regarding the book. Tell them I want the book found. And this monk. Perhaps he can help you with the riddle Liou Chang left regarding the gate."

"Yes, lady." Weak and shivering, Droust lay on his back and stared up at the blue depths of his prison. And, more than likely, his grave.

❦ ❦ ❦ ❦ ❦

"Be still."

Shang-Li gritted his teeth and sat on a bench down in the ship's galley. "I *am* being still." He held his head at an awkward angle. His neck burned like molten metal had been poured on it. Before, he'd hardly noticed the pain. Beneath his father's aggravating ministrations, though, he felt the throbbing ache now.

"You're flinching." His father gripped his shoulder and set him straight again.

"You're hurting me."

"Nonsense. Pain is only weakness making itself known."

Shang-Li concentrated on the steady flame inside the lantern resting in the middle of the table. He pulled air into his lungs through his nose and pushed it out through his mouth as he'd been taught.

Shadows of his father's hands played on the wall. They moved as delicately and smoothly as doves, and the string they pulled through the wound in Shang-Li's neck appeared as thin as spider silk.

"Even a novice to the monastery handles pain more easily than you." His father shook his head in disappointment. "You should have been more disciplined in your lessons instead of running through the forest with your mother."

"I excelled at my lessons at the monastery. And I excelled in the lessons Mother taught me as well."

"See? Modesty was one of the most important lessons you failed to learn. An immodest man challenges both friend and foe, and will know no safe harbor."

Nor any peace from his father, Shang-Li thought and took a deep breath, pushing the pain further from his mind.

He tried to turn his thoughts to the journal lying in the middle of the table. Curiosity had always been his greatest balm. Unfortunately, it was also his greatest weakness.

To his surprise, his father had chosen to forego the

opportunity to explore inside the pages and instead concentrated on tending Shang-Li. One of the sailors had rushed to get the old monk's healer's kit. *Swallow* had a cleric on board, but Kwan Yung had insisted on treating the wound himself.

"Be still." His father hissed in frustration when Shang-Li flinched. "Even a novice to the monastery knows how to sit quietly."

Shang-Li groaned inwardly and hoped that his father was soon finished. It felt like a hive of angry bees had taken up residence in his skin.

Presently, though, his father pronounced the wound properly cared for. After Kwan Yung put his medical things away, they turned their attention to the journal. Despite the pain in his neck, Shang-Li touched the bandage to find out how large an area it covered.

"Don't touch that." His father caught his hand and pulled it back. "You'll foul the poultice."

Shang-Li drew his hand back. "Thank you."

His father bowed his head slightly. "You're welcome, my son." His hand trembled slightly as he finished wrapping his kit in a waterproof cover. "That arrow came close, Shang-Li. Another inch or two, or if it had been poisoned, you might not have made it back to us."

Surprised by his father's concern, Shang-Li hesitated a moment. He didn't know whether to feel thankful or insulted.

He faced his father directly. "But I did make it back."

"Yes. Hopefully this will be the worst of it." His father shook his head. "If *Grayling* did not rest on the floor of the Sea of Fallen Stars somewhere, if she hadn't carried the books we're looking for, and if those books weren't so dangerous, I wouldn't worry any more. There are still a great many things that can go wrong." He put the wrapped kit away. "Let us have a look at that journal you brought back."

The journal's author's name had been Farsiak, an older sailor from Impiltur, He'd had a poor acquaintance with the written language, and poorer still with handwriting. The script was in the common tongue, mercifully not in a seafarer's personal code, but the man couldn't spell very well and often used the wrong word when he wasn't writing about the ship or sailing. Shang-Li struggled through the tangled weave of letters to find the tale.

"*Grayling* took men and stores aboard in Impiltur." Kwan Yung stroked his beard and made notes in his personal journal. "Many of the crew were from the area. Including Droust."

Shang-Li was familiar with Bayel Droust's life. He knew the scribe's story probably as well as his father. Most of Farsiak's comments were no surprise.

Except for the entry that was tucked away, nearly illegible, near the end of the journal.

By the time Capn Porgad chose to throw Bayel Droust over the side of the ship, it were already too late. She were coming for us. Werent nothing nobody could do.

If we had slit Droust's gullet sooner, maybe Grayling and all my mates would have lived. But we didnt. And that night the Blue Lady caught up to us.

CHAPTER FIVE

What Blue Lady?"

Shang-Li looked up from the pages of the journal to his father. "I don't know. A Blue Lady wasn't mentioned in any of the materials you gave me to study."

His father frowned and crossed his arms over his thin chest. "I've read of no Blue Lady. Are you sure you are reading from the section dealing with the loss of *Grayling*?"

Shang-Li held up the journal for his father's inspection. The binding showed a craftsman's hand and the stitching remained tight. "We know when the ship went down. I've read through the other entries. The one before this dealt with a trade with sea elves and a brief battle with kuo-toa. And this section details the sinking of the ship. If you'd let me read further.".

"Feh." His father waved Shang-Li's complaint away.

"Was there any mention of the Blue Lady in anything you read?"

"No. I've never heard any mention of a Blue Lady. Perhaps, it is an epithet of Umberlee."

"You're certain Umberlee didn't sink *Grayling*?"

"No one knows what sank that ship." His father sipped his tea and squinted his eyes in irritation. "More reading. Less questions."

"I seem to recall someone telling me that reading was not to give information, but to lead the reader to ask more informed questions." Shang-Li gave his father an innocent look. "Or has the monastery stopped teaching that?"

"If my eyes could read that hen scratching, or if I had all my tools, I wouldn't have to sit here while you baited me."

Shang-Li grinned. "But they are and you don't." He turned back to the pages. "This Blue Lady seems to have made quite an impression on Farsiak."

"Can we verify the journal's veracity?"

Carefully, Shang-Li flipped the journal's weathered pages. They showed a lot of harsh wear. Judging by the wrinkled and smudged condition of the pages, the sailor— Farsiak—hadn't always taken the best care of it.

Only a few pages on, Farsiak listed the sailors that had gone down on *Grayling* and been lost in the brine.

Shang-Li reached into his bag and took out his own journal. He flipped through the pages until he found the list of crewman they'd confirmed had been aboard the ship. Most of the names matched. There were a few he didn't have, and there were a few he had that weren't on Farsiak's list.

Farsiak had also listed the ship's cargo manifest as well as he knew it. *Grayling* had carried several trade goods and supplies.

"Most of these names are the same." Shang-Li showed

his father the list but knew his old eyes couldn't make out the writing.

His father sipped tea. "Continue."

Shang-Li read through the description of the Blue Lady's attack on *Grayling*. With the sound of the ocean all around them and the creak of the sails grabbing the wind above them, he couldn't help but feel a little trepidation. For all the exploration that had been done, the sea—even the Sea of Fallen Stars—was huge and held many secrets. While he read, his father remained silent and attentive.

When he finished, Shang-Li marked his place with a forefinger. "If such a being exists—"

"We don't know that she does. Men who sail the seas are oftentimes bored. They tend to make up stories and stretch the truth. Much of what you'll hear from them will be idle gossip. This could merely be another fabrication."

Shang-Li raised his eyebrows. "Farsiak seemed fearful of her."

"It could be a tale he told many times in taverns. Or even one that he heard."

"Perhaps." But Shang-Li didn't think so. The description and the awe the sailor had had of the woman rang true. He continued reading.

"I may have found the reason for hiding the journal." Shang-Li looked over the page again and made certain of his translation

"What?" His father peered over his shoulder.

It hurts me to think what went down aboard Grayling. That vessel carried a lot of my friends to their deaths, but I know there must have been some gold on her as well. And I never found none of it during my frantic scurry to save my life.

Cap'n Porgad was ever a man to set store by gold and gems. I never seen him go on a voyage that he didn't turn a tidy profit. And he was tight-fisted with what he got, Cap'n

Porgad was. I was never one to begrudge him his good fortune like some was. The cap'n was always good to me.

But we all wondered how much gold that scribe carried on him. The Grand Council put him aboardship and give him enough gold to keep us sailing, and he spent it like it was water. We knew he hadn't reached the bottom of that particular purse. Me and Tholan were looking for that gold in his berth while the captain set to keelhaul the scholar when the Blue Lady struck.

More than that. We were searching for the scribe's secrets. There was books he had, books he put a lot of store by and protected from everbody. Now and again, me and Tholan would take Droust his supper and we'd catch him studying them books. He always looked angry at them, like they were miserly things and he wasn't getting what he wanted from them.

Me and Tholan took a peek at his journal one night while he was sleeping. He was certain that if he could find the secret of them books, some kind of key to a lock, he would be a rich man. Said wizards would pay him a lot for them secrets.

But then the Blue Lady come. By then it was too late. For all of us. Grayling was sent to the bottom with them books and everbody else, and I was clinging to a timber. If it hadn't been for them pirates that picked me up the next day, I'd have died. The sharks was already circling for their next meal.

"Fools," Kwan Yung snapped bitterly. "Whatever gold was aboard that ship, including the captain's profits, couldn't have been much."

"I thought you just warned me to remember the nature of the covetous eye," Shang-Li said. "If Farsiak believed the gold was there, it didn't matter if it really wasn't."

"Even so." His father trailed thoughtful fingers through his wispy beard.

"Evidently Farsiak intended to go back down there." Shang-Li flipped to the end of the journal. There were a lot of blank pages. "Obviously he didn't live much longer himself."

"Or he lost the book."

Shang-Li nodded, agreeing with the possibility. "This also leads us to believe Bayel Droust knew something about what was contained in the books."

His father grimaced. "Just one more reason we need to find those books and get them back in a safe place. The gate spells General Han used to move his troops have almost been forgotten. That knowledge must not fall into the wrong hands."

"I know."

"Is the location of the wreck marked?"

"Not yet."

"You should find that part."

"Do you want a translation as I go or for me to read it and tell you what I find?"

His father scowled in displeasure. He could be the most patient man in the world, then abruptly change into the demanding sort. "The translation. I want to read his words for myself."

In case I miss something, Shang-Li thought and bent back to the task.

Hours later, Shang-Li heard his father's soft snores coming from the corner of the galley. His small body lay curled on the bench as the oil lantern burned the dregs of the reservoir. His personal journal lay open on the table and the pages rode restlessly as the ship rolled across the unsteady sea. His ink-stained fingers still held a quill.

Shang-Li stood and felt his stiff muscles protest the movement. His flight from the wizard's tower had banged him up considerably, and the continued crouch over a text was never physically relaxing.

He reached into his bag and pulled out a thick blanket. Despite the number of things the bag held, the magic within it always made sure whatever Shang-Li reached for was immediately to hand.

Gently, Shang-Li repositioned his father and wrapped him within the comfort of the blanket. The fact that his father didn't wake as Shang-Li moved him spoke volumes about Kwan Yung's fatigue and sense of security aboard *Swallow*. These days his father didn't often leave the monastery. Not out of any sense of vulnerability, but because he felt his time was better spent there among the books.

One of the sailors walked down the steps, then eased his stride when he saw the old man huddled under the blanket in the corner.

"Sleepin', is he?" The sailor was in his graying years, thick with muscle and scarred by conflicts. His shaggy beard hung to his chest. His complexion was almost the color of burnt butter.

"Yes."

"He's a right insufferable man when he chooses to be."

Shang-Li looked down at his father and smiled. "He is that."

"My da was mean as a snake. Took the hide offa me whenever I did something he didn't like. Which was too often by my lights." The sailor shrugged. "This one, he's a mite too demanding and onerous, but he's smart."

"He is. He's a good man."

"If you ask me, he's lucky to have you."

"We're lucky to have each other." Shang-Li didn't like thinking about the hole his mother's death had left in their lives. But it was there every day.

"Well, at least one of you feels lucky. I hope you can feel lucky enough for the both of you."

"Yes," Shang-Li said quietly. "I do."

The sailor poured himself a cup of tea, then offered one to Shang-Li, who politely turned it down. A moment later and the man was gone back up the steps.

At the table where his father had been working,

Shang-Li looked at his father's journal. The page his father had been studying showed much of the same information on *Grayling* as Shang-Li had copied into his own journal. But there were also new passages that contained Shang-Li's name.

For a moment, Shang-Li was tempted to read the passages. When he'd been a child, he'd sometimes gotten the opportunity to read his father's journals. Kwan Yung was a close-mouthed man regarding his adventures and travels, and he'd never glorified any of the explorations he'd taken part of.

But in those pages Shang-Li had come to know his father as another man. In his younger years, Kwan Yung had traveled much of Faerun, seen beautiful things and passed through horrific events. He had loved and battled and sought knowledge of ancient days and places. He had won and he had lost, as the books he'd written and the scars he carried attested to.

Often, Shang-Li had wanted to ask his father about his travels, but he hadn't been able to. Talking about the knowledge he'd gotten from the journals would have revealed the fact that he'd sometimes borrowed and read his father's work. As a private man, Kwan Yung would have taken more care about where he left journals lying around, then Shang-Li wouldn't have gotten to know the views his father held or the experiences he'd had.

All in all, Kwan Yung hadn't been one to loiter around the monastery either.

Gently, Shang-Li closed the book and bound it with the strap again before one of the sailors felt compelled to leaf through it. He placed the journal on the bench beside his father and returned to his work. Only a few pages further in, he found more mention of the Blue Lady.

Shang-Li worked while his father slept. *Swallow* sailed on gracefully, and the ship's crew came and went without interrupting his work. He was surprised at how soundly his father slept, and for how long. When he was a child, his father seemed to stay up for days or existed only on catnaps.

As his hand idly grazed the back cover of the book, Shang-Li felt an almost imperceptible ridge. He selected a small knife from within his bag and carefully lifted the covering from the backboard.

Inside was a sheaf of paper. It was folded once, in halves, and covered with fine penmanship that showed long acquaintance with writing tools. Carefully, Shang-Li slipped the paper free of the hiding place and took it out. He laid it gently on the table.

Glancing at his father, he knew he should wake Kwan Yung. His father would want to know of any discoveries he might make. Shang-Li started to rise and shake him, then relented. Whatever the paper dealt with, and it might have nothing to do with *Grayling* or Liou Chang's missing books, it could wait until after his father caught up on his rest.

Shang-Li, though, knew he wouldn't rest until he knew what the paper held. He moved the candle lantern closer to shed more light.

Dark blue ink formed carefully articulated symbols on the page. Despite the neatness, however, none of the writing made any sense to Shang-Li. He couldn't read any of it. As he watched, the ink took on an unnatural luster, like it was still wet and about to run on the page.

Hypnotized by the effect, Shang-Li slid his finger onto one of the symbols to make certain it was dry. Consciously he knew that there was no way the ink could be wet. More than seventy years had passed since it had been written.

Unless it was a trick Kouldar set up. That thought didn't set well with Shang-Li. He didn't want to have to explain that to his father.

As soon as his finger touched the symbol, a spark flared to life and popped loud enough to echo in the galley. Pain shot through Shang-Li's finger and he yanked it back. The spark was strong enough that he fully expected the paper to catch fire the way a tree did after lightning struck it. For that matter, he expected his finger to be wreathed in flames as well.

His finger turned blue, and went numb. Then, as he watched, the blueness crept up his finger and slid onto his palm, and the numbness moved with it.

Panic welled within Shang-Li and he started to call for his father. There was strange and powerful magic at work here. Then, as he watched, the mark settled onto his palm. It lay there like an animal, burrowed under his skin.

Shang-Li flexed his hand and couldn't feel anything. There was no pain, no pressure, nothing. His hand moved freely. But his heart thudded inside his chest like a wild thing gone mad.

Mielikki, watch over me, Shang-Li prayed. I may have done something incredibly stupid.

"Do you see him?"

With his eyes closed and the Blue Lady's hand upon his brow, Droust did see the young monk. Her spell tied him to the paper he'd written all those years ago. If he hadn't been witness to her power, he would not have believed it.

"Yes, lady. I see him."

"When I first arrived here, the sea was new to me, manling. But I was strong enough to make it mine. I am bound to this wretched piece of my homeland for the time being, but that will not always be so. I won't allow it. I will not be subjugated as I have been in the past. They thought the depths would kill me, but I found power in this sea, and a way in my dying moments to make it mine. Then I grew strong enough to make the sea nourish the land as well."

Droust had heard the story before. He guessed that Caelynna had arrived during the Spellplague, when the riven worlds found their way back together. Wild magic had been loosed upon Toril and so many changes had been wrought. So many things had been destroyed while others changed forever.

"People are made mostly of water, manling." The Blue Lady changed her grip on Droust's head, somehow finding a way to make it even more painful. But he felt the link to the young monk grow stronger as well. "I rule the water. And I will rule the sea stirred inside men by their hearts."

Droust struggled to cling to his senses only because he knew the Blue Lady would punish him for passing out. He didn't know how he endured the pain. But at last she withdrew her hand from him.

"Good. You did well, manling." The Blue Lady smiled in satisfaction. "Now this monk is mine. We'll find out how good he is, and I'll bring him here." She paused. "You had better hope that he isn't any smarter about Liou's books than you have been."

"Lady, even if you get him here, even if he can break Liou's code, you don't know that you can trust him."

"Do I know that I can trust you?"

Droust hesitated, wondering if it was a trick question. "Yes, lady. I still want to live."

She regarded him pitilessly. "We are both prisoners, you and I. But I live to be free and would risk my life in the doing of that. But you—you want only to live. Even if it is in a miserable existence."

In his fear, Droust didn't have room to be ashamed of his cowardice. That fear was a part of his life. He was certain that the only way he could be free of it was to be dead. He wasn't ready to die.

"We can track the monk now. Soon I will be inside his mind, as I was in yours, and I will draw him to us. In the meantime, order the Nine Golden Swords to find him."

"Yes, lady." Droust watched her go, then turned back to his desk and took out the crystal she had enspelled to allow him contact with the Nine Golden Swords. His fear throbbed inside him. But he did as he was bade.

"Who was the Blue Lady?"

Shang-Li tore a bite-sized portion from the deep-fried bread he held and dipped it into the fish-flavored congee. The rice gruel stuck to the fry bread and he popped it into his mouth.

His father gestured for him to speak. "You were up all night studying the journal. You have a better idea of her from the entries, surely."

Shang-Li did, but he knew his father wouldn't like it. "Farsiak believed she was a goddess."

"Nonsense." Across the breakfast table in the galley, Kwan Yuan dipped his fry bread into sweetened milk and let it soak for a moment. "We know all of the gods and goddesses."

"We did until the Spellplague. Things have changed." Shang-Li's eyes burned. He'd only dozed a short time before his father had wakened him to breakfast, and none of that had been restful. His mind had churned constantly. Stiffness from his exertions and bruising the day before filled his body. He needed to stretch them out and promised himself that he would.

"Why would a goddess make herself known to Bayel Droust?" his father asked. "Why would she destroy *Grayling*?"

"Farsiak felt Droust had been chosen by the Blue Lady."

"Chosen for what?"

"Droust was the only one that the Blue Lady didn't kill that day."

"Except for this sailor."

"He felt he escaped only because she didn't care if he lived or died."

His father nodded. "However, Farsiak could also have

chosen to view his continued existence to her generosity."

"He chose *not* to see it that way. As evidenced by his journal. And the fact that he never put to sea again." Shang-Li reached for another piece of fried bread.

"Feh. Wouldn't Droust have known he was the chosen of a goddess before that night?"

Shang-Li sipped his green tea. "Does one always know when the gods have favored them?"

"Of course."

"We don't all worship the same gods."

His father looked at him.

"Perhaps," Shang-Li said, "some gods choose to follow different paths and enjoy surprises as well as the next person."

Kwan Yung licked sweetened milk from his fingertips. "Some clerics would argue that point."

"I found something else of interest in the book."

"What?"

Shang-Li reached for the sailor's journal and laid it before him. "While I was working with it last night, I discovered a hiding place." He pulled at the cloth and separated it from the binding. Revealed within, the single folded ivory sheet stood out against the dark binding.

Kwan Yung reached for the paper, but Shang-Li closed the book before his father could reach it.

"Not yet." Shang-Li knew he was enjoying the moment too much. Anger flared in his father's hazel eyes and he took that as a warning. Still, he couldn't simply tell his father what he had discovered.

"You try my patience. This mission that we're on is very important."

"I know. That's why I think we both need this instruction." Shang-Li tapped the book in his hands. "We were so intent on what was contained within the book that we didn't question the book itself."

His father looked at book with new eyes. "This is a well made book."

Shang-Li smiled, confident that his father had caught on to their mistake. "The book has been hard used. It was easy to miss the quality of its construction."

Irritation tightened his father's frown. "Feh. The stitching alone gives away the nature of the book. I should not have overlooked that."

"*We* should not have overlooked that."

"Why would a sailor keep a journal in a book so fine?" His father pulled thoughtfully at his chin whiskers. "A captain who wants to make a favorable impression on merchants trusting their cargoes with him might keep such a book. He would be able to afford and justify the expense of such a book. A light-fingered sailor might pilfer such a book from his captain."

"A captain would consider such a book an investment," Shang-Li pointed out.

His father nodded. "The captain of *Grayling* was an honorable man, and a stickler for details. That's why the Council chose him and his ship. If someone had stolen this book from him, he would have turned the ship inside out to find it."

Shang-Li tapped the journal again. "We're in agreement then. There was only one person aboard that ship who had extra books and might not notice if one went missing."

"Droust." His father smiled. "Perhaps your lessons at the monastery were not squandered after all."

"Mother taught me how to read sign in the wild. She taught me to notice variances in everything I looked at. Especially things I thought I already knew. If anything, I've neglected what she taught me this time."

Kwan Yung pursed his lips and shook his head slightly, but he didn't argue the point. "Did the sailor know this paper was here?"

"There's no indication of the binding having been disturbed before I lifted it. If I hadn't felt the discrepancy beneath my fingertips, I wouldn't have noticed it either. The paper was very well hidden."

"You've looked at it?"

"I have. And it only offers yet another conundrum." Shang-Li fished out the paper, unfolded it, and left it there for his father to peruse.

After a brief inspection, his father leaned more closely to the paper and gave it a more thorough examination. He traced the lines with his forefinger, then quickly drew back in surprise.

"Did you feel that?" his father asked.

"The shock?" Shang-Li inquired.

His father nodded and rubbed his forefinger against the ball of his thumb.

"When I touched paper, there was a spark. It bit into my hand." Shang-Li showed his father the indigo spot that had been left on his palm.

Concern darkened his father's eyes. "Are you sure you are well? Books have sometimes been treated with all manner of traps."

"I know. I had the ship's mage examine my hand." Shang-Li made a fist and still felt some of the dull tingling he'd experienced since touching the paper. "He said magic had lingered within the paper, but it was nothing that would harm me."

"We're going to put into port soon. Perhaps we should have someone check your hand there."

"If there are any problems, we can do that, but I don't think that's going to be necessary."

"I've touched the paper several times since the first shock," Shang-Li said. "It didn't affect me again. I think whatever residual force remained within the paper has been expended. I think it was just the remnants of a defensive spell, nothing more. I was surprised it affected you."

"Not in the same manner that it has affected you." His father offered his hand for inspection. His forefinger was unblemished.

An uneasy feeling twisted through Shang-Li's stomach as he cast a surreptitious glance at his marked palm. It's nothing, he told himself again. Still, he made a fist and tried to will the faint numbness away.

"I can't read this page." His father frowned in displeasure. Kwan Yung ran his fingers through his wispy beard. "This looks more like a code than a language."

That was the consensus Shang-Li had reached. "Which leads us to a bigger problem: Droust knew many languages."

"Deciding whether he chose to construct a code in his native tongue or in some other . . . Have you matched this handwriting against a sample of Droust's handwriting?"

"You're better at confirming that than I am."

His father nodded. "I'm also better acquainted with Droust's works." He sighed. "Let me work on knowing Droust better while you remain focused on transcribing the journal. Maybe I can find something that will help us with this code."

Shang-Li tried not to let his disappointment show. He knew his father would divide the labor as he had, but he wished he could pursue the mystery of the note.

"Ship's hit a reef! We're going down! Man the lifeboats!"

In the dream, Shang-Li woke in the hold, where he'd retreated after a storm the night before had liberally drenched *Jakkar's Fox*, soaking her decks. He grabbed his bag and slung it over his shoulder, and grabbed the sword he'd carried then.

Although he knew he was asleep and dreaming, the old fear of sinking returned to him. He felt the cold mist and the light breath of the fog as it surrounded him when he reached the deck. *Jakkar's Fox* was quickly sinking. The merchant ship took on water in her busted prow like a sieve. She waddled and rolled like an ungainly duck.

All around Shang-Li, merchants and their wives screamed in fear. The pleasant trip they'd expected had ended suddenly. A few of them had died that day, and Shang-Li was surprised at how well he remembered their faces in the dream. There had been the silk merchant from Chessenta, a guildsman from Impiltur who was relocating to Westgate in hopes of better business, the twin sons of an investor in the Dragon's Reach that had fancied themselves as ladies' men.

As he had done on that deadly day, Shang-Li helped the passengers into the lifeboats.

Only this time, every person Shang-Li tried to help turned to a corpse as soon as he touched them. They turned to him, hollow-eyed, and breathed their last rancid breath on him, then crumbled into butcher's slops at his feet.

Blessed Mielikki, what was happening? Shang-Li froze as a young girl watched him drop her dead mother to the deck. The little girl ran screaming through the panicked crew and passengers already swamping through water that rushed across the floundering ship's deck. The captain and his crew drew their weapons.

"What are ye a doing there?" Blikaga, the ship's first mate, drew his sword and strode toward Shang-Li.

Shang-Li tried to protest and tell all them that it wasn't his fault, he was only trying to help. But his voice wouldn't work. No matter how hard he tried, no sound would emerge. He backed away, unwilling to fight the men he'd accepted as casual friends. Only a few days before they'd risked their lives together to repel a pirate attack.

"Stop!" The woman's imperious voice rang out.

Everyone aboard *Jakkar's Fox* froze in place.

A moment later, she strode through the billowing fog. Her blue skin marked her immediately, Her beauty was breath-taking and she knew it. Despite the fact that the ship was sinking fast, every person aboard *Jakkar's Fox* watched her, spellbound.

Then she faded from view and a row of monstrous tentacles at least forty feet long burst from the fogbank. Some flailed into men and knocked them overboard while others grabbed men and crushed them to death.

Shang-Li tried to run but there was nowhere to go. With the tentacled monster weighing the ship down, it sank even more quickly. Before he knew it, Shang-Li was in the water. Something grabbed his foot and dragged him down. He fought but couldn't escape.

The Blue Lady's face somehow formed in the water. It wasn't flesh. It looked more like the gelatinous, translucent mass of a jellyfish.

"Come to me, manling. If you're brave enough." She mocked him with her laughter.

Shang-Li woke in a cold sweat and stared around the cabin he shared with his father. He had escaped *Jakkar Fox's* sinking, but it had been a near thing. He'd been tangled in the rigging when he'd gone down. But there had been no tentacled monster, and no Blue Lady.

He brought his knees up to his chest and wrapped his arms around his legs. He knew it had been a dream, but he couldn't help feeling it had been more than that as well. He worked on his breathing, leveling off all the anxiety and panic the dream had brought with it.

Knowing he wasn't going to be able to sleep belowdecks, he grabbed his gear and went out onto the deck. It was the darkest hours before the dawn, the time when the world seemed its quietest. After hanging a hammock, Shang-Li sat there for a long time, then the familiar rocking of a ship under sail finally lulled him back to sleep.

CHAPTER SIX

Vibrations in the wooden floor of the crow's-nest drew Shang-Li from the sketch he was working on. He'd summoned images from the dream and brought them to life on the paper, surprised at how much that effort had given new birth to the fear he'd felt the previous night. Even before he saw who climbed into the crow's nest, his fighting sticks were in his hands.

Yugi, the young sailor that often occupied *Swallow's* crow's nest as lookout, hesitated as he hung onto the ratlines that ran to the top of the ship's mainmast. Constant exposure to sun and salt air had given his black hair an orange sheen and his buttery skin baked pink every day until it looked like coals burned within his flesh. He held up one hand and grinned at Shang-Li.

"Easy. I just came up because the captain ordered me up here." Yugi returned his hand to the ratlines. "We're hoping to be within sight of the coast before long."

Shang-Li put the sticks away and searched for the book he had been working in. The copy he had made of Farsiak's journal sat beside him. The wooden case containing his writing implements sat atop it where he had left it. He pushed himself into a sitting position and folded his legs so that Yugi could enter the crow's nest.

The young sailor leaned back nonchalantly against the edge of the crow's nest. He scented the air like a hound.

"Storm's coming." He scowled. "It'll probably catch up with us toward sundown."

Shang-Li shaded his eyes against the westering sun and spotted the storm clouds rolling off in the distance. "Where are we?"

"Not far from the coast. Close to Urmlaspyr. The captain didn't want to be caught out in the middle of the sea in case a big squall rose up, so we'll hug the land for the next day or so. We'll probably reach the coast in time to drop anchor for the night."

That announcement probably hadn't gone over well. Shang-Li knew his father was in a hurry to return to Westgate for supplies. At least the city wasn't much farther. Weather and wind permitting, *Swallow* would reach her destination in three or four more days.

By that time, Shang-Li hoped to have a location in mind to search. Of course, Westgate offered difficulties of its own. Not to mention the menace of the Nine Golden Swords. He yawned creakily.

"Mayhap you should try sleepin' at night," Yugi said. "Take your nose out of that book for a while. That much readin' can't be good for you."

"I haven't been able to sleep." Shang-Li rubbed his marked hand against his thigh. The blue stain hadn't yet faded. During the last two nights, he'd revisited other sea voyages he'd gone on in the past. In the Dragon's Reach, he'd help find and salvage *Tauric's Cross*, a merchanter that had gone down three hundred and forty years before. In the dream, the hold had been filled with writhing snake-things big enough to swallow a man whole.

Then there had been the time a storm had left *Brass Lantern* overturned. The captain and crew had worked four days to get her right side up again. They had never sunk as they had in the dream, and they had never been preyed upon by shambling creatures that struck quick as lightning.

And in all of those dreams, the Blue Lady had always put in an appearance to taunt him. Shang-Li scratched idly at the blue mark on his hand. He'd cut it with a knife, but only got blood out that morning, none of the blue discoloration.

Yugi smiled. "You're not tired because you're not working on this ship. A sailing man, he's glad to hit his rack every night because he's put in a full day's work."

Shang-Li ignored the jibe. He reached into the cloth bag he'd tied to the side of the crow's nest to keep it from under-foot. He found an apple, a chunk of cheese, and a half-loaf of bread that still felt acceptably soft. Still seated on crossed legs, he took out a small knife and set to his breakfast.

"That's a poor meal," Yugi observed. "Cook's set a fine table this morning. You should wander on down and eat a good breakfast."

"Trying to be rid of me?" Shang-Li used his knife to bring an apple slice to his mouth.

Yugi shrugged. "Actually I don't mind having you with me. I spend a lot of hours up here by myself. After a while I start talking to myself just to have company."

Shang-Li didn't want to go down to breakfast. His father would be there and the likelihood of an argument would ensue. Over the last few days, Shang-Li had gotten no closer to the identity of the blue woman that had destroyed

Grayling. Farsiak maintained throughout that she was a goddess of the sea.

Worst of all, if his father had discovered anything about the mysterious paper, he wasn't sharing that knowledge.

"Can I look at your book?" Yugi gestured toward Shang-Li's journal.

"You may." Shang-Li cut a slice of bread and a slice of cheese, then put them together and ate them. The sharp cheese jarred with a taste of the apple but his stomach rumbled in anticipation of being filled.

"Several of the crew are curious about this sailor's story." Yugi flipped through pages, stopping every now and again as something caught his eye. Mostly it was images of the Blue Lady.

"There's not much to know." Shang-Li cut another wedge of apple. "Farsiak kept up an intermittent log of his life for six years after the shipwreck of the *Grayling*."

"Have you finished copying his book?"

"Yes."

"So what became of him?"

Shang-Li shook his head. "I don't know. It's hard for a man to write of his death after he's dead."

"Aye, I suppose that would be true enough." Then Yugi grinned evilly. "Unless he became a lich or something."

That, Shang-Li told himself, isn't a pleasant thought. But he knew it was true.

"What do you think happened him?"

"Maybe he simply died of old age or in a fight in a tavern." Shang-Li had considered Farsiak's passing while working on the journal.

That was one of the differences between the work he'd learned to do in the monastery and the work his mother had taught him in the forests. In the monastery, a book often led to trails that couldn't be explored. However, in the forests, Shang-Li had learned to follow a trail he'd cut by going forward to find out what it happened, or backward to find out how it had all begun.

Yugi leafed through the pages carefully, his fingers barely touching the edges. His gaze scanned Shang-Li's neat writing but the pages of text didn't hold his interest for long. Instead he studied the illustrations Shang-Li had made. "You're one of the best artists I've ever seen."

"Possibly you haven't seen very many artists."

"Depends on who you want to call an artist. There's men who do tattooing that do beautiful work as well. Just a different canvas."

Shang-Li smiled. "I suppose that's true."

"You don't have to grow up in a monastery to appreciate art." Yugi looked over the top of the page with a sly half-smile. "Of course, you didn't exactly grow up in a monastery yourself, from what I've been told. And you haven't been there to stay in years."

Well, sailors aboard this vessel do like their gossip, Shang-Li thought ruefully. "No, I didn't and I haven't."

Yugi continued turning the pages. Over the last few days he had seen most of the work Shang-Li had done with the translation. "I love the drawings you do of the ship. Is this how she looked?" He held the journal open to one of the pages that showed *Grayling* cutting across the open sea.

"Perhaps. I've never seen her, but I know the kind of ship she was supposed to be."

Yugi turned pages and indicated another drawing. "This one really turns my stomach."

The drawing showed *Grayling* breaking apart amid storm-tossed waves. The illustration was rendered in fine enough detail that crewmen could be seen hanging from the edges of the stricken ship and in the water.

A feminine figure stood atop a twisting wave, riding it gracefully like it was a spirited mount. She had her hand outstretched and it was obvious the sea and the wind obeyed her will.

"Watching gods." Yugi unconsciously touched the charm

that hung from his necklace. "I've never seen a ship go down, and luck willing, I never will. Just the thought of being pulled down into the sea turns my guts to water."

"It's not a pleasant experience," Shang-Li admitted.

The young sailor's eyes rounded in surprise. "You've gone down aboardship?"

"I have. Twice."

"What happened?"

"The first time, pirates scuttled our ship after taking our cargo. Most of us survived because we weren't far from shore. The second time a reef ripped our bottom during a sea quake. Not even the ship's mage had any warning." Shang-Li shut away the pain that accompanied that particular memory. "Many of the crew and passengers didn't survive."

Yugi met his gaze with the honest intensity of youthful inexperience. "You lost friends aboard that ship?"

"I did. Very good friends."

"I'm sorry for your loss."

"Thank you."

Silence between them for a moment. Gull cries sounded overhead and pierced the gentle luffing of a loose sail. Shadowed by the mainsail, Shang-Li looked up into the clear blue sky and saw the line of storm clouds had crept nearer despite the pilot's efforts to outrun it in a parallel course.

Moonwhisper sat on a yardarm only a short distance away. The owl was nocturnal and didn't enjoy the sun as much as Shang-Li did. Despite Shang-Li's offer, Moonwhisper wouldn't remain in the darkness of the hold. Shang-Li knew his animal companion sensed the unease that filled him and refused to be separated even aboard *Swallow*.

The owl's territorial nature awakened with the arrival of the gulls. Feathers ruffling, Moonwhisper shifted on the yardarm and focused on the gulls gliding nearby. His keen talons scored the hardwood. When one of the birds darted too close, Moonwhisper unfurled his wings in warning.

Easy, my friend. Shang-Li slipped into the owl's mind and reassured him. For all the adventures they had shared, for all the distance they were from Moonwhisper's home, the raptor had remained stalwart.

"Do you think it happened like this?"

Shang-Li turned back to the young sailor and found him again studying the drawing of the Blue Lady confronting *Grayling.* "When I read Farsiak's description of those events, that's the image I formed in my mind." It was also one he'd seen in his dreams, again and again. Now it almost felt as though he'd really been there.

Yugi was quiet for a moment and the sound of the gulls' cries echoed around them. A few conversations from the crewmen on deck drifted up to reach them.

"Here, she looks very fierce," the young sailor observed. Then he turned the page to one of the latest drawings Shang-Li had completed. "But here, she looks very beautiful."

Shang-Li studied the drawing and stared into the silver eyes that held so much cold cruelty. She was beautiful, her skin like pale blue marble, and every inch of her feminine. Instead of simply sketching her in charcoal, he'd used chalks to add in the color. Her long hair fell past her shoulders in thick curls. Shells and pearls hung on a few of the ringlets. Dark blue and black armor barely protected her and served mainly to reveal enchanting her assets. A small buckler hung on her left wrist. A crest that resembled rain falling from a cloud lay in the center of it, but Shang-Li hadn't been able to divine its nature.

"She is beautiful," Shang-Li acknowledged. "But many of nature's most dangerous things are. Oftentimes, beauty is just a lure for the unwary."

"You got all of this from the description in that journal?"

Unease spun through Shang-Li. "Not all of it. Some of it comes merely from my imagination." But some of it didn't.

"Have you finished being petulant then?"

Recognizing his father's voice immediately, Shang-Li curbed his irritation at his inability to find something meaningful in Farsiak's journal. He didn't bother glancing up from the snarled fishing nets he worked on. Stymied in his pursuit of information from the journal, unable to get past his father's door and unwilling to seek him out to ask him questions, Shang-Li had turned to ship's chores to occupy his busy mind. He had other books and other studies to attend to in his bag, but he found himself unable to focus on those things.

"I don't know what you're talking about," Shang-Li replied coolly.

His father stood nearby and easily balanced on the rolling ship's deck. "You're playing with ropes like a common sailor."

"Perhaps it's only because I'm being treated like a common sailor."

His father sighed. "I see you haven't given up your petulance."

Shang-Li looked up at his father then. "I'm not one of your students, Father, to be dismissed so casually. I'm here now because you wish me to be, and so did the monastery council."

His father shoved his hands into his opposing sleeves. His students would have quailed at that.

"At the monastery, you are taught to honor your elders. I find it shameful that I need to remind you."

"I was also taught that a man should treat another equally when they share a duty." Despite the easy way the words tumbled from his mouth, Shang-Li wished they were not discussing this. He felt angry at the way he always seemed the child before his father.

A hint of fire flashed through Kwan Yung's hazel eyes. "You think I am treating you as less than an equal?"

For a moment Shang-Li considered denying the line of thought. But it was how he felt.

"Yes."

"How am I doing that?"

Shang-Li lowered his voice so that hopefully not every sailor in the vicinity could overhear. Still, he had no doubt that the crew would learn of the encounter. And their tongues would wag.

"You took that paper after I discovered it."

"Nor have I discussed my findings with you, have I?"

"No." In truth, his father had obviously taken pains to stay away from him.

"You think I have shut you out, don't you?"

"Haven't you?"

His father sighed again but his features softened a little. For the first time Shang-Li noticed how tired his father appeared.

"I keep forgetting how long it's been since you've done any original work at the monastery," his father stated. "These . . . *adventures* you're so enthralled with aren't disciplined things."

Shang-Li started to protest.

His father held up a hand and silenced him. "I would ask that you remember that you're not dealing with one of those skilled amateurs you normally travel with. I am a trained researcher, and I work in a disciplined environment. If anything, I would have shown you disrespect by allowing you to watch me work."

Immediately, embarrassment flushed through Shang-Li and chased away his anger. He *had* forgotten how two equals worked to solve a problem at the monastery. The monks didn't work together. They worked independently, each assessing a manuscript or problem on their own, then coming together to present their thoughts and impressions for discussion.

Working together often tainted critical thinking. More was learned through independent research and discussions than through a joint conjecture at the beginning.

"I treated you as an equal," his father said. "Otherwise I would have invited you to work with me."

Shang-Li bowed his head in embarrassment. "I had forgotten."

"Let us hope that you still retain *some* of the training we invested in you."

Shang-Li knew that his father's words were sharper then they needed to be, but he also felt deserving of his father's ire.

"These books are very important, Shang-Li."

"I know, Father. Liou's books weren't meant for anyone to read. There is too much dangerous knowledge written into those pages. I understand that." Shang-Li thought about mentioning the dreams, but he wasn't quite ready for that.

"I've left the paper in the cabin for you." His father gestured over his shoulder. "I suggest you eat something as well. You need to keep up your strength. You can use the room if you'd like."

"Thank you, but no. I'd prefer to work outside, by natural light, as long as I am able."

His father nodded. "As you wish." He turned and walked away. "We'll talk again when you're finished with your examinations of the document."

As Shang-Li watched his father's retreating back, sadness and anger—both of them new and old—warred inside him. He didn't know why they could find no peace between them. It wasn't his elf heritage or the training that his mother had given him. There was just something between them that seemed insurmountable.

Shortly before sunset, *Swallow* made land.

A storm was brewing on the open sea. Yugi shouted out the news of a land sighting, and they sailed a short distance farther before finding a comfortable cove where the captain felt safe enough to drop anchor. Sailors went ashore only briefly as the storm closed in quickly.

However, the cove was one that had been used before by other ships. The shore party filled a few barrels with fresh water from a nearby spring to replace some of the water that had turned brackish over the last few days. They even managed to find a few succulent berries on bushes near the spring.

Shang-Li went with them long enough to allow Moonwhisper to hunt voles and eat his fill. While he waited for the owl to return, Shang-Li took shelter within a small cave. Wind whipped the trees around and fat raindrops splashed the stone mouth of the cave. Thankfully, the cave tilted up into the short cliff and no rain entered, but that didn't keep out the cold draft.

Working while maintaining contact with Moonwhisper, Shang-Li laid dry wood he'd gathered while in the forest. Shortly after that, a cheery fire filled the cave. Smoke hugged the cave's roof and the dancing flames revealed the crude drawings left by prior bored tenants.

Shang-Li smiled at the drawings. Some had been rendered by scratching a knife point into the stone while others had been created with simple paints made with grease and stone powders. No matter where he'd gone, inside caves and inside towns, men had left their marks. Perhaps the effort met a need to be noticed, and a desire to leave something of themselves behind.

Sitting cross-legged, Shang-Li reached into his back and withdrew the pale white sheet. Although he tried, he discerned no mark left by his father's examination. Shang-Li wasn't sure if he was disappointed. Some clue as to what his father was thinking might have been welcome.

Or it might have influenced your own conclusions, he reminded himself wryly.

He released his breath and focused on the paper. There

was more to it than the nonsensical writing. He was certain of that. A strong force lurked within the paper. The blue mark on his palm pulsed raggedly.

Still aware of Moonwhisper sitting in a tree with a full stomach only a short distance outside the cave, Shang-Li pushed away all thoughts and placed the paper on a stone in front of him. He held his open hand above the sheet and gave his senses over to the magic he felt inside the writing.

At first, nothing happened. Then a vortex swept him into darkness. He thought he heard Moonwhisper call out to him, but if the owl made a noise, it was lost in the sharp crack of thunder.

CHAPTER SEVEN

"Wake, manling."

The imperious command focused Shang-Li's attention. Lost in the soft darkness, the voice drew him like a beacon.

"Did you not hear me?" the voice asked again more sharply.

This time Shang-Li was certain the voice was that of a woman. He was also certain that he knew which woman it was, but he didn't understand how that could be.

Without warning, a strong hand closed around his shoulder and yanked him forward. The blackness went away and was replaced by muted blue. Shang-Li noticed at once that his movements were uncoordinated, slower and heavier as he flailed for his balance.

During his travels in the Sea of Fallen Stars and along the Sword Coast, he had sometimes ventured to the sea bottom in search of sunken cities and broken ships. The gentle rolling hills reminded him of those experiences immediately. Brain coral and reefs dotted the ocean floor, and myriad fish swam all around him.

His breath locked in his lungs at once when he realized he was deep underwater. Frantic, he glanced up and wondered how far he was from the surface. The immediate dark pall above looked daunting.

Surely it was too far to swim.

Instead of gradually growing lighter as it should have, the sea turned pitch black overhead. A few glittering stars flashed in the distance, but from the way they moved he was certain they were luminous fish.

Despite the certainty that he'd never reach the surface, he leaped from the ground and started to swim. A strong iron band closed around his left ankle and jerked him to a stop. Precious air bubbled from his lips as he twisted to free himself.

The Blue Lady stood beneath him and seemed to hold him effortlessly with one hand. Cruelty filled her cold eyes and twisted her full lips into a smile. She looked as beautiful and deadly as Farsiak had described in his journal and as Shang-Li had dreamed her.

"You'll not escape me too easily, minnow." She yanked him back without apparent strain.

Desperate, Shang-Li opened his mouth, thinking maybe she had ensorcelled him. As deep as he was, and he thought he was perhaps deeper than he'd ever been before, the weight of the sea should have crushed him. Yet he lived.

When he opened his mouth, however, salt water trickled between his lips. The thick brine immediately turned him queasy and he thought he was going to be sick. He sealed his lips tightly against the sea.

"Are you drowning, manling?" She mocked gasping for air and took delight in his vulnerability.

Shang-Li doubled over and reached for slim hand that held him with incredible strength. He gripped her thumb in one hand and started pulling. No matter how strong an opponent was, bones still joined together in the same fashion. They still had weaknesses that could be exploited.

If they're human, he told himself.

She yelped in surprised pain and released him. Fire burned within Shang-Li's chest and he thought he could feel his lungs dwindling. He swam upward again, but from the corner of his eye he saw the woman gesture and heard a growled command in an unknown tongue.

Gray bodies knifed through the water around him. In the next heartbeat, the distorted images of six sharks appeared before him. One of them streaked for him and he was unable to get away in time. The hard muscled body slammed against him. His breath left his lungs and he felt hot scratches that scored his chest from the impact.

When he glanced down, he saw that the wounds were deep enough to draw blood. He knew the scent of the fresh blood in the water would send the sharks into a feeding frenzy. He shook his sticks into his hands and knew that he was about to be torn apart.

"Don't try to be too much trouble, manling." The Blue Lady stared into his eyes. "I find myself curious about you, but that won't save you from my irritation." She cocked her head and regarded him again. "You are not totally human."

Shang-Li tried to swim away but wasn't able to elude the sharks. Another collided with his side and scratched him again. He wasn't sure if the impact had broken ribs, but it felt like it might have. The last of his breath escaped him in a cry of pain that slid from his mouth in a stream of silver bubbles.

The Blue Lady gestured toward him and passed her open palm over his face. "Breathe. If I had wanted you dead, you already would be so. You're worth much more to me alive at this point."

For a moment longer, Shang-Li tried to hold his breath. He didn't trust the Blue Lady, and he didn't want to take anything from her. Characters in stories oftentimes became cursed for eating or drinking or taking gifts from a malicious host. And he was certain the Blue Lady meant nothing good.

Then, when he felt about to pass out and his head thudded painfully—no longer in control of his body, he took a breath. He expected to feel the cold rush of the sea fill his lungs and spin his senses away.

Instead, he breathed air. The heaviness and slowness left him as well. When he moved through the water now, he could move as well as he could on dry land. He knew he'd been spelled. He had a ring in his bag that allowed him the same kind of freedom underwater.

"If you try to leave me again," the Blue Lady told him imperiously, "then I will remove my protection from the sharks. And you will once again drown. But I don't think the sharks will let you live long enough to do that."

Shang-Li gazed at the predatory creatures circling him. The black eyes and severely curved mouths left him no doubt about what they would do to him. They were more agitated now, and he knew the blood scent in the water affected them.

Gracefully, Shang-Li swam back down to face the Blue Lady and landed just beyond her reach. He knew the sense of safety brought about by the distance was false, but he chose to take comfort in it anyway.

"Why did you bring me here?" He met her gaze with effort because she seemed so threatening.

"Why do you come seeking me?"

"I'm not seeking you."

She smiled mirthlessly at him. "Yet our paths converge."

"I don't even know where we are."

"You are there, on that ship. Headed for here. I know this."

"How?"

"Don't try my patience, manling." Though her voice was sweet, the Blue Lady's tone dripped with threat.

At her mercy, knowing all she had to do was withhold her spell so he could no longer breathe the sea, Shang-Li nodded. "Lady, I'm looking for books that Bayel Droust had."

"Why? What makes those books so special?"

"The monastery I serve searches for those books. They are important histories."

His form of address and his apparent willingness to tell the truth pleased her and her smile held a bit more warmth.

"Do you know Bayel Droust?" Interest flickered in those silver eyes.

"No. He died long before I was born." Shang-Li didn't bother to correct her reference to Droust. She hadn't spoken of him in the past tense. Common obviously wasn't a tongue she was used to.

"Where are these books you seek?"

"They went down in the ship that Droust sailed on all those years ago, lady."

"How many years?"

Surprised at the strange question, Shang-Li hesitated.

"Come now," the Blue Lady rebuked him. "Surely you know how many years it's been. Manlings have a love of counting years gone by."

"Over seventy, lady."

The sharks continued to circle. Shang-Li still bled into the open water. They tasted him, but they couldn't have him.

"A pittance," the Blue Lady said.

"A lot to my people."

"Half of your people, don't you mean?" She reached out and delicately stroked Shang-Li's left ear tip with her fingers. The touch seemed casual but was delicious. Shang-Li felt as though he were about to melt. "You are elven."

There was no denying that. Nor would he want to. He took pride in both of his heritages. "My mother was an elf."

"I knew of your elven nature. I could sense that about you."

Shang-Li remained silent as the sharks continued to swim around them.

"What makes these books so important that you have to come looking for them seventy years gone?" she asked.

"As I said, they're part of a history of interest to my people."

"The elves?"

"No, Lady."

"These are books that manlings are interested in?"

"Yes, Lady."

"Why did Bayel Droust have the books?"

"He was studying them."

The Blue Lady frowned and her sharply arched eyebrows knitted. "He has not mentioned these books to me."

The constant referral to Droust in the present tense was unsettling to Shang-Li. "Perhaps there was no time."

"There is time now." The Blue Lady grabbed her seaweed robe and whirled around. "There is time now. Come." She started walking away.

Shang-Li thought momentarily of breaking away and trying to swim for the surface. The sharks crowded in, though, and made it obvious that they weren't going to let him swim away.

This is a dream, Shang-Li told himself. All you have to do is wake up. He tried, but in the end he trailed after the Blue Lady.

Something had changed the ocean floor. Where normally only coral and a few plants would grow, riotous life filled the seascape all around Shang-Li. He had been down to the ocean's floor enough times to know that what he was looking at now was in no way normal.

Monstrous crags became cliffs and mountains that offered high precipices and sudden death to a climber on land. In the ocean the fall would only require someone to start swimming. Strange plants, most of them luminous to some degree, stood out against the dead hulks of forests. Blackened tree trunks lay spilled haphazardly in all directions.

And amid those dead forests and new growths lay broken ships. Cargoes of gold gleamed on the sea floor, thrown in all directions by whatever had ripped the ships asunder.

Only a short distance farther on, one of the plants near the trail the Blue Lady followed lunged out at Shang-Li. He caught the movement in the periphery of his vision and spun away as his fighting sticks dropped into his hands.

The plant was easily ten feet tall and stood supple. Vines trailed from branches and struck like whips. Seven purple blossoms with leafy fringes whirled toward Shang-Li. Two of them opened to reveal fanged mouths.

Four of the vines wrapped about Shang-Li's right forearm. Three more caught him by his right leg. Pain filled him when the vines constricted and dragged him toward the gaping mouths. All the blossoms bent toward him.

Shang-Li struck the vines with the fighting sticks and succeeded in tearing them free of his arm. Bloody furrows showed where the vine had taken hold. Before he could set himself to swing again, the vines holding his leg gave a mighty yank and pulled him from his feet. Helpless, he flailed for a moment as the vines reeled him in like a fisherman taking his catch.

He doubled up, folding himself in half, and managed to thrust one of his fighting sticks into the nearest blossom. Greenish pulp exploded from the flower as the weapon plowed through the leafy head. The blossom shivered and let out an ear-piercing shriek.

Shang-Li watched the thing's death throes as he swung his other fighting stick at the next blossom. Even as that one erupted into another gush of viscous green ooze, the third and fourth blossoms bit into his calf and thigh.

Burning pain shot through his flesh and pounded through his temples. He'd been poisoned.

One of the sharks broke free of the Blue Lady's spell and streaked at Shang-Li. Thinking the shark was the greater threat than the blossoms biting into him, he blocked the creature's jaws with one of the fighting sticks and swung the other at his opponent's nose. The shark turned aside and sped away, then spun in a tight circle and headed back more fiercely than before.

The Blue Lady spoke in that unknown tongue again. A whirling mass of black flames formed in the palm of one of her hands. She threw it at the plant. Shang-Li was close enough to feel the sudden heat that warmed the sea. The water boiled up around the plant, then the vines and blossoms drooped in submission.

Shang-Li broke free of the withered vines and crouched to face the oncoming shark. But before the shark got close enough to threaten him, the Blue Lady slammed her fist into the shark's nose. Blood spewed and the predator ricocheted off in an oblique angle to Shang-Li. Breathing hard, feeling the pulse of the poison coursing through him, Shang-Li set himself again and brought up the sticks in a defensive position.

A dozen paces away, the shark's lifeless corpse hung in the water. The black eyes dulled and glazed as Shang-Li watched

She'd killed it with a one blow. He looked at the Blue Lady in surprise. Her slight form didn't look like it could carry that much power. She glanced at him.

"Did the plant bite you?" Concern tightened her features.

"I'm fine." Shang-Li was surprised that he nearly thanked her for asking. But if she hadn't yanked him here to this place, he wouldn't be in danger now. And he was convinced the danger was not yet past.

The Blue Lady walked toward him and studied his leg. "Remove your garments, manling."

Shang-Li felt embarrassed at the request. "I'm fine," he said.

"You're a fool," she told him harshly. "The *dekalinag* vine carries poison. That poison is even now spreading throughout your body."

"I can take care of it." Shang-Li concentrated on one of the magic spells he'd learn from his mother. He touched the corded leather bracelet he wore around his right wrist and brought forth the spell.

A cool wash started at the top of his head, shot down his spine, then split and ran to his toes. In the next moment, the chill flared out to his extremities. When he searched again, the fever that had been building inside him from the poison was gone. A spinning sensation remained within his head and made him feel slightly nauseous.

"It appears you have a few surprises within you, manling," the Blue Lady stated.

Shang-Li met her gaze. "I can take care of myself."

"If the *dekalinag* vine had not gotten you, the sharks would have." She nodded meaningfully at the circling predators. "And if I chose to remove my spell from you, you would no longer be able to breathe and would drown."

"If you say so, lady."

The Blue Lady's silver eyes flashed. "That's how it would be."

"Or I might simply wake up in my hammock aboard-ship." Shang-Li gestured at the surrounding sea floor. "This might all be just a bad dream."

"You're a fool."

"If you'd wanted to kill me, lady, you'd have already done it. You've seen me in my dreams during life-or-death situations plenty of times before now."

"Is that a challenge?"

"No. But I won't stand here and be threatened so casually. Why did you bring me here?"

For just a moment, an almost imperceptible smile

curved the Blue Lady's lips. "You should be very afraid of me."

"Lady, I am," Shang-Li said honestly.

She gathered her seaweed cloak and turned again to walk down the broken crags. "Come. I would show you something."

Shang-Li forced himself to breathe out. He had fully expected the Blue Lady to strike him down as she had the plant and the shark. Nearby, sea currents tore the burned plant to black ashes that floated away. Overhead, the living sharks ripped gobbets of flesh from the dead one.

When he followed the Blue Lady, it was with a mixture of fear and curiosity. The latter had always been the one that had gotten him into the most trouble.

Shang-Li trailed the Blue Lady by a few steps. He gazed in wonder all around him as he saw the strange plants mixed in with the dead trees.

This land isn't from the sea bottom, he realized. He thought of the Spellplague and how the two worlds had been torn apart and put back together again.

"Where did this place come from?" he asked.

"From my home," the Blue Lady answered. She walked alongside a sunken cog buried prow first in the soft sand of the sea bottom. Her boots stirred up puffs of sand that eddied on the current.

"Lady, where is your home?"

"Far." She glanced over her shoulder at him. "Very far by human standards. But I want to go back."

Shang-Li gazed out across the dead wilderness now filled with sea. "Did no one come with you?"

"No one." Her voice hardened. "Make no mistake, manling, I need no one."

Despite the delicate nature of his situation, Shang-Li couldn't help asking another question. "Then why did you take Bayel Droust and the ship he was on?"

The Blue Lady stopped near a huge dead tree that was

at least five or six men thick. Its gnarled roots showed through the sand surrounding it, but it looked unsteady enough to fall over at any moment. She turned and stared at Shang-Li.

"Because Bayel Droust had something I wanted," the Blue Lady answered. She folded her arms over her breasts and for a moment Shang-Li forgot that she was so dangerous and thought of her only as a beautiful woman. "I have taken other ships over the years. His was not the first, nor was it the last." She smiled. "And there will be more."

Shang-Li studied the graveyard of sunken ships and thought of all the lives that had been lost. Thousands of people had perished at her whim, their skeletons littering the strange sea floor.

"This is my new home, your world." The Blue Lady looked content as she made that announcement. "At least for the time being. I don't plan on being here any longer than I have to. In order to make better use of it, I need to understand more of it. There are resources here that I can use."

"For what?" Shang-Li asked the question as soon as it popped into his head.

"My purposes, manling." The Blue Lady drew herself up to her full height. "I don't intend to stay here forever."

"Where will you go?"

"Wherever I wish. This world is as big as my own—a mirror, it seems, in many ways. There are many places I wish to see."

"But why did you summon me here?"

The Blue Lady regarded him for a moment before answering. "You caught my attention, manling. You are drawn to this place. I wish to know why that is."

To better protect herself? Shang-Li wondered.

The Blue Lady sharply gestured at him. Shang-Li felt like he'd been smacked by a large bear. He tumbled through the water and sailed a few yards away. Then, senses reeling, he hung suspended in the ocean. The sharks darted closer.

"I can protect myself well enough," the Blue Lady snapped. "Never think that I can't."

Feeling as though his ribs had been crushed, Shang-Li struggled to draw a breath. When the Blue Lady strode across the sea bottom to him, he tried to move but found himself unable to navigate. He was stuck as surely as a fly in a spider's web.

"I grow weary of you, manling," she whispered into his ear. "You are not as interesting as I'd believed." She was close enough that Shang-Li felt the cold chill emanating from her. Her teeth snapped as she spoke. "Go away and do not let me see you again." She gestured at one of the sharks.

The predator heeled over in the sea and streaked at Shang-Li. The bands of invisible force held him in place. As the shark neared, it grew larger very quickly. By the time it closed on him, it was the size of a small merchant's ship.

The shark's jaws sprang wide, revealing the rows of razor-sharp teeth. Terror flooded Shang-Li. At the last moment, he tugged free of the force. Before he could move, though, the shark closed its maw with him inside.

Blackness surrounded Shang-Li and he couldn't stifle the yell that burst free of his lips.

CHAPTER EIGHT

Caught in the darkness of the shark's maw and his own fear, Shang-Li reached above and felt the slick hardness of the shark's palate and knew that what he experienced was not a simple illusion. The lady's spell still held and he could breathe, but in the jaws of a shark, that hardly seemed to matter.

The shark's teeth parted. For a moment, the darkness was dispelled and Shang-Li saw the deep blue ocean on the other side of the razor sharp teeth. He darted forward, but the rush of water pouring inward shoved him back toward the predator's gullet.

He felt certain that if he tumbled into the belly of the beast he would never escape. He flailed and his fingers found the slimy aperture left by the shark's gill slits. Then the gruesome, smiling mouth closed again and he was once more in darkness.

It's magic, Shang-Li told himself.

He took a deep breath and struggled to focus, but that task proved difficult while hanging onto a shark's gill slit inside the creature's mouth. The shark shook its head from side to side as it swam. Shang-Li bounced off the walls of its mouth and felt the rough edges of the gill slit saw at his fingers. He pushed the pain from his mind and concentrated, hoping to break whatever spell the Blue Lady had cast over him. She hadn't killed him outright. Neither had the shark. The experience now was meant as a lesson in terror.

He pictured the cave's interior and imagined the fire's warmth. For a moment, the sea's chill pulled back from him. Then the darkness melted and he saw the flames twisting before him. He reached for the fire.

Go to the cave, he told himself. You don't have to be here. You can go to the cave. Concentrate. You can free yourself of this.

The fire grew warmer and brighter in his mind. He was almost there.

When he was certain he had built the cave in his mind as best as he could, when he felt the tie to the fire at its strongest, when he was certain he could hold his breath no longer—he released his grip on the gill slit and shoved himself forward.

For a moment, he thought he might be on a one way trip to the shark's belly. Then he sprawled against a stone floor. Choking and gasping, retching up some of the saltwater he had inadvertently swallowed, he pushed himself to his knees.

His soaked clothing clung to him heavily. He grabbed his shirt and wrung water from the material. The sea gushed in a torrent to spatter the stone.

It hadn't been a dream or simple illusion. He had been there. The Blue Lady was real.

As his mind tried to deal with that, Shang-Li crept

closer to the fire to soak up its warmth. He rubbed at his arms vigorously to increase the blood flow. He knew his father would *tsk* in disappointment at his lack of control. At the moment, though, Shang-Li didn't care. The fire felt good and much more hospitable than the bottom of the Sea of Fallen Stars.

Outside the cave, the rain fell in a drumming rush, almost blunting the other sounds that came from without. If Moonwhisper hadn't spread his great wings and opened his yellow eyes in consternation, Shang-Li didn't know if he would've heard the fearful shouts of men.

Moving quickly, Shang-Li gathered the book and the papers, and shoved them into his pack. He slung the pack over his shoulder, shot his arms through the straps, and ran.

Moonwhisper glided out into the heavy rain just ahead of him.

The long hours of constant rain had turned the ground soft. As Shang-Li ran, the earth moved and shifted beneath him. Grassless expanses beneath the oak and pine trees held small ponds that covered treacherous mud slicks. He pounded and skidded through those, never once breaking pace.

Moonwhisper flew above the treetops, almost lost in the blinding rain. Shang-Li traded senses only long enough to spot the ship sitting at anchorage near the foothills of the mountain. Sailors darted across *Swallow's* decks. Others clambered nets to get to safety.

Fierce warriors trailed in their wake. Moonwhisper glided lower and his vision picked out the attackers easily. Despite the long shadows of night and the owl's limited black and white vision, Shang-Li recognized the aggressors as kuo-toa.

The fish-people dwelled in the Underdark, in the twisted maze of caverns and tunnels that ran beneath the surface world. Worshiping dark gods by sacrificing conquered enemies, the kuo-toa rose from the dark depths only to raid coastal villages, attack ships in harbors, or take slaves.

When the Spellplague swept across Faerun, a crack in the sea floor had drained the Sea of Fallen Stars into the Glimmersea, the Underdark's ocean. As a result, the kuo-toa ranged ever wider in their marauding.

Swallow lay a hundred yards out to sea. Canvas flew up lines as the crew made ready to sail. Desperate, Shang-Li borrowed Moonwhisper's sight again as he searched for his father aboard the ship. When the owl glided across the prow, Shang-Li spotted Kwan Yung standing on the prow. His father held a bow and aimed with expert skill. Shaft after shaft sped from his string and transfixed the head of a kuo-toa barely out of the water as they converged on the ship.

Hoarse shouts drew Shang-Li's attention to a longboat still on shore to his left. Nine sailors put up a defense against that thanks a horde of kuo-toa warriors armed with spears, pincer staffs, and harpoons. Two sailors dug their feet into the soft sand of the bank and shoved the longboat into the incoming waves. The battle at both ends appeared to be a losing one.

Shang-Li shook his fighting sticks into his hands, expanded them, and ran for the kuo-toa as soundless as his shadow. The driving rain hampered his vision and masked the screams and hoarse shouts of the beleaguered men.

A kuo-toa pincer staff caught one of the sailors in the throat. Shang-Li recognized the man from a couple of meals they'd shared in the galley during the voyage. He had been young and inexperienced, excited and scared to be on the voyage.

The man dropped his weapon and grabbed the pincers in an effort to get away, but the kuo-toa warrior lifted his opponent from his feet almost effortlessly. In the next instant, the kuo-toa twisted the pincer staff violently.

The helpless man's neck snapped like a dry tree branch. The kuo-toa flicked the corpse away as if the dead man were refuse.

Hot anger boiled inside Shang-Li. He pushed it away, pushed away all emotion, and concentrated on his attack. Moonwhisper glided down before any of the kuo-toa grew aware of the owl's presence. His heavy claws raked the fish-man's brutal features and gouged his eyes.

Black ichor spread across the kuo-toa's face. It squalled in pain and fury as it clapped a hand over the wounds. Angrily, it battered its companions aside and came face to face with Shang-Li.

The kuo-toa stood as tall as Shang-Li, but the creature's body was massively muscled. Even though the kuo-toa was barrel-chested, the fish-man's head still looked too large for its body. The eyes were huge, round disks, black pupils surrounded by amber pools. There were no lids, only protective membranes that gave the eyes a glossy sheen.

A row of razor-sharp teeth curled from the creature's large mouth. Heavy black claws stood out from the fingers and toes, as dangers a weapon as any of those the kuo-toa carried. Moss-green scales covered the body and made the bright gold twists worn for decoration stand out even more strongly.

Moonwhisper had blinded the kuo-toa's left eye so it had to turn its head to look at Shang-Li. Blood leaked between its teeth.

"I kill you," the kuo-toa threatened in a garbled voice. It lifted its harpoon and shield. Iridescent pink and white, the shield looked like mother of pearl salvaged from a giant clam.

Shang-Li batted his opponent's harpoon to the side and closed. Another kuo-toa had turned to face him. He slid past the first kuo-toa, then shifted and slammed his back into the fish-man's iridescent shield. Experience had taught him that the shield was rough and tended to grab opponents. Shang-Li flung his arms out and sank to the ground as the second kuo-toa struck with its spear.

His weight dragged the first kuo-toa's shield down with him, leaving it exposed. The second fish-man's spear sank into the chest of the first kuo-toa Shang-Li had engaged.

Shrugging free of the shield, Shang-Li rolled to one knee, and whipped a backward strike to the outside of the kuo-toa's knee. Despite the creature's powerful build, knees remained vulnerable. Bone cracked with ear-splitting pops, and the kuo-toa sagged to the side. Before his opponent could manage his failing balance, Shang-Li stood and slammed the other fighting stick into the fish-man's throat.

Normally the blow would have crushed a human opponent's windpipe. But the kuo-toa breathed through gills. The fish-man was stunned, but not incapacitated.

The first kuo-toa struggled with the spear embedded in its chest. Using both hands, it had started to pull the weapon from its flesh while howling in pain.

Abandoning its primary weapon, the second kuo-toa pulled a spiked mace from its side and took up a new stance. Knowing he was sandwiched between his two opponents, Shang-Li threw the fighting stick in his right hand as hard as he could at the second kuo-toa's face. The stick's iron-capped end struck the fish-man in its low forehead, and ricocheted up as Shang-Li had figured it would do.

He turned while the second kuo-toa was distracted, just in time to see the first kuo-toa pull the spear from its chest. Grabbing the spear with his free hand, Shang-Li propelled it slightly upward and shoved it through the underside of the kuo-toa's chin. The keen edge slid through the unprotected flesh and up into the kuo-toa's brain.

The fish-man stumbled backward, already dead.

The second kuo-toa struck at Shang-Li with the spiked mace. Shang-Li stepped to the side, put one leg behind the kuo-toa's nearest leg, then slammed his shoulder into the fish-man's upper body. Thrown off balance, the kuo-toa tumbled to the ground and fell on its back. Aware of the second stick tumbling back down, Shang-Li plucked the weapon from the air and slammed it into the kuo-toa's head with a meaty smack.

The vibration caused massive damage inside the fish-man's skull. It shivered and shook like a clubbed fish. Its mouth relaxed, fell open, and it expired.

Walking behind the next, Shang-Li stomped on the kuo-toa's calf and caused its leg to buckle from beneath it. Before the fish-man could recover, Shang-Li pounded its head as well. It sagged and fell forward, taking another kuo-toa down with it.

A kuo-toa with a headdress of preserved squid tentacles pointed a fist at one of the sailors. Recognizing the fish-man as a monitor, one of the kuo-toa leaders, Shang-Li ran up the back of the nearest fish-man and launched himself at his chosen foe.

"I am Gibblesnippt!" the kuo-toa monitor roared fiercely. "Favored of the Sea Mother. I am your death!"

Lightning blazed from the kuo-toa's clenched fist and struck the sailor with enough force to hurl him back over the longboat and into the water. The stench of lightning and burned flesh filled the air in spite of the high winds.

Gibblesnippt roared with laughter and took a two-handed grip on its pincer staff while the other fish-men cheered and their awful voices. "I will feed you all to—"

Before the kuo-toa monitor could complete his dark promise, Shang-Li flipped through the air and landed in front of the sailors. He set himself, a fighting stick in each hand.

Turning its head one way and then the other, Gibblesnippt studied Shang-Li. The fish-man's gills flared and closed rapidly.

"Who are you and why are you so ready to die?" Gibblesnippt demanded.

"If you leave now," Shang-Li said, "I won't kill you as I have killed your companions."

For the first time, the kuo-toa looked back and saw the dead that Shang-Li had left in his wake.

Thankfully, the sailors hadn't been so frozen that they forgot to save themselves. Three others joined the two trying to get the boat out into the surf. Together, they managed the task, but all of them knew the kuo-toa could easily overtake them in the water.

"You're going to fight me with a stick?" Gibblesnippt taunted.

"I'm going to kill you with a stick if need be." Shang-Li didn't move. Five kuo-toa remained before him. Only two of the sailors stood ready beside him. Rain pounded Shang-Li's face and caused him to blink.

Moonwhisper glided overhead, held in check only by Shang-Li's unspoken command.

"You're a very foolish human," Gibblesnippt growled. It gestured with the pincer staff.

In response, two of the kuo-toa drew heavy crossbows and fired. The quarrels flashed through the air as lightning streaked the sky.

Relying on his instinct and training, Shang-Li spun from the path of one of the quarrels and knocked the other from its flight with a fighting stick. As he came back around, he plucked a handful of throwing stars from his clothing and flicked them into motion.

The throwing stars whispered through the air and thudded into the kuo-toa. The sharp blades weren't enough to kill or disable unless they struck an eye, and Shang-Li didn't have time to be that accurate. He slipped his sticks from his sleeve again and launched himself at the monitor.

Gibblesnippt raised the pincer staff to block Shang-Li's advance. Instead of batting the weapon aside with the fighting sticks, Shang-Li rolled beneath it. He came up inside the monitor's two arms, his fists clutching the sticks. Before Gibblesnippt could react, Shang-Li brought the iron-capped ends into both of his opponent's eyes, blinding him at once.

Bellowing in pain, Gibblesnippt stepped back and tried to trap Shang-Li in his grasp. Instead, Shang-Li ducked under the kuo-toa's outstretched arms and took a step to the side. Deftly, the young monk stabbed his fighting stick into his opponent's gill slit and shoved the end through the creature's brain.

A deafening howl ripped from the kuo-toa's large mouth. Blood streamed from its ruined eyes. Blinded and out of control, Gibblesnippt staggered backward and collapsed onto two of its followers.

Four surviving fish-men stood frozen for a moment. The creatures took courage from the leaders. When one of those was slain, the kuo-toa generally retreated until another from among them was chosen.

Shang-Li stayed in motion. He slipped his fighting sticks back up his sleeves and grabbed one of the heavy harpoons dropped by one of the other fallen kuo-toa. Whirling, he threw it with all his strength. The harpoon crunched through one of the kuo-toa's chests.

The stricken kuo-toa fell backward to its knees and cried out for help. None of its companions offered aid. The fish-man struggled to get to its feet, but one of the sailors stepped forward and slashed off its head.

The head thumped to the ground and lay on one side. The visible eye circled its orbit frantically while the mouth gasped.

Without a word, the three able kuo-toa bolted from the fight and ran for the water. The fish-men heaved into the sea and disappeared at once.

The two sailors that had remained with Shang-Li quickly darted forward to search the bodies of the kuo-toa. Their knives flashed as they slashed through purse drawstrings.

Shang-Li didn't think they would get much for their trouble. The kuo-toa didn't put much stock in the idea of surface dwellers' wealth. Still, they wore gold ornamentation and that was worth something.

Just as he started to turn away, lightning blazed and a blue flash caught Shang-Li's eye. He knelt beside the kuo-toa monitor and examined the necklace the fish-man wore. Even after further inspection, he couldn't divine the nature of the device.

But the fact that it was deep blue when nothing else about the creature echoed that color interested him.

Shang-Li closed its fist around the device to pull it free. As soon as his flesh closed over the necklace, he felt the coldness of the Blue Lady on him again. He took his hand back, used his knife to cut free the necklace, and dropped it into his pouch.

The longboat was out to sea and the sailors had clambered aboard. Two of them rowed while the other three fumbled for oars.

Kuo-toa still assaulted *Swallow* in the harbor, but the attacks were less fierce. However, there was no telling when the fish-men would regroup, or how many would arrive. The harbor was no longer safe.

Shang-Li stood. "It's time to go."

The two sailors stood, their prizes held in their fists. They glanced down at the dead men littering the beach.

"What about the others?" the oldest of them asked.

"We can't take them with us and we can't stay to bury them." Shang-Li hated the coldness in his voice. Such a thing was horrible to contemplate, much less do. "We will offer prayers for them when we're able."

Steeling himself, Shang-Li ran for the surf and dived in. When he surfaced, he swam for the ship.

Several bodies of slain kuo-toa bobbed on the water near *Swallow*. Many of them had arrows through their heads, silent truth of the archers' marksmanship aboardship.

As they bumped gently into the ship, a few of the sailors spat at the dead fish-men. Muttered curses floated over the water.

Taking hold of the net draped over the ship's side, Shang-Li quickly climbed aboard. When he saw his father standing on the deck still holding a longbow with an arrow nocked to string, he breathed a sigh of relief.

Kwan Yung didn't look any worse for wear other than a few scrapes on his cheek and chin. An empty quiver and a near-empty quiver hung at his side.

"You are all right?" his father asked.

Shang-Li nodded. "It was a close thing."

Above, Moonwhisper spread his wings and landed in the rigging.

Several of the sailors worked together to hoist the bodies of kuo-toa from the deck. Only a few of the creatures had reached the ship. None of them had survived. All of them got thrown back into the sea.

Captain Chiang joined them. Gray touched the temples of his long hair, which he wore pulled back in a queue. He was somewhere in his middle years, between Shang-Li and his father. The right side of his face held two long scars. He was fit and trim, and had a reputation for being a man who lived by his honor. Both the blades he wore dripped crimson.

"Where did the kuo-toa come from?" Chiang asked quietly. Though his ship had suffered and several of his men were dead, he acted calm and focused.

"I didn't see," Shang-Li said. "The sound of the attack drew me."

"They came out of the water, captain," one of the survivors from the shore patrol replied.

"You didn't disturb them?"

"No. We were just loading the water barrels and they attacked us."

Chiang leaned on the railing and surveyed the harbor. "I've stopped here several times. Other than the occasional pirate ship, these waters have always been safe. I've never before encountered kuo-toa."

"Maybe it was aboleths," one of the crewmen suggested.

The man's words instantly reminded Shang-Li of Bayel Droust's fate aboard *Grayling*. But there had been no talk of aboleths during that attack, no hint that these kuo-toa served the psionic behemoths that ranged over the Sea of Fallen Stars.

"If it was aboleths that put the kuo-toa onto us," another crewman said, "they would have turned us to servitors."

Several of the men shuddered at that. When a human succumbed to the power of an aboleth, he was changed. His outer skin turned into a slimy membrane that allowed him to live better beneath the sea and serve the aboleths. The monsters' appearance was frightening because of their great size and rounded bulk, but few things were as gruesome as the servitors.

"Aboleths didn't have anything to do with it," Shang-Li said confidently.

The captain and crew looked at him. Even his father studied him and waited for him to continue.

"They knew we were there." Shang-Li took the blue stone device from his pouch and held it for all to see in his palm. Even resting there, he felt the magic vibrating within. "One of the kuo-toa monitors wore this."

"What's that?" Chiang made no move to touch the stone.

Several of the crewmen drew back.

"I believe this belongs to the Blue Lady." Shang-Li indicated the device carved onto the stone. At one time, the stone had held the forked wave that was Umberlee's symbol. But that symbol had been carved over, replaced by the image of rain falling from a cloud. "This is her symbol."

"You think they took this from her?" Chiang asked.

"No. I think they're in league with her."

"Why?" his father asked.

The stone grew colder in Shang-Li's hand. A wave of fatigue rolled over him.

"Because I talked to her," he answered. "She's not a myth. And she's not gone. She's still down there."

That announcement started tongues wagging immediately. Chiang silenced most of the men around him with his stern gaze, but they only retreated to talk among themselves farther away. Most of the men didn't believe him. They hadn't heard of the Blue Lady previously, and they hadn't been privy to the conversation Shang-Li had had with his father. Nor had any of them suffered through the dreams she'd woven for him.

"It's unfortunate that you stated that where everyone could hear," the captain said softly. "Some of them may believe you."

"Perhaps," Shang-Li acknowledged. "But they deserved to know. This isn't going to get any less dangerous."

"As you say," Chiang replied. "But such candor—even if well-intentioned—is going to make recruitment hard in Westgate. Even if they don't believe you, most of them will not be willing to follow a madman around. Or someone chasing ghosts. Some of the men aboard this ship now might not come back." He walked away and began attending to his crew and ship.

Without a word, Shang-Li's father took the stone from his hand, wrapped it in a cloth that was woven as much from magic as it was from material, and put it in his pouch.

Shang-Li knew that was wasted effort. Even though the stone was out of sight, it remained malignant and evil. It waited. Just like the Blue Lady.

CHAPTER NINE

Shang-Li stood in the ship's prow and watched Westgate, Old Town and Tidetown, grow steadily closer. When the Sea of Fallen Stars had been full, Westgate had enjoyed a natural deep water port. With the shrinking of the sea, the harbor had fallen away, and the city had needed to rebuild its docks and warehouses closer to the new shore. The new area of the city, the "Tidetown," had ended up squatting in the shadows of the old city.

Because there was no longer much of a natural shoreline, one had to be created. Or rather, the original had needed to be expanded. Those who had built Tidetown worked at their craft. Docks stabbed out into the water and allowed for the transfer of goods. Businesses—taverns, and inns, and warehouses—lay along the abbreviated shore, part along a network of wooden walkways, and part inside caves.

Shang-Li wondered what it would have been like to have seen old Westgate in all its grandeur.

"You've been here before, haven't you?" Yugi stood attentive and ready beside Shang-Li. "Just to Tidetown? Or have you been all the way to old Westgate?"

"I've been to the old city as well. You?"

Yugi shook his head. "Not me. I never got up from Tidetown. The watch doesn't allow rabble or visitors into old town. Especially lowly sailors. So who invited you?"

"No one. And I left old Westgate faster than I went in."

Despite the losses of friends and shipmates only a few days ago, the young man smiled at that. "Sounds like a tale begging to be told."

"For another time."

"I'll hold you to that when we put this place behind us."

"You're planning on shipping out with us?"

"Of course!"

Shang-Li didn't know how he felt about that. After seeing the Blue Lady, after the attack by the kuo-toa, he knew they would be heading into danger. It didn't seem right to bring Yugi along.

As if sensing what the young monk had on his mind, Yugi said, "I don't have anywhere else to go." He nodded at the city. "You think it would be any safer for me there?"

Thinking of the rough trade that went on in Tidetown, as well as the degenerate tastes that were too often entertained in old Westgate, Shang-Li knew Yugi would be no safer there.

Yugi cleared his throat. "So who are we here to see?"

In spite of the danger that waited ahead of him, Shang-Li smiled at the thought of who he was there to see. "Good friends. True friends. Some of the best friends I've ever made."

And he was going to lead them into a blue hell waiting at the bottom of the Sea of Fallen Stars. The realization didn't set well with him.

That night, while the ship lay in harbor, Shang-Li dreamed of the Blue Lady again. He returned to that blue world beneath the sea. For a time he wandered through the forest and horrible things darted out to challenge him. He held a sword in his fists, ready to do battle, but none of the creatures closed on him.

"They won't attack you, manling."

Shifting smoothly, Shang-Li turned to face the Blue Lady across naked steel. She didn't appear to be impressed.

"For the moment, you are under my protection."

"Why?"

"Because I want you to come see me."

"Why would I do that?"

The Blue Lady smiled. "I have that which you seek: The books of Liou Chang."

Unease swept over Shang-Li as he considered the possibilities that declaration brought with it. He wondered how much she knew about the books and what they contained.

"Enough." The Blue Lady's eyes flashed. "And I'm learning more each day."

"What do you want?"

She arched a brow. "From you?"

He waited, unwilling to play into her game.

Uncaring of the weapon he held, she walked around him, occasionally touching the monstrosities that lounged within the strange, underwater forest. "I want to see you, manling, and get to know you better."

Shang-Li knew she was lying. She wanted something from him, but he couldn't imagine what it was. "You won't get me."

"Won't I?" She chuckled. "Your duty requires that you find Liou Chang's lost books, does it not? Would your father walk away from this task when it is so near to completion?"

"We don't know that."

"I have the books you seek."

"Show them to me."

"You disbelieve me?"

"I have no reason to trust you, and every reason not to." Shang-Li moved in tandem with her, shifting constantly to face her without crossing his feet.

"Besides your duty, your curiosity will bring you to me, manling. It is your nature to explore places where no one has gone before."

Shang-Li's eyes cut to the skeletons and corpses scattered across the ground. Some of the bodies looked fresh and sea scavengers worked at the soft flesh. "Plenty have gone on before me."

She smiled sweetly. "But none have returned to carry the true tale, manling." She paused. "You do not even know who or what I truly am." She showed him her shield and pointed to the symbol of the falling rain. "Do you know why I chose this as my standard?"

"No."

"Because the rain is water in transition. It rests in the sea, rises to form clouds that can go anywhere they want to, then falls to earth again to find its way once more to the sea. That will be me, manling. I will rise from this place and create a new empire in this world." The Blue Lady regarded him. "You get to choose whether we work together—or you die."

Shang-Li feared her, but he kept quiet.

"Don't worry, manling. You don't have to choose now. There is still time." Then she pushed a hand out at him—

—and Shang-Li woke in the hammock on *Swallow*. Sweat covered his body and his head felt feverish. He got up and stretched, and wondered how many more of the dreams he would have to endure.

Droust walked through the debris of the latest ship the Blue Lady had pulled from the surface. She had kept some of the crewmen alive this time, given them the ability to breathe underwater as he did, and some of them hid within the broken hull, watching him with fearful eyes.

The burly captain stepped out of hiding and challenged Droust. "Who are you?"

"A cursed man, captain, not your captor. A prisoner just as you are."

"What is this place?"

"You saw the Blue Lady?"

The captain gave a tight nod. "Aye, before she dragged us under I saw her. I'd heard tales of her, but I'd never believed them."

A mistake. Droust didn't allow himself to feel sorry for the man. The captain and the rest of his crew would be hunted and killed by the monsters in the forest. The Blue Lady allowed her pets to play from time to time.

"What are you doing here then?" The captain's anger fixed on Droust.

"I came to see what goods your ship carried."

"Like a thief doing inventory?"

Droust shook his head. "Like a prisoner doing what his jailer has ordered."

Several of the other sailors cursed and stepped forward. All of them were brave now when they faced one man. Droust was certain that hadn't been the case when the Blue Lady had confronted them.

"I says you're a thief, no better'n pirates we've faced over our journey." A large man joined the captain and brandished his cutlass. "What's to stop us from capturing you and using you to gain our own freedom?"

"The Blue Lady doesn't care if I live or die. You would be wasting your time."

Before the big man or the captain could speak again, the monsters lurking within the forest attacked. The awful creatures swam, scurried, and slithered toward the doomed crew. Bravely, the men tried to stand their ground, but none of them could face the sheer onslaught of carnivores. The line broke and they tried to flee more deeply back into the sunken ship. In a moment, blood spread throughout the water and drew the attention of the sharks swimming overhead. Like enormous arrows, the sharks sped down and plucked victims from the ranks of the ship's crew.

Familiar with the carnage and its eventual outcome, Droust sat down to wait until the blood film over the area thinned. He didn't think he breathed it in, but the possibility appalled him. He hardened his heart against the anguished shouts and cries for help.

"Does their death amuse you?"

Recognizing the voice as belonging to the strangest thing he'd ever seen, Droust turned to face it. Only a short distance away in a canyon that had become a graveyard of ships, a vessel peered at him from the eyes of the figurehead of a beautiful woman on the prow.

"No, Red Orchid. Their deaths only sadden me. They remind me of how trapped I am in this place."

"Yet you sit there unmoved as they die."

Droust stared at the figurehead. As near as he'd figured from the coins and other artifact aboard Red Orchid, she had gone down roughly at the same time as the Spellplague had been unleashed upon the world. From his conversations with her, he knew that she hadn't been sentient until that time. She had no memories of her journeys above the sea, only of her isolation and imprisonment here.

The Blue Lady knew about Red Orchid, and would sometimes go there to taunt the figurehead. Or the ship, Droust wasn't certain exactly what Red Orchid had become since being exposed to the Spellplague and whatever magic resided in the land that held Caelynna prisoner. The only reason Droust could suppose the Blue Lady hadn't destroyed the ship was because she regarded her as a curiosity.

Or perhaps the Blue Lady wanted one more thing to hurt and subjugate.

"What about you, Red Orchid? Do their deaths make you feel remorse because you can't do anything?"

Red Orchid looked at him with cold disdain. "If I were able to move, I would fight the Blue Lady."

"You can move."

"Not enough to climb from this cursed hole. And if I could, I would fight."

"Then you would die."

The figurehead was quiet for a time and both of them watched the last moments of the rampant slaughter taking place before them. "This is a death too." Red Orchid's voice was somber. "Watching her take these ships, we die again and again. Only there is no release."

Droust said nothing, watching as a leg floated up from the ship. A shark glided down and took the limb in the blink of an eye.

"She lures another here."

Droust looked at the ship. "How do you know that?"

"I have seen him when she brings him here through his dreams. She taunts him and lures him."

"You have seen into his dreams?" The wonder of that filled Droust for just a moment and chased all the fear and guilt from him.

"I have."

"How?"

"I don't know. Perhaps because I am tied so closely

to her land and to the power she wields. Perhaps that links us."

"What do you know of him?" Red Orchid fixed Droust with her beautiful eyes.

"He is clever and resourceful. He's been very successful recovering other lost antiquities."

"How do you know this?"

"I am in contact with men that work for the Blue Lady on land. They have learned these things and told me."

"And you have told the Blue Lady."

Droust dropped his gaze. "It is what I must do if I am to survive."

The ship growled to show her disrespect. "You only exist, Droust. You don't live."

Droust could say nothing in his defense that she hadn't already heard and discounted.

"Perhaps this one will escape the Blue Lady's clutches." Red Orchid shifted slightly on the front of the ship. Veins of blue lightning underscored the figurehead, showing the remnants of the Spellplague's effects.

"Don't get your hopes up."

"He isn't afraid the way you were. I saw her efforts to claim you in your dreams. You were always frightened. This man isn't."

Embarrassed, face burning despite the chill of the sea around him, Droust drew himself up straight. "This man will bend to the Blue Lady or he will die."

"Can you be so sure?"

"Yes. Already Nine Golden Swords warriors are tracking him in Westgate. They will catch him there and bring him to the Blue Lady to use as she will."

Red Orchid shook her head. "Go root among the dead like the ghoul that you are, Droust. I pity you."

"I have no need of your pity."

"But you do. It must be hard to live so hopelessly."

Droust turned from her and walked toward the ship

while the monsters feasted on the bounty that their mistress had delivered to them. He tried not to think about Red Orchid's words, but it was hard because he knew they were true.

"Are you sure you need the sword?"

Shang-Li sighed as he walked down the gangplank from *Swallow* to the docks. Truthfully, he felt a little overdressed with the long sword resting in a sheath over his right shoulder. He also felt tired and irritable from the lack of sleep.

"Yes, I need the sword."

His father walked beside him and drank in the sights. He was dressed as a proper monk but without the temple insignia. Shang-Li knew most people in Tidetown and old Westgate would assume his father was a beggar. That fact, especially since they weren't there in disguise, was a little embarrassing. He hadn't expected that.

He wished more fervently that his father had stayed aboard the ship. But that would have been too easy.

Several sailors and dockworkers watched as he passed. Most of the glances were unfriendly. A few were speculative and he knew the owners of those wondered how much gold he carried with him. And the Nine Golden Swords walked almost with impunity through Westgate's streets and almost owned the alleys and shadows. The city wasn't a safe place.

"'A sword often represents a challenge,'" his father told him.

"Quoting Barsillus?" Shang-Li lifted an eyebrow when he regarded his father.

"Were I a betting man, I would have wagered you wouldn't have known that quote."

"Barsillus was an interesting man, and he wrote interesting books. Actually, I'm surprised you know of him."

His father harrumphed in displeasure. "Barsillus was an important tactician."

"True, and he practiced his tactics on every kingdom around him. Some historians, rightfully in my opinion, have labeled him a bully."

"Barsillus single-handedly united most of northern Chessenta."

"His book puts it that way. Others felt that he enslaved the surrounding lands."

His father made a rude noise. "History puts it that way."

"Only because Barsillus would have lined his walls with the heads of every scribe that refused to write history the way he wanted it written."

"I've never read that anywhere."

"Father," Shang-Li said, "the man lined his walls with the heads of *everyone* that displeased him. Though Barsillus didn't make that particular comment, the math is certainly simple enough to follow."

"An historian records what is factual and leaves guessing to bards."

"I know several bards who know more about specific histories than I do." Too late, Shang-Li saw that he had left himself open for a swift rebuttal. He blamed his lax attention to the conversation on the fact that he was also keeping watch over them, searching doorways and alleys for possible thieves and assassins. Goddess knew, there would be those in Westgate even without their current trouble.

"Personally, I find that no great feat," his father said. "There are probably fish in these waters that know more about history than you do."

Shang-Li focused on his stride and tried not to sigh. They wouldn't get out of Westgate soon enough.

"Admit it," his father said. "You wore the sword simply to vex me, and to get some petty revenge because I made you work as a server."

"No, that's not it. I'm not trying to vex you. This is a dangerous place."

"All places are dangerous. Were I not looking, I could slip and fall and break my neck."

Not his neck, Shang-Li thought. But goddess willing, perhaps he could fracture his jaw. Or bite his tongue. Even thinking that made the young monk feel guilty, though.

"Wearing the sword is an open invitation to anyone harboring aggressive tendencies," his father said. "It's just as likely there could be some that confront you just to find out if you are worthy of carrying that sword."

"I am worthy of carrying the sword. Anyone seeking that knowledge will get a quick lesson." Actually, the sword was the least of it. Shang-Li was a walking arsenal at the moment. At least his father didn't know about—

"You're carrying so many weapons that you jingle when you walk."

Shang-Li barely held back a flurry of curses. "No, I'm not."

"Petty, vengeful, insecure, obstinate—and deaf. These are not qualities I'd hoped to find in you after your absence, but I can't be responsible for what you fail to learn or what you forget while you're away from the monastery."

"This is my world, Father. I know what I'm doing here."

Kwan Yung gestured at the people around them. "So do the fishermen and the merchant. They also know what they're doing. You don't see them walking around with weapons."

"That's because the fishermen has a filleting knife in his boot and the merchant has three guards who carry weapons." Shang-Li scanned the docks. "Everyone here carries weapons."

"And what would you do if everyone were to throw themselves from a cliff? Would you too throw yourself from a cliff? To be like the rest of these insecure people?"

Mentally, Shang-Li surrendered. "You know, Father, now that I think about it, this *is* about making me work as a server."

"I already knew that," his father said smugly. "But it is good to hear you admit your pettiness. Perhaps there is hope for you after all."

"*You* should have been the server."

"True, and if I were, I wouldn't have spilled the sauce."

Helplessly, Shang-Li ground his teeth and increased his pace. The day could *not* be over with soon enough.

"Who are these people we're going to meet?" his father asked.

"Friends."

"Do your friends have names?""

"You don't know them."

"I could have heard you talk about them."

"I doubt it."

"Why?" his father asked. "Do you not talk about these friends? Do you have some reason to be ashamed of them?"

"The only reason I don't talk about them is because you wouldn't listen. These are friends and a part of my life that you expressly disapprove of."

"That is a large part of your life, you know. And it seems to be growing."

Shang-Li didn't comment.

The alley twisted back and forth between buildings like a broken-backed snake. Halfway down, a man stood in front of a recessed doorway painted a brilliant red.

The man was young and stout. Ginger colored hair fell to his shoulders. His smile was big but disingenuous. He stepped into the alley before them.

"If I could have your attention for but a moment, good sirs, I would very much appreciate it. I will promise not to take up much of your time and to use well what you can generously spare."

Shang-Li feinted in one direction, then reversed and went the other way, neatly stepping past the man. His foot sloshed noisily through the mud, which sucked at his boot as he broke contact.

"A minute of your time." The man pointed at the red door and kept pace with Shang-Li. "Through that door lies Yahlil, the best performer you'll ever have the good fortune to see. She does the dance of the Thirty-Six Veils." The man grinned, showing crooked yellow teeth. "And most of those are very *small* veils."

"Sorry." Shang-Li held up a hand in quick apology. "I've no time."

Undeterred, the barker swung on Kwan Yung. "What about you, good sir? I promise you haven't seen anything like Yahlil in years. She is a woman unlike anything you have ever seen before. Her performance has thrilled nobility near unto—"

From the corner of his eye, Shang-Li watched his father grab the man's ear, tug it and twist it just so, and the man dropped into an unconscious heap in the alley.

"It will be better if we didn't draw attention," Shang-Li said.

His father snorted derisively. "This from the man insisting on wearing a big sword."

"The sword fits in better than leaving a trail of unconscious men behind. You can't just leave men lying in the street."

Ahead, a tavern door opened and two men—one after the other—were tossed out into the alley. Both were obviously very drunk and neither moved after they stopped sliding through the mud. One's chest moved and the other blew bubbles in the muck.

A large man stood in the door and cursed the unconscious drunks. He glared at Shang-Li, who said nothing. Satisfied, the man turned back inside the tavern and closed the door.

Shang-Li stepped around the abandoned drunks.

"Oh really?" his father said as he walked over one of the unconscious men. "I find that unconscious men serve well as the occasional dry spot in this pigsty where you've left me. Maybe someone else will appreciate the providential island I have left."

With effort, Shang-Li breathed out and remained silent as he kept walking.

Lukkob's the Edge Tavern occupied a cliff overlooking the harbor. The narrow street dead-ended at the tavern. It was flanked by shops and a couple of inns. Building the tavern there had been risky to begin with, but Lukkob had compounded the risk by choosing to enlarge the square footage inside the building as his business grew more prosperous.

Unable to claim part of the street because it would have restructured access to the shops on either side of him, Lukkob had built the addition over the cliff's edge. The room's extension hung out over the harbor a good twenty feet and ran forty feet across. Large tree trunks had been fitted into the cliff below at an angle to provide support. Still, on stormy days, the tavern shook and shivered like a luffing sail.

Kwan Yung spotted the tavern and came to a full stop in the middle of the street. A man attempted to drive his wagon over the old man, but Kwan Yung held his hand out and the horse nuzzled it for a moment before turning aside. The wagon's wheels rolled up onto the wooden sidewalk, drawing uncouth commentary from sailors who had to jump hurriedly out of the way.

"We're going into that?" his father asked. "Is it safe?"

"It has been so far."

The old man shook his head. "Folly. I suppose your friend owns this place?"

"No."

"Then why else would a man visit an accident waiting to happen like this one?"

"Lukkob's has got great service. If you know the owner. I happen to know the owner."

"So he *is* a friend," his father said as if that explained everything.

"Yes, but not the friend we're here to see." Shang-Li walked toward the tavern again.

One of the front windows suddenly exploded. Glass shards spun and dropped to the shell-covered street, followed by thin latticework and a big sailor with a bloody nose. The big man rolled and grunted in pain, then pushed himself unsteadily to his feet. He cursed and felt at his hip, then realized his cutlass lay beside him on the ground.

"Obviously this is a well-mannered establishment," his father commented.

"You can wait here, if you like." Shang-Li walked to the swaying sailor and examined him.

The man was a few years older than Shang-Li and corded with muscle from a harsh life aboardship. Blood streamed from the sailor's nose and split lips.

"What's going on in Lukkob's?" Shang-Li asked.

The sailor gestured with his cutlass up, pointing toward the tavern. "Got a pox-blasted dragonborn in there that decided to take exception to the fun we was having with the servin' wenches."

Only lately come from a serving background himself, Shang-Li had to pause and not take exception to the "fun" the sailors were having with the poor woman.

"She decided to take us all on," the sailor continued, "and we would've been able to take her if that tiefling hadn't stuck his horns in."

"A tiefling and a dragonborn traveling together?" Shang-Li asked.

"Maybe. Don't know. They was there when we got off ship."

Shang-Li shook a fighting stick from his sleeve. "Thank you." He rapped the sailor sharply across the temple and the big man spilled unconscious to the ground.

His father shook his head. "Not to question the honor in such a task, but if you decide to go around defending serving wenches everywhere you go, you'll never get anything else done."

"Serving is a task that should be respected. Not just anyone can do it."

"Obviously the ability to carry a tureen of sauce separates those who can from those who can't."

Shang-Li shook his other fighting stick into his hand and continued to the tavern.

CHAPTER TEN

Bloody madness reigned inside the Edge. Men howled in anger and yowled in fear as blows bruised flesh and broke bones. So far, bloodshed was kept to a minimum and there didn't appear to be any corpses among the bodies that littered the floor, but Shang-Li knew that was only because the wolves among the weasels chose not to kill.

The attackers employed their weapons enthusiastically, but to little avail. It was obvious, even in the cramped quarters and vastly outnumbered, that the sailors and mercenaries didn't have the necessary skills to bring down the two warriors standing back to back in the center of the room.

The tiefling, born with thick horns that jutted above his temples, moved with the grace of a dancer. With his dark reddish complexion and reddish armor that echoed the color of blood, he looked like he'd just crawled up from the pits of some Hell. His eyes glowed like fire rubies under the thick ridge of bone that covered his broad forehead. In spite of the devilish cast to his features, he looked young and strangely innocent, even more so with the joy evident on his face and the sparse clump of whiskers at his chin. His shoulder-length dark brown hair swirled madly around him as he moved.

His jagged sword cut the air with authority as he slashed two blades from his throat. He thumped his buckler into the face of another attacker and sent the man reeling backward with a broken and bloody nose.

With a lithe movement, the tiefling shifted and managed to lay the flat of his blade against a mercenary's skull and knock the man out. The move also swept the tiefling's long tail into the ankles of the man behind him. When that man hit the floor, the warrior kicked the man in the head and rendered him unconscious.

"Well met, Shang-Li," the tiefling yelled, grinning the whole time. His blade swept away the weapons of two more challengers.

"Hail and well met, Iados," Shang-Li replied.

"Are you just going to stand there?" Iados leaped to a tabletop and dropped on a knot of men trying to mob his companion. He promptly got pulled down into the middle of the men. "You'd best hurry if you want to join in. This fight won't last much longer. Our opponents are already giving ground."

"If I don't fight, I don't have to settle the tavern bill afterward." Shang-Li stood to one side of the room.

The tavernkeeper, a big-bellied man with his hair pulled back in a ponytail, stood behind the bar and looked irritated. Two serving girls cowered and cheered on the combatants at the same time. "And you'd better have the coins to pay for this, Iados."

With a triumphant roar, Iados emerged in the middle of

his opponents and lashed out with his tail, fists, and feet. Sailors and mercenaries flew backward.

"Consider it a present," Iados proclaimed. "Your tables and chairs have gotten worn, Lukkob You should think on this as a much needed blessing."

"Only if you can pay for what you break." Lukkob reached out with amazing speed and caught a metal tankard speeding toward him. The serving girls cheered again.

"What was the problem this time?" Shang-Li asked.

Kwan Yung stood nearby and dodged the occasional impromptu missile. His face held no expression, but his hazel eyes followed every movement.

"They insulted our serving girl." Iados placed his empty hand on the head of an opponent and vaulted over. As he landed, he whipped his tail out, caught the man in the back of the skull before he could turn, and knocked him flat.

"Me!" one of the young women standing at Lukkob's side said in a prideful way and clapped her hands enthusiastically. "They insulted me." She put her cupped hands to her mouth. "You malodorous swine!"

"When Thava took umbrage with them—" Iados began.

"Honor cried out for vengeance," Thava rumbled in her deep voice. "I only answered to serve my god."

She stood half a head taller than any of her attackers. Ocher scales trimmed in dulled gold covered her thickly muscled body. Her face was low-browed and wide, with golden eyes on either side of her snout. Her mouth was a curved beak that looked capable of snapping a man's hand off without trouble. Darker ocher scales surrounded her neck and coils of scales slightly darker than her body scales formed horn-like structures that curled over her broad shoulders like human hair.

"—the sailors mistakenly thought Thava was fair game as well," Iados finished. "To complicate matters even worse, they didn't know Thava was female. She felt horribly insulted."

"How could anyone not know I was female?" Thava roared

again as she flailed about with the flat of her bastard sword. Despite the possibility that the casual observer might miss the fact that Thava was female, there was no missing the actuality that her heritage had dragon mixed into it at some point. She opened her mouth and roared in the face of one sailor, who promptly fainted on the spot.

Shang-Li grinned. He'd missed the two fiercely these past months.

Iados tossed a man forward, narrowly missing Kwan Yung. The sailor tried to stop himself from sliding across the floor and finally succeeded amid a clatter of chairs. He took a fresh grip on his sword and pushed himself back up, roaring with rage.

Kwan Yung reached over to place a hand briefly on the back of the man's neck and head. The sailor grinned suddenly, then dropped in a boneless heap. Noticing that Shang-Li had seen him perform the action, his father lifted an imperious eyebrow and looked away.

"Are you seriously not going to help?" Iados demanded. He slammed his buckler into the stomach of another man, then whirled, braced himself on his tail, and lashed out with a flying kick that knocked an opponent through the front window.

"If I do, who's going to bail you out when the watch comes to arrest you?" Shang-Li asked.

"Surely the watch will be understanding," Thava said. "This was a matter of honor." She lashed out with a big hand and punched a man in the face.

The man went out like a candle flame in a wind and rolled up against the wall.

"The watch doesn't understand honor nearly as much as you want them to," Shang-Li said. "Now fines and punishment? They're very clear about those things."

Lukkob, the tavernkeeper, placed a tankard of hot tea in front of Shang-Li. "It's good to see you, Shang-Li. It's been a long time."

"It has."

Lukkob looked at Kwan Yung. "Would you like anything, master?"

"Master?" Kwan Yung stroked his beard and smiled in obvious delight.

"I have spent some time in a Shou monastery," Lukkob said.

"To learn to fight, I suppose."

"To learn to read. My father was very adamant about my life taking a different turn than his had. Reading was important to him, and it is to me."

"Ah. So you listen to your father?" Kwan Yung shot a disdainful glance at Shang-Li.

"I did," Lukkob agreed. "He's gone from me now, but I knew him to be a very wise man."

"It is so refreshing to hear a son praise his father," Kwan Yung said. His elbow dug sharply into Shang-Li's back as he bellied up to the bar. "Did you hear what he said?"

"Yes." Shang-Li moved away and blocked a thrown chair with one of the fighting sticks. "He offered you tea."

"Is it good tea?" Shang-Li heard his father sniff the tea he'd been given.

"Very good tea," Lukkob replied. "A special blend that I have shipped in. You won't find better tea in Westgate."

"Then yes, please."

The fight ended quickly. Near the end, with the grunts sounding winded and the blows coming with less enthusiasm, the watch arrived in their burgundy jackets and chainmail shirts. By that time, the mercenaries and sailors had realized they were totally outmatched and had started to flee.

The watch captured many of them before they could get away. Either they would be ransomed back to their ships or places of business by the watch, or they would be put to work for a time building new dock improvements in the city. Either way, their imprisonment wouldn't be wasted.

"Who started this?" a watch sergeant demanded. She had fair hair and a good figure that the chainmail didn't quite disguise. Attractive and self-assured, she commanded instant respect.

"Not us," Iados blustered. "We were beset by these ruffians—"

"We started the actual fighting," Thava said.

Iados rolled his eyes and crossed his arms over his chest. Then he glared at Thava. "Must you persist in always putting the noose about our neck?"

Shang-Li smiled. Thava never lied, not even by omission, much to Iados's chagrin. The paladin's sense of honor had gotten them into bad situations before because her view was so black and white.

"I like her," his father whispered. She's very truthful."

"The two of you?" the watch sergeant said in obvious disbelief. "You decided to take on a whole tavern full of mercenaries and sailors?"

"No. But some of these men made disparaging comments," Thava replied.

"To you?" The watch commander said that with some disbelief. "They must have been deep into their cups."

"To our server."

The watch sergeant blinked. "They made disparaging comments to your server?"

"Me," the serving wench sang out happily and waved her arms for attention as if she'd just won a prize. "They disparaged me."

The watch sergeant shot the server an irritated glance. Then she glanced at Lukkob, who only shrugged and smiled. She looked back at Thava. "I don't suppose it occurred to you to simply ignore those comments?"

Thava drew herself upright and looked almost offended. "No. It did not. Her honor was at stake. As was mine. I live for honor. It is as necessary to me as the air that I breathe."

"Gods save me from paladins." Cursing beneath her

breath, the watch sergeant turned to Lukkob. "You've got someone to pay for this mess?"

Lukkob pointed at Iados and Thava. "Them."

She turned back to the paladin and warrior. "You agree to this?"

"Of course," Thava said. "This is an honorable debt. I could do no less."

"You know," Iados said, "since we're traveling together, you might at least ask my consent before you speak for my purse."

"Then *I* will pay the debt," Thava said.

"No you won't," Iados growled. "You haven't enough coins for all this mess. You keep giving your coins away to churches and paupers."

"Some of us follow a higher calling."

"Some of us like to eat regularly and sleep in dry places."

"Then I assume all the debt and you won't have to pay a single copper." Thava folded her massive arms as she turned once more to the watch sergeant. "I will gladly work off the debt."

The watch sergeant took in the dragonborn's armor with a pained look. "You're a paladin. I can't have a paladin working on a jail crew. There will be arguments and fights every day. The churches will protest. Gods, the headaches alone from that will be too much to bear."

"You can't refuse my offer," Thava said. "I have assumed the debt, and I must pay it. I will insist"

Several members of the watch stepped back.

"I really do like her," Kwan Yung whispered.

Iados cursed and lifted a purse heavy with coins from the inside of his shirt. "*I'll* pay for the damages."

Thava smiled and clapped the tiefling on the shoulder hard enough to jar him to his boot soles. "My companion and I will settle the bill."

"I don't see you reaching into your purse," Iados said.

"I tipped our server for her troubles."

"So you have nothing?" Iados sounded as though he couldn't believe it.

"No. Wealth is an unwelcome burden, Iados. I keep telling you that."

"*I* gladly welcome it."

The watch sergeant, obviously sensing another argument brewing, ordered, "Settle the matter." She turned her attention to Lukkob. "Do you have a sum in mind?"

"I do." Lukkob named it and looked apologetically at Iados. "It *is* a fair price."

Looking at all the damage, Shang-Li had to agree. He tucked his fighting sticks back up his sleeves.

Grudgingly, Iados counted out gold and silver coins and spread them across the bar. His purse was considerably lighter when he returned it to his shirt. Lukkob scooped up the coins and made them disappear.

"Thank you, Iados," Thava said happily.

"You're going to make paupers of us both," Iados complained.

"But you'll have lived with honor," the paladin said. "And honor is its own reward."

"Honor doesn't pay the tavern bill or for lodging." Iados looked gloomy.

"Bahamut always provides."

"Truly? I find your god provides from my purse quite often when it comes to your service."

"Don't blaspheme or question Bahamut. He accepts your faults and you should be grateful for the tasks he gives you."

CHAPTER ELEVEN

The watch sergeant gave the command to her men to take their prisoners from the tavern. Outside, a crowd had gathered to watch now that the violence had come to a halt. A few even dared to come in and have a look around. Lukkob immediately informed them there was a charge for gawking. Some of them still stayed and chose to pay the price.

Thava crossed to Shang-Li and grabbed him in a bear hug that crushed the air from his lungs. "It's good to see you again, my friend."

Shang-Li patted her on the back, then took a deep breath when she finally released him. "I've missed you as well."

"You'll have to tell me of your adventures." Thava smiled, but a dragonborn's features never looked entirely devoid of threat. "I'm certain you have plenty to tell." She reached over and casually righted a table with one massive hand. "We can sit here."

Kwan Yung cleared his throat, managing to sound like as obnoxious as a strangling goose.

"Thava," Shang-Li said, "may I present my father, Master Kwan Yung of the Standing Tree Monastery. Father, this is Thava, a paladin."

Thava's iridescent eyes focused on Kwan Yung. "This is your father?"

"Yes."

"But he looks so . . . so . . . *small*."

"Small?" Kwan Yung raised offended eyebrows and stretched himself to his full height, barely topping Shang-Li's shoulder. "I am not *small*."

"No, of course you aren't, Master Kwan," Thava said quickly. "My humblest apologies. But from Shang-Li's description of you, I'd just expected someone much larger, more fierce, and possessing the temperament of an owlbear."

"That was his description of me?"

"No. It was more the . . . manner he said you had regarding him. The interpretive image was my own." Thava smiled. "But I see I was mistaken. Hail and well met, Kwan Yung, father of my friend. I am most pleased to make your acquaintance."

Shang-Li didn't know if his father was more upset over the description or by the bone-bruising hug Thava insisted on giving him. When she sat him down on the floor again, his father glared indignantly at Shang-Li.

"Please forgive my companion, Master Kwan," Iados said smoothly as he stepped into the mix. "I am Iados Lockhyr. A . . . traveler and entrepreneur." He bowed. "Your son has spoken of you with nothing but the utmost respect."

"You are a much better swordsman than you are a liar," Kwan Yung said.

"I respectfully beg to differ," Iados objected. "I'll wager

that you'll find I am a most excellent liar, this topic notwithstanding."

"Lying is not one of his most endearing qualities," Thava said. "But I feel obligated to let you know that he is one of the best liars I have ever seen. Do not overtrust him."

"Thank you, Thava." Iados looked confused, obviously wondering if he'd been complimented or condemned, but he gestured to the table Thava had righted. "Shall we sit?"

"Aren't you concerned that the men you fought earlier might return?" Kwan Yung asked.

Thava and Iados looked at each other and smiled. Then Iados said, "No. Not really. And if they do, if would be their mistake. We've already paid for the damage to the tavern." He turned to Lukkob. "If I've paid for the tavern, perhaps I could get some service."

Lukkob grinned at him. "Aye. And I'll even name one of the new rooms in your honor when I have them built."

"You're much too kind," Iados replied dryly.

One of the servers brought over a bottle of ale for Iados and Thava and fresh tea for Shang-Li and his father.

"Would you like supper as well?" Lukkob asked. "At least the oven is still of a piece."

"Gentlemen?" Iados asked. "Thava and I had just sat down to eat when we were interrupted." He leaned forward and pretended to speak so that Thava couldn't hear. "But I must warn you: it isn't safe to let a dragonborn get too long between meals. If you know what I mean."

"I take offense at that," Thava said.

"Do so," Iados warned, "and you'll be washing dishes for your supper."

"Perhaps I'm not as offended as I'd first thought." She drummed her large fingers on the table top.

"Supper would be good," Shang-Li said. "We have much to discuss."

His father looked at him doubtfully.

"Lukkob sets a fine table," Iados said, picking up on

the unspoken question. "If you've been aboardship for the last few days, you'll find yourself rewarded. And it will be my treat."

You've just won my father's heart, Shang-Li thought.

"Very well," Kwan Yung said as he moved to take one of the chairs at the table. "Thank you."

Supper came and went, and it wasn't long before the candles on the table guttered in the wind that blew through the broken windows. Lukkob had covered the empty spaces with pieces of sailcloth for the time being, but the bitter wind slipped around them carrying the stink of salt and dead fish. The heat from the fireplace didn't quite fill the room and there was just enough warmth to make Shang-Li long for more.

"You plan to find the shipwreck and the Blue Lady?" Iados asked after Shang-Li had finished his tale.

"I'd rather find only the shipwreck," Shang-Li said, "but I have the feeling that I won't find one far from the other. Given that she has proven to be dangerous in the past, I thought it might be a good idea to look for you two while we were here in Westgate."

"How do you propose to do this?" Thava leaned forward, intent and attentive.

"I've got the coordinates where *Grayling* went down. Ships tend to drift through the ocean when they go down, so I don't expect to find the wreckage there, but it gives us a point of origin to begin with." Shang-Li marshaled his thoughts. "I've dived for shipwrecks before. Sometimes you get lucky and find them in a short time, but you need to know that this could take a while."

"Shipwrecks also mean the possibility of salvage." Iados grinned. "I've dived a few of those myself. If you have good information to begin with and stick to the effort, the time you put into the exploration can be quite lucrative. I'm willing to invest some time after everything you've told me. *Grayling* isn't the only ship that's been taken in that area."

"No." Shang-Li remembered all the ships he'd seen broken and scattered across the sea floor. "But that's part of the problem. This woman—whatever she is—is incredibly powerful and incredibly dangerous."

"Then why is she appearing in your dreams?"

Shang-Li shook his head.

Iados leaned back in his chair, which creaked under his weight. "If she has the book, and the potential to read about these portals, why would she need you?"

Although his father hadn't been comfortable with telling Iados and Thava everything about Liou's books, Shang-Li had make it a sticking point of their continued joint efforts. In the end, it had been Thava and her gentle ways that had won over his father.

His father spoke quietly. "In the seventy years she has had Liou's books, she hasn't opened a portal. We can assume that she hasn't yet learned the power to do so."

"Or that the information was wrong and the spell doesn't work." Iados's tail flicked casually across the floor.

"The information is correct." Kwan Yung didn't raise his voice, but the authority resonated in his words.

"Of course, Master Kwan. I meant no disrespect." Iados inclined his horned head.

"No disrespect taken, Iados. But the spells are a danger if they fall into the wrong hands. I cannot stress that enough."

"And if the Blue Lady thought the spells were deficient, she wouldn't be interested in attracting Shang-Li to her." Thava fixed her gaze on Shang-Li. "But she is. And since she is, I want to point out the possibility that perhaps she needs you to translate Liou's books. You said they were all written in code."

Shang-Li nodded. "They are. I don't know if I can read them. My father and I—and the Standing Tree

Monastery—only want to secure those books before they fall into the wrong hands."

Iados took in a breath and let it out. He scratched at the tabletop with a long talon. "What must books like that be worth?"

Thava frowned at him.

"What?" Iados did his best to look innocent but the horns didn't help him pull that effort off. "I was just thinking."

"In going to rescue those books, you also pose a serious threat to them." Thava studied Shang-Li. "Maybe it would be better if you stayed out of this."

"Sit back and wait to hear?" That appalled Shang-Li. He'd never been one to sit when there was action.

"It would be safest."

Kwan Yung shrugged. "My son and I are also the only authorities on Liou Chang's works. We cannot risk that forgeries are found instead of the real books. We have no choice about going."

"We are at an impasse then." Thava nodded. "There is no way to do this or not do this without risk."

"Exactly as I see it."

"All right." Iados leaned forward again. "So we stock the ship for a long voyage and we begin searching for *Grayling.* What's left of her. What do we do about the Blue Lady?"

"I'm still working that out." Shang-Li looked around the table. "So if any of you have any ideas, I'm open to them."

The candlelight flickered along the tiefling's horns, chipping away the shadows that had gathered in the tavern. The effect made him look even more demonic. His smile was chilling. No one in the Edge sat close by them.

"Sounds dangerous." Iados pulled at his chin whiskers.

"She's pulled whole ships to the bottom of the Sea of Fallen Stars," Shang-Li said. There was no way to make that sound any less threatening.

"Dangerous *is* more expensive."

"Nonsense," Thava said. "You were telling me only a few days ago that you were tired of protecting caravans along the trade roads. You were longing for the sea. And we haven't had a good adventure in several tendays."

Shang-Li hid a smile. Iados had a restless nature and tended to always look for the next patch of green grass.

"I might remind you," Iados said, "that our last adventure nearly killed me."

"Would you rather die old and feeble?"

"I find the whole idea of dying unappealing, if you must know."

Thava snorted. "You enjoy gold and spending gold too much to be careful."

Iados sighed and swirled the ale in his tankard. "This is probably true. Careful doesn't pay very well. And if you pursue safety, you might as well long for a pauper's life." He glanced at Shang-Li. "So how much are you willing to pay?"

"A percentage of everything we find."

"This is not a treasure hunt," his father said.

"Of course not." Thava patted Kwan Yung's hand. "We go to find lost history. That is a noble quest. But Iados?" She sighed and several men closest to them moved away because the noise sounded too threatening. "Iados must find his own reasons for doing things. It is a failing within him that you must accept. He is much more . . . superficial than we are."

"Don't be so sanctimonious," Iados warned. "You know I have a low-retch threshold when it comes to such things. Especially after a big meal."

"I can see why he and my son are such good friends," Kwan Yung stated, "but I don't understand your involvement with either of them."

"I don't question Bahamut's motives for the people he puts in my life," Thava said. "I only know that I was given Iados to look over—"

"I paid the bar bill," Iados argued.

"—and sometimes look out for Shang-Li."

"I thank you for that."

"You're very welcome."

"I am going to be sick," Iados declared. "At least tell me that *Grayling* had a rich cargo on her when she went down."

"Not much of one, I'm afraid," Shang-Li said. "She was on a mission of exploration."

Iados drained his cup sourly.

"But while I talked with the Blue Lady," Shang-Li went on, "I saw several other ships in the vicinity. None of them looked disturbed. There could be treasure aboard them."

Iados leaned forward. "You said you had to recruit crewmen as well."

"Yes. I've got the feeling that several of our crewmen have probably already jumped ship."

"Not a brave lot, are they?"

"Obviously they prefer safe and secure lives," Thava interjected. "Some people do, you know."

Iados grimaced but refused to look at his companion. "Crew shouldn't be a problem. There are many desperate sailors and mercenaries in Westgate these days. There are fortunes to be made if you're strong enough and brave enough. And don't hang about with paladins that long for pious poverty."

"Every gold coin in your purse weighs you down with worry," Thava said.

"If that's true, we're considerably less worried than we were a short time ago."

"You're welcome."

"That wasn't intended as a good thing."

"Eye of the beholder," Thava replied. She picked up a hambone and crunched it thoughtfully in her beak, then sucked out the marrow.

"You want us to do *what*?" Gorrick, *Swallow's* ship's mage, looked apoplectic. He was old and gray, a bent stick of a man in elegant robes. He didn't have many friends on the ship because he was so demanding.

Several of the crewmen started muttering. None of them looked pleased at the prospect of going hunting for a ship sunken by a malevolent spirit or avatar of Umberlee.

Still, it was going better than Shang-Li had thought it might. None of them had charged up the sterncastle from amidships yet. He held up his hands and the crew gradually quieted.

"There is some risk." Shang-Li kept his voice level. He'd had to tell the men what they faced. Captain Chiang hadn't been happy about the venture when Shang-Li had told him in private, but the Captain also served the Standing Tree Monastery. The monastery owned the ship, and he believed in their efforts. Of course, Chiang had never been asked to willingly risk so much before.

"Some *risk*?" Gorrick shook a fist at Shang-Li. "You'd send us to your doom if you have your way." He waved a bony hand at the coastline. "These taverns are full of talk of the Blue Lady and the ships she has dragged down."

Iados leaned toward Shang-Li and whispered. "If I were you, I wouldn't tell them about the dreams."

Shang-Li silently agreed.

"I've been in Westgate for some time now," Thava said. "Until today I've never heard of the Blue Lady."

"I suggest that you don't keep the same kind of company a sailing man keeps." Gorrick's beard quivered with his outrage.

"Way I hear it," someone in the crowd said, "the paladin likes throwing sailors through windows."

"I have been in those taverns—" Gorrick pointed again.

"Wenching and drinking ale, no doubt."

Several of the crew tittered at that. Gorrick had quite a reputation as a would-be lothario.

Gorrick scowled at the crew for the interruption and they drew back from him. "While in those taverns, I've heard talk of the Blue Lady. They say she's the ghost of a ship come calling for vengeance for the pirates that sunk her. They say she went down when the Spellplague came and somehow she was given form and command over the seas where she is."

Several of the sailors spat and reached for sacred symbols.

"The mission we have undertaken on part of the monastery is very important." Shang-Li leaned on the sterncastle railing and pierced each man with his gaze. "You've served on the ship they've given you, eaten of the larder they've provided, and enjoyed fairly comfortable lives. They need you—we need you—at this, our most desperate hour, to be the warriors and sailing men you are."

"I'm not a warrior," someone muttered.

"Aye, and as far as comfort goes, there hasn't been a day that I haven't broken my back working on this ship."

"Gorrick is a hard taskmaster."

The ship's mage glared around. "Who said that? Who dared say that?"

No one owned up to that.

"Think it over," Shang-Li encouraged. "What we plan on doing—"

"Is getting killed," someone interrupted.

"—is important to our safety. The battle you flee from by not coming with us will only be fought at some later date. And it will be worse. Much worse." Shang-Li was convinced of that.

Chiang stepped forward. "You've known me as your captain for a long time, most of you. I'm going with these men to try to find that ship. I would like you to go with me, but I'll understand if you choose not to."

"Because they're a cowardly lot," Iados muttered. Then he let out a painful breath when Thava elbowed him.

Chiang dismissed the crew and it was the most somber leave-taking aboard *Swallow* Shang-Li had ever seen.

That night, Shang-Li woke once more in a dream and trapped at the bottom of the sea with the Blue Lady. He floated in the water as the sharks danced around him.

"Your crew is going to abandon you," she said.

"Possibly." Shang-Li tried to draw his sword but found that his hand passed straight through the weapon.

"Come with me, manling." The Blue Lady arrowed to the surface where a ship was held in the thrall of a storm. Canvas snapped yards and flapped in the powerful winds that keened over the decks. The crew tried to put lifeboats out as the ship started breaking up. One lifeboat did reach the sea, and even filled with crewmen, then a large wave rolled over them and they disappeared.

Shang-Li struggled to be free of the dream. He couldn't bear to watch men dying.

"Do you see them?" the Blue Lady demanded. "Do you see how weak they are in my power?"

Shang-Li said nothing.

"That is you, manling. That is how weak you are. No matter where you go, no matter what you do, I will find you."

Steeling himself, Shang-Li strode toward her. "Are you trying to scare me away? Is that what this is about?"

Light blazed in the Blue Lady's dark eyes, and she smiled. "No. I don't want you to go away, manling."

"Because I'm coming for you." Shang-Li spoke calmly despite the fear that raged within him.

"Because of the books?"

"Because you're an abomination and I won't suffer you to live. There will be an accounting."

The Blue Lady laughed in his face. "And you think you're strong enough to give that accounting? Then come, manling. Come and die." The Blue Lady gestured at the ship and it broke in half. She turned back to Shang-Li. "There were others that thought they could kill me. My own kind exiled me here. But they're going to regret that because I'm going to come back stronger than I was. And when I do, I'm going to have an army at my back. I will invade those lands and take what is rightfully mine. I will take more than that. They will beg for my mercy. And I will not give it."

Horrified, Shang-Li watched as the ship's crew died by the dozens.

"I promise you this, manling. If you come to me, your death will be quick. I will not prolong it. Your foolish courage will be rewarded. But in the end you will still die." The Blue Lady gestured again.

This time a waterspout licked up from the heaving sea surface and curled around Shang-Li like a python. It pulled him beneath the sea, and this time he couldn't breathe. He fought and fought but couldn't escape.

Then he woke in his hammock sucking in wind and covered with feverish sweat.

"We have a problem."

Shang-Li looked up from where he'd been fitting a plank into place on *Swallow's* port side. He hung in a rope harness with tools at his waist. Cool wind sweeping in from the sea warred with the hot sun overhead and his skin was alternately warmed and cooled. He'd sweated so much that his shirt and pants stuck to him.

"If it's about Thava . . ." Shang-Li said.

"No. The crew, what we have of them, seemed to be more pleased about the prospect of having the dragonborn aboard than fearful. They're more afraid of the Blue Lady."

Shang-Li couldn't blame them. "We haven't lost any more crew, have we?" Nearly half of the original crew had fled in the night.

"No. But we have lost our ship's mage."

"Gorrick left?"

"He . . . found more profitable employment." Chiang pulled a folded note from inside his blouse.

Shang-Li took the note and quickly read it. Gorrick's tone was apologetic throughout. But he also pointed out that they were all fools soon to be dead. Finished, Shang-Li returned the note.

"I suppose there's no getting him back?"

Chiang shook his head and put the note back under his blouse. "The ship he took berth on sailed this morning. I was only just given the note by a boy Gorrick hired for the task."

Shang-Li thought about that. Losing the ship's mage wasn't something he'd even remotely considered. And sailing back in the Sea of Fallen Stars without one, even without looking for the Blue Lady, was a foolhardy proposition. "Does my father know Gorrick is gone?"

Chiang hesitated.

"He doesn't, does he?" Shang-Li asked.

"I thought maybe he might take the news better from you."

"No." Shang-Li leaned into the harness that supported him on *Swallow's* side. "He won't. He'll blame me."

"I know your father is committed to recovering those books—"

"Very committed. As he explained to you, the spells contained within those books could allow the wrong person to change all of the Sea of Fallen Stars."

"—but I don't feel comfortable sailing back out there to face what we have to face without a ship's mage."

"I agree." Shang-Li hadn't thought about trying to recover the lost books without a ship, but he knew his father would have him out on the sea in a rowboat if it came to it. That wouldn't have appealed to Iados's larcenous heart at all.

Shang-Li sighed and stared at the plank. Only moments before, he'd felt the carpentry had been hard. Now he knew how easy it had truly been.

"Ship's mages, good ones, are as hard to find as hen's teeth," Chiang said.

"Much harder than that." Shang-Li gave the plank he'd fitted into place a few more taps. Everything seemed water tight. "Are Iados and Thava around?"

"Thava has busied herself helping around the ship. I don't think Iados has made it up from bed yet."

"Manual labor isn't one of Iados's interests."

"No. I surmised as much last night when he wasn't impressed with his lodging aboardship."

Shang-Li hauled himself up the harness and flipped over the railing to land on his feet. He glanced at Westgate.

The city had come to life, filling the streets with pedestrians and carts. Hawkers called out their wares. Hoarse orders, frustrated yells, and curses floated over the placid waters around the docks. Reefed sails snapped and popped in the wind. "If there's a ship's mage to be found in Westgate, Captain Chiang," Shang-Li promised, "we'll bring one back to you."

"A good one," the captain said. "Gods know where we'll be going, we'll need a mage that knows his business."

CHAPTER TWELVE

You know, you could have left me back at the ship," Iados pointed out as he matched Shang-Li's pace. Thava and Kwan Yung trailed behind, lost in one of their increasingly frequent philosophical discussions of the differences between a paladin's calling and a monk's.

"Then we would have missed out on all the complaining." Shang-Li walked the streets of Westgate easily but remained watchful. During his travels, he'd made enemies in the city as surely as he'd made friends, and enemies tended to run in packs in the city these days.

"I could have complained back at the ship."

"You were."

"Not as much as I'm going to complain now." Shang-Li knew that was probably true. "You don't have to feel compelled to excel on my account."

"I told you where the ship's mage could be found," Iados protested. "You could have come here yourself."

"She's an unemployed ship's mage in Westgate. I have to wonder why that is." Shang-Li shot the tiefling a glance, then checked to make certain Thava and his father were keeping pace.

Iados chose to ignore the look. "She's a good ship's mage on all accounts."

"Where's the cynicism I'd hoped for? Something to balance out the desperation I'm feeling?"

"It's concentrating on this long, boring walk through the heat of the day." Iados sidestepped a couple of sailors sprawled in the alley sleeping off rough nights.

"You shouldn't have slept so late. We have a job to do."

"I'm in for a percentage. That, at the very least, makes me a partner. As such, I'm entitled to privileges."

"Like sleeping late?"

"Definitely."

Shang-Li turned the corner by a bakery that filled the immediate vicinity with the pungent aroma of yeast. "Why doesn't this ship's mage have a ship?"

Iados hesitated a moment. "Do you really wish to know?"

"I'm really desperate. I keep seeing images of you, me, Thava, and my father in a rowboat in the middle of the Sea of Fallen Stars if we don't find a ship's mage."

Iados shuddered. "There's not enough ale in all of Faerûn to supply that voyage."

"My point exactly. The ship?"

"It sank."

Cautiously, Shang-Li glanced over his shoulder at his father. Kwan Yung remained contented with Thava's company. Thinking back on it, Shang-Li believed the paladin was the first dragonborn his father had ever spoken to.

"Where did the ship sink?" Shang-Li asked.

"In the harbor."

"That doesn't sound very comforting."

"It could have gone down in the middle of the Sea of Fallen Stars."

Shang-Li shrugged. "When you put it that way, sinking in the harbor does sound better." But he didn't look forward to his father discovering that tidbit of information.

"No one died and the cargo had been offloaded. The vessel had come through serious storms and a sahuagin attack."

"So it wasn't her fault, but they blamed her anyway?"

"Captains and crewmen do like to blame others for their misfortunes. And she was the ship's mage. It was her job to hold the ship together."

"Evidently she held it together long enough to reach safety and get the cargo unloaded."

"Which is why I recommended her," Iados agreed.

"That and the fact that she's the only unemployed ship's mage you know of at present," Shang-Li said.

"Yes." Iados lowered his voice. "There is some talk of her being cursed as well."

Shang-Li swiveled his head around to look at his companion so fast that he tripped over a pothole in the crushed oyster shell street.

"The captain had to blame his misfortune of getting hit by a storm and the sahuagin on someone," Iados said.

"I'm supposed to go back to *Swallow* and tell Captain Chiang I've brought him a cursed ship's mage?"

"I definitely wouldn't do that unless you intend to never lift anchor from that harbor."

Shang-Li walked in silence for a moment. "Maybe there's nothing to the curse rumor."

"Probably not." Iados shrugged. "You know how sailors like to talk."

According to the gossip Iados had overheard, the "cursed ship's mage" was currently rooming at the Splintered Yards, an inn so-named because it had gotten hit several times by storms in the past. A patchwork of timbers covered the exterior and the building held no illusions of pride or grandeur.

A dour old woman with her hair pulled back and a shapeless gray dress stood at the counter . Anxiously, she peered down the hallway and shuffled a deck of cards.

"Need a room, a meal, a drink, or your fortune told, gentle sir?" The old woman awkwardly spread the cards across the scarred countertop. Some of them fluttered to the floor.

"We're looking for someone." Shang-Li picked up her cards and put them back on the counter, then slid a small silver coin onto the counter.

The woman captured the coin with a withered claw and made it disappear as easily as she worked the cards. She swallowed hard and glanced at the hallway. "Who?"

"The ship's mage," Iados said. "I was told she was here."

A scowl darkened the old woman's face. "Have you come to collect from her as well?"

"As well?" Shang-Li asked.

"The captain took her wages and her savings," the old woman said tremulously. "The old flintheart left her here with no prospects and no way of paying her way." She nodded at the rooms above. "I gave her a place to stay in return for cleaning rooms. But there are others that insist she owes them. They went up after her only moments ago."

"Who?" Shang-Li asked.

"Murderous vermin." The old woman spat in displeasure, then quickly checked to see if anyone had overheard her.

"There are a lot of murderous vermin in Westgate," Iados said as he reached to his hip and freed his sword.

"These are particularly offensive." She looked at Shang-Li with wide eyes. "That's who I thought you were. Until I saw your ears and recognized you as elven. They wouldn't let a half-breed among them."

"The Nine Golden Swords?" Shang-Li asked, understanding the mistake that was made because of his Shou heritage.

A woman's scream, filled with fear and rage, ripped from upstairs.

Shang-Li sprinted toward the staircase to his left and ran up the steps three and four at a time. Iados followed at his heels. By the time Thava joined them, Shang-Li held his fighting sticks in his hands. The paladin's massive weight combined with the armor caused the stairs to shudder and quake, and for a moment Shang-Li feared they might collapse. He gained the landing with his sticks held before him.

The dim hallway ran straight and narrow. Doors to rooms sat off to either side. Scars from scrapes and drunken sailors adorned the plain wooden walls. Weak light from outside the building entered the hallway from windows at either end.

A large group of Shou men bearing tattoos that marked them as members of the Nine Golden Swords surrounded a young woman with copper hair at the end of the hallway. She fought against them, but the Shou held her easily. Shang-Li was surprised at how many men had been sent.

"Unhand me!" the woman yelled as she struggled against her captors. "Unhand me, or I swear to Umberlee you'll rue the day you ever touched me!"

"You owe us, woman," a brutish man snarled. He was in his middle years, thick with corded muscle, and had a mustache that curved down to his jawline. "You will pay us back for our losses."

"You lost nothing!"

"That is not how my master views it," the man snarled. He reached out to cuff her.

Ducking the blow, the woman twisted toward one of the Shou holding her and kicked him in the groin.

The man lurched to one side and dropped to his knees before throwing up.

"Well," Iados commented dryly, wrinkling his nose at the sour stench of wine that suddenly filled the area, "he'd obviously been drinking before he arrived here."

"Is that the ship's mage?" Shang-Li asked, nodding toward the young woman.

"I'd say it's a safe bet," Iados said. "There can't be two women in this dump that the Nine Golden Swords would try to grab."

"Well?" Thava demanded.

Shang-Li sighed. "Out of all the criminals in Westgate, did she have to end up in the hands of these?"

"Ah, that's right," Iados said. "You have a history with the Nine Golden Swords."

"Not exactly a history," Shang-Li responded. "More like an understanding."

"I understand that they have orders to kill you on sight."

The brutish man noticed Shang-Li for the first time, then grinned coldly. "Shang-Li? The gods have favored me today. I now have two prizes to bring back. We owe you for the theft you made from us in the Pirate Isles. I'll be happy to take your head as payment for our embarrassment."

The heads of the other Nine Golden Swords turned to glare down the hall.

"Kill him!" the brutish man roared. "Ten gold pieces to any man that brings me his head."

"Only ten?" Iados asked as he readied his sword. "I'd be insulted."

The Nine Golden Swords rushed toward Shang-Li. One of them pulled a crossbow up to his shoulder and fired over the heads of his fellows. Shang-Li watched the quarrel as it leaped free of the weapon, then swept his left fighting stick out and broke the shaft before it hit Iados. The halves dropped to the floor.

"One of these days," the tiefling said, "you're going to have to teach me that trick."

Thava yelled her challenge and drew her bastard sword. In the dim hallway, the blade gleamed and Shang-Li felt the chill of the magic that clung to the weapon.

Two of the Nine Golden Swords grabbed the ship's mage. One slipped a blade beneath her jaw and held it against her throat. They opened the window behind them and forced her through it.

"The mage," Iados said.

"I see her." Shang-Li ran forward, then broke suddenly to the left and partially ran up the wall. He managed two long, deliberate strides before his momentum played out. Just before he fell from the wall, he dived and pushed himself forward to flip over the mob. Two swords slashed up at him, but only one of them was close and he batted it away with his fighting sticks. He landed on his feet behind the Nine Golden Swords warriors.

The mob instantly divided their attention between their front and rear. The brutish man stared at Shang-Li.

"Did you come to give yourself to me?" the man asked.

"I see you haven't gotten any handsomer, Liu," Shang-Li said. He parried the man's blade with his left stick, knocking the blade down to the floor and striking with the right stick only an instant later.

Liu barely managed to get under the blow. He hissed a curse in surprise. At the end of the hallway, the two Nine Gold Swords warriors had disappeared with their captive.

"If I had known you were in the city," Liu threatened, "I'd already have killed you."

"You've tried to kill me before," Shang-Li taunted. "Yet here I am again."

"No more." Liu took a two-handed grip on his sword and slashed repeatedly in carefully controlled blows.

Shang-Li dodged and weaved, forced back by the onslaught. One of the men behind him grew overconfident and lunged, following his sword to its intended target.

"No!" Liu bellowed in warning.

The man didn't have the chance to pull back from his attack. Sidestepping and bending his knee on that side to drop his shoulder, Shang-Li let the man's sword glide over his shoulder without touching him. The sword almost pierced Liu's stomach as Shang-Li batted away his last attempt.

Shang-Li stood, knocking aside the man's sword behind him and then elbowing his opponent in the nose hard enough to lift him from his feet. The man was unconscious by the time he struck the floor.

As he repositioned himself, Shang-Li saw Iados and Thava filling the hallway as they combatted the Nine Golden Sword members. They stepped over the bodies of two or three of them. His father fearlessly trailed behind them.

"Did it really take this many of you to capture a young woman for your master's vengeance?" Shang-Li asked. He batted a series of sword slashes aside, then stepped sideways and delivered a reverse roundhouse kick that knocked another opponent into the nearby wall.

The unconscious man dropped into a sitting position beside the wall, then fell over.

"A point had to be made," Liu said. He feinted at Shang-Li's face, then shifted and tried to skewer his midsection.

Shang-Li dodged out of range, but that only set him up for another series of blinding attacks. Liu's sword clattered along the fighting sticks but didn't manage to find a way through Shang-Li's defenses.

"The way I hear the story told," Shang-Li said, "the ship was lost at sea and the woman was skilled enough to get it back to this harbor before it sank."

"The ship wasn't supposed to be lost." Liu stamped his foot and thrust again, following up almost immediately with a backward slash.

Shang-Li dropped into a low horse stance and the sword cut the air only inches above his head. He thrust his right fighting stick toward Liu's chest, but the man blocked it with his free hand and set himself to strike again.

"If she had done her job, the ship would have been safe."

"Shang-Li, are you going to let them take the ship's mage?"

Recognizing his father's voice, Shang-Li focused on Liu. The man attacked again and Shang-Li defended himself against a flurry of sword blows. Then, when Liu lunged in again, Shang-Li swept the sword aside and charged forward.

Turning sideways, Shang-Li planted his right foot and lashed out with his left. Liu managed to turn away his face, but Shang-Li's foot caught him on the temple and the neck. Propelled by the force of the kick, Liu slammed into the wall with a meaty smack.

After a quick glance to make sure his father and his friends were all right, Shang-Li ran to the window and peered out. The two men struggled with the woman on the slanted roof only a few feet away. Their feet slipped and slid on the damp wooden shingles. Obviously the woman was no stranger to physical encounters, but she was up against skilled opponents.

Shang-Li put his fighting sticks away and stepped through the window onto the eaves. His foot slipped, then found purchase. He found his center, concentrated on his balance, and stepped forward.

One of the men released the woman while the other stepped behind her and held a knife to her throat. The man holding the ship's mage stepped back toward the roof's edge. Unfortunately, the Splintered Yards hadn't been built on level ground. Tucked into the side of the steep mountain that formed Tidetown, the inn hung over a drop of fifty feet on two sides. The Nine Golden Swords warriors had run in the wrong direction. Or perhaps they'd expected their companions to win.

"Take another step, you diseased monkey," the swordsman threatened in the Shou tongue, "and Kim will slash her throat."

Swarthy and wiry, Kim looked the type to slash women's throats. He grinned at Shang-Li and molded himself to the woman's body to present a much smaller target. She tried to pull away from her captor, but his pressed his knife into her throat hard enough to start a trickle of blood that ran down into the hollow of her throat. She stilled.

Twenty feet away, the noise of the battle in the hallway still behind him, Shang-Li halted. He measured the distance and took a deliberate breath. He focused on being calm and stared at Kim's face partially hidden behind the ship's mage's head.

"You will let us by," the swordsman ordered.

"If you release the woman," Shang-Li responded.

The swordsman held his weapon in front of him and slowly closed the distance. As he neared, he drew his blade back, readying for a quick strike.

"She will come with us," he declared.

"No."

The swordsman grinned and kept coming. "Perhaps I will let you have her. My master doesn't care if she's alive or dead. Can I interest you in a dead woman?" Thinking he had the upper hand, he lunged.

Shang-Li bent his left knee and threw his weight and balance to that side. He twisted his right shoulder back and let the sword slide past him. At the same time, he dropped a throwing star from inside his sleeve, caught it in his waiting hand, and flicked it toward the man holding the ship's mage.

The throwing star glittered just for a moment in the sun, then sliced the skin over Kim's right eyebrow. The razor edges nicked the woman's ear in passing. Blinded by a sudden rush of blood, Kim dropped his knife and clapped his hand to his head while he staggered back, partially stunned from the impact.

Already in motion, Shang-Li stepped back and swept the long sword from his back. He turned, left foot forward and right hand gripping the sword hilt at waist level. When the swordsman attacked again, trying for Shang-Li's groin this time, Shang-Li dipped his blade and blocked the attempt. Before his opponent could recover, Shang-Li whipped the long sword's tip to the man's chin.

"Drop your sword," Shang-Li commanded, "and I'll let you live."

The man let go his weapon and sword clattered down the shingles to vanish over the edge. His eyes remained dark and sullen. "One day, monk, luck will not be with you."

"Leave," Shang-Li suggested.

The man turned and fled toward the opposite end of the roof.

"Don't just stand there congratulating yourself, you oaf. Get over here and help!" the woman yelled. She stood at the roof's edge and fought the bloody-faced man off. He'd dropped his knife when the throwing star had hit him, but he hadn't given up the fight. His blood-covered hand wrapped around her left forearm and his left hand flailed for her head.

Instinctively, she shoved him back from her. Then her hands worked in front of her and she spoke a word. A powerful gust of wind slammed into her attacker, driving him over the roof's edge. The ship's mage managed to rip her arm free of the man's grip as he fell, but he grabbed for the roof's edge and caught it with his elbows for a moment. Frightened now, he reached for her and caught her ankle. His bloody fingers lost purchase on the wooden shingles and he fell. She gestured again and a blinding flash of light hit the man in the face. Unfortunately he maintained his hold.

Dragged after the man, the woman fell prone across the roof and tried to find purchase. It was the same move she would have done on a ship at sea tossed during a storm. Despite her efforts, she only slowed her fall. The man weighed her down.

Shang-Li threw himself forward and grabbed her right

hand in his left as she followed the man over the roof's edge. Her yells mixed with the man's fearful screams. Shang-Li tried to hold all three of them on the roof but their combined weight outmatched the purchase he was able to find on the shingles. Several pulled free and clattered down the roof.

Even if Shang-Li had wished to, he couldn't have let the woman fall. She had a death grip on his hand. Pain shot through his fingers and his arm.

He rolled onto his side and lifted the long sword, then drove the blade through the shingles and prayed it would hold. The sword tore through two rows of shingles without pause, then found a support timber and held. The angle was awkward and Shang-Li's head and left shoulder had slid over the roof's edge.

At the end of his arm, the young woman's eyes rounded with fear, but she remained calm and clear-headed. She swung her other arm up to wrap her hand around his wrist.

"Don't let go," she yelled at Shang-Li.

Shang-Li didn't have the breath to respond. He strained against the weight and felt certain his arm was about to tear from his shoulder. If she'd had her hands free, she probably would have unleashed another spell.

The Nine Golden Swords man clung to her boots, but his bloody hand betrayed him and he slipped. Screaming in fear, the man fell forty feet onto the craggy rocks in the harbor at the foot of the steep edge of the coast. The screams ended abruptly.

"Don't. Let. Go," the woman repeated.

The sword split more wood and slipped an inch or so, but it held. The woman swung at the end of Shang-Li's arm.

"Climb," he told her.

"This is your idea of a rescue?"

"Actually, I haven't yet decided if this is a rescue or if you're just going to drag me down with you."

Adroitly, the ship's mage climbed up his arm as though scaling a ship's rigging. When she was once more on the roof, she grabbed Shang-Li by the waist of his pants and hauled him back from the roof's edge.

"Thank you," he said as he sat there a moment and drew a breath.

"You're welcome." The ship's mage stood and headed for the other end of the building.

"You're not going to thank me for rescuing you?" Shang-Li couldn't believe it.

"If you hadn't come along," she told him, "I'd never have ended up on this rooftop about to plunge to my death."

"Only because Liu and his men would have slit your throat in the hallway."

"If they were going to do that there, you gave them plenty of time." She paused at the opposite roof's edge. "Besides that, I was about to save myself. You threw my timing off."

Shang-Li stood. "You're just going to leave?"

She turned to face him. "Staying here now that the Nine Golden Swords know where I am doesn't seem very intelligent, does it? Especially since they appear to want me dead for saving what was left of their blasted ship."

Iados, Kwan Yung, and Thava stuck their heads through the broken window and watched with interest.

"How do you plan on leaving Westgate?" Shang-Li asked.

"On a ship, of course. If I could turn into a bird and fly away, don't you think I'd have done that by now? And there's no way I would ever ride a stinking, godforsaken horse. I'd sooner die."

"If you could have left on a ship, you would have been gone before now."

The ship's mage shot him a dire look. "If I have to, I'll travel with a caravan to the Sword Coast. At least they have wagons. But I'd still be around those stupid horses and all that hair and ordure."

"Do you know those waters like you know the Sea of Fallen Stars?"

"No, but I know seas, ships, storms, and sailors. I can

find someone that needs a ship's mage."

"We need a ship's mage," Kwan Yung said.

Shang-Li shot his father a reproving glance.

The woman crossed her arms and regarded Shang-Li. "You came here looking for me?"

"We do need a mage. But not one that's been cursed. Are you cursed?"

The woman rolled her eyes. "You think I'm cursed?" She glared at him, and she was joined by Kwan Yung, Thava, and Iados.

"No," Shang-Li said. "I'm just saying we don't need a ship's mage that is cursed."

"I'm not cursed," she said in obvious annoyance. "I brought in a damaged ship that most ship's mages would have abandoned. I saved the lives of most of the crew and nearly all of the cargo. Then that thrice-diseased Nine Golden Swords boss decided he'd cheat me of my fee, steal from me, and blame me for everything, ruining my reputation in the process. And you have the audacity to question me?"

"I intended no disrespect." Feeling suddenly foolish, Shang-Li sheathed his sword. "Then we have a deal?"

"No, we don't have a deal," the woman replied. "If you came here thinking I was cursed, and you were determined to attempt to hire me anyway, I have to wonder what you're planning to do. Do you think I'm foolish enough to just go with someone that desperate?"

Iados chuckled and drew the ire of them both. "Oh," the tiefling said politely, "excuse me. Something in my throat. Do carry on. I find this whole discussion fascinating. But you may have to cut it a little short."

"Why?" the woman demanded.

"It appears our victory here hasn't gone unnoticed." Iados pointed out into the street where more Shou wearing the tattoos of the Nine Golden Swords had started to gather. "Maybe we should consider escaping, then working out the details."

Sword in hand, Shang-Li led the way down the stairs. As they reached the first floor, the Nine Golden Swords warriors arrived in force. He leaped from the stairs and hurled himself into their midst, taking several of them to the ground with him. As he rose, he reached out and tripped others into each other, adding to the confusion.

The old woman at the desk fled.

Thava shouted her battle cry and heaved herself over the railing as well. She surged past Shang-Li with her arms outspread, knocking several of the Nine Golden Swords warriors from him and tearing through the front window of the inn in a shower of glass and wooden lattice work.

The ship's mage joined Shang-Li and looked up at him with golden eyes that complemented her copper colored tresses. "Well, I have to say you and your friends know how to fight. We'll have to talk more about this ship of yours."

Shang-Li admired how she kept her calm in the face of so much danger. It made her even more attractive than her looks did. Together, they walked out of the inn, trailed by Iados and Kwan Yung. Then she turned and faced another group of Nine Golden Swords coming down the street. She gestured and spoke, then the patch of ground beneath the running warriors' feet turned to ice. They slipped and fell, tangling themselves.

"Westgate is filled with these idiots these days," the mage said.

"I know." Shang-Li knocked aside a thrown spear, then blocked a sword before skewering the warrior wielding it. "And they tend to run long on memory for enemies."

She drew back her hand and threw a small pellet at another group. As soon as it struck, the pellet transformed into a cloud of gray mist that coated the Nine Golden Swords warriors with frost.

A pair of Nine Golden Swords archers unleashed arrows at them from nearby rooftops. Shang-Li knew he could deflect at least one of them, but the other might strike the mage. He stepped in front of her, hoping to offer her the safety of his leather armor. Instead, she shoved him away and held up a hand.

Instantly, a glowing patch formed in the air in front of them. The arrows thumped into the patch and shattered. Then the mage pointed at the archers and semi-visible arrows shot from her hand to strike both of the Nine Golden Archers warriors, knocking them backward.

"When did you say your ship is leaving?" the mage asked as they continued hurrying down the street.

"As soon as I've secured a ship's mage and squared away the ship."

"Sounds good." She offered her hand. "I'm Amree. Contrary to the popular opinion of Westgate these days, I'm an excellent ship's mage."

Looking at the carnage that lay behind them, Shang-Li nodded and gave her his name. "If you're as good on a ship as you are in a fight, I'd say you were a fine ship's mage."

Amree smiled at him. "And I'm an even better ship's mage than I am at fighting."

"Where we're going, you'll probably have to be both."

CHAPTER THIRTEEN

I thought the Blue Lady was a myth."

Shang-Li paced at Amree's side. Clad in close-fitting pants that allowed her to climb unimpeded, she had inspected all the ship's rigging while she'd worked her spells to strengthen wood, canvas, and rope.

She wore roll-top boots of expensive leather—Shang-Li knew that because the boots were one of her initial demands—a bright green sleeveless shirt, and carried a dagger sheathed at her side. Copper bands with warding sigils wrapped her upper arms. A pouch with her tools and supplies hung across her shoulders.

"She isn't," Shang-Li said. "I've seen her and talked to her."

"And she has the ship you're looking for?"

"It's down there where she is. I wouldn't say she's laid claim to it. There are a great number of ships." And many other things, he almost added before he stopped himself.

Amree trailed a hand along the ship's railing. Shang-Li knew she paid attention to him, but most of her senses were involved in divining any weakness *Swallow* might yet have. She had kept the ship's crew busy for the last three days going over things they thought they'd already done.

Still, none of the crew griped too much about the extra work because all of them knew their lives depended on the ship. She was more demanding than Gorrick, the old ship's mage, had been. But she didn't hesitate to help do the manual labor, often joining in with some of the worst of it.

Amree glanced at him and drew the blue stone and necklace Shang-Li had taken from the kuo-toa monitor from a bag at her waist. "I've also managed to work out what this is." She laid it in his palm. "It's a speaking stone. Powerful spellcraft. It allows the wearer to speak to whomever has a like stone. But this one only works when it's in the same body of water as the other stone or stones."

"These can be used for communication?"

"Yes." Amree frowned. "I don't understand all the spell-weaving that's been done to it, that's beyond my limited means, but I've been able to ferret out some of its secrets."

"That's more than we've been able to do." Shang-Li closed his hand over the stone. "So the other stone can't track us?"

"Not until it's in the water."

"Thank you." Shang-Li dropped the stone and ground it to dust beneath the heel of his boot.

"That was foolish."

He looked at her. "Why?"

"That stone was worth a small fortune to a mage interested in that kind of spellcraft."

"I'm not interested in fortunes, or in the possibility of the Blue Lady somehow tracking us." Shang-Li scuffed away the blue powder left of the stone.

"Thava says you're a monk."

"I was raised at a Shou temple by my father. My mother was an elf. I was also trained in the ways of the forest as a ranger."

"Yet you're determined to try to die at sea. That seems awfully strange."

Shang-Li didn't know what to say about that.

"Well, Master Shang-Li—"

"I'm no master," Shang-Li quickly interrupted. The last thing he needed was for his father to hear that mistake uttered. "I am just Shang-Li."

Amree nodded. "You are certainly an interesting individual."

"Thank you."

"I have to admit, when you told me what you wanted to do, I thought you were an idiot. But Thava vouched for you. For whatever reason, she considers you one of her best friends."

"Yes. As is Iados."

"So, I'll accept you're not an idiot. But are you prepared? Have you ever heard of why the Blue Lady is there at the bottom of the Sea of Fallen Stars?"

"No. I'd never heard of her until a few days ago. The stories aren't written down anywhere I've seen."

Amree smiled, and Shang-Li liked the expression. During the last three days she'd been alternately stern and pensive. She had been robbed of her assets and her reputation by the Nine Golden Swords. Recovering from that was going to be hard, forgetting about it was surely impossible.

"They tell them often around here. My favorite story is that she was a jilted lover who threw herself from a cliff," the ship's mage said. "When she died, she became an undead thing that was drawn to the hearts of ships' captains that cheated on their lovers." She smiled again. "There's nothing like mixing a little romance in with tales of death to make them more palatable."

Shang-Li grimaced. "I fail to see the enjoyment in a tale like that."

Her smile vanished. "You would. You're a man."

"The Blue Lady has destroyed several ships over the years," Shang-Li pointed out. "Not all of her victims could have been guilty of cheating on their lovers."

Amree frowned. "You don't know much about sailors, do you?"

Shang-Li was still trying to find a way to answer that when she walked away.

"You're distracted."

Walking through the shadows of the alley, Shang-Li glanced at his companion. Iados wore a dark cloak that only blunted recognition of his heritage.

"Why do you say that?" Shang-Li asked.

"You haven't said anything about us being tailed?"

"By the two Nine Golden Swords behind us?" Shang-Li frowned and shook his head. "I figured even you had noticed them."

"Even me?" Iados heaved a sigh. "Never mind. Thava asked me to talk to you about another matter."

"What?"

"The ship's mage."

"What about her?"

"Thava has noticed that Amree is very pretty."

Shang-Li had too. "So?"

"So Thava was wondering if you had noticed."

Sighing, Shang-Li shook his head. "Please don't tell me she's matchmaking again."

"Perhaps a little." Iados held his thumb and forefinger an inch apart. "It is a predilection with her."

"It's irritating, is what it is."

"One of her little joys."

Shang-Li looked at him. "Do you remember the last time Thava tried matchmaking?"

Iados scratched his chin, then frowned. "Ah, the were-thing."

Thing was as close as they'd come to identifying the horrible creature. They'd gone on an excavation in Chessenta looking for a cursed tomb. "You got us hunting that tomb," Shang-Li said. "And Thava invited the were-thing along."

"You have to admit, the were-thing made a very beautiful woman."

"And a murderous . . . *thing*!"

Iados nodded and touched a scar along his neck. "True."

"I don't know which of you came closer to getting me killed on that little venture."

Iados clapped him good-naturedly on the back and grinned. "Well, now you have your chance to pay us both back. Aren't you happy?"

Shang-Li growled in displeasure.

Thankfully the shop they were looking for was only a short distance ahead and Shang-Li didn't have to continue the argument. That didn't, however, prevent him from continuing to think about Amree. He was disappointed in himself, but he couldn't help thinking Thava would have been quietly pleased.

"These potions will get you to the bottom of the Sea of Fallen Stars," Vahgren said. "And they will allow you to move freely while you're at that depth."

Shang-Li surveyed the slotted crate that held the magical elixirs. The fluid inside the slender glass vials burned bright sapphire and felt cool to the touch even through the glass.

Vahgren was a gnarled old man with fingers so thin they looked like talons. His skin was permanently stained by different magical ingredients and scarred by acids and other toxic materials. His gray hair stuck out in wild disarray around his prominent nose and gave him the look of a crazed person. But Shang-Li knew of no one better when it came to making magical potions.

Despite the piles, boxes, and sacks of ingredients that filled the shelves, no burglar had ever managed to success-fully penetrate the shop and steal anything. Vahgren's magical wards kept the security tight and were equipped with foul means of death that were legendary.

"I'm glad to hear that," Shang-Li said.

"Bah," Vahgren said. "I'm ashamed that I even had to tell you that. But you were looking doubtful."

"I wasn't looking doubtful."

"He's distracted," Iados explained.

Vahgren's bushy eyebrows shot up as he regarded the tiefling. "Really?"

"A young woman."

Vahgren looked back at Shang-Li, who felt his face grow hot. He should have known Iados would make sport of Thava's machinations.

"A young woman?" the alchemist asked.

"How much for the potions?" Shang-Li asked, ignoring the conversation.

"Oh, they're very expensive. You should know that."

Shang-Li did.

"So," Vahgren said to Iados, "is this infatuation new? Or is it something that's been brewing?"

"New. They only just met."

Vahgren nodded. "Ah. New love. The kind that makes men stupid and women forget about caution. A very dangerous state of mind. You know, that kind of attraction is impos-sible to brew. I know, because I've tried for any number of years. Always failed. But if I ever get it right, I could be a rich man and retire."

"You're already rich," Iados said. "And you'll never retire because you like pedaling your little potions."

"Not so little." Vahgren pointed to the sapphire liquid in the glass vials. "Without me, you couldn't venture to the bottom of the Sea of Fallen Stars."

"It wouldn't be as easy."

"Bah. You couldn't get there any other way." Vahgren waved the thought away as he might a bothersome fly. "I'm more interested in this new love. That can be the most dangerous of magic."

"Could I please just have the potions?" Shang-Li asked.

"Of course." Vahgren bent to tally the figures.

Shang-Li turned to vent his ire on Iados over the whole conversation about Amree, but the tiefling had turned and wandered off.

Despite Amree's displeasure, *Swallow* set sail from Westgate while storm clouds darkened the sky and hid the moon. The canvas sails stood full-bellied in the wind and hardly stood out against the black sky because they were so stained.

Shang-Li stood in the prow and felt *Swallow* rise from the ocean slightly as she gathered speed and crashed through the outgoing tide. A little farther forward, Amree hung onto one of the ratlines and eyed the sails. The glow of the lanterns hung as running lights poured molten gold over her face.

"She is quite beautiful, isn't she?" Thava asked.

Glaring up at the dragonborn paladin, Shang-Li said, "You have managed to incite Iados."

"About what?" Thava's voice was all innocence. Shang-Li crossed his arms and refused to answer.

"Oh," Thava said, "*that*." She smiled, and anyone that didn't know her would have been terrified by the expression. "It's not my fault you're attracted to her."

As Shang-Li watched, Amree moved lithely along the

ratlines and called out orders to the crew. At her commands, they adjusted the sails. Within a short time, *Swallow* ran more smoothly as she headed out into the open sea. Her gait steadied and she gained more speed.

"Shang-Li," Iados bellowed from the stern. The tiefling waved for attention.

Quickly, thankful to escape Thava's well-intentioned attention, Shang-Li abandoned the prow, crossed the midships, and climbed the sterncastle.

Iados pointed to their wake, which gleamed whitely in the darkness and stood in rows like a freshly-turned field. Shang-Li stared into the darkness. In the far distance, the lights of Westgate and Tidetown gleamed whenever *Swallow* rode the crest of a wave. At first Shang-Li saw nothing that could have raised Iados's interest.

Then he spotted the small flurry of weak flames glimmering against the dark water. They were roped or contained at equal distances.

"A ship?" Shang-Li asked.

Iados nodded. "I believe so."

Shang-Li took a deep breath of the salt air and turned the possibilities over in his mind. None of them were pleasant.

"You think it's following us?" Shang-Li asked.

Iados shrugged. "It's possible that there was another ship that wanted to get an early jump on the tide. But this is much too soon for fishermen, and cargo captains like to make the night last as long as they can."

"For the moment, let's keep this among ourselves."

"The captain and the ship's mage need to know."

"I'll tell them." He studied the ship. "Who would follow us out of Westgate?"

"There's only one group I know that could do that on such short notice," Iados said. "The Nine Golden Swords might want revenge on you or the ship's mage, or perhaps both. Or for plunder. Lots of reasons to get out of Westgate so quickly."

"They might not know what we're after."

"No, but you've got a ship as well as a cargo of supplies. And they know you often seek out lost treasures. Either might be enough." Iados smiled cruelly. "All of that together makes us an attractive target."

Shang-Li silently agreed.

CHAPTER FOURTEEN

Four days out of Westgate, the mysterious ship showed up again. The wind had favored them and *Swallow* had taken advantage of it. Despite the provisions, she'd been lightly loaded and skimmed across the ocean surface. After the second day, Shang-Li had grown confident they'd outdistanced the other ship.

Now, it was back.

"Are you sure it's the same ship?" his father asked.

"Yes." Shang-Li peered through a telescoping spyglass. "She's the same design, a cog."

"There are many such ships. Telling one from another must be very hard."

"Not if you have a trained eye, Master Kwan," Amree called down from above. She sat on a yard beside Moonwhisper and fed the owl bits of meat from her hand.

The fact that she'd crawled there without Shang-Li's knowledge irritated him almost as much as Moonwhisper eating from her hand like a docile pet. *Traitor*, he thought at the owl.

Moonwhisper ignored him and greedily accepted another morsel from the ship's mage. The owl even stretched his great wings in appreciation.

"You can tell by the way she handles and the way the crew responds to he r," Amree continued. "Probably in the same fashion you can identify an author's work from the use of words and quill stroke. That's the same ship that followed us out of Westgate."

Kwan Yung preened at that. "Exactly."

"I'm sure not everyone can be taught that skill."

Shang-Li felt his father's gaze on him but didn't bother to acknowledge it. The ship's mage had quickly learned to manipulate the relationship between father and son.

"You can try," his father said with a hint of dejection and disappointment, "but some students remain uneducated nonetheless."

"You have to love what you do."

"And remain focused on what you desire to learn without letting yourself get distracted."

"Exactly."

"Have you eaten this morning, Ship's Mage Amree?"

"As a matter of fact, I haven't, and I find myself famished."

"Perhaps we could continue this appreciation of expertise over a meal."

"Happily."

From the corner of his eye, Shang-Li saw Amree swing lithely and flip away from the yard and the lines. She landed on the deck with a slight thump only a few feet from Shang-Li.

"Keep an eye on that ship," she said as she passed him. "If it starts getting any closer, let me know."

Shang-Li growled an affirmative and watched her walk away with his father. Then he turned his attention back to the ship.

Shang-Li peered at the other ship through the spyglass. There was no doubt that the mystery ship had decided to aim directly for them. All her sails hung from the masts and caused her to resemble a great cloud skimming low over the ocean's surface. She was close enough that he could spot ship's crew eagerly hanging onto the railing. They held cutlasses and other weapons knotted in their scarred fists. Many of them pounded the hilts of their weapons against the ship's side, but the noise didn't yet reach *Swallow*.

"Can she outrun us?" Iados asked.

Captain Chiang nodded. "She's doing a fair job of it now. We're full into the wind and letting *Swallow* have her head. But that ship is built for running. Look at that spread of canvas."

Shang-Li had to admit that the captain was right. The other ship seemed to have more sails grabbing the wind than *Swallow* possessed.

"She's a pursuit ship," Amree declared. "Built for speed. I'll wager she has an improved hull as well, something that makes her cut through the water much more surely than *Swallow* can."

"That ship was gone for two days," Iados said.

"Not gone," Amree corrected. "Still out there. We just didn't see her."

"If she didn't see us, then how did she stay on our track?"

Amree pointed up. "Ever known doves to fly so far from land?"

Shang-Li glanced up and spotted the two white birds

cutting through the pale blue sky. The birds paced *Swallow*, flitting back and forth to overtake her and fall behind again.

"You might have mentioned them before," Shang-Li said.

"I just noticed them this morning, when I was wondering how the ship had kept us in view."

"It would have been better had you noticed them sooner."

Amree shot him an unpleasant look. "Or I might never have noticed them. It might have taken someone pointing them out to me for me to see them. Like some others I could mention."

Chastened, Shang-Li said nothing.

"If they make the mistake of losing sight of us again for a time," Iados said, "I'll take a bow and pluck their spies from the sky."

"I think the time for games has passed," Captain Chiang stated calmly. "I, for one, don't like the idea of being taken by pirates. I won't believe in whatever tender mercies they would offer us for a quiet surrender. It would probably go even worse for you, Master Kwan."

Kwan Yung scowled at the ship. "The fact that they have come all this way makes it apparent these men aren't after revenge for anything my son or our ship's mage has done."

"They've got the smell of treasure up their noses," Thava said.

"That's an idea even desperate men cling to." Captain Chiang looked at his nearby crewmen. "Prepare to repel boarders. And get the archers to their posts."

Fear and excitement warred within Shang-Li as he watched the ship quickly closing the distance. They were at a distinct disadvantage and everyone aboard *Swallow* knew that.

Shang-Li took several deep breaths. His heart rate slowed and a cold calm came over him. He ran his hands along the polished longbow and felt the smooth grain with his fingers.

"We're going to know in short order if Chiang's men have any stomach for fighting," Iados said quietly. "Though our ship's mage seems to be spoiling for a fight."

Glancing over his shoulder, Shang-Li watched Amree standing on the ship's sterncastle. She had her arms folded and her jaw was firm. If she had any hesitation about the coming confrontation, it didn't show.

"She's a scrappy one," Iados said. "You might want to wipe that grin off your face before she catches you wearing it."

Embarrassed, Shang-Li forced the smile away and focused on the approaching ship. The vessel was almost within bowshot. His gaze traveled the ship's railing and the sailors gathered there. Nearly all of them were Shou.

"Well, accuracy isn't going to be an issue for a time," the tiefling commented. "They're packed tightly enough that all you have to do is aim your arrow for the deck and you'll hit one of them."

"True, but their archers are going to be shooting back."

"I'd suggest we concentrate on them at the beginning."

"Agreed." Shang-Li read the ship's name, in Shou, on her broadside: *Lotus Bee*. She was decorated in red and black.

A white flag ran up the main mast.

Captain Chiang stepped up onto the stern deck beside Amree. The captain's leather armor showed wear and tear from past encounters.

A Shou warrior in black chainmail hoisted himself up to stand on the starboard railing. He held himself in place by gripping lines on either side of him.

"Give us what we want," the Shou warrior shouted, "and we'll let you take your ship and leave these waters. We don't want to kill all of you."

Quietly, Shang-Li focused on the man and nocked a goose-fletched arrow to string. He kept the bow pointed down for the moment and had only a little pressure on the string.

"If you try to take this ship," Chiang retorted, "we'll kill all of *you*."

Thava climbed the sterncastle steps and stood beside the captain. She wore her white plate armor and looked fierce as the sun reflected from the polished finish. She had spent her nights cleaning the armor and it gleamed as though it were new.

Despite the appearance of the paladin, the Shou warrior clinging to the ropes laughed. Several of his companions joined him. Shang-Li looked across the water and timed the slow rise and fall of the two ships. "How far would you say he is from us?"

"Two hundred paces," Iados said. "Not an impossible shot from the deck of a ship and the wind against us, but a problematic one. Let him get a little closer."

"I'm not giving up anything from this ship," Chiang replied. "You'll not draw a cup from a water barrel."

"Don't be foolish, captain," the Shou replied. "All we want are the mage and Shang-Li."

"Well," Iados said, "they *do* remember you. Probably not fondly."

"Not at all fondly," Shang-Li replied. The Nine Golden Swords vessel had closed another twenty paces. The archers along *Lotus Bee's* railing shifted a little. "Evidently their archers want to close the distance as well."

"It would be a good tactic." Iados took a fresh grip on the small shield he held.

"If I wouldn't give you a drink of water," Chiang replied, "what makes you think that I would surrender my ship's mage or my passenger?"

The Nine Golden Swords warrior cursed fluently. He released his grip on one of the ropes and drew his sword. He pointed the blade with authority. "I'll take your head, captain. Gods strike me down if that isn't true."

"He's close enough," Iados said.

Shang-Li was already bringing the bow up. Three

fingers on the cord, he drew the arrow fletchings back to his ear until the broadhead rested against his first knuckle. Just as *Swallow* and *Lotus Bee* crested the latest wave, he loosed.

The arrow sped across the water, rising at first, then falling into its final trajectory. Shang-Li already had another arrow in flight when the first struck the Nine Golden Swords warrior in the throat.

Shocked for a brief instant, the man stood paralyzed, then grabbed at the arrow protruding from his throat. He lost his footing and plunged into the sea. At the same time, Shang-Li's second arrow took another man in the eye and knocked him back into his companions.

A torrent of arrows flew from the Nine Golden Swords ship and was just as quickly met by those from *Swallow*. The shafts clanked and thudded against the yards above and whispered through the canvas and lines. *Swallow's* crew took cover, but a few of them were hit. Wounded and dead quickly littered the deck and blood tracked the wood.

Thava took a step in front of Captain Chiang and used her armor to block the arrows that came near. The dwarven armor, rounded to better protect against arrows, kept her from getting pierced but made her an immediate danger to those around her as the deadly shafts ricocheted off it.

Kwan Yung flicked two arrows away with his bow, then loosed an arrow of his own. Another Nine Golden Swords warrior fell into the sea.

"The helmsman," Iados said. "Can you hit him?"

Shang-Li tried to ignore the fact that he didn't know where his father was and concentrate on his targets. He found the helmsman, certainly less than one hundred fifty paces away, and drew an arrow back to his ear. He aimed by feeling as much as by sight. An archer operated far beyond simple visual information.

He loosed the arrow and reached for another. In disgust,

he watched the arrow deflect from a line, but took grim satisfaction when it lodged in the chest of another opponent. His second arrow sped from the bow and this one caught the helmsman under his right arm as he guided his ship into a parallel course beside *Swallow*.

The helmsman tried to maintain his hold, but death sapped his strength and he slumped over the wheel. *Lotus Bee* heeled suddenly to starboard and tracked toward *Swallow*.

"Hard to starboard!" Captain Chiang yelled.

Even though most of the crew responded to the summons, Shang-Li knew it was too late to avoid a collision. He hoped they survived it. They were very far from land, too far to simply hope they could get a longboat to shore, if they even got to one before the ship sank.

"Stay focused," Iados growled. "Pick your targets. The fewer of them there are to attempt to board, the better."

Shang-Li concentrated on his targets, selecting them ahead of time and never checking to see the effects his shafts had. He kept loosing until *Lotus Bee* slammed into *Swallow*. The impact knocked Shang-Li from his feet, but he quickly tucked and rolled to stand again. He rushed back to the railing as the Nine Golden Swords warriors prepared to throw themselves over.

Grappling hooks thumped against *Swallow*. The ships surged against each other again and again, making the deck hard to cross.

"Cut the lines!" the captain yelled. "Keep us clear!"

One of the Nine Golden Swords crew rushed back to the helm and yanked the dead helmsman from the wheel. He hauled hard to starboard to batter *Swallow* again.

Shang-Li stored the longbow with the ropes at the ship's side and drew his longsword. He fisted a fighting dagger in his other hand.

When *Lotus Bee* collided with *Swallow* again, the Nine Golden Swords crew invaded in earnest. Blades and axes caught the sunlight as they sought flesh. Cries, filled with fear and anger and bravado, echoed along the ship like the sonorous cry of one nightmarish beast.

Standing his ground, Shang-Li parried a sword blow, then opened his opponent's throat with his dagger. Beside him, Iados fought like a whirlwind of steel and scarlet death. One of his attackers got too close and Iados blocked the man's axe and gored him in the chest with his horns. The tiefling lifted the man from his feet and flung him as a bull might. The dead man sailed over Iados's head and thumped onto the deck. He didn't move again.

In the stern, Thava stood her ground as the Nine Golden Swords warriors attacked her. Her opponents looked like terriers trying to bring down a bear. She swept half of them away with her shield and the clangor of metal on metal pierced the screams and roars of rage. She swung her short-handled axe mercilessly, lopping off everything that came in contact with her weapon. Dead and dying spilled in pieces at her feet. She didn't fight as she had back at the tavern. Here she strove only to kill and kill again.

Kwan Yung fought nearby and managed to slow some of the men that attacked Thava. He'd traded his bow for a staff and cracked heads and shins with equal aplomb.

Shang-Li gave himself over to the battle. His reflexes, trained in the temple and in the forest, made him incredibly fast and certain. But the sheer numbers of the invaders still forced him back.

Amree gave ground in the ship's stern. She'd gotten separated from Thava and Captain Chiang and was quickly running out of room.

CHAPTER FIFTEEN

Iados," Shang-Li called.

"I see her," the tiefling replied. "Go." His blade lashed out and plunged through a man's eye. Iados yanked the corpse in front of Shang-Li to create a momentary barrier.

Taking advantage of the brief respite, Shang-Li retreated to the mainmast while sheathing his sword over his shoulder. He pushed off the mainmast with his feet and vaulted up into the yards. When he grabbed the nearest one, he flipped and propelled himself toward the stern. He ran lithely across one of the lines, then hurled himself at the nearest canvas on the aft mast.

Catching hold of the canvas, Shang-Li flipped between the sails and landed in the concave surface. When he let go the canvas, he slid down toward the sterncastle just as three Nine Golden Swords warriors closed on Amree.

At the bottom of the sail, Shang-Li hit the boom with both feet and threw himself forward. He cleared the stern railing with ease and ripped free his sword in mid-air. He had the blade in his fist by the time his feet touched the deck.

Amree gestured and spoke a word that vibrated through Shang-Li's skull and stomach. In response, a wave curled over the ship's side and swept her three attackers over the railing.

"The last time I faced them, I was out of my element," Amree said fiercely. "This is the sea, my chosen home. They don't have the same advantage over me."

Shang-Li nodded, but there was no time to talk. New attackers clambered over the railing as the two ships met again.

Suddenly, a wave of incredible pain blazed through Shang-Li's head. He tried to push it away, but it speared through his temples and took away his balance and strength. He dropped to one knee on the deck and struggled to keep the sword up in front of him.

The sky clouded over instantly, or maybe it was a dark fog. Shang-Li tried to figure out which it was, but by then the sea was a roiling mass of water and icy wind that snapped yards and tore canvas.

The Blue Lady's voice reverberated inside Shang-Li's skull. *You have come back, manling. Despite my wishes and my generosity in sparing your life.*

The sea geysered at the ships' sterns. When the gray-green mist cleared, the Blue Lady stood atop a column of water.

"By the gods," Thava whispered as she took a fresh hold of her axe and set her shield before her.

Weakly, Shang-Li forced himself to his feet and faced the Blue Lady.

"I warned you," the Blue Lady said. "I was gentle the

last time. This time I will not be." Then she spoke in a language that Shang-Li couldn't understand.

The storm's intensity picked up. Lightning flashed through the dark clouds and the winds howled. yards snapped like branches and ropes tore liked rotted thread as *Lotus Bee* and *Swallow* were stripped from the top down.

"Archers!" Captain Chiang roared. "Loose!"

The archers overcame their astonishment and fired a ragged volley of arrows at the Blue Lady. The Nine Golden Swords archers reacted even more slowly, but arrows filled the air.

None of the deadly missiles struck their intended target. The howling winds knocked the arrows off course or stopped them cold in mid-flight so that they dropped into the heaving sea. The waves rose higher, until they surged over the bows and the sterns of the ships. All warring between the crews was instantly forgotten as the men struggled simply to survive and remain on deck.

The Blue Lady spoke again, and this time a whirlpool formed behind the ships. Incredulous at her show of power over the Sea of Fallen Stars, Shang-Li watched as the whirlpool widened and pulled the two ships toward the center of the swirling waters. The roar of the surging current nearly drowned all noise.

Men screamed and shouted in fear. Panic rose in Shang-Li and he barely controlled it. He gazed back over his shoulder, searching for his father. Kwan Yung stood at the stern railing and clung fiercely. He spoke, but the gale winds ripping across *Swallow's* deck made communication impossible.

Shang-Li looked at Amree but found the ship's mage remained sure-footed even on the heaving deck. One of her spells kept her grounded to the craft and she walked the heaving wooden surface as easily as she might have crossed a tavern floor. She helped some of the sailors find better grips.

Amree gestured and spoke amid the whirling debris that tore free of *Swallow*. She threw her arms out to her sides and Shang-Li felt a violent wrench pass through the ship as it was pulled in two different directions. The exhausted look of defeat on her brine-soaked features told the tale of her efforts. *Swallow* was trapped.

The ship shifted and jerked as it slid into the whirlpool and the raging waters took her. She stood almost perpendicular in the water as she was pulled down.

"Hang on!" Shang-Li yelled.

Thava tore free of the railing she clutched. The combined weight of herself and the armor proved to be too much for the railing. Despite her predicament, the dragonborn warrior held tight to her shield and axe as she plummeted into the center of the whirlpool. Shang-Li cried out, but she was gone in the blink of an eye. Her armor would drag her to the bottom. She wouldn't be able to escape it.

None of them would.

The realization struck him just as *Swallow* shot down the whirlpool as if she sailed under a full headwind. The ship bucked and bristled as she endured the rough ride. The aft mast snapped off only a few feet above the deck. Then the mainmast shattered in a great *crack* that shoved lethal splinters through nearby crewmen.

The sails tore free and brought a snarl of rigging and broken yards with it. As Shang-Li stared into the yawning horror of the whirlpool, a tangled mass of canvas and rope struck him and knocked him from the ship. Unable to fight free of the knot of destruction, he fell into the water.

Time slowed down just for an instant as he struck the water. Sound changed as the sea filled his ears. He thought about the sapphire-colored water breathing potions he'd purchased while in Westgate and wished that he had one of them now. He held his breath and tried to swim up, but the snarl of rope and canvas bore him steadily down.

All around him, *Swallow* seemed to come apart. Crewmen fell from her deck, as did broken yards and weapons. Her hull cracked and barrels and crates poured out into the sea. All of it fell slowly in the water, and most of it fell at different speeds depending on individual buoyancy. But it all went down. The noise of the destruction echoed curiously in Shang-Li's ears.

He searched for his father but couldn't see him. He hoped that his father had somehow managed to fight free of the stricken ship before it had gone under. He doubted that had happened. And even if his father had somehow gotten free, Kwan Yung would be left to the merciless nature of the Sea of Fallen Stars.

Shang-Li took his knife from his boot and sawed at the rope that bound him. The whirlpool wasn't slowing or losing strength. Everything that had been on top of the water was now pulled toward the sea bottom. Nothing and no one escaped.

Shang-Li's lungs felt like they were going to explode as he slashed at the ropes. Every time he cut a strand, it seemed like he found three more. The water grew gradually bluer and darker as he sank. The light above retreated. Shang-Li didn't know how far down he'd gone, but he felt certain that it might already be too far to recover.

He finally got the strands figured out and slashed his way through just as he plunged toward the blackest depths. Several of *Swallow's* crewmen floated in the sea then disappeared into the darkness below him. He glanced around but could only make out shapes. Finding his father was out of the question.

Then the heaviness of the sea closed in around him and swept away his senses.

Shang-Li woke slowly and saw the impossible world of the sea floor all around him. He didn't know if he'd drawn a breath while he slept, but he didn't now. Desperate, he stared up at the blackness above him and wondered if the sea's surface was up there or if this was death.

Lungs aching for air, Shang-Li pushed up from the sandy sea floor and floated in the water. Despite the knowledge that he'd never make the surface, he swam up all the same.

"Shang-Li. Wait."

Turning at the sound of Thava's distorted voice, Shang-Li spotted the dragonborn standing near a jutting cliff's edge. The paladin still had her shield and sword.

"Take a breath," Thava said. She demonstrated, inhaling and exhaling easily. "It's all right. You can breathe down here."

Unable to hold his breath any longer but still horrified by the thought of drowning, Shang-Li sipped a breath and expected the taste of brine to fill his mouth. A salty tang tainted the air, but there was no water. Strange tentacled creatures the size of small boulders that crawled on the ground, then at schools of multi-colored fish. They were definitely underwater, but they could breathe and move easily.

"I thought you had drowned." Shang-Li swam to Thava's side and dropped to the sandy floor.

"So did I." Thava glanced around uneasily. "I don't know that we're any better for not drowning."

One of the tentacled creatures speared a passing fish. A brief explosion of blood colored the water and the fish fought for its freedom, but the predator stood on its tentacles and hauled its prize into its gaping maw. As it chewed, bits of the fish floated out into the water and other fish darted in for the tidbits. The creature managed to hit two of those before they got away.

"Loathsome things," Thava said. "They thought they could eat me."

Only then did Shang-Li spot the crushed carapaces of the tentacled things lying in the sand only a short distance away.

"Have you seen my father?" Shang-Li asked.

Thava shook her helmed head. "You are the first living

person I found. And when I found you, I feared you were dead as well."

Some of the fear inside Shang-Li's stomach unknotted. If he had survived, then his father could have as well. For the moment he chose to believe that.

"Who were the dead?"

"Four Nine Golden Swords warriors and two of our crew. None of them drowned. All were dead from wounds suffered in battle." Thava paused. "I hated leaving our comrades unmourned and unburied in this harsh place, but I had to seek out the living."

Shang-Li nodded. "Did *Swallow* sink all the way as well?"

"Yes." Thava pointed with her sword. "In that direction. I didn't see her touch the sea floor. But this landscape is strewn with dead and our cargo. None of it is neatly together."

"Ships never simply sink," Shang-Li said automatically. He ran his hands over his gear and found all of his weapons except his longbow. "When they go down, they can coast through the water for long distances, all the while losing crew and cargo."

One of the tentacled creatures crept toward Shang-Li. The thing kept a low profile, barely a hand's breadth above the sand.

"Watch out," Thava said. "Evidently they're not convinced that you're not prey."

Two tentacles shot toward Shang-Li's midsection. He stepped to one side to avoid the first, then slapped the second away with the palm of his hand. He freed his sword and slashed at the thing. The creature tried to get away, but the long sword sheared through most of its body, splitting it open and revealing thick white meat inside. Instantly two of its fellows charged toward it and hooked gobbets of flesh from it with the tentacles.

"Evidently they don't care what they feed on," Thava growled.

Keeping his long sword in hand, Shang-Li gazed around.

In the distance, two bodies twitched and moved on the sea bottom, but that was from the misshapen things that fed on them. No tracks marked the fine sand that covered the terrain.

"Which way did you come from?" Shang-Li asked.

Thava pointed toward the dead men with her sword. "Back that way."

"You saw no one else?"

"Only the dead."

"Were they in a straight line?"

She thought about that for a moment. "More or less, yes."

Shang-Li got his bearings and turned in the opposite direction. "And *Swallow* lies in that direction?"

"Yes."

"Then we'll go there." Shang-Li pushed against the sea floor and swam upward.

"I can't swim in this armor." Thava beat a mailed fist against her breastplate. The sonorous *bong* beat against Shang-Li's ears.

"I'm only going up a short distance," Shang-Li said. "I can see better from up here."

"Stay close."

Shang-Li nodded and swam slowly while Thava plodded across the undersea terrain. Hanging in the water above her, he had a far better view of the strange landscape.

"I've been here before," he said.

"When you spoke with the Blue Lady?"

"Yes."

"I'm no expert in undersea lands," Thava said. Her large feet stirred puffs of fine alabaster sand from the sea floor that quickly settled and left no trace of her passage. "But none of these plants, with all the color and height, seem like they belong here."

"They don't," Shang-Li agreed. He'd ventured beneath the waves on several occasions. He knew the underwater world fairly well.

"I know the Spellplague has twisted and changed things on land. I assume it's possible that the same thing happened beneath the sea."

"The worlds were rejoined. That didn't take place just above the sea." Shang-Li glanced around at the trees and fauna that seemed so misplaced here on the ocean floor. "I don't think the Spellplague can be blamed for all of this."

When he reached the cliff's edge, he peered over the side. The bottom dropped away at least a hundred paces. *Swallow* lay broken and on her side nearly a four hundred paces away. Seeing beyond that distance was impossible. Whatever lighted the land vanished. Men gathered around the stricken ship, standing on the sea floor amid the forest of strange trees and bushes as well as swimming overhead.

Shang-Li tried to spot his father, but the distance was too great. He wanted to swim ahead but he didn't dare leave Thava behind because there was safety in numbers.

"Others survived." Thava stood at the cliff's edge.

"Some at least," he said, still searching for Kwan Yung.

A body tumbled lifelessly from above and landed somewhere in the foliage. Judging from the lack of reaction, Shang-Li suspected the latest arrival was dead. How long would the sea rain dead men from the surface? It was a grim thought and he didn't like thinking it.

He turned his attention to Thava and searched for a way down. The cliff was too steep to walk down, and it ran a long distance on either side. On land he knew he would have been able to see much farther.

"I think I can jump," Thava said. "I may not be able to swim, but the sea should slow me."

"If it doesn't, that's a long way to fall."

"Trying to walk around this cliff could get us into other danger we don't yet know about," Thava said. "There's safety in numbers, and I'd rather chance a fall than whatever predators might lurk out there."

Shang-Li swam over to her. "Take my hands."

Thava chuckled. "I'm too heavy for you to lift."

"Perhaps on the land, but we're not there now. At least I should be able to help control your descent."

Thava took another glance over the cliffside, then hung her axe and shield over her shoulder and reached up for his hands. Shang-Li closed his fists around her mailed gauntlets.

"Together then," Thava said.

Shang-Li nodded. As she stepped over the edge, he kicked his feet and swam up. Her weight and the weight of her armor took him down at once with dizzying speed. They slammed against the cliffside with bone-jarring force twice, and once Shang-Li took the brunt of it. His lungs emptied of air and felt curiously heavy for a moment, then he drew his next breath.

They landed amid ochre and orange trees in a clumsy tangle of arms and legs. Thava flattened two of the trees and crushed several bushes. Shang-Li's head collided with the trunk of another tree and he almost passed out from the impact.

"Well," Thava growled as she got to her feet, "that could have been better, but we are still alive."

Shang-Li groaned as he tried to get to his feet. His head reeled from the collision, but he could have sworn the ground moved beneath him.

Then it yanked from beneath him as a twenty-foot spread of leathery membrane erupted from the sea floor. He only had time for a brief impression of a bat-shape leaping up in front of him as he tumbled backward. Then the creature flipped over in an amazing display of dexterity and came for him. A razor-lipped mouth filled with serrated teeth opened along the front of the creature.

CHAPTER SIXTEEN

Shang-Li threw himself backward, knowing the creature's mouth was wide enough to bite down on his head and shoulders and take them off. As fast as he was, though, the winged maw moved faster. Two barbed tentacles unfurled from the underside of its body and pointed like daggers.

Gods, he thought, why is it everything down here is determined to spear me? Shang-Li barely avoided the mouth, but he couldn't get out of the way of the wing. The thick, heavily muscled membrane slapped against him hard enough that he thought it had snapped his ribs. Fiery pain exploded through his body as he whirled away.

He realized at once that the battering technique was one of the creature's attack patterns. It had flipped him up into the air, exposing and stunning him, and was now coming around for another pass.

Desperately, Shang-Li tried to maneuver in the water. Though he could easily swim, he wasn't built like a fish and wasn't quick enough to avoid the predator's lightning-fast moves.

The creature's sides undulated like wings and it flitted in like a hawk. Shang-Li thrust his sword at the huge mouth and connected with the bridge above the thin upper lip. Seeking to avoid the sudden pain, the creature ducked and shivered. Shang-Li twisted just enough that it passed under him. As it shot by, he folded a hand over the creature's forewing and swung himself aboard its broad back.

Aware of him and obviously not liking the idea, the creature bucked and flipped as it strove to dislodge its unwanted passenger. Clinging to the thing, Shang-Li hung on through the evasive maneuvers as well as the resistance of the ocean against him. While walking at his customary speed, he hadn't noticed the resistance, but now that he moved at the incredibly quick speed of the creature, the environment impeded him.

He shifted his sword and drove it into the center of the creature. Flesh parted easily and a high-pitched scream shivered through Shang-Li's ears. Blood leaked from the wound in the creature's back and swirled around Shang-Li. He thrust again, and the creature jerked and shifted directions, angling upward.

High above the sea floor, the incandescent blue that clung to the land turned pitch black. Shang-Li suddenly discovered he almost couldn't see his hand in front of his face. Worst of all, when he started to breathe in, salt water burned his nose and filled his mouth.

He held his breath and kicked free of the creature when he realized he'd exceeded whatever magic boundaries there were that protected the Blue Lady's realm. He stroked down until the pressure went away and the blue light returned.

Blood streaming from the wounds, the creature tried

to turn around and swoop back down. Before it did much more than reverse its course, three sharks swam out of the darkness and attacked. They ripped flesh from the strange creature with their greedy, darting jaws. It screamed anew and turned its descent into a dive for its life.

The creature didn't make it far. The sharks quickly overtook it, surrounding it, and tore it to bloody shreds. The lifeless body slid through the dark water and quietly disappeared, jerking only when the hungry sharks continued to feed on it.

Shang-Li floated in the water, expecting the sharks at any time to turn their attention to him. One of them separated from the rest and came toward him. Shang-Li lifted his long sword before him and took his fighting dagger into his fist. Then the shark appeared to hit a barrier, jerked, and turned away. Quietly thankful, Shang-Li swam closer to Thava.

"Something prevents the sharks from coming here," the paladin said.

"The Blue Lady," Shang-Li said. "She can also allow them into this place, though."

"Not a pleasant thought."

"No. But it does mean, at least for the moment, she doesn't intend to kill us."

Thava looked around at the tentacled things gathered in the knobby knees of the strange trees. "Perhaps, but there appears to be no shortage of other things that are prepared to kill us and feast on our bones."

Shang-Li surveyed the strange forest in front of them. "Ready to proceed?"

"Cautiously," Thava suggested and continued.

Shang-Li lost count of the things that slithered and crawled through the strange forest as he and Thava trekked across the sea floor. He kept track of the big ones, the ones that were aggressive enough to attack without provocation or invading their territory, and the ones that slyly lay in wait in camouflaged areas. Amidst the bones of humans, they also found the remnants of several sea creatures. He wondered how heavy the toll was on the environment with all the predation of the strange things that lurked and hunted in the Blue Lady's domain.

"This place is an abomination." Thava kept her voice low. "I've been in ghoul-infested crypts that were safer than these waters." The paladin shifted her axe and kept watch. She didn't act nervous, but she appeared more wary than Shang-Li had seen her in some time. "Have you a plan for getting us out of here?"

"Not yet." Shang-Li glanced at the sharks circling over-head. "Even if we were able to avoid the sharks, we're too deep to simply swim up. We'd never make it."

"As Iados says, things are never impossible. Some of them just take miracles to get done." Thava smiled crook-edly. "We'll find a miracle, Shang-Li. Or we'll make one."

"I know." But what he hoped for most of all was that the others were still alive. He trudged up a long, sloping hill, deciding to keep with Thava now that the forest was so thick he sometimes lost her when he swam above it.

At the top, he peered down into a ragged canyon and saw several wrecks cracked and broken on top of each other, like tinder laid for a fire.

"They didn't fall like that." Thava peered down at the scene as well.

"No. They were placed there to get them out of the way."

"The Blue Lady doesn't strike me as a caretaker."

"No, but she might get them out of her way after she's taken the salvageable cargo. And when she's able to escape this place and begin attacking the coastal cities, gold and other goods would help her raise a mercenary army and navy."

Thava lifted an arm and pointed. "Someone is down there."

Straining his eyes, Shang-Li took only a moment to

spot the men milling around the pile of broken ships. They moved raggedly, wary but untrained in the ways of warriors as they formed a loose perimeter. Then Shang-Li spotted a familiar figure and his heart leaped.

"Iados." Happiness resonated in Thava's voice. "He lives."

"As do many of the crew. But I don't see my father among them."

"Your father isn't frail, my friend. He can take care of himself. We will find him."

Shang-Li wished he shared Thava's certainty. But finding Iados and a dozen crewmen was a good start. As he walked down the hillside, he felt more hopeful.

"Shang-Li! Thava!" Iados trotted forward, shaking a tentacled thing from the end of his sword. Blood streamed through the sea around him. The tiefling's face split into a smile. "I knew if I had survived that, surely fortune would favor the two of you as well."

"We've had to work at it." Shang-Li pointed to the corpse that tumbled through the water from the end of Iados's sword. "There are plenty of those things about, and several others besides."

Iados frowned and cursed. "Too many, if you ask me. It's a wonder that they haven't started eating each other." He paused and looked at the treeline. "Or perhaps they have and this forest would be overrun with them otherwise."

"Have you seen my father?"

Iados shook his head. He nodded toward the men with him. "We met up with each other along the way and decided to see what we could salvage in the way of weapons and stores from these ships. For the most part, our efforts have been largely unrewarded."

"You mean you haven't found any treasure." Thava grinned.

Iados scowled. "I'd had hopes. But these ships have been picked clean."

"The Blue Lady does have a use in mind for the treasure she's finding." Thava snorted. "She's no better than a pirate."

"Perhaps not, but she's more powerful than any pirate I've ever crossed blades with."

"Are the crew armed well enough?" Shang-Li glanced at the sailors as they crept along the ships.

"I believe so. But weapons aren't going to turn them into first-class fighters."

"I know. But maybe they will give them enough of an edge to stay alive." Shang-Li peered up into the constant blueness. "I haven't found any way to tell north."

"Nor have I." Iados glanced around. "We're going to have to map by landmarks. And there's no way of knowing how much time passes down here either. I haven't a clue how long it's been since we sank."

"We don't know how big the Blue Lady's domain is either." Thava stared at the ships. "Though with as much damage as she has done, I would say that her range is quite large."

"*Iados!*" One of the sailors screamed in terror. "Over here!"

Quickly, the tiefling drew his weapon and trotted to the man.

"Oldyr and a couple of the others went over there! They were attacked by those things!"

Shang-Li drew his sword and scanned the nearby forest. A flurry of activity in the brush line along the ship's prow drew his eye. One of the sailors had gotten seized by a man-shaped creature. At first Shang-Li thought the sailor had gotten trapped by his opponent's ropes, then he saw the "rope" writhing and knew that they were tentacles.

Despite his efforts to free himself, the sailor remained stuck fast. He dug his heels into the ground but was dragged slowly toward his captor.

Blue lightning flickered in the man-shaped thing's body.

"Spellscarred," Iados growled.

A tremor of unease shivered up Shang-Li's spine. During his travels he'd seen a few of the spellscarred, those people and things warped by an encounter with the plaguelands, remnants of the terrible Spellplague.

A change wasn't always for the betterment of the individual. In Chondath, one of the Spellscarred had been left without his bones. He lived as a blob in a butcher's tub for all to see. Yet another boy had been changed by the plaguelands and given the ability to heal almost instantly from wounds that would have killed another man.

More often than not, the plaguelands created monsters instead of granting power. But that fact didn't keep some from seeking them out and trying their luck.

And then there were those unfortunates that encountered the plaguelands despite their best efforts.

Shang-Li swam forward. Iados and Thava already closed on the battle. A few other sailors took up arms as well, but they followed behind.

The shambling mockery of a man wasn't alone. Three others lurked in the relative darkness of the brush. The cobalt flames coursed through their bodies as well. Closer now, Shang-Li felt certain they'd once been human. Their features had changed and ran together like melted wax, and the flesh had turned a mottled plum. But they wore the tattered remnants of clothing.

Their heads came to severe points, as if their skulls had been hooked by something and drawn upward. Yellow eyes peered out beneath a bony ridge of brow that curved into the creatures' cheekbones. The squat, heavy bodies promised strength and durability. The tentacle had sprouted from the center of the thing's hand.

"Help me!" the sailor squalled. He tugged fiercely at the tentacle that had roped him but couldn't free himself. His feet stirred up small clouds of silt as he fought to keep his distance.

"Let him go," Iados commanded.

The sea shamble—Shang-Li could think of no other name that fit—glared at the tiefling, but there was no indication of whether it understood. Turning its attention back to the imprisoned sailor, the sea shamble grabbed the tentacle with its free hand and hauled the sailor in closer.

Shang-Li swam down and drew his dagger with the intention of cutting the sailor free. A second sea shamble lurched into motion with surprising speed. It lifted its arm and pointed at Shang-Li. A blur launched from its palm and became the tangling spirals of a tentacle slightly thinner than Shang-Li's little finger.

Before Shang-Li could avoid the tentacle, it wrapped around his right ankle and quickly climbed all the way up to his thigh. When it constricted, Shang-Li felt the blood flow to his leg shut down. A burning ache made him immediately wonder if the thing carried some kind of poison as well. His senses faded a little and he became convinced that it did.

He raked the dagger through the tentacle, sawing frantically through the muscular length. His senses continued to splinter, and double-vision filled his head. He unwrapped the tentacle from his leg, sickened by the way the thing continued to wiggle despite being severed from its host.

Iados blocked a tentacle from another with his spear, quickly tangling the obscene length around his weapon. He shoved the spear into the ocean bed and held on fiercely as the sea shamble sought to drag him in. Then he drew his sword and slashed the tentacle free. The sea shamble stumbled backward as dark purple blood spewed from its wounded appendage.

Feeling started to return to Shang-Li's leg, and blinding pain knotted his muscles. He shoved the agony away and swam toward his opponent.

The sea shamble darted away as Shang-Li closed. It threw its other hand forward and a tentacle shot out of the palm. The sword vibrated in Shang-Li's hand as he hit the tentacle, but the thing wrapped his weapon. Yanking his sword free, Shang-Li slashed through the tentacle, and swam toward his attacker.

Growling, the sea shamble launched itself at Shang-Li. The thing opened its hideous mouth and revealed jagged, curved teeth.

Shang-Li planted both his boots against the sea shamble's chest. Rough hands grabbed Shang-Li's ankles and the sea shamble tried to pull his feet into its mouth.

Rolling to his side, Shang-Li arched his body and stabbed the sword into the sea shamble's face. Purple blood spewed into the water around the creature's head. The blue fire scarring its body flickered brightly, then dimmed and finally went out.

Shang-Li swung his sword and cut the sea shamble's head from its shoulders. The thing collapsed slowly and tentacled predators closed in on the corpse at once. Shang-Li turned to give aid to his companions.

Thava held a tentacle in her mailed fist. She yanked and the sea shamble flew through the water and landed at her feet. She placed a heavy boot at the center of its chest and bore down. Then she swung the battle-axe in both hands and cleaved the creature from crown to chest. A cloud of blood erupted into the water.

The sailor that had first gotten caught floated listlessly. His eyes stared sightlessly through the sea. One of his hands loosely held a couple of gold coins that worked free of his fingers and drifted down to the ocean bed.

"Gods, these things are foul." Iados swam back to join Shang-Li.

"There are more of them lurking there." Thava freed her axe with a jerk. "Perhaps we've outstayed out welcome in this place."

Shang-Li looked at the floating dead man and remembered his visits from the Blue Lady. "There's no place down here where we will be welcome."

Shang-Li, Iados, and Thava headed up the salvage party, taking turns scouting ahead as they retreated from the sea shambles. They found another shipwreck a mile from their last position, a warship. The deck was charred black, and the sails were scorched tatters that wafted on the ocean currents. Arrows and crossbow quarrels stuck out from her hull. An intricately carved woman hung at the mast, smudged in places by the same fire that had threatened the ship.

"She went down hard," Iados remarked quietly. "Hard to say if the fight was one she won or lost."

"The shape she was in from the fire, I'd suggest you could probably split the difference," Shang-Li said.

"I doubt there's any cargo left aboard her," Thava said.

"We should look all the same." Shang-Li swam toward the ship. "At the very least I'd like to know her name so I can perhaps get word to her home country. If she went down recently, there may be families that still wish to know the fates of the crewmen."

Strangely, even underwater *Red Orchid* stank of smoke and death, her crew's demise clinging to her.

Shang-Li swam over the ship with his spear in his hand and landed on the charred deck. Charcoaled wood splintered and floated away. He stamped on the deck and listened to the empty echo. Her bottom had been ripped away either by the attack of the Blue Lady or her ill-fated descent underwater.

Her crew hadn't been spared either. Many skeletons lay scattered across the deck and on the sea floor nearby. Several of them still clenched weapons.

"They also drowned," Iados said softly. He knelt by a dead man sprawled beneath the mainmast. "Why? Why did they drown and we did not?"

Shang-Li shook his head. "Because the Blue Lady wanted us to live."

"How long would you say this has been down here?"

"Since the Spellplague," Shang-Li answered. "Otherwise it would be somewhere else."

Iados flicked his tail, obviously irritated with himself. "Yes. I wasn't thinking."

The sailors cautiously entered the hold. Most of them had learned in the past that any sunken vessel quickly turned into a habitat for sea creatures. They'd also learned that everything in the plaguelands came equipped with huge, bloodthirsty appetites.

"You do not have permission to come aboard this vessel," a female voice boomed.

Shang-Li took a step back and readied his spear. Iados freed his sword and plucked a dagger from his belt with his tail.

"You need to leave this ship at once," the voice insisted.

"That's not the Blue Lady," Iados commented.

"Definitely not," Shang-Li agreed. He tried to find out from which direction the voice came from, but the sea dispersed the sound.

"Shang-Li," Thava called from the ship's prow. She had remained on the ground and in close proximity to the ship.

"Yes?"

"I told you to get off the ship," the female voice continued.

"You need to see this."

Shang-Li swam forward and dropped down to the prow. The deck there was almost burned as badly by the fire as the rest of the ship.

Thava stood in front of the ship and gazed at something below Shang-Li. "What's going on?" Shang-Li asked.

Wordlessly, the paladin extended a hand and pointed at the ship's figurehead.

Her head was just below the prow, her hair swept back and scalloped into the hull over her out flung arms that held the ship as if to ward it from danger. Her feet crossed at her toes. Flickers of blue flame danced along her wooden flesh.

"Well," Iados said, "whoever carved it had an appreciation for the feminine form."

Shang-Li silently agreed, but he focused on the blue flames that twisted within the figurehead.

"*She* is the one talking." The paladin held her battle-axe at the ready.

"You were told to leave this ship," the figurehead stated. "If you don't do so now, I will take action."

"A talking figurehead isn't so unusual." Iados leaned calmly on the railing and peered down. "I've seen them before. Usually they're spelled to act as lookouts for the ship's captain. A parlor trick and a decent enough security effort."

The figurehead looked up and the wood creaked as it moved. "I am no parlor trick."

"Of course," the tiefling said in a much quieter voice, "she could also be a spy for the Blue Lady."

"And I am no spy," the figurehead insisted. "I protect this ship. The Blue Lady sank us in the middle of a battle while we were on our way back home."

"Who are you?" Shang-Li asked.

"I am Red Orchid."

"The ship is called *Red Orchid*."

The figurehead fixed him with her obsidian eyes. Blue flames swirled within the depths of her gaze. "I am the ship. If I could free myself, I would destroy the Blue Lady. She killed my captain and my crew."

"When?"

"On the last day I ran before the wind," Red Orchid replied.

"How long have you been down here?"

The petulant look of a troubled child framed her face. Then anger pushed the expression from her lovely wooden face.

"You ask too many questions," Red Orchid snapped. "You have been warned to leave the ship. Do so now."

"And if we choose not to?" Iados inquired politely.

"Then I will make you." The blue flames twisting within Red Orchid's wooden body blossomed.

The ship rocked violently beneath Shang-Li. Timbers cracked and burnt planks snapped and fell away like a dog shaking off water.

"Get out of the hold!" Shang-Li roared at the sailors still within the ship.

Most of *Swallow's* crew had shied away at the sound of the figurehead's voice and now hung in the water a short distance away. Three men swam from the hold to join their companions.

Shang-Li pushed off the deck and away from the tangle of broken ratlines and tattered sails.

The ship's prow changed as Red Orchid melted into it. Her face formed in the wood, taking over the whole prow, and her mouth opened in a predatory smile. Blue flame crackled and rushed along the ship. Unbelievably, the ship surged forward a dozen feet across the sea floor. More timbers cracked and debris fell away from the ship like snow. A massive impact slammed into Shang-Li and knocked him backward.

"Go away," Red Orchid admonished. "Go away or I will destroy you."

"She's crazed," Iados said as he pushed up into the water near Shang-Li.

"Perhaps," Shang-Li said. "Or maybe she only wants to be left alone."

"Have you ever seen anything like this?" Iados asked.

Shang-Li shook his head as he watched the beautiful face snarling defiance on the ship's prow. "I haven't even heard of anything like this."

"It's spellplague," Thava said as she walked over to join them. "Maybe she was an animated piece of wood before, but now she's realized into something more complete."

"How would you know that?" Iados challenged.

"You can feel the life force within her," the paladin replied.

She kept her battle-axe in her hands as she surveyed the ship. "I think she became more real once she was exposed to spellplague."

"Leave her," Shang-Li answered. "She's got nothing aboard her that we require."

"Doesn't the idea of leaving a sentient being trapped in this place bother you?" Thava asked.

"Yes, but I don't see any way to free her. Do you?"

Reluctantly, Thava shook her head.

"As far as we know," Shang-Li continued, "we're all trapped down here."

CHAPTER SEVENTEEN

Swallow lay surprisingly intact amid the broken underwater forest. Other than the splintered masts and the cracked hull, she looked serviceable, and much of her crew—including Amree—had survived the descent.

Shang-Li also happily noted that Moonwhisper sat on one of the remaining yards. Somehow the owl had managed to remain with the ship and hadn't gotten lost in the swirling waters.

When Shang-Li briefly touched the owl's mind, he discovered the fear and confusion within Moonwhisper. As best as he could, Shang-Li comforted Moonwhisper and left him perched there.

Several bodies lay in a heap in a clearing a short distance away. The clearing had been made by the ship as it caromed through the forest. Most of the dead were Nine Golden Swords warriors, but some of them belonged to *Swallow's* crew. The bodies jerked and moved as they lay there and Shang-Li had at first thought some of them might yet live. Then he spotted the tentacled creatures burrowing through the tangled limbs and bloody torsos.

"Foul creatures," Iados snarled as he stood on *Swallow's* prow and gazed down at Shang-Li. "We can't do anything more for the dead. If we tried to keep them here for a proper burial, they would only have attracted more carrion feeders."

"More are going to come along soon enough," Shang-Li said.

With a nod, Amree stepped from the prow and floated to the sea floor. She landed in a faint cloud of sand that quickly settled. "At least for the moment those dead men provide a distraction for those creatures. I take it you've discovered that we can't swim toward the surface past a certain point?"

Shang-Li tried to mute the helplessness he felt. "I have. Whatever spell that's in this land, or that the Blue Lady has laid, only provides air and light here."

"Even without bars, it remains a prison." Iados growled in his throat and flicked his tail irritably. "I hate prisons."

"We're not going to stay here," Thava said.

Iados considered her. "If you were to shed that armor—"

"I won't. And even if I did, I still wouldn't be able to swim to the surface. None of us could do that."

Iados smiled at her grimly. "I suppose it is possible to walk back to the mainland to reach the coast. Though that would be a perilous and long journey."

Shang-Li shook his head. "We can explore, but I doubt the spell that allows us to breathe underwater extends to the coast. Otherwise there would have been sightings of the Blue Lady in those places."

Amree waved an arm toward the ship. "It's also possible we could raise *Swallow*. If the three of you would get busy instead of standing around working your jaws."

Shang-Li and the others turned toward Amree.

The ship's mage gazed at them with perturbed expression. "Unless you want to just waste time around here and wait for the Blue Lady to kill you?"

"No one said she's going to kill us," Iados said.

"She didn't drag us to the bottom of the Sea of Fallen Stars for a tea party," Amree replied. "You can stick around for that if you want to, but I'd rather hold my destiny in my own hands."

"You haven't had your destiny in your own hands since we sank." Iados smiled weakly. "I mean no offense, mage. I prefer to have a more—"

Amree crossed her arms and lifted an eyebrow. "Defeatist attitude?"

"Don't mistake cynicism for giving up." Iados gripped his sword hilt. "I'll fight until I draw my last breath. But I have no intention of underestimating this creature." He gazed meaningfully at the pile of dead men. "We weren't as prepared as we should have been."

"We didn't have time to prepare. She hit us more quickly than we'd expected." Shang-Li silently chided himself. "I should have known the Nine Golden Swords were in contact with her."

"She was already in contact with you, Shang-Li." Thava dropped her mailed hand heavily on his shoulder. "She already knew where you were. And whatever she wants from you—"

"Liou Chang's books translated."

"—that has saved our lives." Thava shrugged. "And no one could have prepared for this. Even after all these stories we heard about her, I wouldn't have thought she could do this."

Iados stomped on a small tentacled thing that tried to sneak up on him. "If she wants Shang-Li, why hasn't she come for him yet?"

"Maybe she's just letting us get used to the idea that she

has us exactly where she wants us," Thava suggested. "Or maybe creating that whirlpool exhausted her."

"Either way," Amree said, "you can wager that she'll be along soon. Our lives are only saved for the moment. And if you ask me, I'd rather die trying to get out of here than sit around like a sheep waiting to be butchered." She looked at the surrounding terrain. "This may be a prison, but it's ripe with possibilities. I intend to exploit some of them."

Shang-Li nodded. "What do you need us to do?"

Amree gestured toward the sunken ships in the distance. "There's a graveyard of preserved vessels out there. We need two masts and spare wood. Canvas and rope, if there's any to be salvaged."

"Maybe we could find a better ship than *Swallow*," Iados suggested.

"I've spent days putting magic into this vessel," Amree told him. "I can't just easily transfer that over to another ship. And I'd rather work with the strength I've laid into *Swallow* than hope for the best with another ship. She's worth salvaging."

"I agree," Captain Chiang stated as he came up to join the ship's mage. The captain certainly looked worse for the wear, but his spirits seemed intact.

"All right," Thava said. "We'll head up scavenging parties. We'll also need a guard around the ship. There are a number of misbegotten beasts lying in wait in these waters."

"I'll have the quartermaster draw up posts for your scavenging crew and to defend the ship," Chiang said.

"Have you seen my father?" Shang-Li asked.

"He's below," Chiang answered. "In the hold. He's all right, but he was concerned about you. He'll be glad to know you survived."

Shang-Li swam toward the ship, telling Iados and Thava he would rejoin them momentarily to begin the salvaging effort.

❦ ❦ ❦ ❦ ❦

Kwan Yung stood in the debris scattered throughout *Swallow's* cargo hold. All of the goods and supplies lay in a jumbled mess. A handful of crewmen worked among the debris to Kwan Yung's specifications as he walked and swam throughout the ship. He carried a glowstone, a magically imbued stone that shined light when needed.

The orange gleam of the glowstone gave the hold an eerie appearance and reminded Shang-Li of volcanoes he'd ventured through on other endeavors. His father's shadow loomed largely over the ship's interior.

A cut split Kwan Yung's left eyebrow and his eye had swollen partially shut, but he otherwise appeared none the worse for wear. He barked orders to the sailors, directing them where to take the cargo.

"Father."

His father turned and smiled for the briefest moment. Then his control returned and the smile went away. "I see you lived."

"I did."

"Then you should make yourself useful. Amree seems to most hopeful she can give new life to this vessel." His father looked around and sighed. "Better had we not sunk at all."

"The Blue Lady could have killed us outright."

"Maybe." His father paused to yell at another sailor who had evidently been putting a crate in the wrong place. "Then again," he added, "perhaps she did all that she was able by sinking us."

"If she could create this place—"

"She didn't."

"What makes you so sure?"

His father sighed. "Were you not trained to think at the monastery?"

Shang-Li refused the bait. The last thing they needed

right now was another bout in their unending argument about his education.

"No one mortal could have built that world out there, Shang-Li," his father declared.

Perhaps a goddess? But Shang-Li dared not put that thought into words.

"And before you think it, that woman is no goddess," his father said.

"I never thought she was," Shang-Li said as earnestly as he could.

"What you see out there," his father waved to indicate the expanse of underwater land outside the ship, "is a mistake, a gross error created by magic and whatever evil the Blue Lady was capable of. This land doesn't belong here. Your eyes tell you that. So it came from someplace else and was only brought over by the Spellplague."

"You think she came here alone?"

"Possibly. Or she killed whoever else came over with her. She's powerful. You know that because she's able to survive here. But why is she trapped here?"

Shang-Li thought about that and understood where his father was going with his thinking. "Because someone trapped her here."

"Exactly. Whoever it was had to be very powerful. Otherwise the Blue Lady would have overcome whatever spells keep her chained here. Or possibly the Spellplague strengthened the enchantments that bind her here. This prison was created especially for her. Maybe her escape attempts drew her to our world when the Spellplague hit. She could have been locked away for a very long time."

"Whatever the true answer, we don't have much time. You should get to work." His father turned back to the activity in the cargo hold. "We have to clear this area of all supplies that were ruined during the sinking." Then he turned back to Shang-Li. "But there are other things you should keep in mind while you're out there."

Shang-Li waited.

"*Grayling*," his father said. "If that ship is down here somewhere, I would like to see Liou Chang's books salvaged. They are much too powerful to let lie in the wrong hands. Find them, or find out if they were destroyed."

Shang-Li nodded. His father's interest in those books went without saying.

"Also, we need water."

That surprised Shang-Li.

His father frowned a little, obviously displeased. "Perhaps you haven't gotten thirsty yet, Shang-Li, but you will." He waved a hand through the water easily and stirred sediment that floated in the sea. "We can breathe this, by whatever magic exists, but we certainly can't drink it. And as soon as we open any water kegs down here, they become fouled as well. I think it's safe to assume we're not going to find any fresh water in this place."

"Even if we find fresh water or wine or ale, how do we drink it without it becoming fouled?"

His father waved him to the ship's stern. There, an empty barrel had been upended and tied to the bulkhead. "Stick your head in there."

Shang-Li did and discovered an air pocket that nearly filled the barrel. Breathing the air inside the barrel was easier, but it tasted stale and stank of the barrel's previous contents, turnips.

"The air will quickly go bad," his father said. "But it will give us a place to drink. We'll put up more as we need them. We can't eat down here either without swallowing sea water. Whatever the spell is that allows us to breathe down here, it's very selective."

"How did you get the air in the barrel?"

"The ship's mage conjured it. She intends to use that spell, on a grander scale of course, to raise the ship when it's time." His father smiled appreciatively. "That young woman is very intelligent. Quite the thinker."

Shang-Li looked around the ship's cargo hold and realized how huge the job would be to fill the hold with enough air to carry the ship to the surface. "Do you think she can do it?"

His father hesitated. "I hope so. That would depend on how well the hull's integrity has held together."

"Patching the leaks could take too long," Shang-Li said. "The Blue Lady has ignored us so far, whether to let our fears grow or because she needs to recover, but that will end soon."

"I know."

"We could line the hull with sailcloth. It's designed to catch the wind."

"That task would take a lot of sailcloth."

"Some of the other ships that are down here will have salvageable materials. Some of it will be sailcloth."

His father nodded. "I'm glad to see that the ship's mage isn't the only one that can think." He looked at Shang-Li. "You had best get going."

Shang-Li nodded, but he disliked the idea of leaving his father with this ship. The Blue Lady's would doubtless be coming for *Swallow*.

Shang-Li swallowed sour bile. Worse yet, the Blue Lady could chose to end the water breathing spell that protected them at any moment and they would all drown. He hoped that the breathing spell wasn't hers to control and was a part of the land or the Spellplague, or whatever the mixture between all things involved might be.

"Be safe, Father." Shang-Li bowed slightly.

"And you, my son." Kwan Yung bowed and touched Shang-Li's shoulder briefly.

Shang-Li leaped up and swam away, negotiating the maze of sailors ferrying cargo. When he glanced back, he saw that his father had already turned his attention back to his duties.

Shang-Li swam through the cargo hold and out into

the open sea. Even though he knew *Swallow* was no real place of refuge, he felt the disappearance of the protection the ship offered.

It felt like hours later when Shang-Li returned with the latest salvage they'd recovered. Finding planks and pulling them free of ships was hard work, especially when they were constantly threatened by the sea shambles and the other denizens of the strange forest.

He drank water from the barrel and tried to hold his breath against the stink of turnips. He had a handful of raw fish fillets in the same manner, then laid down to rest on a pallet of bedding that felt soggy. Despite the discomfort of the bed.

He felt like he'd only just closed his eyes when the Blue Lady called to him.

"Wake, manling. You don't get to sleep all the time."

Equal parts angry and fearful, Shang-Li opened his eyes. He felt for his fighting sticks but they were gone. He stood before the Blue Lady unarmed. *Swallow*, his father, and his friends were nowhere in sight. He was dreaming, he realized and he relaxed a little at that. Even though he was certain he wasn't safe, his father and friends would be.

He hoped.

The Blue Lady stood in front of a ruined stone building that had once been multiple stories. Several sections had collapsed, but part of the building stood and would have offered shelter if it had been on land.

"What do you want?"

Amused, the Blue Lady smiled and cocked an eyebrow. "Such insolence, manling. Haven't you discovered that you live now only at my whim?"

"Do I?"

"Yes." She walked toward him, totally unafraid. "More than that, your father and your friends live through my generosity as well. Perhaps I should kill one of them to show you how much power I wield here."

Shang-Li backed down immediately. "That isn't necessary."

The Blue Lady shrugged. "I don't mind killing. I'm actually quite good at it. You should know that from all the ships you've seen that I've brought down over the years."

"Why do you target the ships?"

"To gather wealth, of course. Walk with me."

At first, Shang-Li was going to resist the command, but a trio of sharks swam close to him and got him moving. He fell into step behind her and thought of how her turned back might give him an edge, if only he'd held a weapon. If only he weren't dreaming.

"Honor will only get you killed." The Blue Lady walked up a flight of stairs that followed the outside of the building.

"You seek revenge and to expand your power. That will get you killed quicker."

"Only if I fail, manling. And I don't plan to fail."

"You're here, which means you've already failed once."

The Blue Lady halted at the top of the steps. Her dark eyes blazed silver fire, and for the first time Shang-Li wondered if she had taken on some aspect of the Spellplague after her long exposure as well.

"I didn't fail, manling." Her voice was as cold as the gales that swept the far north. "I was betrayed by someone I was foolish enough to love. I should have crushed him as I'd set out to do. Instead, I spared him and let him get close to me. I don't make mistakes like that anymore."

"Who threw you out of the Feywild?"

"People who feared me. People who feared my passion and my vision."

"Your vision for what?"

"My father held a kingdom in the Feywild. I intend to get it back. And you are going to help me. You might find the secrets in Liou Chang's books. If you can translate the information I need about the portals that General Han used, I will let you live."

Shang-Li said nothing.

"If you don't, I'll keep killing everyone on that ship until you agree to help me. And if you don't, I will kill you and find someone else from the Standing Tree Monastery. Now that the monks know the books are here—and I'm sure you or your father has let them know—they will send someone else if you're not heard from again. And you won't be." The blaze in her eyes faded. "Think about my offer, manling. If you do as I ask, I will let you and the others live."

"If the creatures in the forest don't kill us?"

The Blue Lady smiled maliciously. "Think of them as the sands in an hourglass, manling. More of them will catch your scents. As soon as enough of them gather at your ship, they won't wait to hunt you singly anymore. They'll come for you in force. By then, it will be too late to save everyone."

"I have to choose between dying and living under your subjugation? That's not much of a choice."

"It's still a choice, manling. And I can be more generous." The Blue Lady waved at the room below them. The roof had been ripped away and the interior lay exposed. Inside the room, gold ingots, coins, and gems lay in disarray.

"My treasury." The Blue Lady folded her arms. "Do as I ask, if you're able, and I can make you wealthy as well."

Shang-Li looked at all the treasure and knew that Iados wouldn't believe it when he told him the tale later. The tiefling would be disgusted that he'd missed out on the tour. But wealth had never left much of an impression on Shang-Li. Poverty was another matter and he couldn't help think about the good that could be done if the treasure could be reclaimed and put into the right hands.

"Think about what I have said, manling." The Blue Lady leaped into the ocean and swam away. A large shadow lifted from behind the building's ramparts—an enormous squid that trailed her like an undulating shadow.

"Now go."

Shang-Li woke with a start and shoved at the hand on his shoulder.

"Easy." Amree looked down at him with concern. "Another bad dream? Or a visit?"

"A visit." Head swimming, Shang-Li sat up and felt chilled to the bone. "A bad one."

"Did she tell you why she's stayed away? Was she weakened?"

Shang-Li shook his head. "It was her choice. She's giving us time to think."

"You mean she's giving *you* time to think. She hasn't been in contact with anyone else."

Shang-Li nodded. "She wants me to translate Liou Chang's books."

"Can you?"

"I don't know. Possibly. I'm good at what I do."

"I thought you were a monk with ranger training."

"I'm also good with translations. My father trained me to work in the monastery library. I'm nearly as good as he is."

Amree smiled. "I've seen the two of you fight. That isn't all he's trained you in."

"No, I suppose not."

Her smile faded. "Translating those books is going to endanger a large portion of the Sea of Fallen Stars."

"If not all of it." Shang-Li took a deep breath to clear his mind and let it out. "So doing that isn't an option. I don't trust the Blue Lady."

"Good. If you did, I'd be tempted to tie an anchor around your neck and leave you here."

"Thanks." Shang-Li smiled.

"Why don't you try to get back to sleep? I can keep watch for a while. If you look like you're starting to dream again, I'll wake you."

Shang-Li closed his eyes and tried to think of good thoughts, but they seemed really far away at the moment. Finally, he slipped over into the darkness of true sleep.

After he woke, the salvage started in earnest. Iados, Thava, Shang-Li, and *Swallow's* quartermaster and ship's pilot had pieced together a map of the terrain drawn it onto the interior of the cargo hold. They had also marked sites they could retreat to if the Blue Lady came calling.

Back at *Swallow*, Shang-Li swam through the hold and found the area better organized and better lighted. Chunks of glowing coral in short lengths of fishing nets hung from the hold. The combined light made the submerged cargo hold more navigable.

"Put it here," a sailor instructed Shang-Li, Thava, and Iados as they carried in a stretch of canvas holding salvaged goods. Thankfully the load of casks, barrels, and crates resting on the canvas remained buoyant in the sea, and they were easy to manage.

Shang-Li guided the canvas down to the bottom of the hold. "Nothing's marked," he told the sailor. "These might be anything."

"Anything's better than nothing. I will hope for a cask of wine that has not yet soured." The sailor smiled. "Do you have any idea how long the ship this is from has been down?"

"I've never heard of her. The name didn't turn up in the research my father and I did."

"We will hope it has not been overlong. If there is

anything to be had."

"Where can I find my father?"

The sailor pointed toward the mass of coral lighted in one corner of the hold. The light blazed through a sheet of canvas.

"Amree has managed something of a ship's galley there where we can eat and drink," the sailor said.

Shang-Li thanked the man and swam up toward the hold. Thava and Iados joined him and they floated above the floor of the cargo hold.

Tentatively, Shang-Li pressed his hand against the belled canvas. Surprising strength pressed back against his palm.

"Is there not a way in?" Iados asked.

"Go under," Amree called. Shadows moved across the rounded canvas. "If you pull apart the canvas, we'll lose the air."

Shang-Li swam under and immediately spotted a rectangle cut out in the center of the floor. Catching hold of the opening, Shang-Li hauled himself up and through. As soon as he emerged into the air, he felt drenched. His sodden clothing dripped all over the floor. He looked down at the mess he'd inadvertently made and was fascinated.

"You've dived before?" Amree sat on the floor in the corner of the small area created by the canvas. Fatigue darkened her eyes. A bloody bandage wrapped her right hand.

"Yes," Shang-Li responded as he made way for Iados and then Thava, who both experienced the same waterlogged effect he'd suffered. "Many times. Nothing like this, though."

"Nor have I. "

Kwan Yung sat on a wooden cask and grilled fish fillets over heated coals. A large pot of clam chowder simmered on another set of coals. He worked quickly to keep the food coming.

Sailors sat on the floor and scooped thin wine from an open cask. They ate quickly from bowls, tearing at the fish with their fingers and drinking the chowder. Then they headed back out to keep the rotation going. The canvas covered area was filled to near bursting.

"One of the sailors that came in earlier said you were attacked," Amree said.

"We encountered a group of spellscarred humanoids," Shang-Li said. "I think they were changed by the wild magic."

"From this world or hers?"

Shang-Li shook his head. "They wore remnants of sailors' clothing, but there was no way to identify them."

"There wasn't much left of any humanity in them," Thava said. "They were little more than predators."

"That seems to be the way of everything in this place," Amree said. "Did you find any salvage?"

"Planks. Sailcloth. Some goods, though we don't know what they are yet."

"You've given them to the quartermaster?" his father asked.

"Yes."

His father handed them three bowls, then quickly ladled soup into them.

For the first time Shang-Li noticed that he smelled the food. "Why couldn't I smell the food outside?"

"It's part of the spell I used to create this bubble." Amree laid her head back against the canvas. It shifted and rolled slightly, marking the constant movement of the sea that Shang-Li hadn't noticed while in the water. "I drew the air from the ocean and I have to cycle the good air in and the bad air out. Otherwise the air in this place would make us sick." She smiled a little. "It's strange to know that the bad air we gather in here could be more harmful to us than the sea outside."

Kwan Yung took fillets from the coals and passed them out. There was enough for Shang-Li, Iados, Thava, and all the sailors presently inside the canvas to have one.

"Have you found any sign of *Grayling*?" his father asked.

"Not yet. But we didn't go any farther than the ship we found today."

"How big is this place?" Amree asked.

Shang-Li shook his head. "It would take days to find the edges, and we'd lose too many in the forests. Finding *Grayling* is going to be difficult."

"Yet it must be found," his father said, tugging on his beard. "You cannot fail in this."

"I know."

"If we do not take back the journals of Liou—"

"Father, I know," Shang-Li said. He stood, irritated and exhausted. What did he have to do to get his father to see he was doing what he could? The weight of the missing books lay heavy on his thoughts. The others were staring at him.

"I'm going to sleep," he said, and abruptly left the air pocket, still seething.

Shang-Li sat up on the floor of the cargo hold, his heart pounding and his mind jumbled with thoughts.

Around him, the ship creaked and rolled with the constant movement of the ocean. Several small fish had invaded the ship and pestered sleeping sailors. Every now and again a startled yelp would wake everyone as a sailor discovered a crab had wandered into his clothing. Thankfully the guards posted at the cargo hold entries had turned away most of the tentacled things that tried to creep in as well.

"They keep getting in." Shang-li turned to see Amree sitting on a crate, watching him.

"You should sleep" she said. You're going to need your rest."

"And you don't?"

Amree sighed and folded her arms. "I've got a ship to watch over, and she's currently in unsafe waters."

Shang-Li glanced at the canvas-covered air bubble in the corner. "Does that spell strain you?"

Amree shook her head and her red tresses floated on

the water. "No. It's set. Maintaining it isn't necessary. It's self-sufficient for the moment." She paused. "What is going to be difficult is expanding that air bubble to bring the ship to the surface." She gazed around the hold. "Even if we manage to get enough canvas to hold the air necessary to lift the ship, we're not going to lift quickly. Nor will we be able to steer *Swallow*. She'll go where she has need to, mostly up, but there will be some drift with the currents and the tide. More than likely we'll still be far out to see and away from any help. We may even drift into the territory of the sahuagin. Or the aboleths." She pulled at the bandage on her hand.

"Let me see your hand," Shang-Li said.

"My hand is fine."

"Has anyone tended to it?"

"No one's had the time."

"Not even my father?" Shang-Li found that hard to believe.

"Your father," Amree said, "has been busy feeding everyone. He's still up there now taking care of that. He's the one you should be worried about."

The sharp ache of guilt twisted in Shang-Li's stomach. He hadn't given a second thought to his father's chosen task.

"Where is the ship's cook?" Shang-Li asked.

"Lost. Somewhere in the sea. A few of them were, you know."

Shang-Li did know. He also knew more had been lost to the predators in the strange forest.

"May I please see your hand?" he asked.

"Now you're a cleric?"

"I'm a monk," Shang-Li replied. "One of the first things we're trained to do is care for the body. Our own or someone else's."

Gently, noting how tense the young woman was, Shang-Li took her hand and guided her to a sitting position in front of him. He carefully unwrapped the cloth from her hand. The fact that the cloth didn't feel saturated still amazed him, especially when he considered how wet it would be when she entered the air bubble.

"How did you injure your hand?" Shang-Li asked.

"A broken timber slipped," she said as she watched him. "I tried to grab it."

"Not a good idea."

"I wasn't thinking."

Beneath the bandages, the palm of her hand was red and swollen with infection around a four-inch gash that ran crossways across her flesh. The tear wasn't very deep, though the flesh was thin enough there that the muscles and tendons were revealed. Fresh blood rose from the wound and faded into the water.

A fish swam over to her and hovered over her palm. Shang-Li brushed the fish aside and it swam away.

"I don't know how you did anything with this hand," Shang-Li said.

"I tried not to."

"You should have told someone."

"Everyone was busy trying to stay alive."

"Who cleaned the wound?"

"I did."

"You didn't do a very good job of it."

"Is criticism one of the services you throw in with your care?" she asked sharply.

"Yes," Shang-Li said, "but thankfully it's just as free as everything else I'm doing."

Amree tried to withdraw her hand.

Shang-Li held onto her fingers. "There are splinters in there that have to come out. And I'm going to have to suture your palm back together."

Involuntarily, Amree closed her hand and didn't look happy.

"What's wrong?" Shang-Li asked.

She grimaced and looked embarrassed. "I don't much care for needles."

Shang-Li retreated long enough to get a small knife and

tweezers from a cleric kit. He added a curved needle and fine gut. Then he sat cross-legged in front of Amree once more.

"This is only going to make me dislike you more," she threatened.

"That's a risk I'll have to take." Shang-Li took her hand and held it gently but firmly. "This is going to hurt."

She turned her head away and didn't move while he removed eight good-sized splinter fragments. Once he was satisfied the wound was clean, he threaded the needle.

"You were lucky," Shang-Li said in a soft voice. "None of the muscles, nerves, or tendons were damaged. Except for the tear in your flesh, your hand is fine. Once I close the flesh up, it will heal fine."

"If it doesn't it's going to be expensive to have a cleric bless it back to normal."

Shang-Li looked into her eyes. "If we leave it untended, you could lose your hand. Maybe sicken and die before we get out of this place. At the very least you'll bleed and attract predators. And if you're going to create enough air to raise this ship to the surface and keep us protected while you do that, you're going to have to be healthy."

"You don't look the part of a seamstress."

"Are you ready?"

She took a deep breath, held it a moment, then let it out. "I am."

Shang-Li pushed the needle through her flesh, felt her tense, then slowly relax a little. He pushed the needle through the other side of the slash, then pulled the ravaged flesh together and tied the first stitch.

"I'm going to put a lot of small ones in," he said. "Spacing them out might discourage scar growth. This should leave little in the way of damage."

"All right."

"Just keep breathing." Shang-Li threaded the needle once more and began again.

CHAPTER EIGHTEEN

Shang-Li swam with a heavy spear clutched in one hand. Given their present circumstances, the spear seemed a better choice than his fighting sticks. Thava and the sailors who followed him also kept their weapons out, ready for the Blue Lady's creatures to attack.

Iados swam and scouted a head of them. The tiefling's tail twitched like a cat's as he surveyed the sea floor. They'd already learned many creatures liked to conceal themselves in the loose silt and the brush. And all of them appeared ravenous.

The forest continued on as far as Shang-Li could see. He'd never seen anything like the environment he watched around him. As a ranger, he'd been trained to feel at home in the forest. But though he'd tried to find some familiar bits of this one, there was no closeness, no safe harbor. The forest just felt *wrong*. It didn't feel dead, but it felt something close to that.

Ahead, Iados waved and indicated that he'd found the first shipwreck of the day. Dodging through trees and brush, Shang-Li swam forward and Thava picked up her pace. The rest of the salvage crew trailed after them.

Holding the spear in both hands, Shang-Li dropped toward the sea floor near the ship wreckage. The vessel hadn't fared as well as *Swallow*. She lay broken almost in half, her masts broken and splintered, and her deck largely gone. Cracked timbers and shattered planks lay beside the ship.

"She's a cargo ship, isn't she?" Iados asked. Like Shang-Li, he carried a heavy spear.

"I believe so." Shang-Li used his spear to test the ground in front of him. He stabbed the long blade experimentally into the silt to see if anything lurked beneath the debris.

Curious fish swam nearby, and a few of them fell prey to the tentacled things that hid in the nearby brush. The hunters brought the writhing fish to their maws and ate greedily. Sharks had followed the scavenging crew from *Swallow* and now circled lazily overhead. The predators were patient hunters but every now and again one would drop down and hit the unseen barrier. Whatever force contained them discouraged them time after time. Shang-Li hoped that continued to be the case.

Thava stood at the keel and brushed away the algae that covered the bowed planks. "Her name was *Bokhan's Pearl*. Does that mean anything to you?"

"No," Shang-Li replied. "The ship we're searching for is called *Grayling*."

"Judging from the shape of most of the ships that the Blue Lady took under," Iados said, "I wouldn't hold out hope that you'll find much of her."

"I don't need to find much of her," Shang-Li replied. "I only need the captain's cabin to be intact." And somehow airtight, he thought, gods willing. "Let's see what we can salvage." He swam down toward the broken ship but remained vigilant.

He touched down on the ground a short distance from *Bokhan's Pearl*. With Thava on one side of him and Iados on the other, Shang-Li boarded the ship.

The interior was dark. Cargo lay broken open and in disarray. Nothing looked as if it had been disturbed since the ship settled on the sea floor, but the damage from the storm that had taken the vessel down was apparent.

Skeletons, their bones picked clean and gleaming in the blue glow that permeated the area, lay scattered around the hold.

"What killed them?" Iados shifted one of the skeletons with a foot, making certain it didn't rise up to grab hold of them.

Shang-Li knelt next to the nearest one and surveyed the remains carefully. The skeleton was intact and didn't show any signs of combat damage or residual harm from the ship's sinking. Tattered clothing clung to the skeletal legs and ribcage. An amulet hung around the dead man's neck.

"I don't see any signs of past wounds," Shang-Li said.

"This one suffered combat injuries," Thava said from a few feet away. "Axe blows. A sword thrust through the ribs. But all the bones show signs of healing. This person lived through those attacks. Whatever killed them wasn't violent."

"Storms are violent," Iados observed. He remained on guard and watched the ocean around them.

"They didn't die in combat," Thava said.

"Then how?"

"Drowning would be my guess," Shang-Li answered, and he felt the grim reality of the situation close in on him.

"That doesn't make any sense." Iados shook his head. "Why did they drown if we don't?"

"I don't know," Shang-Li replied. He didn't bother to point out that could at any moment since he felt certain the thought lingered constantly in their minds. "Perhaps they drowned before they reached the blue light. Maybe the Blue Lady chose not to help them."

"And where is she?" Iados asked impatiently. "If it was so important for her to have us down here, why hasn't she come to claim her prizes?"

Shang-Li couldn't answer that either.

"I'm tired of waiting," the tiefling declared with an angry snap of his tail.

"Until we know more about her," Thava stated, "you're only waiting for your death. Better we should take this time and learn. The battle will come."

Most of the ship's cargo was ruined, contaminated by the ocean or strung out in pieces across the floor. Some of it lay half-buried in the silt.

Shang-Li prized at one of the planks near the ship's stern. The wood remained good, but the vessel had been constructed well and intended to stay in one piece.

Shang-Li braced himself against the ship's hull and managed to rip the plank free. Handling it in the water was much more difficult than on land. Whatever magic allowed him to move and breathe beneath the ocean didn't apply to the things they scavenged from the ship. The plank moved slowly through the water and made the job hard.

However, the water made the heaviest prizes easier to manage. Two sailors carried a mast that would have taken a block and tackle and a crew of stout men to raise on land.

A short distance from the ship, Shang-Li dropped the plank on a pile of others that had been salvaged. Thava stacked another.

"How long do you think we've been at this?" the paladin asked. "The men are tired, and they've been through a lot today. If it is still the same day."

Shang-Li nodded. No one needed to be overtired, but

the need to finish the task Amree had set before them remained on his mind. Staying focused was hard when he thought about the Blue Lady and how she might close in on them at any time. When he let himself get fatigued, he couldn't help thinking she was deliberately letting them labor on their escape just so she could yank it away from them at the end. "Let's finish up with what we have, tie it off, and get back to *Swallow*."

Thava nodded.

Swimming up, Shang-Li called the salvage crew in. They sorted through the timber, canvas, and cargo they'd gathered. Then they swam in freight teams to haul their salvage back.

Shang-Li held onto a corner of sailcloth and swam. The weight of pots and barrels weighed the center of the sail-cloth. It also slowed progress because it fought the ocean in an ungainly fashion.

But it went.

Although he glanced around him and saw no one, Shang-Li couldn't shake the feeling he was being watched.

Shang-Li tracked the darting shadows all around him as a matter of course. Never before had he noticed how restless marine life seemed to be. It was always moving.

What are you doing, manling? The Blue Lady's voice lay chills all along Shang-Li's spine.

Looking around, Shang-Li realized he could no longer see his companions or the load he'd been tugging along. She has you in her thrall, he thought.

You've had time to think over my offer, manling. Now I want to know if you're worth the time I'm taking to keep you alive.

"You're not keeping us alive." Shang-Li thought of the dead sailors they had lost over the last couple days. "We're keeping ourselves alive."

I'm keeping you from dying more quickly.

Shang-Li didn't answer. No matter what he said, she would only turn it against him.

Do you see your friends? Are you even awake?

Hesitantly, Shang-Li hung in the water. He didn't know if he was awake, or what had happened to the others or the salvage.

There is someone I'd like you to meet. He is my guest—

"Prisoner, you mean?"

—and I expect you to treat him with respect once I introduce you. If you harm him, I will kill everyone that is there with you.

Shang-Li didn't have a response for that. "Who is the guest?"

You will know him. He will test you, your knowledge, and see if you are the one I need. If not, I will kill you and let my pets have you. But at least it will go more quickly.

Anxiety twisted Shang-Li's guts but he kept his focus and forced himself to be calm. They were running out of time. "When is he coming?"

Soon.

Pain flooded Shang-Li's temples as her power filled him. Then she was gone, and the sorrow of her leaving left him almost shattered him. He breathed through the feeling and it quickly went away. When he blinked again, he found Iados glancing in direction.

"Are you all right, Shang-Li?" Iados had him by the shoulder.

"Yes. I . . . what happened?' As he looked around, Shang-Li saw they'd spilled the canvas with him.

"I don't know. It was like you were in a trance."

Shang-Li shook his head and it felt heavy and slow. "It was the Blue Lady."

"She's able to contact you while you're awake?" Thava sounded more concerned.

"Her power over you is obviously growing," Iados said. "That's something we hadn't considered."

Shang-Li had, but he hadn't wanted to bring it up. Even now, he didn't know what to say, or how to tell them exactly when they would no longer be able to trust him.

Since no one could tell by the horizon or by the eventual fall of darkness how much time passed, the hours were marked by candles that burned in the canvas bubble. After everyone had six hours sleep, interrupted by a two-hour guard shift in the middle or at either end of the cycle, Captain Chiang roused his crew and the "day" began anew. The schedule was hard to keep because there was no way to mark time while away from *Swallow*.

Shang-Li, Iados, and Thava once more headed up the salvage party. They didn't return to *Bokhan's Pearl*. An infestation of sea shambles in the area nearby had been enough to dissuade them of that.

"I hate the way they watch us." Iados stared bleakly at the inhuman things that stayed mostly hidden in the treeline. "I don't know if they're waiting on us to catch us unaware, or if they're spies for the Blue Lady."

Shang-Li shook his head and regretted it. For the last couple of days, he'd been plagued by ferocious headaches. His sleep and even an increasing number of his waking hours were interrupted by nightmares.

"I don't know."

"And where is this mysterious person the Blue Lady told you she would send?" Thava kicked at a scuttling thing that had crept too close and latched onto her boot.

"I wish I knew."

"Because it's not like we're going to have friends down here," Iados said.

"Have you had time to consider my offer, manling?"

Startled, Shang-Li glanced up into the shadows of the hold they were currently sorting through. The Blue Lady floated in the water in front of him, glowing with an incandescence almost as bright as the glowstones they'd hung in nets on the wall. Out of habit, Shang-Li reached for his fighting sticks and this time they fell into his hands effortlessly.

Amused, the Blue Lady smiled. "Still you cling to your desperation."

"Would you have it any other way?" As he looked around, Shang-Li saw that he was alone. Iados, Thava, and the others were no longer in the hold. He hadn't seen them leave.

"No. Desperation drives you, manling, but it is an elixir to my kind. You work so hard, dream so big, and yet you live so small and so quickly."

Shang-Li tried to keep his thoughts focused on the Blue Lady and not think of the gamble they were putting together to raise *Swallow*.

"I know all about your pathetic ship, manling. You're only foolishly wasting your time trying to get it from the sea bottom. I brought it down here, and it shall remain here. You can do all that you may to fight me. In the end, your frustrations and panic will only feed me more."

Emboldened by his own fear because it turned him numb, Shang-Li strode toward the Blue Lady. "You say you laugh at us, at our efforts to free ourselves. But we haven't been down here over eighty years, have we?"

"Careful, manling." Dark fire flashed in the silver eyes. All amusement slid from the Blue Lady's beautiful face. "Don't overestimate your value."

"What does it feel like to be trapped so long?" Shang-Li stopped within striking distance. "At least I'm here with my own kind. My friends and family. What do you have?"

"You brought your friends and father here to die with you, manling," she said. "Does that knowledge really make you feel all that smug? Is that something you can take pride in?"

Despite his pain and uncertainty, Shang-Li made himself meet her gaze and hold it steadily. "Not pride. Solace. I won't die alone. Can you say the same thing?"

The Blue Lady moved so suddenly Shang-Li didn't even see the blow coming until he was struck. Nearly knocked unconscious by the blow, Shang-Li sailed backward and was slowed by the water until he drifted to the bottom of the hold.

"You will have only a short time to prove yourself now, manling. If you cannot do what I wish for you to do, I shall take great joy in breaking you."

Slipping into and out of focus, Shang-Li watched the Blue Lady fade away. Then Thava's face was in his. Concern pulled at her features.

"Shang-Li. Are you all right?" Thava turned his face to survey the damage that was surely there.

Tasting blood, Shang-Li tried to sit up. The dragonborn restrained him.

"Easy." Thava pulled a cloth from her pack and wiped at his face. "What happened to you? I didn't see you fall." She looked over her shoulder. "Did anyone see what happened to him?"

One of the sailors stepped forward. "Didn't see anyone hit him. He crossed the hold, talking like he was talking someone—someone I couldn't see—then he was flying backward."

"It was the Blue Lady." Shang-Li fought free of Thava and sat up. Groggy, he got to his feet. "You didn't see her?" He looked at the sailor.

The man shook his head. "There was nobody there."

"She was here." Iados touched Shang-Li's face and the pain caused him to flinch.

"I didn't see her," the sailor said.

"None of us saw her." Iados growled irritably and flicked his tail. "It's not going to do a lot of good posting guards if she can come right in unseen."

"There are still plenty of other things out here that we need to be on guard against." Thava watched Shang-Li. "Are you sure you can stand?"

"Yes. Thank you."

"What happened?" Iados asked.

"I think she's growing less fond of me." Shang-Li wiped at his mouth and it came away stained with crimson that quickly lifted into the water.

"Well, that can't be good."

"No," Shang-Li said. "I would agree."

"Did a shipwreck fall on you?" Amree stared at Shang-Li when she came to join him at eveningfeast.

Shang-Li brought her up to date on his latest visit from the Blue Lady. He was grateful the fish fillets and crabmeat was so tender because his jaw still ached and was swollen. Despite his hunger and fatigue, he hated wasting time eating and trying to sleep when the Blue Lady was looming ever nearer. But he knew he couldn't keep up the salvage work without dropping. Sitting there and lying there still felt like wasted time, and time was growing precious.

"Maybe she's all threat."

"If she were," Shang-Li said, " we wouldn't have as many sunken ships to choose from."

"True." Amree picked at her bandages for a moment.

"The canvas is coming along." Shang-Li nodded at the canvas lining the interior of the hold. "Is it airtight?"

"It will be. Long enough for us to get to the surface. After that, we have to hope the repairs we did to the hull holds. Otherwise we'll be back down here again."

"If we don't drown."

"We've rescued some longboats as well." Amree pointed at the collection of them in the hull. "Before we attempt to leave, I'm going to have those lashed to the upper decks.

If we can't hold *Swallow* together, we'll put to sea in the longboats."

Shang-Li frowned at the thought of that.

"I know." Amree grimaced. "It's not what I would want either. But I don't want to come back to this place."

"I would imagine that would be the end of us. We're barely tolerated now."

"*You're* barely tolerated. I'm surprised the rest of us are allowed to live." Amree shuddered. "And I'm beginning to have serious misgivings about that."

"Why?"

"Killing us would be easier. If she's keeping us alive, maybe there's another reason for it."

"Like what?"

Amree shrugged. "I don't know. But I know people like the Blue Lady don't do anything without a purpose. There was a reason she saved as many of us as she did. And why she hasn't had her pets close in on us before now."

"I hope you're wrong about that."

"Me too." Amree smiled at him bravely. "But I don't think that I am."

Shang-Li's meal was even less appetizing that before with that thought on his mind, but he forced himself to eat.

"I do have another idea," Amree said after a few moments. "The ship you and the others found? The living one."

"Red Orchid."

Amree nodded and looked thoughtful. "I've been thinking about her a lot."

Shang-Li had too. He felt bad about leaving the ship trapped in the Blue Lady's domain.

"One of the hardest things we're going to have to do is keep *Swallow* upright as she floats to the surface. The currents are too unpredictable, and we have little control over her ascent. But I was wondering if Red Orchid might have more control."

"Because she's alive?" Shang-Li thought the idea was intriguing.

"Yes. I need to find out if Red Orchid the being is the whole ship or just the figurehead. If she can control the ship's movement the way she does its shape, she would be ideal to help guide *Swallow* to the surface. If we could transfer her to this ship."

"You don't know if that's possible."

"Not until I ask her."

Shang-Li shook his head. "I don't like the idea of you being gone from the ship."

Amree arched an eyebrow at him. "Because I won't get things done? Your father—"

"Because you won't be safe." Shang-Li gestured past the ship's hulls. "You haven't seen everything out there. It's incredibly dangerous."

"Oh, and handling a ship on storm-tossed seas during a battle isn't?"

Shang-Li closed his mouth and curbed his immediate response. He waited a moment. "I could talk to Red Orchid."

"You're not a ship's mage. You don't speak the language of ships."

"I spoke to her before. Red Orchid speaks Common quiet well."

She looked at him. "Shang-Li, you're doing the best that you can do, but you can't do it all. I'm a ship's mage. Red Orchid, for whatever else she may be, is a ship. There's no one down here with us that speaks ship better than I do." She paused. "And I want to meet her."

Shang-Li hesitated for just a moment. "All right."

Standing close by with his spear in his hand, Shang-Li watched as Amree approached Red Orchid. The figurehead's eyes watched the ship's mage and shifted across the prow of the ship.

"She's going to talk to the ship?" Iados sounded as though he couldn't believe what Shang-Li had told him.

"That's what she said."

Amree stopped a good dozen paces from the figurehead. The prow already bowed a little like it was about to change shape again.

"Hail and well met, Red Orchid," Amree greeted. "My name is Amree. I'm a ship's mage."

"Hail and well met, Amree Ship's-Mage." Red Orchid glowered over Amree at Shang-Li and Iados. "At least you're more polite than the others."

"I've had time to prepare to meet you."

Red Orchid shifted, relaxing a little. "You wanted to meet me?"

"I've never even dreamed of something like you. Of course I had to meet you." Amree looked at the figurehead. "May I come closer?"

"Of course. I am not afraid of you."

Amree ran her fingers along the prow. "Are you the ship or the figurehead?"

"I'm whatever I wish to be. I . . . am." Red Orchid shifted a little, like someone that realized she suddenly intrigued someone else.

"Were you yourself above the water?"

"I remember bits and pieces of things of those times." Red Orchid frowned, and the disappointment seemed to carry in every line of the ship. "But I do not know that."

Amree continued walking around the ship. "What are your earliest complete memories?"

"Only this place."

"I was told you can change your shape."

"I can." Red Orchid the ship quivered like a wet dog. The prow melted into a the stunning face of a woman again.

Even at the distance from where Shang-Li stood, he saw the smile on Amree's face.

"That's incredible." Amree trailed her fingers over the ship's chin. "You're beautiful."

"Thank you," Red Orchid said smugly.

"Now see," Iados whispered to Shang-Li, "you could have won her over with charm."

Shang-Li shook his head.

"Do you wish to sail again?" Amree asked.

"I can't master the shape long enough, and I don't quite know how to fix the damage I've received." Red Orchid's "face" disappeared and was replaced by the shape of the prow again. "During the years I've lain here, I've tried to reassemble myself. Even if I could, though, I can't empty the water from myself."

"Could you leave this ship?" Amree stood in front of the ship's figurehead.

Red Orchid hesitated, as petulant as a child. "I don't know. I've never tried that. I've never had any reason to."

"I have another ship. One that has a place for you. If you can separate from this one."

The figurehead's eyes grew large in concern. "How would I do that?"

"Could you pull yourself into the figurehead?"

Red Orchid shook her head. "Then I would be so small."

"It would only be for a short period of time. I promise. Then you could be part of a larger, healthier ship."

"I don't suppose Amree asked Captain Chiang about this," Iados grumbled. "*Swallow* is his ship."

"His ship happens to be sitting on the bottom of the Sea of Fallen Stars." Shang-Li snorted. "I think the captain would make a deal with the Bitch Queen herself if he could get his ship above the waves again."

"Why do you come to me if you have another ship?" Suspicion was etched into Red Orchid's words.

"We have another ship, but she is just a ship. She's timbers and iron, blood and sweat, but she doesn't have your strength or your awareness. You are more than a ship, Red Orchid. I think you're strong enough to help us keep control of *Swallow* when we lift her to the surface."

"What if we fail?"

Amree placed her hand on the ship and smiled. "Would it be any worse than where we are now?"

Red Orchid paused. "What if separating from this ship ends me? What if I am actually all of this ship?"

"I don't know." Amree drew her hand along the prow as though comforting a child. "I do know that the only way we can find out is to try."

Red Orchid was silent for a long time. Then she turned her face up toward the surface. "What does it feel like to run before the wind? I can scarcely remember."

"It's the most beautiful sensation in the world."

Red Orchid smiled. A dreamy look relaxed her face. "I am ready to be free of my grave, ship's mage. One way or the other."

"Carefully!" Amree cursed as Shang-Li jerked on a pry bar to loosen the figurehead from the ship. Wooden dowels shrieked in protest and at least two of them broke with vicious cracks.

Chastened, Shang-Li stopped what he was doing and looked up at Red Orchid. "Are you all right?" he asked.

Pain turned her face pale and made her features look azure in the blue light. The unintended echo of the Blue Lady's appearance left Shang-Li slightly unsettled. He almost expected the Blue Lady to talk to him and tell him it was all a trap, that they were wasting their time while she closed the net around them.

"I'm fine." Red Orchid stretched a bit on the prow, then became still again. "Becoming so small is hard. I feel more trapped than ever."

"It won't last long." Amree took the figurehead's hand

and squeezed it gently. "I promise. No longer than we need take to get from this ship to ours."

Red Orchid nodded and they continued.

"Gently," Amree admonished Shang-Li.

"I know." Shang-Li set the pry bar and began again. He worked at the figurehead, but couldn't help feel that the task was taking far too long to do.

"What's wrong with her?" Shang-Li stared up at the figurehead mounted on *Swallow*. Since they'd disconnected her from her original ship, Red Orchid hadn't spoken.

"The toll of moving her was higher than we'd expected." Amree floated in the water before Red Orchid and worked with various things she had from her craft.

Shang-Li didn't know what the items were that the ship's mage used, but he knew they were things a ship's mage used to put strength and power into a craft. He felt the surge of *something* that emanated from Amree's efforts, and he knew it was stronger, more focused, than anything she'd done aboard *Swallow* before.

"She had to . . . *diminish* herself to fit within the figurehead." Amree took a black pearl from her pouch and held it in her hand. When she closed her hand, her fist glowed with purple light that bathed Red Orchid. "She's never done that before."

During the swim back from the ship to *Swallow*, Red Orchid had finally stopped speaking and seemed unable to hear. Even while getting hung on *Swallow*, she hadn't uttered a word.

"Is she going to be all right?" Thava asked.

Amree shook her head irritably. "I don't know. I've never seen anything like her. Maybe more of her remains within the ship we left behind. Maybe she wasn't able to squeeze all of herself into the figurehead."

"Wouldn't she have known that?"

"She doesn't know what she is either." Amree sounded discouraged. "This is new for both of us."

"Perhaps all she needs is time." Kwan Yung leaned over the railing over the prow and peered down.

Shang-Li looked at the inert figurehead and *Swallow's* only partially repaired broken hull, and he thought about the increasing strength of the Blue Lady's *visits*. "Unfortunately, time is the one thing we don't have."

Another salvage crew swam toward *Swallow*.

"This can't be good." Iados turned to face the approaching group. "They started out after we did."

Yugi, the young lookout, swam at the forefront. He was excited and out of breath as he coasted up close to them and stopped. "We found *Grayling*."

Grayling was nestled in a canyon that was hard to see while swimming. Broken merchanters, warships, and fishing boats littered the ocean floor under the canopy of strange trees. Tentacled creatures hung like obscene fruit from the branches of the trees. When anyone ventured too close, the creatures launched their tentacles and pulled their prey in to them.

Shang-Li and the others battled the creatures and drove them back from the trees nearest the canyon. Even in those depths, the blue light coming from the land chased away the gloom after a fashion.

The first ship lay on her side. Shang-Li took some of the glowing coral Amree had created from her kit and held it to shine around the vessel. Barnacles covered her stern but he found part of a name. He used his dagger to clear away the barnacles and found:

Wavecutter.

"Do you know her?" Iados asked.

"A merchanter," Shang-Li said. "She was in the documents we researched. She went down a few years after *Grayling*."

"Shang-Li." Thava called from ahead, waving her glow-stone to get his attention.

Shang-Li swam over to her and saw a few fresh corpses lying on the ground near another ship. They'd been savaged by predators and most of the soft parts of the bodies were gone.

"They haven't been down here long. Not long enough to have come down with *Wavecutter*." Shang-Li swam to one of the men and held the glowstone closer. Crabs and other small carrion feeders scuttled away as he turned over the body.

Only shredded gore remained of the man's features. Even if Shang-Li had once seen the man, he wouldn't recognize him now.

"Someone's alive inside!" a sailor called out.

The man lay on the floor of the captain's quarters. He was human, in his middle years, and scarred from life at sea. He was pale, close to death.

Weakly, he held his hand up to ward off the brightness from the glowstone. His swollen tongue protruded from his cracked lips despite the water that surrounded him.

"Who?" he whispered.

"No one who means you harm." Thava held out her empty hands but her great size still made her threatening to see.

The man glanced at Iados. "Devils? Come to fetch me to some pit and torture me?"

"No," Shang-Li answered. "Where's your captain?"

"Dead. Thirsted to death." The man grabbed at a dagger near his hand three times before securing a hold. "Like all the rest of the crew. I think I'm the only one left."

"We have water."

The man laughed weakly but it quickly turned into a cough that racked his body. "We've got water too." He waved toward the ship. "But we couldn't drink any of it because of the curse on this place. Blasted spellplague," the man said. "Keeps us alive down here, but fouls out water before we can drink it. Every mouthful you take is tainted with brine. Makes you sick."

"We can get you a drink," Shang-Li said. He reached into his bag of holding and pulled out a large bladder normally used to carry spice powder. It was airtight and contained some of the air Amree had created back at *Swallow*.

One of the sailors found an empty barrel, lined it with tarp, and tied it to the mainmast. Shang-Li pushed the bladder into the barrel and squeezed the air out. Huge bubbles formed and collected at the top of the barrel, then the space grew bigger.

Thava picked up the sick man and carried him to the barrel. Once he was inside, once he'd discovered the air pocket trapped inside, he gave a glad cry of understanding.

"Gods, let me drink," he croaked. "All this wet around me, and me parched as a frog in the desert."

Shang-Li handed over one of the bladders of water they'd brought with them. "Go easy with it or you'll make yourself sick."

The man took the water in his shaking hands. "I've been without water before. I know to pace myself." Even so, his past experience didn't help him now. A moment later, he emerged from the barrel and threw up. The bile formed a cloud in the water that immediately attracted a small school of fish to feed on the debris.

"My name is Kulher," the man said a short time later. Looking better rested and more healthy, he sat cross-legged in front of Shang-Li. "This ship is *Lysinda*, named for the captain's oldest daughter. We were a cargo ship until the Blue Lady decided to pull us under."

"Do you have any idea why she picked you?" Iados asked.

"No." Kulher shook his shaggy head. "We've run these waters for years. We knew to stay away from the domain of the Blue Lady, even though most of us were convinced she was a legend captains with ill luck blamed for losing their ships."

"You saw the Blue Lady?" Shang-Li asked.

"Only for a moment, before the storm struck us, broke us up, and dragged us under."

"How long have you been down here?"

Kuhler shrugged but shivered. "Long enough for a lot of men to die from thirst."

"Probably only a few more days than we have," Iados said.

"We should have thought of the trick with the water barrel."

"Unless you could have made air," Thava said gently, "it wouldn't have done you any good."

"The ship's mage died when the Blue Lady took us. We'd barely entered the water when a shark snatched him and bit his head off." Kuhler looked forlorn. "I lost me a lot of good friends on this voyage. Men who have stood with me through bad times and hard times." He paused. "I feel guilty for asking, but do you have a way to get out of here?"

"We're working on it," Shang-Li said.

"Why does she bother to bring the ships down if she's not going to do anything with them?" Iados asked as he swam beside Shang-Li back toward *Swallow*. He flicked his tail in annoyance.

"The next time I see her, I'll ask her."

Iados regarded him. "You would, wouldn't you? It would probably be the last thing you did before she killed you."

"She hasn't killed us yet. I remain hopeful about that."

"Or foolish without just cause," Iados growled. "She may be busy with other things, or we're so insignificant she doesn't care. Maybe she derives pleasure from watching her captives thirst to death in the ocean."

Shang-Li showed his friend a lopsided grin. "You're such an optimist."

"Well, down here the glass would always be full, wouldn't it?"

"She said she planned to break away from here. So

whatever the Spellplague has wrought also binds her to this place."

"She has a very big cage," Iados commented. "Still, once you know where the walls are, size doesn't matter. You'll still feel the confinement."

Shang-Li swam deeper to examine the other shipwrecks. The goods aboard *Lysinda* would stand them in good stead for days, and the salvage potential seemed enough to finish making repairs on *Swallow*. He focused on finding *Grayling*, wondering if the presence of *Wavecutter* harbored some hope of finding the ship in the tangle of dead ships lying in the canyon.

He found two other ships, *Garnatok* and a slave ship that had dozens of skeletons in her cargo hold, but not *Grayling*. As he approached the next ship, Yugi called out to him.

"Shang-Li! Over here."

Heart pumping a little faster, Shang-Li told himself not to get his hopes up. Even if Yugi had found the ship, chances were good that everything aboard her—including the precious books—were ruined.

Upon first sight, Shang-Li's hopes diminished. The ship lay broken in two, and much of her starboard side was ripped away. Not even much remained for salvage. Still, he landed on her broken hull, took a fresh grip on his spear, and freed the glowstone from his bag.

"Is this it??" Yugi asked as he came to stand behind Shang-Li.

Shang-Li held up the coral so the light played over the prow where the ship's name was proudly displayed. The paint had faded over the long years, but it was still legible: *Grayling*.

"Yes."

"All this for books?" Yugi asked. "Truly? That's the only treasure you want?"

Cautiously, Shang-Li shined the glowstone down into the hold. Things moved below, but they were fish and other scavengers, nothing large enough to offer him much threat.

"It is," Shang-Li replied. "You've seen my father, and you know that he serves the Standing Tree Monastery. They don't search for treasure."

"I've heard that they don't turn it aside when they find it neither," another sailor said.

Shang-Li didn't argue the point. The monastery was self-sufficient but they did a lot with what they were given. When the monastery did well, the villages around them prospered as well.

"No gold aboard this ship?" the sailor asked.

"She was an explorer." Shang-Li stepped over the side and swam down into the hold. The lighted coral barely held back the darkness. "The only gold she might have been carrying will be in the captain's strongbox and perhaps in the pockets of her crew."

"Could be worth a look." Two of the sailors split off and swam toward the ship's waist where crewmen slept.

"If an air pocket remains aboard this ship, I want to know about it," Shang-Li said. "And don't open anything that could be watertight. We can't lose those books."

He swam through the darkness, usually only able to see a few feet in front of him. The darkness seemed to magnify the darkness, make it appear to be larger and deeper than it actually was. He went through the cabins one by one. All of them were open and flooded. He had to swim down to enter the ones on the starboard side and up to enter the ones on the port side because *Grayling* lay on her side.

Sand had filtered in as well and provided a layer of lighter coloring in the shadows. Eels slithered across the sand and bared the wood in places. A squid squirted away into hiding.

Bayel Droust's cabin was easy to recognize once Shang-Li got there. A fine powder of sand had drifted over the writer's tools and ink bottles, but they looked otherwise unharmed.

Shang-Li put the glowstone on the edge of the over-turned desk behind, gathered those things, and put them into his bag. He couldn't imagine Droust leaving the items behind out of choice.

He found an oilskin bag that felt like it contained a sheaf of paper Droust would have used to send letters. But under a tangle of loose clothing, another oilskin pouch held a stack of what looked like books or journals.

Shang-Li felt the shape again with his hands to reas-sure himself of his immediate conjecture. He smiled in the shadows and couldn't wait to get back to *Lysinda's* water barrel to confirm his suspicions. As he shoved the bag into his own, he noticed a shadow on the wall in front of him.

Someone had followed him into the room and now stood in front of the glowstone. The light played over a naked blade.

CHAPTER NINETEEN

Shang-Li shook his arms and his fighting sticks dropped into his waiting hands as he turned. A Shou man wearing the tattoos of the Nine Golden Swords lunged into the cabin and thrust his spear at Shang-Li's chest.

Shang-Li turned sideways, and the spear slid by less than an inch away and thudded into the wall behind him. Taking a step forward, Shang-Li whipped the stick across the man's face, then snap-kicked the warrior in the groin.

His opponent dropped to his knees, gagging and spewing a cloud of bile into the water around him. Shang-Li went forward and hammered the man at the base of the skull. The Nine Golden Swords man slumped slowly through the water as he lost consciousness.

Outside in the main hallway, the passageway was taller than it was wide with the ship on her side, and there was precious little room to maneuver. He chastised himself for allowing the salvage crew to get separated. He'd known the area wasn't safe, but it had seemed safe enough.

Three more Nine Golden Swords warriors blocked the way he'd come. Their weapons reflected the orange light from the coral he'd left in Bayel Droust's cabin. Without a word, they started forward, filling the passageway.

Shang-Li backed toward the other end of the ship. Stairs led up to the top deck. A shadow crossed his field of vision and he dodged back just as the attacker waiting outside the cargo hold thrust his sword into the hold.

Shang-Li slid his weapon into the man's sleeve and jerked his arm above his head. He blocked the sword with the other fighting stick. Setting himself against the underside of the deck, Shang-Li pulled with all his strength.

The Nine Golden Swords warrior came through the hold and slammed into the opposite wall.

Shang-Li ripped free his fighting sticks and propelled himself through the cargo hold as the three other men charged his position. Darkness above filled his peripheral vision and he turned swiftly as he swam.

Thava stood on the ship and held her battle-axe across her thighs. "We have guests," the paladin announced.

"How many?" Shang-Li put his fighting sticks away and drew his sword.

"I've spotted at least a dozen." Thava smiled grimly. "But you can subtract two of those."

"I counted five inside. One of them is down but not finished."

"It appears the Nine Golden Swords were more fortunate than we were after the storm."

"Or the Blue Lady spared them," Shang-Li responded, then he concentrated on staying alive as the surviving warriors boiled from the hold.

Despite their bristling blades and zealous nature, the Nine Golden Swords warriors weren't used to fighting underwater. Shang-Li took advantage of his swimming ability and shoved himself into a long dive over their heads.

The unexpected move caught the men by surprise and they ducked back, but not before Shang-Li slashed through one man's sword shoulder to disable him. By then Thava had leaped from the ship's side and crashed into the other three. They fell, bowled over by her armored size and weight.

Thava kicked one of them in the head to render him unconscious, then clove another man from crown to the nape of his neck. The remaining man ran for his life but he didn't get far before the paladin brought him down with a throwing axe. The flat of the blade crashed into the back of his head and he crumpled.

"What do we do with the ones that still live?" Thava asked.

"If I had my way," Iados said as he stepped from the brush that hugged the canyon wall, "we'd slit their throats and have done with them. Let the Blue Lady's little beasties fill themselves up on them for a while and buy us some time."

Thava shot him a look.

"Except that I know that isn't your way," Iados went on.

"And it never will be," Thava vowed.

Iados sighed. "I must admit, I sometimes long for the simpler days before I became your traveling companion."

"You're fortunate that I saved you from yourself." The paladin recovered her throwing axe.

"So what then does wise Bahamut say? Do we take these men as prisoners?" Iados gestured to the fallen Nine Golden Swords warriors.

"No." Shang-Li took a fresh grip on his sword. "Now that we know these men are out here, we'll try to steer clear of them."

"That could be difficult."

"I won't have their murders on my hands. It's one thing to kill a man in battle, but I won't slit his throat when he's helpless."

"That's why you should kill them in battle when the chance presents itself." Iados flashed an evil grin. "I assure you, I took no prisoners, nor did I leave any that I crossed blades with that live to challenge us later."

Shang-Li swam up over the ship and spotted the sailor that had waved him over to *Grayling*. The man floated slackly in the water. Blood flowed in streams away from the sailor's slit throat.

"You can tell that's what *they* were doing," Iados said as they swam past.

"We'll gather our people," Shang-Li said, "get what salvage and cargo we can haul this trip, and take it back to *Swallow*. If we're lucky, it will be enough to tide us over until Amree gets us to the surface."

As they swam back within sight of *Swallow*, the first thing Shang-Li saw was the blue energy of the Spellplague flickering through the ship.

"She's alive," Thava said as she leaped up from the ground to see across the dense brush.

At the front of the ship, Red Orchid shifted and moved as if coming awake. Amree still floated before her, gesturing and using a wand that glowed orange and wavered like a flame. Shang-Li took solace in the fact the creature was still alive, but he checked his hopes. Just because Red Orchid had survived didn't mean she was whole, or even that she could help them keep *Swallow* under control once they started for the surface.

And the Blue Lady's messenger had still not appeared.

He chased the dark thoughts from his mind for the moment and continued swimming toward the ship.

Upon arrival at *Swallow*, Shang-Li swam into the hold and crawled into the air space Amree had created. The bubble was considerably larger and lines had been run to keep the ship from floating up from the sea floor prematurely. The feat buoyed the hopes of all aboard. But *Swallow* wasn't yet seaworthy.

"You found *Grayling*?" His father abandoned the kitchen to one of the sailors, wiped his hands on his apron, and joined Shang-Li at a table they'd salvaged.

"Yes." Shang-Li removed the oilskin pouch he'd found aboard the shipwreck. He hadn't wanted to chance opening it anywhere else rather than chance the sea destroying the books after all these years.

"These are Liou Chang's books?"

"Let's find out." Shang-Li untied the clever knots that kept the protective pouch sealed. It took effort to keep himself calm. He upended the bag and the books slid into his waiting hand.

All of them were journals written by Bayel Droust, and all of them were from times before *Grayling* had sunk beneath the waves.

"Regrettable." His father clapped him on the shoulder.

Holding his anger and frustration in check, Shang-Li pushed the books away from him on the table. "They're still out there. I failed."

"No, my son." Kwan Yung's voice was soft and carried only to Shang-Li's ears. "If this mission meets with failure, it is *our* failure. Not yours to bear alone." He paused. "Besides, the books are still out there, as you have said. We haven't failed yet."

Shang-Li returned to the world outside, feeling more tense, more anxious. Amree was still using her magic to soothe Red Orchid. A dozen sailors were checking nad tightening the lines. If they didn't find the journals of Liou Chang, all the efforts would come to nothing once the Blue Lady used the portal spells to escape her prison.

He approached Thava and Iados, who were explaining to Captain Chiang how they had found the *Grayling* and been attacked. Captain Chiang nodded to Shang-Li as he came near.

"Do you know where the Nine Golden Swords' ship is?" Captain Chiang asked.

"No," Shang-Li said. "We didn't see them again after we left the canyon."

"Gods willing," Iados growled unpleasantly, "the ones we left behind became meals for some of the monsters we've seen down here." He glanced at Thava. "I suppose you have no objection to that?"

"As long as I don't have to watch, no." Thava lounged against the ship's hull with her helm next to her.

"Then we don't know if our enemies are near or far," Chiang stated. He didn't look happy.

"Near enough," Shang-Li said.

"But we don't know if they've a mage that has figured out a solution to eating and drinking while underwater." Chiang smoothed his beard. "They could be in dire straits. Desperate men make mistakes."

"Desperate men," Iados said, "also do desperate things. And they didn't act like men thirsting to death. They were fit, able. We'll do well to post extra guards until we're clear of this situation."

Chiang nodded. "Agreed. I'll amend the roster. It will cut back on the amount of sleep the men are getting. They're not going to be happy about that."

"It beats waking with a knife in your throat," the tiefling pointed out.

Chiang gave him a thin smile. "It would have been better if the survivor you brought back was a warrior. Or, gods willing, a wizard. That way we would have had more defensive capability instead of just another mouth to feed."

"Perhaps, but I think it's going to be a while before we see *better*."

Amree swam toward them. The ship's mage looked worse than she had the last time he'd seen her, worn down and exhausted, but she was no longer favoring her injured hand.

"How is Red Orchid?" Shang-Li asked.

"Better. Getting stronger. I think she's acclimating to the ship well. She seems to be herself and says her strength is quickly coming back."

"How soon before we can float the ship?" Shang-Li asked.

"Come see," she said, and led them back into the hold. Treated canvas, coated with tar so it was virtually airproof, covered the ceiling.

"We've nailed over the holds to contain the air as I make it," she said. "And I'm continuing to make air every day, but I can't do that and make repairs at the same time. Attending to Red Orchid has also set me behind in my schedule, but I think the good she will do will offset that." Seated on a crate, she drew her legs up and encircled them with her arms. "However, as I've considered our situation, I've realized we have a new problem I hadn't counted on."

"What?"

"Ballast. In order to get *Swallow* to float faster, we're going to have to rid her of the ballast. I can't make enough air to overcome all that weight."

Shang-Li looked at the rocks that covered the bottom of the cargo hold.

"What's the problem?" Iados asked. "Getting rid of the rock only makes sense. There's less weight to lift. Seems like the only set back there would be having to move all of it."

"That will be a chore," Amree agreed. "But ballast aboard a ship is important."

"Only if you're attached to all those rocks."

"Those rocks," Chiang said, "keep the ship balanced while in the ocean. If a ship is not properly weighted down, she would turn over every time the wind blew. She'd float like a cork on the water and have no control. Every time we take on cargo, it has to be carefully configured. We take on more cargo, we offload ballast. We don't take on enough cargo, we have to load ballast."

"So if *Swallow* goes up without ballast," Iados said, "there's no guarantee she'll be right side up on the sea surface. Even with Red Orchid's help."

"Or, if by chance we do go straight up, she might not stay that way. If she falls over on her side in the ocean, we could right her again because we have longboats that weren't destroyed. And we'd need to be able to shift ballast to aid in that." Amree glanced at Shang-Li. "Though I would like one or two more longboats. Supply boats filled with food and water. Just in case the ship doesn't survive and we do."

Kwan Yung came out of the dry area and stood beside them. Still embarrassed by his mistake, Shang-Li found himself watching Amree intently, rather than catch his father's eye.

"We'll have to pull them into the dry area and get them properly stored before we try to ascend." Amree bit her lip. "There's also another problem."

"We seem to be harvesting a veritable bumper crop of them as we sit here," Iados commented.

"I don't know how far down we are," the ship's mage said. "I've seen what happens to men who stay down too deep too long and come up too fast. Sometimes they die, but when they don't they are left with withered and weak bodies."

A chill passed through Shang-Li as he remembered the sailors he'd seen that had suffered the malady while helping with salvage operations or treasure hunting. They'd gotten caught out in the depths when their water-breathing potions had become exhausted and had swum as quickly as they could to the surface. Most hadn't made it, but nearly all of the others had been left crippled. No one knew why the sickness struck.

"A person, maybe two," Amree said, "I could protect from the sickness. But I can't protect this ship's crew from something like that."

"We still have the water-breathing potions," Shang-Li reminded. "We could all drink one of them before we begin the ascent. The potion should protect us."

"Are you willing to bet your life on that?" Amree demanded. "The lives of this crew?"

Shang-Li looked into her eyes and remained calm. "I know that if we remain here," he said, "we're going to die. There are too many things in this place that are only too happy to hunt us."

Amree gazed fiercely at the tarp. "I just wish I could create enough air *now* so I would know. One way or the other. I don't like waiting. When I do, my mind has more than enough time to figure out all the things that could go wrong."

Kwan Yung spoke softly but his voice drew all of them. "Once you have planned for everything bad to happen that you can, once you have made all preparations, it is always better to plan for things going right. Let planning take over when—and *if*—there is need." He nodded toward her. "You should get some sleep. We all should. The time will come when we will need it."

"Awake, manling."

Drowsy and worn, Shang-Li opened his eyes and was surprised to find that he was still in the hold. The light from the glowstones staved off some of the sea's chill. He looked around and saw many sailors slumbering around him. His father sat at the table and read through Bayel Droust's journals, though Shang-Li had read through enough of them that he was certain nothing of consequence to their present predicaments would be found.

The Blue Lady stood in the center of the hold and looked around with casual disdain. "So this is what has been occupying your time?" She walked toward the canopy of air that had swelled so large in the emptiness.

Swallow twisted at the ends of the ropes anchoring her to the sea floor. Over the last few hours, she'd threatened to pull free of the moorings twice. Only Red Orchid's warning about the slack had prevented that.

The Blue Lady touched the air-filled bubble with a long-nailed hand. She smiled coldly. "You fight against the sea. I had to accept it as my home even though it fought me at first."

Soundlessly, Shang-Li rose to his feet. His fighting sticks dropped into his hands.

"You would only be wasting your time, manling." The Blue Lady peered at him. "And if you wake your friends, I'll kill them here and now, and I'll destroy this ship."

Shang-Li forced his breath out. "What do you want?" He spoke softly so he wouldn't wake the sleeping sailors or alert his father, though he didn't understand how Kwan Yung could be unaware of the Blue Lady's presence.

"I have masked myself and you to them. If anyone looks, they'll see you still sleeping there."

Shang-Li looked back at the spot he'd just vacated. He gazed in stunned fascination at himself sleeping there, and was surprised at how haggard and thin he looked. Cold and fearful, he turned back to the Blue Lady.

"I don't want them to be harmed."

"Good. Then you will come to me. Follow."

Tucking his fighting sticks back into his sleeves, Shang-Li walked through the sleeping crew. No one, not even his father, noticed his passage. Nor did the guards Captain Chiang had assigned to their posts. Even brave Thava remained unaware of him as he passed by her.

Shang-Li had never seen a spell so powerful.

In the forest, the tentacled things and the sea shambles drew back from the Blue Lady.

"They know you are under my protection. They will not harm you."

All the same, Shang-Li stepped warily and watched all the creatures as they trailed after him. He felt confident he could escape them if it came to that, but possibly not if one of them seized him first. And definitely not if more than one got hold of him.

Only a short distance farther on, the Blue Lady came to a stop and pointed her sharp chin at a man standing in the shadows of the swaying trees. "Follow him to my home. There we will see if I was wrong in keeping you alive. If I was, you will die to pay for my mistake. But if I was right, you can live to serve me."

Shang-Li knew that would never happen, but he didn't say so. He concentrated on the figure beneath the tree. There was something familiar about the man.

"Come forward."

The man stepped from the shadows and Shang-Li recognized him.

"I am Bayel Droust." The man spoke politely, but the fear of the Blue Lady was alive in him.

"You should be dead by now." Shang-Li spoke before he thought about it. Instead, Bayel Droust only looked the same age he had in the drawings Shang-Li had seen of the man. He should have been old for a human, older than Shang-Li's father.

The Blue Lady waved that away. "Long life is part of my gift to Bayel Droust for his continued obedience. But I shouldn't reward all those years of failures. As you can see, I can be generous."

Droust said nothing in his defense, only kept his head bent and his gaze resting on the sea floor. "Yes, lady."

The Blue Lady turned to Shang-Li. "Follow him. I will

be waiting for you. If you do not, I will bring doom to all of your friends."

Without another word, the Blue Lady disappeared.

"You are Shang-Li." Droust lifted his eyes. "Of the Standing Tree Monastery."

"I am Shang-Li, but not necessarily of the Standing Tree Monastery. I work with them and with my father, but I am my own man."

"She thinks you can decipher Liou Chang's books."

"Perhaps." Shang-Li tried to temper his immediate dislike of the man and not think of all the deaths that might have been prevented if Droust had somehow gotten word to the surface world about the Blue Lady. Then he realized that wasn't fair. He didn't know what Droust's circumstances were during the intervening years.

"Do you know what secrets the books hold?"

"The secret of portal travel, you mean?"

"I do." Droust shook his head and frowned. "Though it would doom you, and perhaps me, I pray that you aren't successful. If you are, all of the Sea of Fallen Stars is in danger. Perhaps all of Faerun. She will amass an army and bring war to our world from another plane."

"I know that."

"Then why did you agree to come?"

"Because I don't want my friends killed."

Droust muttered a curse. "She will only kill them anyway. She hasn't let anyone go from this place. Even her lackeys, the Nine Golden Swords warriors she lures down here, are never freed. She doesn't want the surface world to know anything about her."

Shang-Li knew that, but having the possibility put into words was disheartening.

"We must go to her citadel." Droust stepped up into the water and started swimming.

"I suppose it would have been too much trouble for her to bring us along when she left."

"She was never here. That was only an image. Down here, she's very powerful."

"She's powerful on the surface as well." Shang-Li swam after Droust.

"Yes, but she's more vulnerable the farther she goes from this place."

"Why?"

"The other eladrin that banned Caelynna from the Feywild tied her to this place. The curse they used was twofold. She is stronger here, but she's tied to this place as well. Leaving her could kill her."

"Stronger than she was there?" Sea shambles moved below Shang-Li but couldn't keep up with the two of them. Tentacled things reached from the tree branches but fell short.

"I believe so, though I don't know for sure."

"Do you know why they exiled her from the Feywild?"

"Because they weren't able to kill her." The land elevated slightly and some of the terrain looked familiar. "She made enemies. Powerful enemies. Other than that, I don't know."

Shang-Li looked at the other man. "All these years you've been down here, you've never learned more than that?"

Droust rolled over in the water to face him. "For the last seventy years," he said in a harsh voice, "I have spent every waking hour of every day wondering if I was going to live. I've seen thousands of people die in that time, or stumbled over their corpses when I searched shipwrecks at her orders. I haven't had the luxury of learning much more than how to stay alive, and how miserable such an existence can be."

Chastened, Shang-Li decided not to ask any more questions about Droust's motivations. His actions spoke even more eloquently of the terror he'd been subjected to. The man had trouble making eye contact and constantly searched all around him for creeping things.

"I wasn't trained for this." Droust resumed swimming. "Not fighting. Not survival. I'm a scribe. A good one. And

I couldn't even translate Liou Chang's books. I've failed at the one thing I'm good at."

"I might not be able to translate it either."

"I've consoled myself with thoughts that my failure could possibly be the greatest thing I've ever done. But if you translate those books and find that spell, you need to know she'll kill you. And probably me as well. And definitely your friends. She'll use them as she has used others."

"What do you mean?"

Droust took a breath and let it out. "Caelynna, the Blue Lady, sometimes sacrifices groups of those she has allowed to survive their plummet into the sea because she can use them for other things."

Cold dread squirmed within Shang-Li's stomach.

"That's right," Droust whispered. "She hasn't let them live just because she wanted you to have company. She was waiting on the moon cycle. Tonight it will be full. And when it is, she can have her creatures descend on those people in that ship and kill them all. The ritual requires blood and power, and it allows her to reach into the Feywild for things—creatures as well as plants. She transplants them here and lets the spellplague residue change some of them into even more dangerous things." He glanced at Shang-Li. "Perhaps some of your friends will come back as those morbid creatures."

"The sea shambles?"

"I hadn't heard them called that, but the name is a good one. As far as I know, they have no other name."

"How long is it until moonrise?"

Droust shook his head. "I only know that Caelynna has been preparing for the ritual for the past few days. I knew she wouldn't do it with you there. Not until she was certain you weren't able to translate those books." He paused. "And she may decide to replace me with you. Otherwise she'll kill you." He looked at Shang-Li. "I don't know which to hope for."

CHAPTER TWENTY

The citadel looked exactly as Shang-Li remembered it. Tumbled down and scattered, with only a few sections remaining, the edifice didn't look grand or imposing, though a hint of past majesties remained.

"Did this come from our world?" Shang-Li asked. "Or from another or the Feywild?"

"I don't know. There's writing on some of the buildings, but I don't recognize any of it. And there are three iterations of the same language, possibly generational changes, or there are two languages, and one possibly has iteration. I'm not certain."

Shang-Li's curiosity rose immediately, then died just as suddenly as he spotted the squid-looking thing lurking behind the main building. "What is that thing?"

Droust looked, then shook his head. "It's another of Caelynna's possessions that has no name."

"She created that as well?"

"No. It was here from what I gather. She conquered and enthralled the creature. Now it does her bidding."

Shang-Li looked at the creature. "But it's not free?"

"Nothing," Droust said morosely, "that lives within this place is free."

Shang-Li swam after Droust. Together, they swam through the sunken remains of the citadel. What remained of the buildings was beautiful. The stone was mostly white and pale pink even in the blue glow. None of it was cut; all of a natural shape and size, chosen specifically to fit into the structures. Long covered walkways, some of them broken, ran on different levels from one section of the building to another, allowing for many outside areas that probably once offered magnificent views of the building and the grounds.

"I have another place where I work." Droust alighted on a balcony that overlooked the collapsed center of the building. In the past, it might have overlooked a flower garden, judging from the space before it. "But this is where Caelynna keeps Liou Chang's books under lock and key and guard."

As soon as they entered the hallway, a group of Nine Golden Swords warriors waited with swords in their fists.

"Ah, the monk," one of the Nine Golden Swords said. A predatory smile stretched across his face. "I'd heard you survived. For now."

Shang-Li ignored the man as he walked past, but he listened to the man's breathing to see if there would be a shift that noted movement on the man's part.

"Another time, monk," the warrior promised. "When you aren't a protected plaything of the Blue Lady."

Almost immediately, Shang-Li dismissed the man from his mind. The Nine Golden Swords were the least of his worries at the moment. Above the sea, the day was draining and the full moon would wax. He couldn't stay inside the citadel without warning his father and his friends, and he couldn't leave Liou Chang's books in the hands of the Blue Lady.

The hall continued for some distance before turning to the right. Droust pointed to a door flanked by four Nine Golden Swords members. They bared their weapons at Shang-Li's approach but offered no direct threat.

"They don't like you." Droust halted in front of the door and waited as one of the Nine Golden Swords members used an ornate key on the lock.

"We share a long and blood-soaked history," Shang-Li said. "I have never cared much for thieves and murderers. Obviously the feeling is reciprocated."

The Nine Golden Swords warriors merely grinned and cursed him. One of them spat at Shang-Li, but the effort was wasted under the ocean.

Droust led the way through the doors into a large, ornate library lit by massive glowstones. The sea remained locked outside the doors as though a wall of glass separated the interior of the room from the hallway. One of the Nine Golden Swords warriors stuck his head through the opening and his wet beard dripped onto the floor as he grinned evilly.

"Caelynna understands she has to keep this room dry if I am to work." Droust walked behind a dressing screen, then pointed to another on the other side of the room. "You'll find dry robes there. Get out of your wet clothing. You can't get the books fouled."

Shang-Li walked behind the other dressing screen and reluctantly took off his leather armor. He didn't like being left so unprotected and unarmed in the midst of the Nine Golden Swords, but he didn't want to ruin the books either. Once he was dressed in the simple gown, he joined Droust at a large marble table in the center of the room.

Despair filled Shang-Li as he looked at the empty shelves that lined the walls.

"I know," Droust said. "I felt the same way. When I was given this room, the shelves were full of books."

"Where are they now?"

"Molded. Ruined. A long time before my arrival. Caelynna chased the water from this room and set it up for me to work on Liou's books. I had to throw away the old books. Nothing of them could be saved. It was one of the hardest things I've ever done. I've worried for years about all that was lost of whomever lived here." The scribe peered around the room. "I'd never thought I'd ever be cloistered away for so very long in one place." He glanced at Shang-Li. "But you're probably used to that."

"No." Shang-Li had loved the monastery, but he had loved the forests and even the cities more. Mostly he had loved the adventures, the new experiences that came on a nearly daily pace. "Where are the books?"

Droust hesitated. He crossed the floor and took a crystal from a gold chain around his neck. As he pressed the crystal near a blank section in the bookshelves, a keyhole appeared. The scribe thrust the crystal home and twisted.

A moment later, a thick stone door opened on a stone box that suddenly appeared. Droust reached into the box with reverence and took out two books. He turned and carefully brought them back to Shang-Li.

Handling the books delicately, Shang-Li placed them side by side on the table and began flipping them open one at a time. With them juxtaposed, he hoped that he could pick up any redundancies Liou Chang might have used in his code work.

The passages were written in script that Shang-Li didn't recognize from any of the languages he knew or was familiar with.

"They're written in artificial languages," Droust said.

"I know." Shang-Li carefully turned the neatly lettered pages. "I've read some of his other books. My father made me translate much of Liou's work while I was growing up at the monastery. He's an authority on Liou Chang."

"Then why isn't he here?"

"Because my father is an excellent academician, but I'm better at breaking codes. Besides that, the Blue Lady wanted me here." Shang-Li looked at Droust. "I'm going to ask you a simple question, and I want you to think about your answer before you give it. Do you understand?"

"Yes."

"Do you want to escape the Blue Lady?"

Droust's face pulled tight in consternation. "What are you talking about? That's foolishness. It can't be done."

"But if it could?"

The scribe held his tongue.

"It's better if you live another seventy years or more in captivity to the Blue Lady?"

Droust lowered his gaze. "No. It's not better."

"Then let me secure these books so they won't be damaged by the sea." Shang-Li returned to the dressing screen for his bag. "Does the Blue Lady watch over you while you're here?"

"Sometimes. But she's going to be deep into the ritual she's preparing to sacrifice your shipmates."

Shang-Li thrust the books into the bag and they promptly disappeared. Despite the addition, the bag was still almost weightless. Then he dressed himself in his sodden clothing and armor.

Droust changed as well and stood ready, though frightened.

"Can you use a weapon?" Shang-Li asked.

Droust shook his head. "As I said, I'm only a scribe."

"Then do your best to stay out of the way."

Droust looked toward the door where the Nine Golden Swordsmen stood guard. Though the doors were closed, their voices outside were loud as they swapped lies and told of conquests with women and games of chance.

"They will never let us by."

"That's our second option." Shang-Li crossed the room and began examining the walls. "Doesn't it strike you as strange that in a room this large and—once upon a time—so important would only have one exit? Especially in a building as the size of this one?"

Droust looked thoughtful and scared. "I've never thought about it."

That's what comes of leading a cloistered life, Shang-Li thought. The edge on your curiosity dulls. He slipped a fighting stick from his sleeve and tapped on the wall.

"You think there's a secret passageway?"

Shang-Li snorted. "Of course I do. Anyone in a citadel like this would want one in case of attack, or for the household staff to use to stay out of sight. Or perhaps for spying on guests."

"I've never noticed one."

"Have you ever looked?"

"No."

"Perhaps that's why. Now be quiet and let me listen." Shang-Li worked slowly, taking his time as he went around the room. Finally he located a section he thought was hollow from the sound of his taps.

Slipping his knife from his boot, Shang-Li pried around the edges of the stones. Even after all the years of being at the bottom of the sea and surviving the Spellplague, the mortar remained tight and complete. After a while, he thought he'd been mistaken about the hollow space, that perhaps it had only been a void after all. Time leaked away from him, slid like oil from a clenched fist. He couldn't bear the thought of his father and friends dying without having a chance to defend themselves or escape.

Then his clever fingers found a release near the juncture of wall and floor. The release only moved a fraction of an inch, and even after all this time it moved smoothly. Locks *snicked* open.

Droust let out a strangled cry and looked back over his

shoulder at the entrance. For a moment Shang-Li thought perhaps the scribe was going to shout a warning. He tightened his grip on the fighting stick and readied himself to ram it into Droust's throat to silence him.

Visibly shaken, Droust watched the door, then turned back to Shang-Li. "They didn't hear that."

"Good." Shang-Li stood and opened the hidden doorway. It only moved a few inches, blocked by fallen stone. The opening wasn't large enough to squeeze more than his head through.

"What's wrong?" Droust pressed in close to him and tried to look for himself.

"The passageway's partially collapsed." Shang-Li held out his glowstone. "But the passage continues. What's in the room next to us?"

"A sitting room. Perhaps a place where library guests went to eat and compare notes."

"Is the door locked?"

"No. The guards use it to store provisions and clothing."

"All right. Then we go there."

Droust stepped in front of Shang-Li. "You can't be serious."

"I'm not staying here. Not when my father and friends are at risk and unaware of the danger they're in."

Droust pointed at the doorway. "There are four men out there. Warriors."

Shang-Li shook his fighting sticks out into his waiting hands. "I didn't say it would be easy." He looked at Droust. "Now are you with me? Or are you the first opponent I have to take down?"

Apprehensively, Droust stepped aside.

"The Blue Lady won't be quick to kill us." Shang-Li strode for the door and forced his fear away. "Those men have standing orders not to kill you. You can wait here and claim that I overpowered you, or you can come with me."

Droust hesitated only a moment. "I'll come."

"Try to stay out of the way. We're going to the room next

door and find the passageway there. Then we try to lose ourselves until we find a way out."

"All right."

Shang-Li nodded toward the door. "Open it."

Trembling visibly, Droust pulled the door wide.

The two Nine Golden Swords closest to the entrance turned to face the door, but they didn't move as if they were expecting trouble. Shang-Li stepped among them, feeling the ocean close around him again as he walked from the dry room into the sea-filled passageway. A chill permeated him and he couldn't resist the unconscious reaction of holding his breath when the water surrounded him.

He swung the fighting stick in his right hand in a backward strike that caught the man on the right in the temple. The warrior sagged and fell slowly toward the floor. The other warrior thrust his sword, but Shang-Li parried it with his fighting stick and pivoted on the ball of his left foot to deliver a roundhouse kick with his right foot that caught the man in the jaw and knocked him back into one of his companions.

Forcing himself to breathe, Shang-Li stepped between Droust and the other Nine Golden Swords warriors. "Move! Quickly!"

Droust scuttled out of the library and headed up the hallway to the next door.

"Big mistake, monk." The warrior on the right advanced and readied his sword. "The Blue Lady only needs one of you alive."

Shang-Li stepped toward the man, feinting to the right, then blocking the man's sword thrust with both his fighting sticks. Spotting the second man up and swinging now, Shang-Li spun his head down to his knee and turned around to sweep the man's legs from beneath him. As the man fell backward, Shang-Li went smoothly from the spin into a hands-free cartwheel over the other man's sword. Using his left stick to shield his right arm from the man's backward blow, feeling the impact numb his arm, he stepped forward and dragged the end of the right stick along the man's sternum. The Nine Golden Swords warrior screamed loudly and dropped to his knees right before he passed out.

The final guard sprinted backward and let out a yell.

Other guards came on the double, filling the other end of the hall.

Shang-Li turned back and saw Bayel Droust opening the next door. The scribe made it inside just before Shang-Li followed at his heels. Droust cursed helplessly as he fumbled his glowstone from his pouch and held it aloft.

Mold and debris filled the room. Broken shelving hung on the walls and a table looked like a squashed bug in the center of the floor. Someone had cleaned one corner of the room, and provisions were stored there as well as polearms.

"Check the wall." Shang-Li slid a stone shard under the door and kicked it hard to set it. The stone wouldn't hold against an assault for long, but he hoped it would last long enough. By the time he reached the opposite wall and the first blows and curses from the arriving guards beat at the door,

"Here." Droust indicated a wall section that was almost a match in location to the one in the last room. He shoved timbers out of the way in his haste to clear the area. "I can't find the locking mechanism."

Shang-Li knelt, found the release, and swung the door open. Hinges creaked in protest at the unaccustomed movement. Thankfully they were fashioned of stone and not metal. Otherwise they would have rusted away.

The pounding at the door and the curses gathered intensity. The alarm was doubtless already being delivered throughout the citadel.

Droust peered cautiously into the passageway. "We don't know where this leads."

"Away from here." Shang-Li shoved past the other man and took out his own glowstone. "For now, that's enough."

He closed the door and locked it. The Nine Golden Swords warriors would struggle to find the secret of the door as well. Hopefully by the time that they did, Shang-Li would be lost to them within the passageways. He held the glow-stone up and went forward as fast as he felt he could across the debris-strewn floor.

Only a short distance farther on, the passageway forked. Shang-Li examined each of the new paths but saw no markings that indicated where they might lead. He chose the one on the right just so they could keep moving. Thirty feet later, as near as he could figure, he turned another corner and found a set of stairs leading down.

"Should we turn around?" Droust stood at Shang-Li's back and peered down.

"No."

"What do you think is down there?"

"Haven't you ever prowled through a castle or manor house?"

Droust shook his head. "I think that would have been frowned upon."

"Probably. The thing is, all passageways eventually lead to the kitchen or from the kitchen."

"We don't want to go to the kitchen."

"Actually, the kitchen would be good. Kitchens lead to wine cellars with their own entrances from the outside, as well as sewers."

"You're assuming the lower part of this building still exists."

Shang-Li started forward again, conscious of time slipping past him. "We have to assume it does. Otherwise we're going to be backtracking."

A short time later, Shang-Li stared in disbelief at the utter destruction that had been left of the kitchen. Tumbled down stone blocks filled the area and rendered it impassible.

"Back." Shang-Li slid by Droust and went back the way they'd come. "We still have the other fork to explore."

Long minutes later, Shang-Li followed the other passageway up steep steps that twisted in a lazy spiral. Unfortunately the new path didn't have any side doors that allowed them to exit. And the passageway kept going up. Occasionally they heard the loud voices of the Nine Golden Swords warriors on the other side of the wall, but they were gradually leaving those behind.

"This isn't good."

Shang-Li paused while every nerve in his body screamed at him to be moving. His father was out there—in danger. And Shang-Li had delivered Thava and Iados into the greatest foe they'd ever faced.

"Why?" Shang-Li held the glowstone so it shined into Droust's face.

"The upper part of the citadel is off limits to everyone." Droust sucked in air because they'd been moving quickly. "This is where Caelynna works her strongest spells."

"She wouldn't trap herself." Shang-Li turned and went on. "There has to be a way out." His legs burned from the sustained effort and the fatigue that had been built up over the last several days. He pushed away the pain and tiredness and tapped reserves he'd been trained to access in the monastery.

Then the passageway leveled off. Lifting the glowstone, Shang-Li studied the hallway and found the latch for a doorway a stone's throw ahead. He glanced at Droust.

"Do you know where we are?"

"No. But this has to be in the upper portions of the citadel, as I said."

Shang-Li pressed his ear to the door and listened intently, but heard nothing. Then he dropped to a prone position on his chest and smelled at the juncture of the door and the wall. Only the smell of rot and the sea filled his nostrils.

Cautiously, he drew his fighting sticks, hid his glowstone and made sure Droust did the same, then disengaged the lock and opened the door.

On the other side, the room was silent and still. Rubble covered the floor and cracks parted the ceiling in places, though none of them were large enough for them to crawl through. The door on the other side of the room stood ajar, but a streamer of harsh blue light cut through the darkness and power hummed around Shang-Li.

"It's Caelynna." Droust plucked at Shang-Li's sleeve. "She's beginning the ritual.

Shang-Li's heart sped up a little and he wondered if he was already too late to help his father and friends and the rest of the ship's crew. Despite the fear clinging to him even more heavily than Droust, he crept across the room and peered out.

The top floor of the citadel was made in the round. Other doors, broken or missing, framed five other room off the main room, which was circular. The design gave the citadel's master a common area for his guests to meet. A brick firepit sat in the middle of the circular room. Two doorways led from the common room.

The Blue Lady floated in the water above the firepit. Her hands stayed busy as she sang or spoke in languorous syllables that Shang-Li didn't recognize. They sounded like the elven tongues he knew, but these words were decidedly different. Despite the soft sibilance of her voice, the words came out harsh and sharp, as if filled with razor-sharp thorns.

Sharks swam around her in lazy circles, weaving a protective net.

Shang-Li had never killed anyone from behind, never ambushed anyone with lethal results, but as he stood there, he was sorely tempted. If he could have struck without alerting the sharks and getting intercepted, he felt certain he would have.

Shang-Li looked back at Droust, wanting to make certain the main remained stable. Evidently the Blue Lady wasn't too concerned over their escape. Why would she be? She planned on killing everyone.

The Blue Lady stopped speaking and an azure tear formed in the water and glowed. Unconsciously, the Blue Lady raised her hands in defense. For just a moment, fear eroded the confidence on her face.

A male eladrin's face, handsome and eerie and cruel, formed in the azure tear as it grew larger. He spoke in a harsh voice that filled the large room with thunder. Shang-Li recognized the name Droust had referred to her by: Caelynna.

The Blue Lady interrupted the man's guttural venting with her own. She laughed at him and mocked some of the words he used.

Angrily, the eladrin thrust his head and one arm through the azure tear as it grew large enough to allow him. Lightning suddenly filled the room. One of the bolts smacked into the wall near Shang-Li's head and he was blown backward.

CHAPTER TWENTY-ONE

Blind and deafened for a moment, Shang-Li held onto his fighting sticks and rolled to his feet. He'd been trained to fight blind, and he already knew where he was in the room and how large the room was. He even remembered where most of the debris was. Crossing his arms over himself, he waited for the first of his foes to arrive.

When someone grabbed his forearm, Shang-Li almost lashed out. Then he recognized the weak grip as Droust's, not a Nine Golden Swords warrior seizing him or the razor-slash mouth of a shark. He blinked his eyes and made out shapes through the shadows of the room.

"Are you all right?" Droust leaned his head close to Shang-Li's as he whispered.

Shang-Li nodded and tried to slow his beating

heart. He stared at the door, expecting discovery at any moment. When it didn't come, he returned to the doorway and peered out.

The sharks floated in the water, their flesh torn and bloody, all of them dead weight now. The Blue Lady stood in the midst of swirling currents that lashed her hair around. She held out a hand to the azure tear and squeezed it down to nothing. Then she whirled on her heel and marched from the room.

Cautiously, certain that at any moment he and Droust would be discovered, Shang-Li hid. Then he thought of his father and the others and knew that he couldn't balk. Hiding in that room wasn't an option.

He stepped out into the circular room and chose the door opposite the one the Blue Lady had departed through. He shoved one of the floating shark corpses from his path. Then blue incandescence dawned again over the fireplace.

Turning with his fighting sticks in his hand, Shang-Li watched as the azure tear formed again. He grabbed Droust and got the scribe moving toward the other door, following at his heels.

"Hold," a voice ordered in Common. "If you would save your lives, listen to me." In the azure tear, looking smaller and pained, the eladrin male stared at Shang-Li. "We have a common enemy."

Shang-Li halted. After seeing what the eladrin had done to the sharks, it was doubtful he would reach the doorway without suffering the same fate. "What do you want?"

"I am Fergraff, a prince of the Shining Valley," the eladrin said. Only his face showed in the azure tear now. "I have a boon to ask, but I think it's one that you would willingly take up."

Hesitating, Shang-Li knew that every moment he wasted put him that much later to reaching his father.

"You can't escape Caelynna's wrath, Shang-Li." Fergraff spoke with conviction. "She's grown powerful there in that place, and it's our fault. When we banished her from the Feywild, we didn't know she would master the elements of that sea as she has. We expected her to be imprisoned, not becoming an even stronger menace to us."

But you didn't care if she became a threat in our world, did you? Shang-Li thought. Not until she became a threat to yours again. The question was on the tip of his tongue but he held it there.

"Caelynna calls to us, taunting with her plans." Fergraff's image shimmered a little, as if the connection to the Feywild wasn't secure. "We know what she's pursuing."

Shang-Li kept himself from reaching for Liou Chang's books in his bag.

"Even if she isn't able to glean the secrets from the books she has in her possession," Fergraff said, "Caelynna will keep searching for a way to come back here."

"I don't have time for this." Shang-Li shifted. "My friends, my father, are in danger. I have to go."

A look of irritation flitted across the eladrin's cruel face. They didn't like the other races to begin with, and getting talked to with such casual irreverence had to go down hard.

"You must stop Caelynna before she can perform the ritual. But you're not strong enough to do it on your own."

"Then help us," Shan-Li said.

"We can't. If we step through the gate into your world, the spells we have holding Caelynna in the sea will be broken. She'll be able to come back here with all her increased power intact. We won't be able to stand against her."

Shang-Li grew angrier as he realized the eladrin didn't intend to take an active part in confronting the Blue Lady. He didn't know if they were afraid of her or afraid of the realm she'd created.

"If you're not going to help, we're done here." Shang-Li turned to go.

"Wait! We can help. We just can't join you there. We must preserve the our powers as much as we can in the event we are forced to face her here."

"Moral support isn't going to do much good." Shang-Li put venom into his words as he thought of his father and the others.

"We can give you a weapon to fight her. One that will be powerful enough to damage her. And we can get you back to your ship." The eladrin's face hardened. "Whether you live or die after that is up to you."

"What weapon?"

"A very special one, and one that you will feel at home with." Fergraff shoved a hand through the azure tear. In his hand, he held two fighting sticks.

"I already have those."

"Not like these." Fergraff shook the fighting sticks and blades flicked open to stand at ninety-degree angles to the sticks. "And together, they are more." He flicked the blades closed again and shoved the two ends of the fighting sticks together. When he removed his hands, they'd joined and lengthened, becoming a staff a few inches longer than Shang-Li was tall. Then the eladrin shook the staff again and the blades shot out the ends of the staff. "You can use this?"

Amazed and impressed at the sheer beauty and chilling threat of the weapon, Shang-Li accepted the staff. The wood tingled and felt alive in his hands. "I can use this. But how—" Even as he wondered how he could separate the staff into two parts, it separated and became two fighting sticks the right size. He flicked the blades out, then in, then joined the staff and made the blades flick at the ends again.

"It is our gift to you," Fergraff said. "Use it in good health, and we hope that you are successful."

Shang-Li separated the weapon into two fighting sticks again and slid them up his sleeves in place of his original fighting sticks, which he shoved in the back of his belt.

"Thank you for the gift." Shang-Li bowed slightly, but he never took his eyes from the eladrin's cruelly beautiful face. The dead sharks floating through the room provided a grim reminder of the Feywild's power. "Now about my return to the ship."

Fergraff tossed a black pearl into the room that descended slowly and burst into an oval a foot from the floor and just out of Shang-Li's reach. "That way will take you to your ship."

Shang-Li hesitated.

"You can trust me or not," the eladrin said in a cold voice. "But what good would it do for me to give you a weapon against Caelynna and not allow the use of it?"

"Thank you." Shang-Li stepped toward the spreading oval and felt the pull of it at once.

"You must hurry once you are there. Caelynna will not tarry."

Just before he entered the black pearl oval, Shang-Li glanced back at Bayel Droust. The scribe hesitated and looked helpless.

"I've got the books," Shang-Li said. "If they are not recovered—and I promise that I will see them destroyed before I allow them to fall into the hands of the Blue Lady—you know she will blame you for this. There won't be any reason for her to keep you alive."

"I know." Gathering himself, Droust followed Shang-Li into the blackness.

Once he entered the spell, Shang-Li's senses whirled and he felt lost. Fear ran rampant within him, and he knew that was part of the dark magic touching him as it worked on him. Droust keened and moaned, and Shang-Li couldn't find it within himself to fault the man.

Then, as quickly as it began, the spell ended. Shang-Li spewed out into the water above *Swallow*. His senses reeled so much that he at first didn't recognize the ship. Then he spotted Thava standing at the ship's prow gazing up at him. An instant later, Droust vomited forth into the sea as well. The scribe whirled end over end as he flailed awkwardly.

Turning in the water, Shang-Li tried to spot the Blue Lady

and her horde above the forest but saw nothing. Shambles and the tentacled things moved within the trees and brush, but they kept their distance from *Swallow*.

The ship shifted and rocked on the undersea currents. Ropes tied to stakes driven into the sea bed and some of the nearby trees held her down. Shang-Li hoped Amree had been able to make enough air to allow them to surface. He swam toward Droust, grabbed the man by his shirt, and pulled him down toward *Swallow*.

Thava met Shang-Li as he dropped to *Swallow's* forward deck. "How did you get up there? The last I saw you, you were sleeping. You've done so much lately that we let you sleep."

"That wasn't me. The Blue Lady took me and left an illusion behind. Get the others. We have to go. She's on her way here now with an army." Shang-Li ran to the prow and called the sailors in from their work on the hull. No more time could be afforded patching it.

He looked down at Red Orchid.

Red Orchid stretched herself on the prow and met his gaze. "We could have used more time, Shang-Li, but I am ready."

"Mielikki willing." Shang-Li quickly posted lookouts, then went below to find his father and Amree.

"We need more time." Amree looked as though she was about to fall over as she stood within the air bubble she'd created inside *Swallow's* hold.

"If I could make that happen for you, I would have. But all the Blue Lady was waiting on was the moon." Shang-Li glanced at his father. "We brought Liou Chang's books back with us." He held out the bag that contained the books.

His father took the books and nodded. "You've done well."

"Only if we live to tell of it."

"No." Kwan Yung shook his head. "Keeping the books

from the Blue Lady was success enough. I would like to return them to the monastery—"

"But if that doesn't look possible, we have to destroy them."

His father nodded and pain showed in his hazel eyes. "Of course, but I would rather concentrate on our escape."

"So would I." Shang-Li glanced around and saw Thava and Iados gearing up for contact.

"She's coming!" someone yelled. "The Blue Lady is coming!"

Shang-Li dived through the bottom of the opening at the bottom of the hold and through the tear in the hull. The tear was much smaller, but it hadn't been closed yet. They needed it for ease of access to get into the hold.

He shook the fighting sticks into his waiting hands and felt the power of them thrilling against his flesh as if they sensed the coming battle as well. His body flooded with blood and he cleared his head to ready himself mentally.

Over the top of the trees, the Blue Lady and her horde of creatures and Nine Golden Swords warriors swam toward *Swallow*. She rode the giant squid, which pulsed like a heart as it stayed at the forefront of the approaching danger.

"I see you have new toys." Iados stood at Shang-Li's side and nodded at the fighting sticks.

"Gifts." Shang-Li brandished them and black lightning seemed to shimmer through the wood. "They're supposed to be dangerous to the Blue Lady."

"Gods willing." Iados took a fresh grip on his blade.

"Remember the plan." Shang-Li flicked the blades out of his fighting sticks. "We fight them off only as far as we can breathe. Then we have no choice but to crawl within the ship."

Iados nodded grimly. "That's one detail I won't forget."

Captain Chiang stood in the sterncastle above. "Cut loose forward."

Red Orchid picked up the command. "Cut loose forward."

Immediately Shang-Li cut three of the ropes holding

Swallow down. He grabbed hold of the last rope with one hand and quickly threaded it through the belt of his leather armor. Iados, Thava, and two of the sailors did the same. *Swallow* angled upward.

The Blue Lady and her group swam faster, closing inhumanly quick.

"Cut loose stern," Captain Chiang ordered.

"Cut loose stern." Red Orchid's voice sounded strong and confident. Blue lightning threaded through *Swallow* and lit her up brightly in the water.

As soon as the lines were cut, *Swallow* rose toward the surface, slowly at first, but she gained speed quickly.

"No!" the Blue Lady shouted. She abandoned her mount and swam ahead of it.

"That squid is going to be a problem," Iados grumbled. "You might have mentioned that she had that."

The sharks reached *Swallow* first and attacked immediately. Shang-Li swung both fighting sticks, sinking the blades into the predators' flesh again and again. Streamers of blood trailed through the water. Iados split one of the sharks open with his sword. Thava swung her axe and caught another in the teeth, then the heavy blade cleaved away the top half of the shark's head.

The sailor in front of Shang-Li screamed in horror as a tentacled thing struck him in the face and a shamble grabbed him around the legs. Before Shang-Li could reach the man and offer help, the tentacled thing thrust an appendage through the man's eye and deep into his brain. Racked by death throes, the man released his weapon and stopped fighting. Unable to do anything else, Shang-Li cut the dead man free.

Red Orchid grew large and fierce at the prow. Her arms reached nearly ten feet in length and she broke and ripped Nine Golden Swords warriors and sea shambles alike as she battled.

The Blue Lady swam for Shang-Li and avoided Red

Orchid. "How did you escape?" she howled.

Shang-Li ignored her. The water was already getting hard to breathe, and the darkness around him told him that they were rising out of the safe zone. He held onto his fighting sticks and slashed at a Nine Golden Swords warrior that tried to impale him with a sword.

The Blue Lady's eyes blazed. She spun and threw a hand toward *Swallow*. Something shimmered through the water, then *Swallow* rocked violently onto her side. Blue lighting coursed through the ship as Red Orchid worked to right her.

"Shang-Li!" Iados scrambled up the line that led back into the ship's hold. "Come on!"

"You've doomed yourself, manling." The Blue Lady swam and effortlessly paced the rise of the ship dragging Shang-Li after it. "If you want to live—if you want your father to live—you'll surrender yourself and the books to me now. You can't get away." She threw another spell at *Swallow*. This time, in spite of the sea, part of the hull caught fire.

Amree swam from the hold. She had a rope tied around her upper body. She gestured toward the hull and another shimmer quieted the flames, leaving only scorched planks behind. Then the ship's mage spun toward the Blue Lady and flung out her hands. Bright sparks shot from her fingers and raced across the distance.

Before the spell reached her, the Blue Lady waved again. Something glimmered in front of her and the bright sparks extinguished with horrific cracks less than a foot in front of her. The bright explosions and sound seemed to leave her dazed. Recovering, she hurled another spell at Amree, but blue electricity from the ship's hull streaked out to intercept it.

Choking on the black water, Shang-Li watched as the squid wrapped its tentacles around Red Orchid and tried to pry her from *Swallow*. Red Orchid fought valiantly, but Shang-Li knew the squid was too large and too strong. Red Orchid would be ripped free of the ship and destroyed.

Brazen and bold, confident that she couldn't be hurt by him, the Blue Lady closed on Shang-Li. "I can let you live, manling. Give me what I desire, give me the secrets of those books and I will let you live. You and your father can be liaisons for me with the surface world. You can have good lives."

No longer able to breathe, Shang-Li couldn't answer. Instead, he struck with one of the fighting sticks. The Blue Lady put up an arm instinctively to block the blow and keep it from her face. The blade glowed with black fire, and cut deeply into her arm.

Howling in pain and surprise, the Blue Lady fell back. She clutched her wounded arm to her and glared at Shang-Li with murderous rage. "Now you have failed. There will be no mercy. I will destroy you all."

Shang-Li grabbed the rope and started up toward the ship. *Swallow* tossed and jerked out of control as Red Orchid desperately fought the squid. The blackness masked the ship from him and he couldn't clearly see how far he was from the hold. He climbed the rope as his lungs threatened to burst in the water he could no longer breathe.

CHAPTER TWENTY-TWO

Strength flagging, Shang-Li tried to hang onto the rope that shivered like a captured snake seeking escape. He hauled with one arm and reached with the other. The sea pressed against him now as the magic protecting the Blue Lady's lands waned. Pressure built up in his ears and he grew afraid they would burst. Pain throbbed through his skull and his lungs threatened to turn him inside out.

Then the rope jerked forward. For a moment he thought *Swallow* had shifted and nearly knocked him loose. With the next jerk, he realized that something—some*one*—was hauling him in. He focused on conserving his strength as the ship took shape before him. The huge shape of the monstrous squid wrapped around Red Orchid like some kind of obscene growth. Blue lightning flickered along the ship's hull.

Just when he was certain he could no longer hold his breath and his strength was fading, Shang-Li banged against the edge of the broken hull and slid inside. His head broke the water and he sucked in a lungful of air. Before he could recover, Thava yanked him up with one big hand and handed him a flask with the other.

"Quickly." The dragonborn pressed the flask against Shang-Li's lips while he was still taking deep breaths. "The water-breathing potion."

Remembering the damage that could be taken during a swift rise from the depths, Shang-Li took the flask and drank the contents. Almost immediately his breath turned to normal and the pressure in his ears from the ocean pressure subsided.

Swallow jerked again.

"The giant squid has Red Orchid." Shang-Li started for the hold, then saw that the air-filled canvas blocked the way.

"You can't go that way." Iados scowled. "We've got to hope she can hold her own until we reach the surface."

"She will." Amree spoke confidently. "Red Orchid is strong."

Two heads, both of them belonging to sea shambles, thrust through the opening in the hull. A sailor harpooned one of them and forced it back outside. Thava stomped the other shamble's head flat, breaking bone and smearing blood on the hull. The corpse slipped back through the water.

Shang-Li stumbled through the water and over the loose ballast covering the ship's hull as *Swallow* tossed. "Red Orchid's taking a beating."

"She's keeping us right-side up." Amree watched the air-filled canvas with concern.

"How much longer before we reach the surface?"

"I don't have any idea of how deep we were or how fast we're rising."

Iados cursed. "Not nearly fast enough."

Kwan Yung stood nearby. He locked eyes with Shang-Li and nodded. Another blow, this one from the Blue Lady Shang-Li was certain, rocked *Swallow*. All of them save for Kwan Yung and Amree feel to the floor. A half-dozen or more sea shambles clustered around the hull break like barnacles and tried to force their way inside. Shang-Li seized the fighting sticks and joined the battle. In short order the sea shambles were dispatched.

A moment later, pale light dawned against the canvas straining against the hold.

Swallow popped up, then settled back down into the water and rolled over onto her starboard side. The rent in the ship's side showed a patch of blue sky and white clouds.

"We made it." Iados's words sounded like a cheer.

"Not yet." Shang-Li climbed the floor of the ship and up the wall until he reached the rent. Thava and Iados followed at his heels.

"Haul that canvas down," Amree shouted at the sailors she'd selected to trap the air in the canvas. "If you don't keep that air in *Swallow's* guts, we're going to end up back at the bottom of the sea."

Shang-Li hauled himself through the rent and stood once more in the warm moonlight. His heart sang for just a moment, then the Nine Golden Swords warriors, the sea shambles, and the tentacled things all surfaced and clambered up onto the overturned ship. Fighting sticks in both hands, Shang-Li advanced into the fray. He smashed creatures with the sticks, then used the blades to block the swords of the Nine Golden Swords warriors and pierce their hearts and throats.

He moved with surefooted grace on the slick hull, never making a faltering movement. He hammered a tentacled thing, ducked beneath the sword thrust of a warrior, and swung, flicking the blade out unconsciously. The point sank into his attacker's temple and dropped him to the ground without a sound. He kicked the dead man free of the blade and moved to the next opponent.

With a harsh battle cry, Thava pounded past Shang-Li and rushed to the ship's prow. Whirling her axe over her head, the paladin leaped from the ship and into the center of the squid Red Orchid fought. Fearlessly, Thava sank the axe into the creature again and again. A tentacle slid free, dismembered and wriggling, and sank into the sea.

The Blue Lady exploded from the ocean on a plume of water only a few feet from Shang-Li. She leaped and landed on the ship next to him, a spear clutched in one hand. Without preamble, she struck at him with the spear.

Shang-Li blocked her attack with the sticks, then stepped smoothly sideways and took the attack to her. He drove her back at first, then she took an extra step backward and threw a hand out at him. A sudden blow struck Shang-Li and knocked him from his feet to sprawl on his back.

"You're a fool, manling." The Blue Lady came at him with her spear. "You should have taken the offer I tendered to you. It was generous. At least you and your father would have gotten to live." She thrust with the spear.

Shang-Li blocked the blow with a quick movement of his foot. The spear point bit into the hull and dug divots from the wood. The Blue Lady drew back to strike again and he knew he wasn't going to be fast enough to prevent her from at least wounding him. Before she could strike, thick ropes of webbing formed in the air and wreathed around her. Shang-Li rolled and got to his feet.

The Blue Lady burst through the webbing, roaring with rage, and turned to face Amree. The ship's mage spoke a spell and a whirling ball of fire filled her hand. She threw the fireball at the Blue Lady. Shang-Li felt the heat of the fireball as it sizzled past him. A massive wall of wind met the fireball only a few feet in front of the Blue Lady. The flames twisted and roiled around her, but they never touched her. She threw her hand out and blue-white beams sped from her fingers and became icy spears.

Iados joined Shang-Li and together they rushed the Blue Lady as Amree staggered back.

"Fools!" The Blue Lady shifted her attention to Iados and Shang-Li. "You only hasten to your deaths."

Iados clutched a shield in front of him and leaped into the air as lightning shot from her hand and assumed a serpentine shape. The serpent-lightning lashed out and Iados managed to get his shield in front of it, but the impact sent him spinning backward ten feet along the pitching hull.

Shang-Li ran across the hull, thrown off stride by the shifting footing. The Blue Lady turned on him and threw a hand out. Kicking his feet out, Shang-Li slid across the deck under a glistening orb that suddenly burst and hurled razor-sharp projectiles in all directions. A few of the projectiles ripped into the back of his leather armor and one tore through the side of his neck. Warm blood flowed down into his armor and across his collarbone. When he reached the Blue Lady, she leaped over him, but he'd expected that.

Flicking the blades of the fighting sticks out, Shang-Li caught them in the ship's hull to stop himself, but immediately caught a burst of blue lightning that knocked him up and away. Red Orchid was striking blindly at anyone trying to harm the ship. But her attack may have saved Shang-Li's life because the Blue Lady thrust with her spear and pierced the nearby deck.

Blue energy crackled and lashed out at the Blue Lady, hammering her backward. Iados pounced quick as a cat, slashing at her with his sword. But his weapon only dulled on her spear and against her skin. The Blue Lady laughed at him and tossed a few snarled curses in his direction as she drove her spear at him.

"You can't harm me with that weapon," the Blue Lady stated.

"Perhaps not," Iados replied grimly as he dispatched one of the sea shambles that had scrambled on board, "but I can be a distraction."

"Only until you're dead." The Blue Lady lunged at him again as Shang-Li gathered himself.

Iados batted the spear aside with his shield and sword again and again, moving backward constantly and taunting her. "Perhaps you can't harm me with that weapon either."

Growling in rage like an animal, the Blue Lady continued her attack. Moonlight glinted from the force of her attacks. Amree attacked once more with a spell that seized the Blue Lady and lifted her from the ship in an invisible grip. The Blue Lady freed a hand and waved. Crackling waves of power dispelled the invisible grip and she dropped to the pitching hull.

Shang-Li closed on her, attacking with the enchanted blades of the fighting sticks. She managed to block most of the blows, but she gave ground at every attack and some of them got through. In seconds she was bleeding from a half-dozen small wounds.

She levitated from the deck and shouted, "Enough!" With a gesture, a storm gathered and black clouds obscured the pale moonlight. In the space of a drawn breath, gale force winds whipped across *Swallow* and tore at her exposed sails. Waves crashed against the hull. Timbers creaked and Shang-Li grew afraid the ship was going to be torn to pieces. Blue energy coursed down *Swallow's* length again and again.

Amree touched a necklace tight against her throat, then flung out her other hand. Deadly red missiles streaked from her fingers and underscored the darkness surrounding them. The missiles crashed against the Blue Lady and jolted her, drawing forth screams of pain and rage. Amree prepared herself again, still clinging to the necklace. Then a sea shamble stood up on the hull and wrapped its misshapen arms around her.

"Iados!" Shang-Li yelled across the thunder and crash of the waves. "Get Amree!"

Without hesitation, the tiefling hurried to the side of the ship's mage, but a dozen sea shambles stood up on the hull.

A small, lean figure struck out of the darkness. Kwan Yung launched himself from the deck and swung a sword at their foe. For a moment, the Blue Lady fell back, then she stretched forth a hand and invisible force wrapped around Kwan Yung and lifted him from the ship's hull. She held him aloft and cursed.

Shang-Li's heart sank. He had known his father wouldn't be safe on the ship, but if things went badly, as they looked like they were going to do, he'd assumed he would be dead before he saw anything happen to his father. Standing bowed by the storm lashing *Swallow*, Shang-Li blinked through the stinging salt of the sea spray and tried to figure out his next move.

At the prow of the ship, Red Orchid and Thava still battled the squid—but it was impossible to tell how the battle was going. Thava either had hold of the creature by one tentacle and was fighting her way toward the center mass, or the squid held her and was drawing her toward its mouth.

The Blue Lady turned her beautiful face toward Shang-Li and smiled. "I still have use of you, manling. I can still be generous. I will let you live if you lay down your arms and swear allegiance to me. But I will no longer spare your father."

True fear pierced Shang-Li. All those years Kwan Yung had appeared implacable and invulnerable. But Shang-Li knew that wasn't so. His father was mortal, and he was the bravest, most stubborn man Shang-Li had ever known. He couldn't imagine a world without his father in it.

"Or," the Blue Lady said, "you can trade your life for his. Perhaps he's as good a scholar as you are when it comes to deciphering Liou Chang's books." She paused and gloated as sea shambles and Nine Golden Swords warriors clambered over the hull and massed for an attack. "Lay down and die, manling, and I will let your father live. Choose!"

Shang-Li focused and drew the calm into his body that his father had always instilled in him, and he drew upon the stubbornness that he knew came from his mother and her people as they lived unfettered in the forests of their homeland. Both had taught him skills, and neither had raised someone that would quit. He felt the turbulent power coursing through his fighting sticks.

"No," he said. "*You're* going to have to choose." He joined the fighting sticks into the staff as he sprinted forward.

Just in front of the line of sea shambles and Nine Golden Swords warriors, Shang-Li planted the staff and vaulted over their heads. The storm winds howled and crashed into him as he left the ship's hull. He landed atop a sea shamble, ran across two more, then flipped into the air. He flicked the blades out at both ends of the staff and thrust it toward the Blue Lady's heart.

Surprised by the attack, the Blue Lady drew back in the air, unmoved by the winds that she had summoned. Her hold on Kwan Yung failed and he dropped to the ship's hull.

Shang-Li dropped to the deck and gathered himself again. Then he sprang once more to the attack, chasing the Blue Lady forward toward the prow and the writhing mass of tentacles that Thava and Red Orchid battled.

"You forfeit your life, manling."

Remaining focused on the Blue Lady, Shang-Li bashed a Nine Golden Swords warrior from his path, knocking the man back into the rough sea, and gaining speed. *Swallow* moved more sluggishly beneath him and he knew she was taking on water. Either the canvas air pocket ripped or the sailors hadn't been able to keep the opening sealed.

More red missiles struck the Blue Lady and lit her up in scarlet fire for a moment. Shang-Li took heart in the knowledge that Amree still lived, and if she lived there was hope that Iados did as well.

Hurt and distracted, the Blue Lady searched for Amree and threw out a hand. By that time, Shang-Li had reached the ship's prow and ran out of hull. Surefooted as a deer, he leaped for one of the squid's rising tentacles and caught it with one hand. As the creature flicked its tentacle, Shang-Li took advantage of the power and movement and launched himself at the Blue Lady. He gripped the staff in both hands and aimed one of the blades at her heart.

The Blue Lady moved at the last instant and the staff missed piercing her heart, instead passing through her chest just below her shoulder. No longer able to maintain her levitation because of Shang-Li's additional weight or the pain from the wound, she dropped into the sea.

Shang-Li clung fiercely to the staff as he plunged below the waves. At first he held his breath, then he remembered the water-breathing potion was still in effect. He breathed in easily and moved with fluid grace despite the water.

The Blue Lady flailed at him, striking his face and smashing his cheekbone. Shang-Li's eye swelled shut immediately and he breathed through the incredible pain. He kept his fists locked around the staff. As they sank in the depths, the Blue Lady drew a dagger and attacked him, plunging it through his leather armor into his chest, seeking his heart. No effort was made to keep him alive now. The dagger bit deeply.

Afraid that if he pulled the staff from her he would lose her and she would be free in her element, Shang-Li separated the staff into fighting sticks again. One of them held fast to the Blue Lady, and the other came free in his hand. Both of them glowed with black fire.

They struck again and again as they sank. Blood streamed around them as they dropped toward the azure glow of the Blue Lady's realm. Finally, she stopped moving, and Shang-Li didn't have the strength to strike again. He had no strength left in him and knew blood spewed from him. Sharks circled and drew near.

Then strong arms wrapped around him from behind and a soft cheek pressed against his face. Amree disengaged Shang-Li from the Blue Lady, then swam up with him toward the surface. With his head back, Shang-Li saw the moonlight growing brighter. Then he saw nothing at all.

EPILOGUE

Two days later, Shang-Li sat in a longboat with bandages covering his wounds. The few healing potions they'd had had saved his life, but until they were able to reach a cleric or get more potions, he had to heal naturally. Pain flooded his every waking moment.

"Easy, easy," Red Orchid shouted as longboat crews pulled at *Swallow*. Ropes connected them to the ship and they gradually righted her as other crewmen shifted the ballast in the ship's hold. But *Swallow* came up to the surface, water dripping from her furled sails. A moment later the ship sat at anchor on the Sea of Fallen Stars. Some of her yards were broken once more, but the hole in the hull was patched and she was more or less watertight.

Shang-Li shook his head in wonderment.

"What?" his father asked. "Did you think Amree would not be able to do as she'd set out to do."

"Not that. I'm just surprised that so many of us are still alive."

Thava and Iados labored in the longboats with the rest of the surviving crew. Amree called out directions from the ship's prow.

"We lived," his father stated simply. "We fought for ourselves and the gods favored us. Hopefully we still have many things to accomplish to justify their trust in us."

"Or maybe we were lucky."

His father snorted. "Even your mother wouldn't have agreed with that."

"You're right."

Reaching into a basket at his feet, his father handed him a bowl of cooked rice. The provisions had come from one of the cargoes they'd managed to rescue. "You need to eat. Get your strength back."

Although he didn't feel hungry, Shang-Li did as his father bade him. It wasn't worth the argument, and he knew his father wouldn't give up.

"Do you think we've seen the last of the Blue Lady?" Iados asked hours later when they'd returned to the ship.

Shang-Li stood at the railing where sailors worked on repairs and peered down into the calm ocean. As soon as the Blue Lady had vanished into the sea, the storm had abated.

"I do," he told the tiefling. "She was dead. No one could have lived through that."

"You did."

"I had help."

"You do realize there are probably several fortunes lying at the bottom of the sea down there. As well as a potential door to somewhere else."

"You do realize that in order to get to any of that treasure, much less return home safely," Amree said behind him, "you're going to have to have a fit ship. And you're not going to have that if you don't get to work."

"Harpy," Iados said beneath his breath.

"I heard that." Amree walked away, already giving orders to the ship's crew

Shang-Li glanced up at the broken and splintered yards. Moonwhisper sat there looking regal and distant, doubtless thinking of mice and other small snacks.

Kwan Yung walked up with a cleric's kit. "Come." He gestured at Shang-Li. "Let me rebind your wounds." He waved to the deck. "Sit."

Shang-Li sat and held still as his father checked the stitches. The flesh was raw and abraded. Thankfully there didn't appear to be any permanent damage, but healing would take time.

"This may hurt," his father warned. "Do not cry. I don't want you to shame me."

In spite of the pain and everything they'd been through, Shang-Li laughed. For a moment. His father smiled at him. Then Kwan Yung started working on his wounds and the real pain began.

"Do you regret coming with me on this quest?" his father asked.

Shang-Li thought about that for a moment. "No. It made me remember."

"Remember what?"

"When we used to do things together."

His father shrugged. "Sons turn into men. You can't be someone's son forever. We will argue and disagree. We will see the world differently."

"Or," Shang-Li said, "we could start seeing some of the world together and find things we can agree on."

His father looked at him and smiled. "Sometimes the son can teach the father new things. I would like that. I find the monastery too lonely at times."

Quietly, Shang-Li reached forward and gave his father

a hug. To his surprise, thought it was in public and such things weren't supposed to be done in public if at all, his father hugged him back.

His father patted his shoulder. "But do not think I will let you forget you spilled that sauce on purpose in the Pirate Isles, Shang-Li."

"Of course you won't."

FORGOTTEN REALMS®

Ed Greenwood
Presents
Waterdeep

BLACKSTAFF TOWER
STEVEN SCHEND

CITY OF THE DEAD
ROSEMARY JONES

MISTSHORE
JALEIGH JOHNSON

THE GOD CATCHER
ERIN M. EVANS
FEBRUARY 2010

DOWNSHADOW
ERIK SCOTT DE BIE

CIRCLE OF SKULLS
JAMES P. DAVIS
JUNE 2010

Explore the City of Splendors through the eyes of authors
hand-picked by FORGOTTEN REALMS® world creator Ed Greenwood.

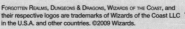

FORGOTTEN REALMS

The New York Times BEST-SELLING AUTHOR

RICHARD BAKER

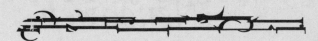

BLADES OF THE MOONSEA

". . . it was so good that the bar has been raised.
Few other fantasy novels will hold up to it, I fear."
—Kevin Mathis, d20zines.com on *Forsaken House*

Book I
Swordmage

Book II
Corsair

Book III
Avenger
March 2010

Enter the Year of the Ageless One!

MARK SEHESTEDT

Chosen of Nendawen

The consumer, the despoiler, has come to Narfell. His followers have taken Highwatch and slain all who held it—save one.

Book I
The Fall of Highwatch

Book II
The Hand of the Hunter
November 2010

Book III
Cry of the Ghost Wolf
November 2011

Vengeance will be yours, the Master of the Hunt promises.
If you survive.

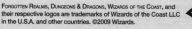

OPEN UP A WORLD OF ADVENTURE WITH THE

DUNGEONS & DRAGONS®

ROLEPLAYING GAME STARTER SET

RUN THE GAME

Build your own dungeons and pit your friends against monsters and villains!

PLAY THE GAME

Explore the dungeon with your friends, fight the monsters, and bring back the treasure!

GRAB SOME FRIENDS

AND THE

STARTER SET

AND

START PLAYING TODAY

playdnd.com